# WHITE DOG

**Rupert Whewell** was born in 1969 in Buckinghamshire. He attended Clifton College, Bristol, and then graduated with a degree in English literature from Downing College, Cambridge, in 1992, writing his dissertation on 'How inconsequential are Sterne's writings?' After a short time working in advertising in Hong Kong, he settled on a career as a recruitment consultant. He established his own firm, Bateman Gray, in London in 2003, specialising in placing bankers.

He enjoyed reading and kept abreast of contemporary literature and art. His parents moved to Scotland, where his love of hill-walking was born. He was a good sportsman, with skiing and climbing eventually becoming his way of life. Chamonix became his second home. He counted skiing down Mont Blanc as one of his greatest triumphs. He loved the Alps and rode the Étape de Tour twice, one of which took in Alpe d'Huez. Golf was also a sport he enjoyed and continued throughout his life.

With his fiftieth birthday looming, he joined a group setting out to climb peaks in the Nanda Devi area of India in May 2019. An avalanche brought about his early death in the Himalayas, together with the loss of his seven climbing companions. He is survived by his mother Elaine, brother Andrew and sister Lisa, having no children of his own. *White Dog* is his first novel, published posthumously.

# WHITE DOG

RUPERT WHEWELL

First published in 2022

Hardback ISBN 978-1-913532-98-7
Paperback ISBN 978-1-915036-00-1

Also available as an ebook
ISBN 978-1-913532-99-4

Typeset by seagulls.net
Cover design by Dom Forbes
Project management by whitefox

# **CONTENTS**

# FOREWORD

## By Lisa Whewell Anson

This book has been a long time in the making. Rupert always loved writing, and talked often about his desire to write a book. Distracted by a full life and being present with his friends and family, it remained in the background, referenced and variously started without real progress. In his late forties, he started to put pen to paper in earnest and *White Dog* was born.

What is the book about? It tells the stories of individuals connected to the world of art and finance. Set in a period of fundamental change, with the advent of new international elites and the arrival of their wealth – breaking like a wave on London and elsewhere – *White Dog* tells the story of the deforming effects of this new class. It is about how money recasts the world for its own ends, how art became an asset class, how everything now has a price, and how most things can be repurposed to serve as capital. In his turbulent career, our protagonist – equally in thrall to it and dismissive of it – is drawn into these new and private worlds, and is both fascinated and appalled by the trade-offs, the money, the venality and the ability to corrupt and influence the wider world.

My brother Rupert was a very special person; not just to me – as a lifelong presence – but to his many friends. His tragic death on 26 May 2019, in an avalanche whilst climbing the Himalayas in the Nanda Devi region of India along with his seven colleagues, cut short his life at forty-nine years old. It is something I will never get over and will never forget. Those gut-wrenching moments when we were told they were missing, at the time not realising that the group had

been killed nearly a week before. The endless calls to send out heli-
copter searches, desperately clinging to the last remaining hope that
they were alive. We had numerous and intense conversations with
the Indian Mountaineering Foundation (IMF) and their incredible
rescue teams, who were fighting the weather as they undertook a
three-week journey to recover the bodies. The outpouring of grief
from his many friends and their sharing of amazing stories about
Rupert was a remarkable display of human connection; one of the
most remarkable I have ever known. His memorial, held in London
on what would have been his fiftieth birthday, was attended by three
hundred friends and family members and was a celebration of life of
which he would have been proud.

At his memorial, many tributes were made, highlighting the
significant impact Rupert had on many lives:

> *He loved to party. He was loud, excitable in a gathering, fun to be
> around. A good and reliable friend. I always felt he was just a little
> disappointed by us adults. We made too many compromises for his
> liking. We were too preoccupied by things he felt were unimportant.
> His school reports show it from an early age: he did not follow the
> signs along a conventional path.*

Rupert never wanted to grow old. His most remarkable achievement was that he lived his life as he wanted, free from convention,
expectation and material possessions; rich with human connection,
humour and the big outdoors. He left no immediate family. He left
a big impression.

Two years on and I miss him every day. I have taken on the task
of finishing and publishing his book, which he left 80 percent
complete. Rupert's passion for words was lifelong. Commended in
the WH Smith Young Writers' Competition in 1982, he went on to
Cambridge to read English and developed a reputation for being
'vocabulous', a word concocted by friends to describe his fabulous

vocabulary. He would carry phrases that tickled him like others carry grudges. Words delighted him. Always looking for a pithy insight, he would turn words and phrases around in the light of his impish intelligence before deciding that they were worthy of inclusion in his extensive lexicon. He loved word play and verbal duelling, much evident in this book.

I can see him laughing at me and the irony that I am the one left finishing his 'great unfinished novel'. It was important to me to see his story through and share his writing. This has been done with the help of the team at whitefox and John McDonald, who has artfully filled in the writing gaps. My thanks to them. It brought me closer to Rupert, and I hope it will keep his memory alive for those that knew him and will entertain others who did not.

I want to pay tribute to his climbing colleagues, to whose memory this book is dedicated. I did not know them, although our families are now all intimately intertwined through the events of that fateful day on top of the world. Alongside Rupert in their final ascent were:

- Martin Moran, UK, team leader, whose body was never recovered
- John McLaren, UK
- Richard Payne, UK
- Ruth McCance, Australia
- Ronald Beimel, USA
- Anthony Sudekum, USA
- Chetan Pandey, India, IMF liaison officer

Our thoughts remain with all their families.

Two people were central to events as they unfolded after the tragedy: Mark Thomas, a close friend, who was leading the second group in this party and was the first to reach the site of the avalanche and to raise the alarm; and Wing Commander Amit Chowdhury from the IMF, who was in constant contact and provided a lifeline of communication and determination as he led the three-week recovery operation in extremely difficult conditions, which his team conducted alongside the Indo-Tibetan Border Force. Both were pillars of strength in our darkest days, and I will always be grateful to them.

Although we cannot hear him anymore, there was, in his passions and in his writing, a message he left to all of us. He thought we were getting life wrong. For him, real life was seeing the ridiculous for what it is and seeing the sublime for what it is. Most of life is laughable. Words can be sublime. Mountains can be sublime. I hope that we all remember, as his voice fades from our memories, that his priorities were different from most of ours and that his treatise on life was written in his actions and his passion – a passion that had a profound influence on his family and his many friends.

This book, in which Rupert's unique voice is resurrected one last time, is dedicated in loving memory to my much loved and greatly missed little brother. Friend. Son. Hero-Uncle.

## CHAPTER 1

# IF YOU'RE SCARED OF WOLVES, STAY OUT OF THE FOREST

The rear door of the large chalet opened silently and easily. Ryder stepped out into the Alpine night, allowing his eyes a moment to adjust. He could see footsteps in the snow, leading off into the cold, deserted darkness. At least, he thought it was deserted, until he saw the flare of a match. He moved a few paces forward, to be free of the interior light. That's when he noticed the dark shape of Pavel Muransky, and the glow of his cigar. It was several days later than had originally been arranged, and Ryder had found the chalet empty when he arrived. He'd deposited the painting in the spacious living room and stepped outside.

Now he watched in silence as the bluish backlit smoke billowed around Muransky's big Slavic skull, which rotated like a deck-mounted cannon, with the glowing muzzle coming to bear on him. The Russian beckoned him over – Ryder noticed the bottle as he approached. Away from the chalet it was dark, and he couldn't tell what the bottle contained. Muransky filled his glass first, then another one for Ryder, which indicated his arrival was anticipated. Ryder brushed snow from the log seat and sat beside the bigger man, taking an exploratory sip from the glass – it was whisky. He nodded approvingly, half hoping this might prompt Pavel into speaking. It already felt like a contest – one of first-move disadvantage.

The Russian sat up from his slumped position, trying to rouse himself. Ryder noticed the bottle was almost empty.

'I have kept you waiting . . . Sorry, business.' Pavel's hand rolled over and away in a dismissive flourish. He seemed to find amusement in his accentuation of the word 'business' – the catch-all. An excuse for everything; an explanation for what couldn't be – or didn't need to be – explained. Cursory, yet complete.

Ryder shrugged it away, thereby making it something approaching an acknowledgement, if not an apology. 'I've been amusing myself watching people having what they consider to be fun, going up in mechanical lifts and then returning to where they started.'

Ryder said this as if it was adequate to describe his feigned nonchalance. He tapped out a cigarette and was about to light it.

'Wait! Have a cigar.'

'No thanks.'

'Why not?'

'Unhealthy.'

Muransky laughed that big Russian guffaw of his, and scoffed in the way only Russians can scoff. 'Unhealthy, my *zhopa*!'

There was a line to be aware of around the rich. For Ryder, it was knowing that they viewed him as something to entertain them. He wasn't too craven or fawning – unlike others who threw themselves, unprincipled, at the beck and call of the obscenely lush. For him – well, he had to do it his own way. OK, he could just about manage the sucking up if he had to – not often, only if he was absolutely certain he'd benefit from it. He reckoned it was a pride thing, but he didn't care to look any deeper. Better not to.

And then there were the errors of delusion – of mistaking proximity to wealth for being wealthy yourself. He'd made enough of those mistakes, gone a bit hard at it, got dragged into the game of overextending. Sooner or later you had to pay. He'd been a bit too wild too early in his commercial life, forgetting he was no more than a disposable item to certain people. Someone once warned him, in apparent seriousness: *Just remember, you don't have tits.*

Now, that was a rule to live by!

Ryder had developed his own set of codes. Then again, he wasn't too good with rules. But at least by having them, he had the option of applying them if he wanted to – if the situation merited it. His job was to offer the filthy rich the things they didn't have, couldn't buy. He lent them dimension, extended them, made them appear to have depth, recast them, elevated them, compensated for some deficit. They obviously weren't lacking in material things, so it became a question of intellect, or insight, or *recherché je ne sais quoi. What do you add to my life? What do you bring?* He had to remember, of course, the issue of limited attention spans and glances could quickly turn elsewhere. It was all fashion, despite what they said. And don't expect gratitude. That price would never be paid.

And so he was here, in Switzerland. Yet, despite all his rehearsals for this meeting, Ryder already had some leverage he could use, if it was required. Back before he'd even known the Russian, he'd paid into Pavel's favour bank. Ten years ago, he'd been asked by Seth Silver to expedite, and that was the actual word used, an introduction to his old school for Pavel's son. He hadn't given it much thought – it was something he could do, so he did it. At the time, it was a favour for someone else, but now – well, it did no harm to be remembered.

'How was Charterhouse?'

Muransky didn't answer, just gave Ryder a quizzical look, as if he didn't know what he was talking about. Never expect gratitude – remember! The Russian was a big man – imposing, very wealthy, gruff but gracious, of enigmatic age; Ryder reckoned him to be about fifty. A child of perestroika and glasnost – of champagne and stagnation. Nobody really knew how he'd made his money and most people didn't care. Ryder was fascinated by Pavel, or the idea of him, though the stark fact of the Russian could leave him cold. Of course, he'd never admit to such awe. He knew a few Ukrainians and

Georgians, but nobody like the big man. He was like the cold wind off a glacier – exhilarating, but dangerous if exposed to it for too long. Ryder couldn't help wondering what the guy was *really* doing here at this ski resort. Hardly just collecting?

Pavel seemed somehow morose, despite the whisky, and Ryder wasn't going to go all entertainer on him. He knew better. He'd been waiting days and he'd wait some more for this bear to emerge from his den – in his own time. For now, outside the comfort of the chalet, he could feel the cold working its way through his inadequate clothing, and he wished Pavel would decide to go in. He hunched up his shoulders and screwed his neck down so tight it felt as though a few vertebrae might crack like thin ice.

'Every man should have a place of refuge . . . a sanctuary.'

Pavel sounded wistful. Ryder indulged him. 'Is this yours?'

'Christos, no! This is recreation. This has mountains, but that's all.'

Ryder looked down over the valley to see the little grouping of lights perched amidst the hulking forms of the dark, white-capped mountains. They seemed to huddle together for warmth and company, camped together on some hard frozen ledge. Was someone on their balcony, down in the little *dorf*, smoking and drinking and looking back at him? If so, what would they see? Verbier smeared across the face of Mont Gelé, bursting over its sides, a very Swiss version of a carnivalled pleasure dome? They'd see the arterial road and its swathe of bright lights, bars, hotels, shops, and branch roads contouring out and diminishing in size, as they ascended like tinsel twine on a Christmas tree.

What they wouldn't see was the missing illumination of the massive unlit chalets in the middle of the season. Obscured plots, reservoirs of dumped-down currency, inferred by the absent light. Dark body energy.

'Maybe you do need your own Kehlsteinhaus. I hear the best people often do.'

'Typical that you would know the name of the Eagle's Nest, Ryder.'

'Typical? How?'

Pavel shook his head and laughed.

'Because you're no eagle.'

'What am I, then?'

Muransky didn't answer the question, at least not out loud. He saw Ryder as something serviceable, but not totally in his control. Maybe a small white dog – something he'd stick down a hole. A terrier. Something that had pride and independence but could still be relied on to come back with the rabbit. Though, at that moment, Ryder looked more like a cat, prepared to suffer indignity rather than relinquish its hauteur. Wanting the warmth of the chalet, but suffering the cold for the end-result reward. A Machiavellian moggie. Maintaining the belief that it was his own choice to remain outside.

Pavel waited a few minutes more before relenting, then he clapped Ryder heavily on the back, almost shattering his clasped and frozen jawbone.

'Let us go inside.'

As the interior of the chalet enveloped them in its glow, the Russian fetched a heavy pair of boots, a thick coat and a big fur hat, and insisted that Ryder try them on. When he did, under protest, Muransky roared his approval.

'For next time you go out in the cold.'

Ryder caught sight of himself in a mirror – he looked like a child, swamped in a man's clothes. Still, he didn't care, as long as they did the job and kept him warm. Right now he was beginning to feel like a human being again, and it seemed Pavel was starting to shake off whatever was troubling him.

Muransky poured the remainder of the whisky and discarded the empty bottle. He began to tell Ryder about his grandmother, who'd worked for a scientist in Siberia.

'His name was Belyaev . . . I think.'

In the old Soviet times, they had run a scientific programme to study and understand how wolves had developed into dogs – to learn the underlying basis of domestication. But instead of wolves, they had to use more manageable silver foxes from the fur farms. They selected and bred the tamest to see how heritable that characteristic was. Within a few generations, they had a far more domesticated fox – one that was curious around humans rather than scared or aggressive. Over successive generations, the foxes came to have the characteristics and behaviours of dogs. What surprised them was not just the speed of the change, but also the associated alterations in physical appearance. The foxes came to look like dogs, with floppy ears and dappled pelts.

Pavel paused and the darkness returned to his face, but he was happy to keep talking. Well, maybe not happy, but forced to form and shape what was in his head. Ryder felt like an adjunct, necessary and redundant at the same time. It was one part soliloquy, one part incoherent ramble, serving only Muransky's nominal need for an audience to keep at bay what was really on his mind. Like a man who'd gone through the four phases of denial, anger, bargaining and depression, and was now at the fifth. Resignation.

Ryder sat back and stopped even looking for an opening to get him onto the subject of why they were here – to get him to buy the painting. He tried to figure out how Pavel's being drunk could be used to that end. He didn't mind what he'd given up to be here. He'd always made accommodations for clients and their foibles and demands, and that was called professionalism – or as much as it could be called professional choice. Pavel was rich enough, carried that latent level of threat about him; or, as Ryder preferred to think, was just interesting enough to be pandered to. His background was the great unknown, sufficiently compelling that all opportunities to encounter it should be taken. What he was and had done was only surmised, garnered – guessed at. And that's what set him apart.

Which was why this story was unusual. A freewheeling memoir, a lugubrious admission, a skein of personal history. Maybe it was easier to be candid with someone apart. Fewer complications, fewer consequences. Well, that's what he thought at the time – but it was going to work out in a very different way for Ryder.

The experiments on the foxes had to be conducted in secret because of Lysenko's doctrinal orthodoxies, which rejected the Darwinian/Mendelian ideas of genetics. But that danger of the early years was replaced by the neglect of post-communism, and the money dried up. People sought to fund it privately, with the sale of domesticated foxes as exotic pets. But it wasn't enough and, eventually, they had to kill the specially bred animals for their fur. Because of their ears and colouring, the pelts were worth less than they would have been had they been left as nature intended.

Ryder wondered if there was supposed to be some moral to the story – some proverb or maxim. But Pavel had nothing to add, nothing by way of explanation.

'I bet they'd still piss on your carpet.'

Pavel retrieved another bottle from a cupboard and filled their glasses again. He seemed to be laughing, but not at Ryder's glib remark. Silently, without any felicitous sound. Laughing, but morose at the same time.

'If you are afraid of the wolf, do not go in the forest.'

Pavel grinned as he said it – a loose, liquid grin. Ryder wondered if he was drunk. He'd never seen Muransky affected by the amount he drank, and he could drink a lot. He wondered what the Russian meant by that remark and if it was directed at him. Just an exuberant expression? Or a warning?

'Stalin.'

'What?'

'He said it . . . about going in the forest.'

'I see.'

But he didn't really. Ryder never quite knew where he stood with Pavel – something beyond the sheer Russianness of him. OK, there was the impenetrability and all that, the not knowing what he'd done to get his money. But it wasn't just that; it was as though there was a heavy veil between what Pavel seemed to want of Ryder and what he actually needed. It had an inscrutability about it – at least, until now. Now it seemed as if the Russian had come loose. The mask of his face was no longer securely in place. Something had pierced it. Ryder had never seen him look, by turns, manic and jumpy, nonchalant and offhand.

It was always understood that Ryder would never ask about Pavel's activities in Russia, beyond what was required by KYC. Don't ask and you'll be told no lies. Their relationship was based on understood rather than agreed elements of trust and discretion, elegantly circumscribed by history and wit. And without recourse to London or Moscow rules.

How had he been drawn into the role he now served? Ryder had no answer to that, except for time and place and happenstance. He'd always had a fascination with Russians – well, wasn't that the point of his world, that it threw him into contact with people he had to rub along with to survive? But why did the Russians, in particular, hold his fascination? Was it because of the stories he'd heard from his mates in the art business – about way back, when the older dealers were faking it and making it? Of Moscow in the '90s, with its fatal convulsions and attractions?

Half the bottle later, Ryder decided to just leave the painting where it was and ask Pavel to take a look the next time he went for a piss. When he did, the Russian decided to urinate off the balcony and not walk past the picture. Ryder joined him as he leaned back to take in the clear sky above, both men competing for distance with their streams. This casualness and blokey camaraderie was all very well, but Ryder couldn't wait any longer.

'I've left it out for you to see.'

'Shall we, then?'

Ryder zipped up his trousers.

'You should see it alone.'

The Russian shrugged, as if to say, *your choice*.

It was two cigarettes later when Ryder felt he needed to go find out where Muransky had got to. He stepped inside to see the painting bathed in light. Pavel had taken one of the existing pictures down and the Picasso had stolen its place. The discarded painting lay against the chalet wall, to one side, far enough away so as not to detract from the privileged spot that *Nature Morte* had taken up.

Pavel sat immobile on the modular sofa, facing it.

It was always a question of judgement – what to say, what not to say, when to interrupt, where to cut across their experience of the work. No one wanted to steal that moment away, not least the dealer trying to sell it. After all, people became attached through looking. That was at the heart of it. That was the irrational attraction – the key element. There was a time to talk and a time to shut up. He'd learned that it was a mistake to butt in at the wrong moment. Better to let the buyer form their own attachment, their own reaction to the painting – let it take some part of them, yet remain outside them too.

The ceremony, the act of intimacy, the initiation.

It was important for the client to be immersed before the intrusion of words, of price, of mundanity. To believe that it wasn't just another chattel. That they knew what they were looking at, even though, of course, they never could. Ever. What they saw was completely subjective and not what the artist had seen. So how could they know what it meant – how could they presume to know anything about it?

Nevertheless, Ryder always liked to take the romanticised view; it stood in marked contrast to the curiously joyless functional buyers who seemed to involve themselves in a world of acquisition for outward-facing reasons. But, just as nobody was entirely irrational, Ryder needed to speak – to overlay it. Not just to describe it but to place it, to make it real as an object in time and space, to make it legitimate through its paperwork, its history, its provenance.

To convince.

To make the deal.

It surprised him that Pavel was taking the process so seriously. He'd had the Russian down as the possessor type – but that didn't seem to be the case on this occasion. Ryder didn't want to have to cut short his rapt attention, but it had to end sometime.

'I can leave it with you overnight.'

'Three million dollars, you say?'

And there it was, the breaking of the spell. Ryder nodded as Pavel turned to look at him. It always had to happen, but there was pleasure in delaying the moment when the mercantile world reasserted itself.

Art, at least, had that going for it – that there was a natural tension between its effect and its financial value, something that couldn't be said of other asset classes. And there he was again, thinking of art as an asset class. But that was partly why it remained interesting to him. Sometimes he thought he put more premium on the money than on the art itself. Though tonight, it seemed that wouldn't be a distinction he needed to make.

'Leave it overnight. Come tomorrow.'

\* \* \*

Morning broke and Ryder reckoned it had all gone very well the previous night. It wasn't until he got to within thirty yards of Muransky's chalet that he realised something was off. He'd already seen the police car, but it wasn't until he turned the corner that he encountered the group of officers standing outside on the driveway.

Their attention was immediately drawn to him.

## CHAPTER 2

# BEGINNINGS

Barnabas Price – *Mister* Price to his staff – was the London head of Boulets, the international auctioneers. He liked the Monday morning meetings; they gave him an opportunity to talk down to his department heads – to expound his personal and, as he believed, inimitable mantra. They'd heard it all before, of course, in one form or another, but they still maintained the pretence of listening.

'It's not for us to understand them, nor to explain them. We are not their friends; they are clients.'

He paused for effect. Someone yawned. He frowned.

'I'm greedy . . . and I want you to be too. It's the essence of our trade, greed and vanity. Commission always trumps conscience.'

Price liked to think he was motivating them, transferring greater urgency and energy to their endeavours. But his words were mainly aimed at the younger staff members, like Ryder, because the others were too set in their ways for his urgings to make the blindest bit of difference. At another level, he was doing it for his own egotism, adding a flourish here, a gesture there, like some thwarted thespian. He'd been in the game for thirty years and was entitled to this weekly performance, but he was beginning to resent the fact that too many of them treated it as entertainment. His waggish tone wasn't meant to amuse, it was meant to animate – like good king Henry before Harfleur. They'd become far too comfortable.

Maybe he ought to fire a few of them, see how funny they thought it was then.

Sometimes he wished he'd never left Sotheby's.

The captive audience comprised about twenty people. They looked, for the most part, an eccentric bunch – like academics who'd got waylaid at the dog track. In fact, some of them looked more like bookies than fine-art and antiques dealers. An unruly bunch, with their own specialisations and their own little fiefdoms, and very few of them had much real commercial savvy. Price knew them, knew he had to elaborate and improvise every time. He needed to pick on someone to get through their complacency.

'You . . . Ryder.'

'Me?'

'Yes, you. As our newest head of department – albeit a temporary one, I must remind you – what are our favourite things?'

'Raindrops on roses and whiskers on kittens?'

Everyone laughed – except Price. He loured down at the twenty-five-year-old.

'You think this is humorous?'

Ryder didn't answer; he disliked being picked on by pompous people. Price decided to leave him alone for now, and expanded his gaze to take in the rest of them.

'Death, divorce and debt. Our three horsemen of the apocalypse . . . or should I say *opportunity*. Indeed. And you are here to avail of such opportunity. Our horsemen's Sancho Panzas, guiding them, advising, bringing in the business that befits your level of responsibility and salary.'

More desultory laughter.

'And you, young Ryder, remember what happened to your predecessor, the unfortunate Richards.'

Ryder didn't know what had happened to Richards, so how could he remember?

Price was reaching the climax of his performance. He took centre stage and lifted his arms in a final, dramatic pose.

'Right, don't let me down. All of you go, get out of my sight and bring me back gold.'

They all stood up and began to file lugubriously out of the meeting room. Price watched them go, amidst the scrape of chair legs and the bovine heft of it all, mumbling to each other and looking far too casual, even before they got outside. Price called back his man from modern art, who'd taken to bringing one of his subordinates with him to the meetings. The fellow was a hustler, he made far more commission than anyone else, so he believed he could write his own rules. Price needed to slap him down just a little, before he got too big for his Basquiats.

'Nigel . . . your man . . ?'

'He needs to learn, Mister Price.'

'Of course, of course. But ask me first.'

'Yes, Mister Price.'

And that was that – it only left Ryder to be dealt with. Price didn't know about Ryder – wasn't sure about him. He might turn out to be a huge pain in the proverbial. But he was young and there was a certain élan about him. Commercial – that was it – he was commercial, unlike most of the unholy relics he'd inherited. And 'commercial' in Price's book wasn't a slur, a handicap. Commercial was good. So, he was minded to persist with Ryder, despite his impertinence. In any case, the young man had been rather forced on him with Richards's going – and he could always keep an eye out for someone to replace him in Furniture.

If it came to that.

Ryder returned to the improvised bureau in his department. The fact that furniture took up more room than anything else made management less disposed to provide a proper office. Space had to be justified. So, for the moment, the furniture people were camped in amongst the Danersk chests and Aldeburgh cabinets. Ryder was thinking about what Price had told him when he took over the job – that you learn more about a man by how he spends his money than by how he makes it. He hadn't thought of it quite that way before.

He didn't even know if he believed it, but, for all his outward absurdity, Price was a shrewd enough character underneath.

Ryder was trying to equate the statement with what he himself thought – if you could have a good rummage in someone's drawers you'd find out a lot about them. The difference between what they wanted you to know and what they withheld was what made them interesting. He decided to try Price's theory out on Bentley Brooks, who was slumped forward in his chair, making the first cup of tea of the day.

'So, what do you reckon, Bentley?'

'Please elaborate.'

'You find out more about a man . . .'

'Or woman?'

'. . . by how *they* spend their money than how *they* make it.'

Bentley unfurled himself from the kettle.

'I don't know. Give me some money and I'll spend it, then you can tell me.'

Brooks was an enigma to Ryder. In his late twenties, he appeared to be a man of no appetite or ambition, entirely content in a role for which he was evidently overqualified. He didn't seem to resent Ryder getting the head of department job over him, and was blasé to the point of catatonia. Nothing was worth overexciting himself about, it seemed. And what kind of a name was Bentley anyhow? He said it was Old English and meant 'from the moors'. Ryder could believe that. Despite looking closely for signs of rancour and frustration in him regarding the promotion, there was none. It was as though he was perfectly content to just be and do enough. Bentley seemed to have worked out that there was no point in anything except getting through to Friday. Ryder wondered what he did at the weekends, but was unable to come to any conclusion.

Price suddenly appeared. He hovered for a moment or two, considering the hygiene implications of taking a seat beside them in their low-level confederacy, then decided to remain standing. He surveyed the young lackeys with their hands cupped round their mugs of tea. Ryder spoke first, admitting his superior to the conventicle.

'Make Mister Price a cup then, Bentley.'

'No . . . no need. I won't be long.'

Price said this in a tone of near panic, in case he might have to bring his lips into contact with a grubby-looking mug that some porter had salivated into previously. He squinted his eyes at Bentley. 'Could you . . . ?'

That was Price. He sometimes didn't feel the need to finish a sentence, a request – expected the person addressed to understand its implications. He sometimes spoke in half-sentences. Dealt in semi-statements. Requests that weren't fully formed. Innuendoes, even, where he couldn't ever be accused of intimating anything too directly. Just a prompt. A tincture of intention. A vocal intonation.

Bentley took the hint and sidled off into the antique undergrowth, taking his mug with him. Ryder tried to postpone the inevitable bollocking – or what Price considered to be a bollocking. 'I'm down to a house clearance in Gloucestershire this afternoon . . . quite a grand family, apparently. There should be some good stuff.'

'Very good, very good. But . . .'

'The mother died. I'd guess they'll want to shift it all.'

'Excellent, Ryder. We like death, don't we?'

'We need more lots for next month's sale . . .'

Ryder kept rabbiting. Price put his hand up to end the small talk. 'About the meeting . . .'

'Meeting?'

'Just now . . .'

Ryder knew perfectly well what was coming, but he tried to look innocent and accommodating.

'You must, Ryder, try not to be so flippant.'

'Flippant, sir?'

'Yes, flippant, Ryder.'

'How so?'

'You know very well . . .' Price paused, looking for the right blend of impeachment and assuagement. 'I realise that young men nowadays have a tendency towards recalcitrance, but it's not in your best interest to be insubordinate.'

'Recalcitrance?'

'You know what I mean.'

'Must run in families, sir.'

Price gave him a confused look – what was he talking about?

'Like wooden legs.'

Bentley came back, as he'd been instructed to by Ryder whenever Price dropped by for a sermon.

'Anyway, we'll leave it like that, shall we?'

Ryder shrugged. Price would have preferred an acknowledgement in words – to him, shrugging seemed slightly workman, mildly irritating. He could accept it from Bentley, but it smacked of insolence from Ryder. It was going a bit too far.

'Take Steel with you this afternoon.'

The order to Ryder reasserted his authority. Price tapped his knuckles twice on the back of Bentley's chair, then turned and left the furniture department to settle back into its somnolence.

* * *

It wasn't that he didn't like Charlie Steel – Steel was OK, he knew his stuff, he'd been in the game a long time. He was fairly decent company too, if you didn't mind the chip on his shoulder, but Ryder still resented his presence and Price knew it; that's why he'd sent him along, as a further reprimand. Caught in these thoughts, he was a little late cranking the steering wheel of the van over as they hit the deep long curve of the exit from the M4 onto the M25. He had to force it and hold it as the slack Renault Master heeled and then set itself on a solid list for the duration of the bend. The thing was not to touch the brakes.

'Yes, and do mind the bend, it can catch out the unwary. Oh no – sorry, my mistake, we're already . . .'

Steel had a habit of sarcasm – a sort of just-behind-time precognition thing. Pointing out the error under the guise of helpful comment. Ryder made a mental note to try it out on Price.

'I can stick to the speed limits all day, if you want?'

He could be caustic himself when he decided to be.

'No, that will only make it longer.'

It was a badge of some pride in the business – the number of miles hammered out around the country in vans. If you weren't doing the miles, you weren't doing the job. Steel, of course, had clocked up many times over what Ryder had, and was bitter about that. All those years on the road and now this novice doing the driving. Ryder reckoned if he made that stick, he'd always have ascendency over the man. Bitterness was a clincher – if you could lay that charge on anyone, they had to show their colours. It was like ippon in judo or karate or whichever martial art. Still, if he were Steel, he'd be bitter too – middle-aged, middling success, most of it behind him – check your rear-view mirror, man! What good would his erstwhile erudition do him now? How would it sustain him? He could see his future, more of the same – only less so.

For Ryder, the mileage medals were still very much ahead of him, and that's why he always jumped behind the wheel on these two-handed expeditions. He sent Steel a sidelong glance – a look that would have to serve as an acknowledgement of the steering error. Steel gave him a wan smile, then flicked his eyes back to the road, indicating that Ryder might want to do the same. Ryder made a conspicuous show of looking as they joined the M25. From there they headed towards the Chilterns, down the large escarpment and onto the Oxfordshire plain, then north-west, skirting the Cotswolds. It was only there he could believe he'd escaped the outreach of London – as though he could no longer be seen. There was no sight of cities, and the green and pleasant land lay spread out before them.

\* \* \*

Ryder angled the front left of the van and edged it as far as he could up to the grassed verge. His elbow was slung out the window, and the old dear in the Volkswagen Polo trying to pass in the narrow lane wasn't doing a very good job of it. There was miles of room on her side, but she was reluctant to shuffle past as he inched his way forward. They should teach this in the test – or, in her case, the geriatric retest. C'mon love, he thought to himself, but with a fixed smile on his face so as not to spook her.

'Maybe if you came forward, I could just squeeze by.'

She came forward, but not enough, so he gestured with his hanging hand for her to keep moving.

'You shouldn't bring such a large vehicle up this road!'

She rolled her window down when they were level, but only as far as she might within a monkey enclosure. Her voice was shrill, no doubt someone in favour of restoring the death penalty for shabby people and shoplifters – and white-van drivers.

Steel leaned across the cab. 'Good afternoon, madam.'

He used his very best ingratiating voice, before Ryder could retort in a less emollient manner – one that would certainly send her scurrying to the nearest beadle.

'Could you possibly direct us to Devonshire House?'

She frowned – certain that they were en route to rob the place.

'Well ... I don't know ..'

'We're the auctioneers ... from London.'

Charlie was trying to reassure her that they weren't a couple of muggers come to murder them in their beds. Ryder wondered if the London bit really helped, but had to admit Steel had called it right when she lightened her frown.

'I suppose it's all right. A mile or so along, on the left. You really can't miss it.'

Charlie smiled back warmly. 'Thank you, madam.'

Her face subsided into a smile. The outbreak of niceness had righted the situation. Ryder didn't care; he thought there was absolutely no need to be so servile and sycophantic about it. Up to him, he'd have dragged her from the car and driven it past himself, then kicked her up the arse for being so fucking snooty.

The private drive was long and Ryder decided to keep his speed up, otherwise they'd be speaking to the next generation by the time they got there. There were signs suggesting a speed limit of five miles per hour, but he was in a mood after the incident in the lane and he doubted if some private policeman would jump out of the undergrowth with a radar gun. Steel was hanging onto the door handle to steady himself over the potholes and rough patches of gravel. It was only when they broke from the cover of the trees and came steaming out into the open, in sight of the main house and with a plume of dust rising behind them, that he felt he had to say something.

'You should slow down, Ryder, to the speed of a trotting horse.' He was trying to make a joke of it, to disguise his concern. 'The gentry won't want to see a white van trying to break the sound barrier along their dilapidated driveway.'

Ryder conceded and slowed. He concluded that Steel could fit easily into this world. Charlie's feigned attempts to mock these people had a certain acuity of observation, but lacked any spite or twist. Unconvincing. In reality, Steel was comfortable with it all; it was a milieu he wanted to be part of. He was of its cloth. A second-son priest who knew more about morality and commerce than his blue-blood parishioners? But what else did he have, apart from a line in disaffected humour? And where had that got him?

Ryder, on the other hand, wanted none of it – none of what he considered to be obscene. An inbred elitist with a lisping sneer?

And a bowtie on his ballcock.

## CHAPTER 3

# GREEN AND PLEASANT

Their visit took a little more than a couple of hours. They declined coffees before they began their tour of the house – they weren't builders! The daughter seemed keen to guide them around, but, in truth, she'd just get in the way. Once she convinced herself that they wouldn't make a beeline for the silver spoon drawer, she was happy to leave them to it. They each set about it with notebook in hand, aware of the other but working independently – also aware of where the other's glance and time were spent. For Steel, it was within his normal modus operandi, and Ryder took it as such. Though he felt, no doubt, there was some kind of test element to it. How's your knowledge, boy? What did you miss?

Ryder wondered what the ancestors of the current owners did to get the coin to build this pile. *Behind every great fortune there is an equally great crime* – the phrase was attributed to Balzac, but it might have been someone else. One of the slogans beloved of the shouty marching left, who'd been marching a very long time and probably would do so for a long time to come. *Property is theft* – now that was definitely the French anarchist Proudhon. But it wasn't a very revolutionary day. In fact, Ryder couldn't help musing that all this aristocratic theft couldn't have happened without the collaboration of the plebeians who manned the armies and the scaffolds and the expropriations and the taxations. The lackeys who turned on their own class and who believed the panjandrums were their betters – even today. What did the word 'majesty' mean in a modern setting? Or 'highness', for that matter? They still bent the knee and tugged the forelock. They elected scoundrels who robbed and pillaged at will, and thanked the toffs for crapping on them from a great height. Ryder had always advocated that such a delicate flower as democracy should never be entrusted into the horny hands of the proletariat.

When they completed their tour, they returned to the kitchen. The brother had arrived on the scene and, in the peremptory fashion familiar to his class and sex, took over from the sister. This time they accepted a cup of tea, the provision of which was delegated to the girl, in fine bone china. Ryder took a sip and returned the cup to its saucer, but not before turning the saucer over to see the maker's mark.

Steel was spelling out the details of business, how there was a pending sale in which their objects could be lotted, but it would need to be expedited quickly. Always fix a timeline. Make them think a deal could fall away with prevarication. Ryder had heard the Charlie spiel enough to know it and its variations. He'd yet to work out how much of it was for his own benefit and how much he extemporised to keep it lively for the client. It certainly wasn't required as insurance against the unexpected question that never materialised. What the client got was the same set of preliminaries – a dance around what they thought they knew and what the dealer put them straight on. Of course, the end point was always the same. Value.

Ryder lounged in a deep but unremarkable chair, observing them, seeing the earnestness of the sister and the graspiness of the brother, with his stuttered attempts to get to the money moment – trying to interrupt and move things on impatiently. The brother stood, while the others sat, trying to establish a position of mastery. Hugo Baskerville in front of the fire. What he wanted was what he couldn't have – a guarantee of how much it would all sell for. Charlie seemed to bend, then snap back, in his attempts to make it clear that he could only give minimum estimates, to avoid disappointment.

'But you have experience in these things, don't you?'

'Selling goods always carries risk and a degree of uncertainty, sir.'

'Yes, but you've done this many times, haven't you?'

'I have indeed, so you must trust me to know what I'm talking about.'

Instead of certainty, Steel did the right thing in offering him something else – trust. If they offered him certainty, he'd then suspect them – and he'd be right. So no, not certainty. He wanted to trust them, trust what they said, trust them to get him what he now thought it was all worth. And what he thought it was worth was the figure Steel gave him. That was now not just anchored, but had become an established and cherished amount. And if it turned out to be wrong, it was OK – as long as it was wrong on the right side. Both the brother and the sister had now come to trust Charlie. That was the trick. Trust was the prize. Trust served up in ten minutes of talking.

The brother signed the preliminary documents of sale, which Steel ceremoniously produced from his battered artist's satchel. A nice touch. The sister had to sign them too, so the brother shovelled them over to her. After an hour of lifting and sweating, they'd packed what would fit and what they could manage into the van. Charlie got the brother to sign off on the inventory and they were back outside.

'Odd, isn't it, how little time it all takes.'

Ryder was sitting on the grass, smoking what he considered to be his most deserved cigarette of the past week.

'Yes, especially when you consider that some of this stuff hasn't moved for centuries.'

'With the weight of it, you can see why.'

'Right, well, chop chop. Let's skedaddle.'

Ryder got up without a retort. 'Skedaddle' – who used that word anymore?

Steel was upbeat – all energy and eagerness. Still, Ryder could let him have that; he'd done his job. He jumped into the cab on the driver's side and took his time on the way out. They passed the baronial gates, with their stone lions either side. Heavy enough to be difficult to move, good enough to be worth the effort.

'I know a rather good pub around here.' Steel wanted the reward of a drink.

Ryder looked at his watch.

\* \* \*

The Trout had a smattering of cars outside it. A couple of dog walkers huddled around the back of some estate car. A stern and alarmed woman looked at them as they pulled onto the gravel – a relation of the old bag in the lane, Ryder wondered? He let Charlie go get the beers. Seemed only right as, technically, he was the senior man. And, if they only stayed for one, well then, why should he pay? In any case, Charlie being middle-class, he probably needed to go for a piss.

Ryder secured an empty table outside. There were no extenuating factors in play, such as good-looking girls, so an easy choice. He sprawled himself in elongated ease, both arms slung over the back of the bench and both legs extended to full length underneath. He laid his head back to feel the late-day sun on his face.

'Proper beer for me; loutish lager for you.'

Ryder let it slide. Anyone who'd just bought you a beer got to say what they wanted – but only once.

'Do you ever consider that such comments mark you out as an old fogey?'

That was letting it slide.

'Do you ever consider that people say things to annoy you?'

'They would only annoy me if I valued their opinion.' Ryder sat up straight to get hold of his lager. Steel shook his head as they raised their glasses to each other in an underplayed way. 'What happened to Richards?'

'Who?'

'My predecessor in furniture.'

'Don't you know? An unfortunate accident.'

The first taste was so good it induced a second and a third in quick succession, until half of Ryder's pint had been swallowed in a matter of seconds. He winced at the coldness and the gas remained for a while, before relaxing into that dreamy appreciation of what he'd just tasted. That was good! He held the rest of the pint up to the sky and it looked like a second splendid sun. The light on the riverside bathed the bank and backlit the fly-life low on the water, as the swallows and martins flicked and skimmed their runs. This simple delight seemed to lull Ryder into accord, suspended from the whole getting-and-spending business.

'What unfortunate accident?'

'Nobody knows for sure, but some say a light bulb exploded inside his anus. There was a lot of blood.'

Charlie Steel had long since stopped directly trying to tell Ryder about the vagaries of the auctioneering business and its obscure denizens – not wanting to induce that irritation of the bright and the young who'd already worked it out and resented any suggestion that they didn't know everything. So the younger man was surprised when the beer began to loosen Steel's tongue and he started a discussion about the market, laced with recollections of the early years. He seemed to be edging towards some greater comment about the business and its future, and he could see he had Ryder's wavering attention when he said there was a difference between serving tastes and creating desires.

'At the height of this racket you could play, which is to say *manipulate* elements . . . conduct them.' Steel was warming to his theme, giving it a musical orchestration. 'You're selling something over and above the physical piece. And not just the provenance and history, but some amalgam of the buyer's own background too.'

He said there was a higher register, a deep and complex interaction taking place. Then he smiled, as though beginning to suspect rhetorical flourish, or perhaps interrupted by his own self-consciousness because he was talking to someone in the trade.

Ryder's fickle interest began to be replaced with dissonance. Was there anything that annoyed a young male cynic as much as being caught out as an idealist? It seemed ridiculous that Steel could hope to manipulate desire in others when he seemed so nullifyingly content with his middlebrow lot. The man was a bit of a cultural eunuch – one that Ryder had no desire to emulate. His equanimity and his acceptance of his lot disgusted Ryder; just taking a sliver of the cake. Where was his ambition? His appetite? Ryder wanted a slice, not a sliver – maybe even half the cake. Still, at least he'd seen that there was still some stirring within Charlie, something thoughtful, something that had a passion for it all.

Steel withdrew with the suggestion that maybe it was all an advanced form of the sell, like ivy wrapped round the trunk of a tree. He was pleased with that final poetic curlicue.

Ryder yawned. Charlie nudged his now-empty glass along the bench.

Once Ryder had left for the bar, he pondered the possibility that it wasn't the buyer alone who was manipulated in the act of the sale, but the seller too, as some implied negative of the buyer, also subject to doubt, fear, greed and love. Dealers were buyers too, were they not – enthusiasts as well as cynics? Of course, they convinced themselves that wasn't the case, and the powers that be at Boulets reminded them of monthly figures, transactions, revenues; prose, not poetry. Then again, despite his regular exhortations, he'd still chosen that world.

Ryder came back with two more drinks, which would never be as satisfying as the first. After downing his lager in just a few gulps, he observed that he was probably already over the ludicrous limit, so it was time to get back on the road. Steel took longer to drink his pint of real ale, and Ryder smoked a cigarette while he waited. It was then that he noticed a woman moving round the patrons of the pub garden, with little bundles of green and white flowers in her hand. She was trying to sell them, but getting nothing but scowling rebuffs from the bourgeois Grenache-guzzlers. She approached Ryder and held up a bunch to him.

'Buy some lucky heather, sir?'

'How is it lucky?'

'It grows on the graves of fairies.'

Steel gave her a hard look. 'She's a pikey. Tell her to piss off.'

Ryder got between them. She turned to leave.

'Hang on, what's your name?'

'Lola, sir.'

'How much?'

'A pound.'

Ryder only had a fiver.

'Keep the change.'

The woman was young, maybe Ryder's age. She was very good-looking, in a dark sort of way, with jet-black hair and olive skin. She wore some kind of long traditional dress and had large silver hoops in her ears.

'That's kind of you, sir.'

'Where do you live . . . Lola?'

'On the road.'

'Which road?'

'All roads.'

It touched something inside Ryder, something he wasn't even aware of. It conjured up images of Kerouac and Cassady and the hippie trail, and a different kind of freedom to that of money. It was something he might do some day – leave everything behind. But not before he made his fortune, so he'd have that safety blanket to wrap round himself.

Lola turned away again, and Ryder followed as she crossed the pub car park. Charlie called after him. 'Where are you going?'

'Get yourself another pint, I won't be long.'

The woman was nervous, wondering why Ryder was behind her.

'Why are you following me?'

'Listen, Lola, I'm an art dealer. Do you have anything I might be interested in?'

'And what would you be interested in?'

'I won't know till I see it.'

She stopped walking and looked him up and down, slowly.

'Come, then . . . I'm close by.'

She gave him the invite, even though she was suspicious of this Gorgio and what he wanted. Ryder didn't think there would be anything – it was just there was something about her, the name, it was in his head – *la-la-la-la Lola*. This one most definitely wasn't Ray Davies's trans person and Ryder wondered about kismet, about fate, if there was order in the universe or if everything was just random chaos.

Past the car park, the woman crossed the road and went through a gap in the hedgerow into a field. There was a caravan in the distance, an old-fashioned horse-drawn bow-top wagon, with the animal grazing nearby.

'What if I don't have anything?'

'Then, no harm done.'

Ryder didn't know why he was doing this. It was outside his normal parameters of persistence with a woman. It was as if the feyness of her was making him move, dragging him along, almost against his will. He was stepping into the unknown here – the previously unexperienced. And who was to say a bunch of bandits wouldn't jump out and mug him at any second? Maybe she did this all the time, lulled the lascivious into a false sense of scurrility.

Ryder was wary, even though he'd asked for this – nobody had forced him into the greenery of the field. There seemed to be some kind of latent menace in the air as they walked together towards the horse and wagon, as if the trees were watching him, as if the ground was alive to his movement across it and the sky was touching him with cyanic breath. He kept looking over his shoulder. The surrounding landscape was like a wilderness, a wild sylvan expanse of dark woodland and feral meadow. He never knew there were places like this in Gloucestershire; it was more in tune with somewhere like Slovakia, where he'd been once on a school excursion. Or maybe it was just his overactive imagination.

Despite the opacity of the sky and the sinister greenness all around him, Ryder absorbed the near-to-nature sense and elemental feel which was so close to being oblivious. It felt like the kind of ambience in which a man could lose himself and hide away from the gobbling and grunting of the barcoded world. He sometimes thought there was too much waste – people took more than they needed and, because it was more than they needed, they wasted most of it. But would he feel the same way if he ever struck gold?

He followed the woman, even though he knew it was crazy. Right? On the high blue evening over the wild green of the field. A strange place, with a dark, subliminal beauty which he'd seen once before in an arthouse film about a remote area close to Kashmir, with silver water and lush wild lotus and heady air – the only difference here was the absence of snow-capped mountains.

The evening was eerily still – calm and clear. Ryder shaded his eyes against the lowering sun and looked out across the glass-green surface of the land. The woman was humming a tune to herself, one he didn't recognise, and he was beginning to wonder if she was actually there or not. Maybe he'd fallen asleep after the pints of lager and he was now dreaming all this. Or maybe he was in some kind of trance. He'd heard stories about people being hypnotised by gypsies into giving them stuff, only to wake up and discover all their cash was gone and unable to fathom how it went. Maybe – but she was exquisite, with huge green eyes, and her name was inside his head. *Lola!*

'What's your name?'

'Ryder.'

'Like the man from Brideshead.'

She'd read Waugh? Lola laughed at his scepticism as they reached the bow-top caravan.

'Why are you alone out here?'

'I'm waiting for the rest of my people. They move slower than me, but they should be here by nightfall.'

The inside of the caravan was ornate – baroque even. Rococo and chinoiserie and filigree and enamel, without being gaudy or ostentatious. Ryder hesitated before entering. There was a small fire burning in an epergne stove, which seemed unnecessary, given the heat of the evening. Yet the interior was cool – not cool, exactly; *tranquille, reposant,* spiritual even – it was a milieu never before experienced by Ryder and he was a little unnerved by it, even though he tried not to show it.

There wasn't much light, except for that coming through the small windows and from the dancing red shadows of the fire. A scent of lilac filled the air. Ryder felt uneasy – off guard. This wasn't what he'd expected when he set out with Steel that morning. Although it might have seemed to someone outside his head like a crazy, spontaneous excursion and not something he'd normally do, the subliminal force that had made him follow the woman was more powerful now than ever. It required something of him. It was waiting. But he didn't really know what he was doing or what he was expected to do.

Or maybe he did.

The emanation seemed to be coming from the woman. And, while it was distant before – vague, ethereal, somewhere remote inside his head – now it was close up and personal. In his face. It was outside his scope of experience. The woman stood across from him, watching him. She could see he was nervous – unsure of his surroundings or even himself. Out of sync with the poetry of nature – the shadows and dusky twilight and strangely hued chiaroscuros and dancing silhouettes.

'What would you like to buy?'

\* \* \*

By the time he got back to the pub, Charlie Steel was half-pissed.

'Where in God's name have you been?'

'Doing business.'

As they left the country lanes and filtered their way to the M40 junction, it was as if their little excursion into the bucolic had never happened. The pastoral hinterland had retracted behind them, leaving no trace of their visit.

## CHAPTER 4

# THE CROSS KEYS

Once back in the London traffic, Ryder's thoughts got supplanted. They drifted as he bounced between the lanes, and aligned themselves to the night ahead. He reckoned that now he'd started drinking, he should keep it up – go down to the pub after work and hopefully have some chat with the new barmaid in an attempt to get the gypsy woman off his mind. Then push on to meet other people, preferably outside the auctioneering trade, and take the night as it came.

The Cross Keys was the obvious choice, even though Ryder wasn't all that enamoured of the partisan atmosphere there – it detracted from the release he liked to experience when he frequented a pub after working all day. It had been going on for at least a year, but had only become apparent to the regulars fairly recently. It was a sly battleground between those who saw themselves as local and legit, who treated the forays of a new tribe into their territory with amusement at first, and the after-workers, who came mainly on Fridays for happy hour. Just a few at first, and then they started to arrive in greater numbers and more often, extending their trespass to Thursdays and even Mondays, which had become the hair-of-the-dog day after the weekend. They could no longer be so easily ignored, despite the fact that they were very good at ignoring the locals.

Summer evenings in The Cross Keys now smelled of Chanel instead of cigarette smoke. That was OK for the air-conditioned cyberjoints round the West End, or the politiclubs full of egotistical men and unapproachable women. Guys too interested in catching a glimpse of themselves in the mirrored walls, and women waiting for something indefinable. Or legal eagles working themselves to death, or exchange people pouting, or theatrical types talking shit. Where they had to be seen. Had to be chic. Had to be self-consciously cool. But not here, not in the immutable Cross Keys.

The publican wasn't sympathetic to the gripes of the natives, and even took on extra staff to cope with the additional demand. The regulars had always assumed he was one of them and on their side, even when he began introducing what they considered to be borderline heresies. They gave him the benefit of the doubt; it had to have been forced on him involuntarily by the brewery. But the guy had a dry, taciturn manner that spoke to strength, and enough years of experience to neither get too excited nor intimidated by anything. So, when the fridge appeared and the Chardonnay started to be stocked, he took the jibes graciously as he pulled the pints of Dogbolter and Davy's Old Wallop.

The regulars smirked at first, making light of it, taking the piss, having their bit of fun at the newcomers, who had names like Alistair and Aurelia and caricature faces and fancy drinks. There was so much ammunition it was almost a sport, and the landlord could have sold tickets to spectators had he been minded to. But he was only interested in keeping the drinks flowing at the busy times and he needed more hands, so he hired the new barmaid to help out. She'd been working shifts for a couple of weeks and she was efficient and breezy, and pretty enough to attract Ryder's attention. She could also look after herself, had that way around men that some women have – easy and familiar, but with a line that can't be crossed.

Ryder saw her as a challenge.

The Cross Keys seemed to lie marooned between one tide and the next, a still-just-about-living outpost of the old Fulham. Tucked away amongst regular terraced streets, the big power station, and light industrial units with security fences guarding the weeds on the forecourts. And, of course, Chelsea Wharf itself, just a few hundred yards away. The backwater sense was enhanced further by the busy North Bank road, which swept away from the river as if it wanted nothing to do with the area – traffic rat-runs that Ryder knew how to negotiate. It was a sort of unlovely cut-off, near to other, shinier things – to the cash that was swilling about but not necessarily in the right direction.

To the regulars, there was now their side of the pub and the 'other' side, and the line shouldn't be blurred but it often was. The interlopers were even taking over the space outside, which had been pretty much ignored by the natives until they saw the lovelies using it and then claimed it was theirs. The trouble was, the longer you held ground, the greater entitlement you had to it, and the newcomers were taking over more and more – coming earlier and staying longer. Issues of possession and territory and occupation seethed just under the surface, unnoticeable to the casual passer-by. And the landlord was compliant, because he knew how much money they were prepared to spend. He told the regulars they should drink extra and even suggested they should be more adventurous with their choice of tipple – the ultimate heresy!

Ryder eventually got to leave work and head to the pub. He'd let Charlie Steel out of unloading, which could have been construed as some kind of unvoiced apology for deserting him earlier and not explaining why. Ryder was young and fit, but he considered it demeaning to have to lug furniture around unaided, so he collared one of the Irish porters and offered him a score if he'd hang back and help. The guy's mates jeered him for taking the bribe, as they sloped off to their Guinness and green cabbage.

In mutual surly silence, they hoofed all the lots into the store together. It only took about twenty minutes, quicker than carrying it out of the big house with Steel. Ryder managed a sullen 'thank you' to the Irishman and got a grunt of acknowledgement when he handed over the twenty. Then the guy was off to join the other porters in one of the unlovely pubs they frequented. Maybe it was to do with the price of a pint, or maybe being away from all but their own; Ryder didn't care much either way.

He could tell the Keys was busy, even before it came into view. It had that hive noise. He could see people out on the street as he turned the corner, hear the sound of chat and laughter. He'd had half a thought to swerve it, but decided against that, only because the new barmaid would be serving and he really needed that distraction from *la-la-la-la Lola*.

He pushed his way through to a place least occupied which was close to the locals. He wasn't one of them, but he wasn't one of the Julians either. He was impartial – an outsider, a fence-sitter – so they were merely wary of him rather than hostile.

Someone grabbed his arm, just as he was trying to catch the barmaid's attention. 'Ryder . . . what are you having?'

'Pint of Stella, please.'

It was a reflex response, before even turning to see who'd offered.

Maurice Mears was a nice enough guy. A bit put-upon, which was why he was at the bar, brandishing a fat pink fifty that, no doubt, belonged to Hugo Swanson. Hugo was Mears's boss and the biggest producer in the London office of Boulets – and he let people know it. He never went to the bar himself and believed paying relieved him of that chore. And there were always enough lackeys around him to do the legwork. It was Mears's turn on this particular occasion. You got away with what you could get away with – didn't you?

In exchange for his pint, Ryder was roped into helping to carry back the round of drinks. He was handed some glasses and a bottle of champagne, which he thought was ostentatious in a pub. All right in clubs, but not in pubs.

Swanson was in full flight when they arrived at his table, but was happy to interrupt his train and take control of the bottle and glasses, distributing them where appropriate. A tight circle had formed around him, like a small duchy that had declared independence from the rest of the patronage. Ryder could imagine him issuing his own currency, each coin featuring his leonine profile and mane of hair and promising its bearer simultaneous flagrancy and distinction. He hadn't seen the man grace the Keys for work drinks before, confirming the level of neoteric colonisation. Maybe it was the height-of-summer-heat that had tempted him out amongst the minions.

Swanson seemed to hold a certain dark aura for many people within the firm. Everybody had a view of him, and they were all happy to express it. Ryder was intrigued rather than anything else – for all the barbed words pointed at Swanson, they couldn't eradicate the fact of his success. Did they not understand that their interest was setting him apart from them? Anyway, why would he care? There was much that was dreary in their approach – accusations of arrogance and conceit which might have hit the target, but instead just bounced limply off. Others, in their own minds, thought they were taking him down, but Ryder found that a ridiculous position. It didn't affect the man, not a single jot. The only question Ryder had was why, if he was so good, was he still here? Why wasn't he at Christie's or Sotheby's?

'Ahh, well done, Maurice . . . and look what you've found, one of those van people from furniture.'

Swanson gave Ryder a slightly effeminate look that indicated he was only playing. He continued to busy himself with the wine and glasses, as though it was him who'd undertaken the precarious journey to the bar. He popped open the champagne and filled the glasses of two of the other members of his department. They were called 'the Swans', not just because they worked for Swanson, but because the girls were tall and attractive and sleek and graceful and blonde, and they breezed around together. They had that dual wattage that people could only ignore by denying it, which of course was itself a reaction. Ryder's opinion was, if you had it flaunt it – and if you didn't have it, you should get it.

They were wearing Ballantyne and Aquascutum and Nicole Farhi, and smelled of Givenchy and Valium. Swan1 looked at him with a faint smirk. 'We were deliberating whether the behaviour of an artist in life should affect the way we consider the value of their art.'

It was a welcome-to-our-world gauntlet.

'An everyday pub topic, I see.'

She seemed pleased that she'd dropped him in it, or thought she had. Ryder looked sideways towards the window for a moment, as if for inspiration, then back at her.

'Well, I guess I could kick off with Nietzsche and say the artist is someone who steps outside and releases himself from the normal rules of morality.'

That wiped the smirk from her face.

He continued with a quickfire spiel, dancing through a speedy review of the subject. He could see Swanson trying to jump in and regain the mic, frowning heavily as if he was giving weight, if not birth, to a major academic treatise. Ryder bounced through a list of the saleroom greats – the whorers, absinthers and syphilitic wastrels who'd graduated to Paris. Then he threw in a few scribes – Verlaine, Rimbaud and Henry Miller. He avoided all reference to anyone British, then jumped over to the greats of abstract impressionism and their heroic shagging and drinking and threat – or was it heart – of violence. It had slightly vortexed on him, and he needed to wind it up before it icarused itself.

'So, yes, without their lives there's not much left. But tell me what you think.'

He was reversing the situation, putting her in the hot seat.

She was on the point of answering when Swanson reasserted himself with a low guttural tone that served notice of what he was going to say. He complimented Ryder for an amusing carousel ride and wondered why he wanted to work in furniture, leaving no doubt that he looked down on that department. Ryder wanted to answer that paintings was a closed arena, open only to those of a certain bloodline, but couldn't get it in. He would have said, had he been able, that it came with a certain overbred polite milieu in thrall to a tight roster of clients in an even tighter circle of dealers. At least he got to work with the very best pieces, whereas he'd be slung to the backwaters of twentieth-century art in paintings.

Swan1 came back, still aiming at Ryder, either impressed with his previous response or determined to show him up as a charlatan. He didn't know which.

'Do you suppose we should hold buyers and collectors to the same standard?'

'Is there a difference between buyers and collectors?'

'You know what I mean.'

'Do I?'

'If the collection is good enough, should we overlook how they came by the cash to buy it?'

They all looked towards Ryder with insider expressions of smugness and amusement. Swan1 had brought something else to the debate – the spectre of money. Swanson breathed in deeply. He gave Ryder a raised-eyebrow look, as if to say, *See what you could have if you worked in the right department.*

'If you've got it, why not flaunt it?'

Ryder's answer was as much aimed at Swan1 herself as it was at her question. She seemed to recognise that, and it made her smile.

'Really?'

'Sure. Money is money and art is art. We shouldn't get all self-righteous about it.'

To Ryder, it seemed that Swanson had arranged and composed this little scene – his own circle – a school of Hugo – followers of Hugo. A coterie that set itself apart and remained aloof from the realities of the world. It was a conscious effect that Swanson wanted to maintain. A separateness, something impermeable and clean, like alabaster. Ryder had brought it back down to earth, thrown mud at it, burst the bubble of pretension.

He stuck with it for a while longer – not that it wasn't interesting, but it had its limits. He drained his glass and reckoned it wasn't going to refill itself. Anyway, he wanted to get back to the barmaid. As he slipped away, he was amused to hear Swanson returning to the topic, restating the question and asserting that the Popes were every bit as bad as Caravaggio. He wondered how long the crash-mouthed savant could exist on that plane!

Ryder eased his way through to the bar and was lucky enough to get served by the new girl. He felt the need to order two pints – one just seemed suspect and tragic.

'What time d'you finish?'

'Eleven.'

'What you doing then?'

'Early night. Tomorrow's gonna be another working day.'

In the words of Paul Simon. She even sang it.

'*And I'm trying to get some rest . . .*'

He joined in.

'*That's all I'm trying . . .*'

'*. . . to get some rest.*'

'What about the weekend?'

'Working on my tan.'

'We could do that together.'

She slapped his hand, laughing, and took his money.

But it wasn't a no. Was it?

Now that the barmaid was out of the frame, at least for tonight, Ryder grew bored of The Cross Keys. He considered going on somewhere else, but decided to get an early night too – tired after all the lugging and lifting of the day. As he walked along Black Lion Lane, the barmaid's hologram could no longer overwrite Lola's in his mind, so he switched over to Swan1. He had to wonder why Hugo felt that one tall blonde wasn't enough. Then, every dealer knew that a matched pair of anything would always attract greater attention. Was it also an index of status? Virility?

Ryder decided it was all a bit obvious, a bit naff really, but a long way short of the full Heffner. Was Swanson fucking them? No, wrong question – how often was he fucking them? Together? Separately? How many different variations had he attempted? Was he still generating new ones, the sick deviant? Probably not that sick, and not that deviant. It didn't bother Ryder, it was nothing to him, but the play-back/review function of his mind kept slipping back to the bow-top wagon and had to be constantly reset.

The faux pas, if that's what it could be called, was that Swanson paraded it in a way that made the girls look dissolute and dumb – which Ryder now decided they weren't, or at least not Swan1. The other one might be as thick as congealed pig shit for all he knew. Until now, they'd seemed to him like paired cats, belonging to some Egyptian high priest. Now they were individuals – different, dichot-omous – and, as such, they could be separated.

Even though they were still Swan1 and Swan2, Ryder was making himself think of them in other terms – he even remembered their names, and which belonged to which. It annoyed him that their puffed-up middle-aged boss sought to grant himself status and potency in such an un-English way. He felt like shouting, *For fuck's sake, man, you're as conven-tional as it gets, stop behaving like a Hollywood casting director*. But no, it wasn't that – objectionable though it was – he was old and they were young and the public presentation that they were fucking was repulsive. That, during office hours, they belonged to him, fell under him.

Ryder had heard Hugo refer to them as his daughters, and that was the lie – a reverse psychology claim that this wasn't some sexual chore-ography. They somehow gave legitimacy to Swanson. After all, what was he without them? And that, in a way, answered Swan1's question. They were his works of art. Others could have their Vermeers and their Van Goghs – he had his Swans. He was both buyer and collector.

'Ryder?'

He turned to see one of the women approaching along the street behind him.

It was sultry and still in Black Lion Lane, and Ryder could hear the howling of a lone cat in the distance. Which one was she – he wasn't sure until she came closer and then he could see it was Swan2. What did she want from him? Had Swan1 sent her to tell him he was a fake and a philistine and he'd never be a fine art dealer? Was she going to prove him wrong by proving Hugo right? He wanted to shout at her to go back, but he was caught in the headlights of hesitation. She came alongside and slipped her arm through his.

'Are you going my way?'

'Which way is that?'

She was the wrong Swan and he wanted a woman to supplant the gypsy, not some lightweight version of that woman's pseudo-sister. He'd intended to get some respite with the barmaid in her uncomplicated bed, with no career and no veneer and no neurosis, but – as that wasn't going to happen – beggars couldn't be choosers.

They walked without speaking, and Ryder was surprised to find it wasn't an awkward silence, just the sound of two people without anything to say. He looked away from her eyes, which were trying to scrutinise his secret schemes and low-down lies. He shuffled his feet and she smiled.

'I liked the way you handled that.'

'What?'

'Katie . . . in the pub. Hugo put her up to it, of course, when he saw you at the bar with Maurice.'

Ryder was feeling slightly oppressed by it all, pierced and underestimated by it, the paltry success, the sanctimony. It all seemed so insignificant compared to the earlier sense of freedom in the field. Still . . .

'Didn't you want to stay with the others?'

'No, I was bored . . . like you.'

He felt like a thief in the night, stealing this woman to satisfy some desire to justify himself. There was an unfamiliar misgiving inside his head, and a little worm of self-doubt was burrowing itself into his usual unscrupulousness. But it was too late to feel remorse or regret, with Swan2's velvet voice vibrating on the strings of his soul.

Ryder looked up into the sniggering sky – the moon mocking him and the stars smirking. Her head rested itself on his shoulder, with the anticipated sin of what was coming reflecting itself in her lovely eyes.

And Charlie Steel always said there were no bad men – only bad women.

## CHAPTER 5

# SWAN2

The problem wasn't work; it was the nagging restlessness that stole up on him. Maybe it was the unclear path ahead, but he was only twenty-five, for fuck's sake. The work was fine – it was other things, ingenious anxieties that found him out and bored their little drill-like mouths into him. Those invisible worms of self-doubt. But even that didn't cover it – they were invisible and came from within, not without. He could variably try to ignore them, drown them out, outrun them, give them vent, starve them, or exalt in them.

He didn't suppose he was unique, if he thought about it, but he reckoned he probably felt it more than most – that fatal flirtation with the neon. If it let him alone, it was only for a while, until it reasserted itself – the conviction that there must be something brighter, something righter, that there was always something more interesting going on somewhere else. Then again, things tended to turn out differently to how he imagined.

Just look at last Monday.

Ryder came round to the day slowly. His eyes opened and dimly registered the curtains, which weren't doing much good against the low morning sun – more a diffuser than a barrier. He peered at them, wondering at their drab barren brownness. Who could have actually chosen them? Who could have actually designed them? Funny, it never bothered him when he hadn't been drinking.

The sheets seemed to have deserted the bed and lay on the floor, but his left forearm was pinned down by the blonde head that lay on it. He tried to extract it slowly, to a whimper of complaint. His arm felt dead and heavy when he finally managed to free it. He rolled over onto his back and lay there like an expired pharaoh in final prayer, looking up at the ceiling and waiting for feeling to return to his arm.

He began to replay the evening, bringing it to mind – phrases, lines, looks. Laying them down, trying to assemble and edit it all, filing them away. It was as though if it wasn't recalled it hadn't happened. But he wasn't doing too well. Alcohol had the ability to obliterate all else, its after-effect was doing it now, and in the act of trying to remember, he was feeding the oblivion. That's how obsession started – and also how it ended. It was too early to say which seed fell onto what ground. The inconsistency of desire – he loved how the art world had a register for it all and, in its formulation, made it more allowable.

Fire and air – from baser elements.

The siren call of Swan2, who had since become Anna, and who'd stayed over every night since their initiation last Monday, commanded him in a swirl of shape and desire. Halogen images of Lola still hovered – would it matter to this body lying next to him what was going through his mind during sex? Sometimes a girl just wanted to be fucked, with no strings and no sentimentality.

He slid his hand under the tangle of her hair and began the slow, tidal process of waking her up. After a while, her pliant body turned and her head buried itself into his chest. He traced his fingers lightly down her exposed back and she wriggled in closer. Maybe good sex was good sex for reasons he had no idea about – maybe it was purely instinctual, a restless internal energy that had no connection to merit as a rational human being. Her voice had that husky morning texture when she spoke.

'That was different.'

'Different good? Different bad? Indifferent? Out-different?'

'That's not a word.'

She bounced herself off the bed and sashayed to the bathroom. She'd developed a habit of dropping something into a conversation, then choosing not to explain it or follow it up. It irritated him – as if it was his responsibility to do it for her, to intuit what she was thinking. That was the trouble when someone got to know you, or thought they knew you; they began to read you, work you out, see the patterns – the shortcuts. He felt something was being asked of him, eliciting something from him, attempting to curb him. Was she expecting to spend the day with him? Did he need to make excuses? Did he even feel the need to make excuses? He reached down to his crumpled jacket and fished out a lighter from the fist of shrapnel in his pocket. How had that got there? Had he been through enough rounds at the bar to accumulate all that rubbish?

He found a crushed packet with two cigarettes left in it, pulled one out and stuck it in his mouth, then climbed out of bed. Anna had locked the bathroom, so he walked naked through the patio door which led to the feral garden, and pissed on the wild-growing weeds. Her voice followed him.

'Are you smoking out there?'

'No.'

'You know I hate it.'

The tangled mass of the garden had been beaten back only far enough to accommodate a barbecue some weeks before. The cat was laid out in the sun, giving him a one-eyed glance of minimal concern. He cocked his head so he and the animal looked levelly at each other.

Ryder didn't like domestic cats, couldn't see the point of them. Dogs were different; they were good for certain things, like chasing sticks and barking at birds. Cats did nothing but eat and shit and expect gratitude for their existence. He scraped the foot of one of the metal chairs across the paving. That made the little fucker sit up and adjust its eyeballs. Ryder didn't know who the cat belonged to, if anyone at all, but the wall of his flat was its preferred morning haunt, catching the early slide of the sun. Maybe the cat thought the wall was his, and the garden too, and all the gardens that fell between this street and the one behind. It wasn't boxed into these little lots, but free to roam wherever it wanted.

He'd become used to seeing the cat, but wouldn't go so far as to say he could ever be friendly with the animal. That would give the cat an opportunity to treat him with even more disdain and contempt. Ryder flicked the butt of his cigarette at it, and it hissed amidst a small shower of sparks then laid its head back down in a casual recline as though it'd have him believe he'd failed to disturb it. Maybe he should concede to giving it a name? Maybe Capote, after all unnamed cats?

He knew he wasn't going to spend the day with the girl who was now in his shower – he couldn't face it. He couldn't sustain the effort and, besides, it was something that had run its course. He lit the other cigarette and wondered if there was an optimum time to split up. He found it all slightly ridiculous, all slightly laughable – his own presumptions as much as hers.

The early warmth of the sun on his face brought back some of the night before to him – not all, just disjointed bits and pieces from which he was able to form a narrative.

Swan2 liked to go clubbing – Club 49 in Chinatown or Jakata or Stringfellows or the Metro Café. These places went in and out of vogue daily, and there was always somewhere new where the 'crowd' was going. Proprietors lived or died on the whim of the beautiful people, the hedge funders and political climbers who mixed easily with pop stars and television celebs and sports personalities. With all these shining people, the West End streets looked as bright as the heavens on a clear night, all shining at one another in their own private firmament. Their lights mingling and intermingling until the whole town was ablaze. And the ordinary people looked on from the sidelines and made happy clapping noises from a distance, not daring to get too close in case they got burned. Wondering at the beauty of it all, dazzled by the light and down on their knees giving thanks that they were so uniquely blessed with such wonderment that was psychotic in its extreme self-delusion.

Ryder preferred more orthodox places, like the Velvet Lounge or Blues Alley. Discreet places, where a man could have a drink and talk to a beautiful girl without wondering if she *was* a girl or a half-boy and without the whole fucking world looking down his throat. Places where the bar staff knew him and what he liked to drink, and didn't expect a twenty-pound tip for mixing an overpriced caipiroska.

Last night he'd sat at the bar, drinking a pint of Stella, while she shook her tits at the throng of teratogenetics on the small dance floor. She'd come back over with sweat on her forehead, and stuck her hot tongue into his ear.

'For Christ's sake . . .' Ryder pushed her away.

'Come and dance.'

'Don't want to dance.'

'You're so oblong.'

'What the fuck does that mean?'

She didn't know, it was just one of those 'in' expressions. 'Why are you in such a mood?'

'I'm pissed off with this place. Look at them, they all want to fuck themselves.'

The place was really getting on Ryder's nerves, and so was Swan2. It had only been a week, but it looked like the time had come to part. She let her hand slip between his legs, but he eased it away and knocked back the rest of his pint.

'I'm going.'

'But I don't want to leave yet.'

'You don't have to.'

He put the empty glass down on the bar and walked away across the crowded club. Swan2 watched him go, but she didn't follow. She wondered why she was even with him, him being so oblong and all. But there was something about Ryder that she hadn't seen in any of the other men she'd been with. He did something to her – and it wasn't just the sex. He treated her like a woman, not a girl, and she wanted to be treated like a woman. She could take it.

Swan2 decided to stay at the club, for a while at least. She knew he didn't love her, whatever that meant. What was love, anyway? People loved their dog, their kids, their mother. That was love. The thing between a man and a woman wasn't love – had nothing to do with love. It had something to do with movement and smell and taste and touch and violence and sound and sense and light and dark and addiction and compulsion and hope and despair. But it had nothing to do with love. She ordered another cocktail.

Ryder didn't go straight back to the flat. He called into the Cadogan hotel bar and had a few more pints of Stella. The strong Belgian pilsner was beginning to take effect and he felt restless and disoriented, as if something was happening or going to happen and he didn't know what it was. He thought about Swan2, who preferred to be called Anna, and hoped she wouldn't come back to the flat tonight. It was over, the brief thing they had – if, in fact, they ever had anything. Good for the week it lasted, but when something was over it was over and it shouldn't be dragged out until it turned ugly. He ordered another pint.

It was quiet when he got back, in the solitude of the early hours. He lay on the bed and allowed the coolness to calm him down. Everything was outside where it ought to be; didn't intrude on him, on his inalienable right to be alone. Silence came and lay beside him – touched him nervously – covered him and kissed him. He though about Lola again – about why he'd been attracted to her in the first place. Her wry smile, the way she looked at him, the way her voice spoke to him, the touch of her hand on his. Had she known what she was doing? Had he? He was afraid her bohemian exterior might be masking underlying emotional problems. Dangers. Time bombs. What if he took things further with her – that's assuming he was able to find her again. Would he be in control? Of what? Who'd be in control of who?

'Ryder . . . let me in.'

Ryder continued to lie on the bed without moving. He heard Anna's voice coming from outside the flat.

'Ryder . .'

He wanted to get up to let her in, but couldn't. His body wouldn't move. It was immobile, as if he were dead and rigor mortis had set in. He heard her voice again. Urgent. Louder.

'Ryder . . . let me in!'

He didn't want to let her in, but she wouldn't go away. She kept shouting. He had an in-built bitch meter, and it was flashing red now. Eventually, he forced himself off the bed and made his legs walk to the door – tried to stop his legs from walking to the door. He didn't believe she'd be outside, even though he could still hear her voice. It was a dream. He hoped it was a dream. Wished it wasn't a dream.

He opened the door.

'What took you so long?' Swan2 pushed past him into the flat. 'Were you asleep?'

'I think so.'

She began to kiss his ear and her hands were inside his shirt. She pushed him backwards into the bedroom. He didn't resist. He removed the rest of his clothes while she removed hers and he fell on top of her in the bed. She could tell he was angry, even though they were supposed to be making love. He was really attacking her. Brutalizing her. Trying to make the smug-faced girl underneath him submit to his displeasure.

She manoeuvred herself into the sixty-nine position, and blew him along her white teeth and pink tongue. He buried his face in her silken vulva, breathing hard and dribbling little bubbles of residual lager. The dysfunctional properties of the beer delayed the inevitable, and the two bodies writhed on the bed for longer than either of them could remember, with a couple of cigarette breaks and trips to the bathroom for Ryder, which made his dick go down a little and Swan2 had to get it going again. But it had to be finally brought to climax – so Ryder flipped her over onto her back and entered her in the missionary – which was the way it worked best for him. She kissed his face as the spasms shook his body, and lifted herself up to him to pronounce the pleasure – letting out little sounds of her own, which he never knew if they were real or just for his benefit, nor did he know if he cared that much.

Now, he finished his cigarette and stubbed it out by really grinding it into the stone flagging, as if he had a grudge against it, regretted having smoked it. Anna seemed to be in a hurry when he went back inside. She threw back her still-wet hair and pinned it, while Ryder tried to work out what he was going to say. But she seemed on the point of leaving, which meant he might not have to say anything.

'I've got to go.'

He made a half-arsed show of saying she should stay, that they could, well ... then petered out. Tempting as it was, she couldn't. She had plans. She kissed him goodbye, then left.

He was delighted to be on his own again. While she'd saved him the trouble of getting rid of her, he still managed to resent that she could do without him. That wouldn't prevent him from finishing with her for good on the phone. It already felt like it had fallen off into the past.

Was that bad?

\* \* \*

It was Sunday afternoon, he was hungover and shagged out – the last thing he needed was Jonnie, his elusive flatmate, even if he did still pay rent. Jonnie'd got serious about his girlfriend a while back, and now seemed to just run in and out for stuff. Ryder was still naked.

'Ahh, male recumbent nude. How have you been, Ryder?'

'Make me a cup of tea and I'll tell you.'

'Heavy night?'

Ryder didn't answer; it'd be stating the obvious. Jonnie looked far too happy as he headed to the kitchen. Ryder followed.

'You look sickeningly happy. You know what I've told you about that?'

'Could you please put some clothes on if you're going to be critical?'

Ryder picked up his shorts and shirt from the floor.

Other people's happiness was just about tolerable, provided you were happy yourself. Otherwise, it was completely unacceptable.

'I've come to tell you I'm moving out.'

'Oh no! Where am I going to find someone who I like and who's never here? Have you no consideration?'

'Sorry.'

'You know I won't be able to replace you.'

'That's the nicest thing you've ever said to me, Ryder. But it's not like I'm dead.'

'You might as well be. Don't tell me, that's the second-nicest thing I've ever said?'

'Close.'

In the time they'd shared the flat, the two men had developed an engaging double act, played out mostly for public consumption. It wasn't planned that way, but it had made them a hub of interest and amusement. And you needed some profile – some buzz – for people to want to be around you. But Jonnie had moved on, or grown up. He'd moved away from what he'd been a few years before. Back then he'd been a party version of his real self – wilder, louder, funnier, more on it. More everything. He was happy to drop it all when he met Sophie – the bars, the wildness, the trips. None of it made sense with her; it was before her. He didn't want Ryder to meet her, but it was inevitable, and Ryder told her it was great because now he wouldn't have to pay a cleaner. It was the last time she came to the flat. Now Jonnie was also done with this place.

Jonnie stirred the tea and wondered if certain things needed to be said, and decided they didn't. He handed the cup to Ryder.

'There you go, mate.'

'Mate' wasn't a word they used. 'Mate' was for taxi drivers or for talking yourself out of a fight. 'Mate' was the glue you needed to try to stick something back together.

'That proves it.'

'Proves what?'

'The cat was right.'

'How so?'

'The cat said you're a cunt, Jonnie, in the same way your sister said it, and the time before that when your mother laid out the same claim.'

'Fuck you, Ryder.'

'No thanks.'

Ryder threw the tea into the sink. He ran the tap until it went cold, then lowered his mouth and gulped away. He rummaged in the cupboard, found a can of anchovies past their sell-by date, which he opened and drained then emptied onto a plate. He went outside and looked for the cat, who was nowhere to be seen. Nevertheless, he made a show of putting the plate down and withdrawing with a flourish that would have impressed an audience at the Royal Opera House.

Jonnie picked up the stuff he'd come for and made his way to the door. There was one more thing to be said.

'By the way, I won't be paying any more rent.'

## CHAPTER 6

# THE KNOCKOUT

This particular day off began at 04:45. The alarm was placed just out of his arm's immediate reach and slapping arc, which meant he had to move to stop it. There was nothing good about such starts – the auto-function piss and shower, too early for appetite, an undrinkable cup of tea which he slurped mechanically, then spat back out. *Eat a live frog in the morning and nothing worse will happen to you the rest of the day*, according to Mark Twain. All that really meant was you anticipated something bad happening, so you pre-empted it with something worse. What if something bad didn't happen? Then you were eating a frog for no reason – every day?

Ryder didn't know what had brought the Twain quote into his mind – in any case, it was ridiculous, maybe intuitive in a hokey way, but fuck-all good to him. There were worse things out there than eating frogs. He grabbed his jacket and headed through the door, forgetting for a moment where he'd parked the van. He always made a point of leaving it at least thirty metres away from his flat, so as not to wake any of his immediate neighbours on the early-start mornings. Anyone further away – well, he didn't really care about them. Still, he did try to park in a different spot each time. Was that being considerate? Or was it perversity – instead of disturbing one small group, who might have got used to the early sound of the van, he preferred to spread the disruption over a wider area?

He didn't see another vehicle for at least five minutes, darting his way down the rat run until he joined the M40. Dawn's light showed itself first in his mirrors. Looking straight ahead, it was still night, but behind him he could see faint fingers of light in the sky. It was as if he'd created it as much as perceived it. There was a simple and profound pleasure in seeing the dawn heralded overhead, available only to those up early enough to feel special. Virtue rewarded. We few, we happy few – and gentlemen in England still abed shall think themselves lazy bastards. Then a sense of sky formed – tendrils of clouds, half seen, no longer created. And the spell was broken, the camaraderie of predawn drivers ended. Now there were too many vehicles to be remembered in flowing cups, as the colouring sky continued forming.

Ryder stopped for coffee after two hours. It was better than his tea, but that didn't make it good. But it was wet and hot and went well with a bacon sandwich. He decided against a second, which would never be as fine as the first, and concentrated on the map and catalogue which plotted his day. He wasn't sure why, but he'd made a decision to put something into force – to make something happen. Maybe it was the need to flaunt his acumen in response to Swanson, who'd implied that furniture was just a bit too artisan, not quite as important as the visual arts. He wanted to mark himself out as someone who could have done art, but had chosen to do furniture instead.

And it wasn't that he needed the stamp of cool; he spent a lot of his time doing a good job of detracting from the pseudo-cool things other people did. But why did he feel this sense of emptiness, of being left out in the cold? He didn't know what the answer was. It was no longer enough to just get by. Making a living didn't quite cover it, even the side business, which was what today was about.

Since he'd started in this game, Ryder had a private sideline going on. Why shouldn't he? Why wouldn't he? He saw it as working to the fullest of his ability – furniture might not be the most glamourous end of the business, but it was one he could make pay, twice over. As acting head of his department, and on his own account.

Given that he spent so much time travelling around the country to look at stuff on behalf of Boulets, why would he not also do some of it on his own behalf and utilise the network of auction houses and dealers that he was familiar with? Trading for himself was more than just a way to earn extra cash; it was also a means of building a plexus of useful contacts and connections. The travelling helped too; it was one thing to look through endless catalogues, only everyone else was looking through them as well. Nothing could replace getting your boots on the ground and doing the miles – covering the ground. You never knew what you'd find. Ryder was getting himself known and, in some places, that was fine. It helped with the good regional dealers. He could remain anonymous in other places and that was fine too – sometimes it was an advantage not to be known.

He'd had a few touches. Nothing special, not enough to retire on, but more than beer and petrol money. And he liked holding the folding. He liked the tactile sense of cash, especially when he was outside the trade. Always fifties – it impressed people to peel one off a wad in a bar or restaurant. A fifty looked money, even to the City guys who watched zeroes on screens all day.

After deciding to squeeze in a couple of auction-house viewings that he otherwise wouldn't have looked at, he settled on his route for the day, drained the dregs of the coffee and left the café. Today, he'd picked a plain white van – no name, no number, no gothic calligraphy to set it apart from the plumbers and builders. He said he liked it for its handling, unconnected to its lack of livery, so no nosey fucker would get suspicious. And, anyway, Boulets sometimes liked to do things without advertising their intentions. So how was this different?

Ryder parked the van as far away from the rural auction house as he could and sauntered in unannounced and unnoticed. He nodded to a couple of porters on the way, more in greeting than recognition. He carried on to the display area, with good light coming through the battery of mesh glass windows in the timber-framed roof. In fact, the light was so good, you half expected to find bird shit on the lots of furniture laid out in serried rows underneath. Ryder proceeded down the walkways. There was a certain 'pile 'em high' bonfire-night quality about it all – and, for the most part, it was what he expected to see. He wondered about all the mahogany pulled out of tropical forests and transported around the world – all the craftsmen, all the hands – through time. The indignity of it was too much, the mass-ness of it, like some jumbled recreation of the wood's original forests. A reliquary for what once was.

There were three lots he wanted to look at and they were average. There was some turn to be made on them, but nothing to get excited about. It was as he was going outside for his first cigarette of the day that he noticed Lot 180. It was catalogued as Georgian but, if he wasn't mistaken, it was a Ming temple cabinet. An easy misattribution to make, because some Ming pieces didn't have the oriental design associated with Chinese furniture – they were older and plainer than what was normally seen.

The great uni-controllers of China were all gone, that ambivalent line from ancient dynasty to Marxist mediocrity, dissolved in the waters of pecuniary necessity. The new leaders were accountants, not dogmatists. Budget men and investment bankers and entrepreneurs. The global labour pains of the late nineties had given birth to a new world and brought a new market force into that world. Tough. Screaming. Hungry. A new star was shining from the East. The Chinese were building up a vibrant economy on a bustling manufacturing base, along with sophisticated financial services fuelled by a highly educated workforce. The old bogey of China's human rights record was being trampled into the dust of the Wild East boomtown that everybody wanted a piece of. The country was rich in natural resources and cultivating a healthy stock market. Tycoons were being created who wanted to buy back the heritage that had been stolen from them by the colonialists.

And price didn't matter.

He stopped and pretended to look at the lot next to it. Then he got down on one knee to tie his shoelace and have a closer look at the legs. He really wanted to pull it out and check the backing and the interior of the drawers. He needed to know – to be sure – but he had to be content with what was immediately visible, for fear of attracting the attention of other sharp-eyed dealers. But what he'd seen was enough to cause a flush of excitement. Ryder loved a misattribution. Along with the opportunity to make money, there was something infinitely satisfying about it. Pretention was found out and superior knowledge rewarded. But it was the idea of substantial gain that excited him right now. He didn't even want to do the figures, as though someone might read his mind and steal his bonanza. If he was right, this could make his year. That a lot had been miscatalogued wasn't exactly news; it happened more often than people knew. Ryder didn't bother to leave bids for the other lots.

He'd be coming back.

When he finally got into the van and shut the door behind him, he went full drummer-on-the-steering-wheel and stamped his feet on the floor, simultaneous to a loud 'YESSSS!!!' He could just about think again, in spite of the adrenaline. He breathed in slowly and allowed his heart rhythm to gradually return to normal. The thing was not to get too carried away – not to fuck it up. What if this? What if that? How does this fail? His immediate problem was cash. He had four grand on him and the piece was listed at three to five. It might be enough – then again, it might not.

He got back to the auction house about an hour before he figured Lot 180 would come up. He felt nervous, just being there was making him skittish, as though what he knew was leaking out all over the floor. He imagined everyone looking at him, knowing what he was thinking, waiting to foil his plan. He tried to tell himself it was a sleepy provincial auction and these hicks wouldn't know a Ming from a Malouf if they tripped over it. He positioned himself in the wings, leaning against the wall, where he could scan the other bidders.

To Ryder, people gave themselves away pretty quickly – the middle-aged couples out for a bargain, the first-timers who didn't quite know how it worked, the enthusiastic glee-clubbers moving forward when their lot was about to come up, the looking-arounders seeing who was bidding, the nervous, the know-it-alls. Then there were the auction veterans, the quasi-retired, the teachers, academics, amateur historians, the local parochials passing the time. All of those could be ruled out, and that was almost everyone in a place like this. He scanned some more, looking for the one guy, and it would be a guy, who was paying no attention to what was going on around him.

That's when he saw O'Malley.

Peter O'Malley had something of a reputation, and the situation had suddenly become dangerous – Ryder's worst fear. He moved towards the exit, deliberately bumping O'Malley on the way out.

'Sorry . . . cigarette.'

O'Malley followed him out, as Ryder knew he would. The man was short and stocky with a wide-boy look about him. He eyed Ryder coolly as he came over and gestured without speaking for a light. O'Malley grinned as he handed the lighter back, as if to say, *Let's see how we play this little hand*, each of them recognising something of the same creature in the other.

O'Malley spoke first. 'If I was to guess, I'd say you're after something in particular.'

Ryder was the taller of the two, and looked down on the shorter man in his practised, non-committal stance. O'Malley was unfazed by this and stood as full square to him as his stature would allow.

'I saw that carry-on in your van earlier.'

'So?'

'So now you're back and it seems this might be the time for a talk.'

Ryder smiled nonchalantly, even though he felt like punching the guy. 'Tell me what you're in for, then I'll say what I'm in for.'

O'Malley scoffed. 'Oh yeah, why don't I do that!'

'Look, it'd be better for each of us if the other wasn't here, wouldn't it?'

'Doesn't mean we both can't win.'

Ryder knew what was coming next, but he let O'Malley spell it out. What he was suggesting was known as an auction ring – a knock-out. A situation where two or more parties operated or colluded in such a way as to manipulate the process in order to pay less for an item than they knew it to be worth. Ryder hadn't been involved in one before, and he knew it was illegal. But it would be a great story to tell in a bar and it had just a tinge of the Robin Hood about it. Who had sympathy for the auction house – and, as for the seller, maybe *caveat emptor* should have a corollary? The fact that it was against the law didn't seem to hinder people from advertising their involvement, and they were even regarded as heroes for their insight and intrepidity – all the more adventurous for that element of illegality.

'I'm O'Malley.'

'I know.'

'And you're Ryder ... of Boulets.'

'Which of us should bid?'

One negotiation ended and another began. O'Malley knew which piece Ryder was after and he'd spotted the same misattribution. It was decided they'd split the profit fifty-fifty and that Ryder should be the one to bid, only because he was less likely to be recognised than O'Malley. That meant, if the bid was successful, the item would come into Ryder's possession and he'd have first option on its resale. The word 'trust' wasn't mentioned throughout this engagement, because its mention would have emphasised the irony – considering the reason for the pact was the distinct lack of it. Mentioning it would've seemed like a deception in itself. Besides, the basis of this deal was hard cash, and Ryder only had so much of it, a fact he didn't mention to O'Malley.

\* \* \*

The problem with trust was that, when there was so little of it that mentioning it seemed like a form of deception in itself, it almost became self-guaranteeing. Almost. O'Malley couldn't see Ryder when the bidding on Lot 180 started. Where was he? Better not fuck it up! Ryder could see him, looking all edgy with his head bobbing around. The basis for furniture valuation was depth of market and comparable sales. It differed from the art world, whose dynamics weren't the same. The catalogue estimate seemed fair, one of those moving catch-alls, if it had been what they thought it was. A sale was a dynamic process with its own energy and rhythms, so why bind it too tightly, why anchor its supposed value too closely to a single figure? Of course, people then thought the valuation was a mere figment, that it had no basis, no solidity. Even the experts couldn't say, and that was the great unspoken in this world – the fear that it had no basis. Everyone wanted to see it go wrong at some level.

Ryder knew that a similar Ming piece had sold for almost £200,000 at a London gallery only three months previously. And he wasn't sure if O'Malley knew exactly what it was worth. He felt a strange assurance at that moment, as if the outcome was already known. Time just had to spool out to reveal what had already taken place. And yet its remaining uncertainty was what made it exhilarating.

The fight or the prize?

The bidding was slow; there was slack if steady interest. Starting at £1,500, it lumbered its way upwards. Ryder bid at £1,700 and again at £2,100. There were six bidders to begin with, including himself. Two dropped out at £2,500 and he could see two of the other three. A county-looking late-middle-aged woman, elegantly dressed. Must be buying for herself, he thought. And a bluff, tweeded man in a checked shirt who might have been a farmer or ex-military. Ryder might have been good at judging buyers, but there was always the odd time they'd confound him. There were all sorts of people who collected, and they could be experts in their areas of interest. The older ones had plenty of time, and usually money too.

The bidder he couldn't see was behind Ryder and was quick to bid it up – sending the message he was serious. As bidders dropped out, the few who remained became more visible and now Ryder paid greater attention. It was down to three when the lot broke through its upper estimate of £5,000, accompanied by a collective exhale. A current transmitted itself through the auctioneer and pinged off all the objects and people in the room. Every bum on every seat rotated this way and that, a few degrees, with each additional bid. Ryder didn't like people being able to see him; it was why he always stayed close to the back. His bidding was no more than a gesture now, he just nodded slightly with a half-blink and stood motionless with his arms crossed.

Down to two and the insistent quick bidding of the man behind him became irritating. Ryder took exactly the same number of seconds to respond each time. In that delay sat the hope and then the disappointment of the other bidder. If the man had earlier taken it for lack of resolve, he'd now have to think again.

The pattern continued upwards in bids of £100 – £6,700, £6,800, £6,900. Ryder's timing was metronomic and evenly spaced. It was clear to him, when there was momentary hesitation in the other bidder's response, that he would now win. He stayed on beat. The other man kept going for three further rounds, then hesitated again. The auctioneer put it to him at £7,700 and he confirmed. Ryder followed suit. The hammer finally fell at £8,000 – just on the limit of Ryder's fifty-fifty pocket. He blew an inward sigh of relief.

There was another collective exhalation, then the mass resumption of conversation, like glass breaking. The auctioneer nodded confirmation to him and he acknowledged, then attention moved on to the next lot. Drama over. Ryder watched his acquisition get moved off by a pair of porters. A good time to slip away. He went outside for a cigarette and waited for O'Malley to find him.

O'Malley was all smiles and hands outstretched, as if celebrating a goal, forgetting that they were supposed to be inconspicuous and separate. Ryder could only manage a half-smile – how much better would 100 per cent profit have been! The £8,000 was gathered together and a handshake followed, insincere on Ryder's part.

'Buyer's premium?'

'Five per cent here.'

'Let me pay it, Ryder, for the great work you've just done.'

'Very good of you, O'Malley.'

'I want half of it back from the resale.'

O'Malley also wanted details of how Ryder was going to go about that. Who would he approach? How much would he ask? How much would he settle for?

'I think it's worth a hundred and twenty thousand.'

'That much?'

'Maybe less.'

Ryder just wanted to get going. It'd been a tense day and he was tired, with a long drive in front of him. He didn't want to spend time chinwagging about the trade and getting to know O'Malley. It got to him that people felt the need to tell him about themselves – wouldn't it be nice if, once in a while, someone wasn't out to convince him they were great and their lives important? It was that sort of behaviour that got him all riled up, and then he had to reply in kind. But, in seeing only the brash certainties and missing the underlying insecurities, it allowed Ryder to box people in and kick against them. For him, this made his own naked individualism a nobler enterprise.

'Don't forget, Ryder ..'

'What?'

'I know how to find you.'

## CHAPTER 7

# HOLMES

Lucien Holmes lay sprawled on a sofa whose rococo magnificence was out of place in his bunker of an office at the back of his premises. One arm was thrown over his face. It lent him an aspect of woe, should a painter choose to represent the scene. Grief-stricken male figure recumbent. Actually, he was on the phone – he was always on the phone. The call was taking so long that he wrapped his arm over his head as a change of position. He looked down at his toes and wriggled them absently. It had long been his habit not to wear shoes or socks when he was in the shop. But now he no longer bothered to put them on even to speak to people who came in – his so-called customers. And he only spoke to them if he couldn't get Gerard or Cassie to do it.

Generally, his staff knew they should try to deal with anything that came up before bringing it to him. So when he saw Cassie walk in and look at him in that slightly pissed way, he knew he'd have to get off his arse. On this occasion, he didn't mind so much. He wanted to end the call and this was as good an excuse as any. She stood there, waiting, as he rounded off the conversation, inspecting the nail on his big toe at the same time. Holmes liked Cassie; she had the air of someone who wouldn't take any shit, even from him. And now she looked sullen, sarcastic, like a bored schoolgirl waiting to chop some boys down to size.

The caller on the other end was reluctant to go and, for Cassie's benefit, Lucien started yakking his hand like a glove puppet and feigning a yawn, to indicate he was bored and doing his best to extricate himself. Holmes seemed to be perpetually bored, except with Cassie – in fact, he told her she was the only thing he'd never be bored of. They both agreed to treat it as the truth – which it sort of was.

'Well, you do that and give me your answer. Bye.'

He hung up abruptly, mouthing the word 'cunt'. Then he pulled a big, oversized smile, the one he did just for her and no one else, or at least that's what he said. She called it his 'Mack the Knife smile'. He liked that.

'Why can't they all be like you, Cassie, instead of the multitude of cunts who afflict me?'

She didn't take him seriously for the most part, which was why it worked so well. To her, he was a forgivable reprobate spaniel, whereas to most other people, he was an opportunist hyena. It helped that Holmes had known Cassie since she was born – he used to knock about with her father, who had a reputation for being on the fringes of the law. One day she'd walked in off the street and said she wanted an interesting job, and he was the most interesting man she knew. She was eighteen. And here they were, ten years later.

'There's someone outside to see you.'

'A cunt?'

'You'd probably designate him as such.'

She rarely used the c-word herself. Not that she wouldn't, but her view was, once you started, where did you stop? And, at work, she saw it as her role to try to keep Lucien contained for as long as possible and not cause contention from the outset. Not that the work boundaries were all that clearly defined. It was a standing joke that Holmes had got to the point where he clearly objected to people coming into his shop – people who wanted to deal or see him about something or wanted something from him specifically. They seemed to have a misplaced belief in his magical abilities – that he could turn water into wine. Trouble was, the more he told them they couldn't come in, the more they wanted to, and the more interesting and in demand he became. That trick was OK for nightclubs and exclusive restaurants, but why did they all feel they had to have a piece of him?

'Why can't Gerard deal with it?'

'I knew you were going to say that. Because he's not here.'

'And what was I going to say after that?'

*'Can't you deal with it, Cas?'* She said it in a whiny voice, mocking him. 'The answer should be obvious, otherwise I wouldn't be in here.'

She had him on a spike, giving him her withering look that made him feel like he better appease her. A look to be used sparingly – like certain words.

He threw his head back at the sheer unreasonableness of the world, at how he had to do everything himself. He jumped up and off the sofa, like a wrestler flipping back onto his feet, ready to go again.

'Right, let's go see what this clown has to say for himself.'

'Clown?'

'Cunt, then.'

He threw her a sidelong glance as he passed by – a 'you're really making me do this?' look. Cassie shrugged and told him he might want to put on his shoes. He flicked his hand in dismissal.

Holmes had one of those shops people rarely went into – even Holmes himself. And, when he *was* there, he didn't want to be disturbed. It was an imposition to have to deal with people, especially ones he didn't like – and that defined practically everyone he knew. Not that he found it unpalatable to be there; quite the opposite.

'This is where I like to lie low during the day.'

It was just irritating when Gerard wasn't there and Cassie couldn't cope. Surely that was the point of employing people – to act like buffers? To get between him and anything annoying?

It was doubtful if Holmes ever cared that much about anything, but he'd become incorrigible as he got older and more successful. It was as though he'd come to understand just how central he was to the enterprise he was involved in: dealing. People were buying a piece of him, of what he brought to the transaction, the pheromone that exuded from him. He was never that sure if it said something about him, or about all the others. The world could walk by his shop and never come in. He wasn't interested in that world. He had a globe of his own, there in his display window, for the taking or leaving. If you took it, you had to accept that Holmes could tilt it on its axis.

Gravity and wealth, these things coalesced in certain places – in people and postcodes.

The people who did come in – well, most of them weren't that interesting, but what could he do? Some of them had money, of course – most of them. But even those, Holmes didn't care about that much, could take or leave. If they came in, it meant they wanted something from him, not the other way around. And he no longer had to worry about making a living, at least not in an ordinary way – not in a mundane, boring, grafting, everyday way.

As it happened, the cunt outside very definitely did not have money, yet here Holmes was, barefoot in the street, peering into the back of an unsigned white van. But that niff of a deal was in the air; even if he thought the possibility was remote, it still got the adrenaline in him going. He could have fun with it, mess with it, play about with it a bit – and who knew? Maybe.

He'd strode out ready to go to war with whatever was asking for his attention, but it was something of interest, as it turned out.

Holmes barrelled over to Ryder, who noticed he was barefoot. He pulled himself up onto the tailgate of the van, which heeled over slightly and then righted itself.

'Right, so where's this thing that, apparently, I'll definitely want to see?'

'And then you'll want to buy.'

Ryder stood to one side, to reveal the blanketed form of the cabinet. Holmes looked at him as if he was an idiot.

'I can't see it.'

Ryder was about to speak, then decided to keep his mouth shut and just drew the tapes through to release his prize. He pulled the sheet off and let it drop, giving the action a stripper's touch of theatricality.

Holmes stepped forward and looked. Not averting his eyes, he pointed a finger at Ryder.

'Who are you?'

'Ryder.'

'And who's Ryder?'

'A dealer.'

'Really?'

People drove stuff round all the time, but he normally knew them, and they normally said they were coming. This was speculative – very speculative. Maybe this young fellow just wanted to meet him, to be able to say he'd encountered the great Holmes and tried to do business with him?

'This is interesting, you know. Well, I guess you do know.'

'That's why . . '

Ryder stopped in mid-sentence, because Holmes held up his hand to cut him off. He reckoned he didn't need to say anymore as he watched Holmes circle the Ming like a cat round an injured pigeon. Ryder could see the dealer's sharp interest, even though he was frowning and looked to be fretting as he moved round the cabinet, gauging its proportions in the pinched environs of the van. What was the point of interrupting him?

Holmes was completely given over to his appraisal, as though Ryder wasn't even there. His sceptical expression was replaced by one of suspicion as he tapped the surface and examined the joints, pulling out drawers and stretching his hand into the space to check the hidden workmanship. He traced his fingers over its length and width to savour its exquisiteness, to take it in. Then he stood up straight.

'Where did you come by it?'

'Gloucestershire . . . rural auction.'

'How much did you pay?'

'Well . . .'

'Oh, come on, Ryder!'

Holmes's insistence was disconcerting. It wasn't done, asking people how much they'd paid. But this was Holmes and he did whatever he wanted.

'Two hundred,' Ryder lied.

'Two hundred what? Buttons? Dustbin lids?'

'Thousand.'

'And you could afford that?'

'I have a partner.'

'Who?'

Ryder hesitated again. This guy was too much. Who did he think he was? He could have taken the piece to someone else – he'd been told Holmes didn't ask questions.

'Peter O'Malley.'

'That cunt! You don't want to be doing business with him.'

'I had no choice.'

'I see . . . a knockout.'

Ryder was not going to comment on that remark.

'Anyway, you were right. I do want to buy.'

It was audacious. Most dealers wouldn't be so upfront, they'd hedge and haggle and feign disinterest to begin with. But this was Holmes – there was no feint, no game, no bluff, no guile. It was so definitive that Ryder thought the work was done – all the practised lines, all the rehearsed arguments, rendered obsolete straight away.

Holmes grabbed the side of the van and stepped down awkwardly, hurting his knee. He grimaced, unseen by Ryder.

'Why don't you bugger off and have a chat with your partner about what you'll take for it?'

'Well, I know roughly . .'

'Come back tonight at seven.'

Holmes didn't wait for, or need, an answer. The pain in his knee had subsided, so he marched back in through the doors of his emporium, with his name writ large across the frontage – solid, yeoman-like, reassuringly plain.

So that was Holmes, Ryder thought to himself. He'd always wanted to meet the legend and now he had.

He'd be back at seven, with the number that was already in his head.

\*   \*   \*

Ryder returned to Holmes's shop that evening. It was shut – why wouldn't it be? The heavy cage grille had been pulled across the front, with a lock the size of a house brick securing it in place. The interior was dark, with the only light coming from the window display. Ryder couldn't help but look. The items on show seemed transubstantiated somehow. Their light, framed by the darkness, cast a sense of disembodiment out into the street. There was a theme, of course – Far Eastern, as it happened, but not Chinese. Coincidence? A rare Vietnamese temple vase with a blue dragon motif on a black background; a Cambodian carved stone statue of a bare-chested female deity with an ornate headdress; an imperial Japanese lacquered case, on which the sharpness of the craftsmanship seemed unbelievably impossible. They seemed to float, hardly tethered by their physical components. People would want them, that desire compelled by them being on the other side of impenetrable glass. He imagined how his polished-up Ming cabinet would look in such a setting – exquisite, priceless.

Ryder went to the door and pressed the bell. No response. He pressed it again, beginning to think that Holmes had changed his mind and this wasn't going to happen after all. No one came. The light stayed off. Then he saw the rough notice that had been sellotaped onto the inside of the glass door, but had come loose and fallen to the floor. Two words, scrawled in large green felt tip: 'RYDER – GASWORKS'.

The cab took ten minutes to get to Gloucester Road. It wasn't ideal to have to come to this place, and Ryder hoped it wouldn't be the same doorkeeper as the last time. The incident replayed itself in his mind as he walked up to the entrance. Why was it that when you were rejected by something, it became of greater interest? Some rule of attraction? Almost Newtonian. It was totally unreasonable, of course – even at the time. When he heard his own words of complaint, he knew he wasn't going to change the outcome.

Well, there was nothing else for it now – he'd been planning to ignore its existence for a few months, but Holmes was in there, so that's where he needed to go.

The last time Ryder had been up to its thick exclusionary door, the slot window had opened, some words were exchanged and the slot had closed again. He'd stood there for a while, thinking the door might unlock, but it didn't. And that was that – looking like a tit in the arse end of West London with a girl he'd dragged there on the brag that he could get them in. That was his previous experience of this place – on the wrong side of the unforgiving slot with that little French fucker behind it. The snail-eating shit had been all uppity with him, and he'd called him a charmless fucking Napoleon in return. That might have been recoverable, but it led to a mix of heavy invective from which there was no reprieve. The recollection made him wince.

Ryder swore he'd never come back, but the place was an unofficial hangout for many of the art crowd, somewhere you needed to be seen if you had insider aspirations. As ever, hasty action was to be regretted at leisure. How could he have known at the time that this would be the thing to foul up his plan? Even as he was preparing himself to apologise and do whatever it took, he could feel himself kicking against it, half reforming the attitude that had got him into this situation in the first place. Still, maybe someone else would be behind the slot.

He knocked. The peephole swiped open and there were the beady Gallic features he'd hoped to avoid. The eyes, beaklike conk and pursed lips of the truly self-righteous inerrantist. The guy was in no hurry as he looked Ryder over, enjoying that his abuser had come back to ask to get in again.

Ryder figured that he might as well get on with it, since any hope that the guy wouldn't remember seemed to have fled.

'I want to apologise . . . you know, for the last time.'

The man's eyes lowered but kept on Ryder, who could no longer see his mouth. If he had, he'd have seen the ghost of a smile, as the doorkeep anticipated exacting his revenge.

Ryder blabbered on. 'It was wrong of me . . . and I'd like to say sorry, fully and completely. I was drunk and showing off to the girl.'

He felt like a stripper in some Amsterdam slot gallery, being observed by disembodied eyes. It was demeaning and he wanted to poke a freshly sharpened pencil through the slot and into them. Yet he kept grovelling – there was too much at stake.

'I believe I may have appelled you, in terms that might have been construed as offensive. Believe me, they weren't meant to be and were offered only in jest.'

'You called me a French . .'

The guardian at the gate broke off dramatically, happy to prolong Ryder's discomfort.

'You called me . . . I shall not use the word.'

'Sounds entirely possible, but I have little memory of it.'

'And you did so repeatedly.'

'As I said, I'm extremely sorry. I wonder if there's any way . .'

'Oh, you want to get inside?'

'Yes.'

'And I thought you had come only to apologise.'

'That too.'

Ryder detested the servility of what he was having to do. He wasn't really into abasing himself and he'd gone as far as he was prepared to. Fuck Holmes anyway, for putting him in this situation.

He tried one last time.

'I have a rendezvous with Mr Holmes.'

'Holmes, did you say?'

Ryder nodded contritely. He could see the name Holmes carried some weight in this place, but he decided to let the pervy little voyeur pretend it was his idea to have a change of heart. Let him have his pathetic jobsworth power – for now.

'I think I am preparing to forgive you.'

His eyes continued to fix on Ryder, to play the game of keeping him outside, extending the time over which he had control. Eventually, he withdrew and slid the screen slowly shut. Even then, he made Ryder wait and, after a totally unnecessary delay, he opened the door. Ryder felt like kicking him in the crotch, but he didn't. This was just a club, he told himself, but for now it was a club he needed to get inside.

And where was Holmes?

## CHAPTER 8

# THE GASWORKS

The Gasworks was a club in the same way as Holmes's emporium could be described as a shop. It wasn't untrue, but it was definitely misleading. It was both a drinking joint and a fuck-you, and you'd be disappointed if you arrived believing in the basic tenets of service expected of an establishment that described itself as a bar/restaurant. That was wilful misrepresentation. The whole point was to keep people out, but not through some concept of maintaining exclusivity or a mysterious brand élan. It was more a policy of not letting wankers in. Of course, the theme-pub twats tried – the more you rejected people, the more they wanted to see what they were missing. It was how they created heat in the plastic-and-platitude establishments.

But not here.

No, The Gasworks belonged to the conspicuously cool, and you had to be part of that *tableau vivant*. Wankers were taking over everywhere, and The Gasworks had developed an exclusivity way beyond that of platinum and roped-off areas. No clipboard jobsworths here – just the grille, from which you were inspected and either admitted or rejected, on the basis of first sight being right. No discourse. No recourse.

The Frenchman's name was Nicole, which he announced as if they were meeting for the first time. His appearance, now that Ryder could see the rest of him, was fastidious and he had an OCD air about him. Maybe he was only ever perfunctory when he looked at people through the slot. Ryder, instead of sticking him in the eye or kicking him in the crown jewels, offered his own name and his hand. Nicole took it in a limpish way, like he was inspecting the manicure, or lack of one. What a strange little fruit – a kumquat – a quince.

Nicole swept along a corridor and conveyed Ryder through to the bar. He was sure this personal touch and attendant cordiality was to do with Holmes and not himself, not that it mattered. What mattered was, he was here. And, now that he was finally inside The Gasworks, he was curious to see the source of such headiness, having heard so much about it. People always overdid their describing of places, but the innards of The Gasworks matched up to everything he'd been told. It was a splicing together of the profane and the insane – a playpen for the bastard offspring of Hieronymus Bosch and Divine the Drag Queen. By the time he'd found Holmes, he felt like he'd walked into a Pogues song.

That was the clientele. The backdrop was just as exotic – a hoard of stuff that had been hooked, fenced, won, lost, or passed through on a handshake and a lie. For a trial that would never be held, in which the names had been changed to protect the guilty. Full of oddity to his dealer's eye – pornographic chess pieces, dishevelled leather chairs, defrayed décor, gaudy gilt-framed paintings of uncertain provenance – like a ship had tipped out its cargo from a ten-year tour of the more erogenous zones of the world. The place exuded a sense of unseen decay, as if some pathological hoarder had been given free rein to unburden him- or herself, aided by a group of dissolute dipsos.

This place looked like it already shouldn't exist. Art people were always on about the patina of a piece, the accumulated dirt, the layer that gave the expression of age, of history, of use or even misuse. The Gasworks had its own patina – a bit scuffed, slightly grubby, as though the surfaces should never be cleaned, marked as they were by drink, argument, drugs, sex and god only knew what else. In here, they didn't trust stuff to be clean – clean was fake and sterile and prudish; gunge was good, just like greed in the 1980s.

Everything about the woman behind the bar told Ryder that she ran the place. She didn't just run it, she *was* it. Almost six foot tall, with a blonde beehive that made her look even more intimidating. She wore a miniskirt that was too tight, with a boob tube and big hoop earrings. A cigarette dangled from the bright red of her lips. This was her club and these were her people. She was queen over all she surveyed, and Ryder could see why the likes of Holmes could fondly slide into the embrace of the place.

Holmes was standing at the far end of the bar with a crowd who looked to have taken over that section. The dealer was gesticulating theatrically and he delivered what Ryder assumed was the punchline, because his retinue hooted in amusement. He could hear the laughter above the rest of the noise. Filthy. Ribald. Belly. Ryder waited, allowing Holmes the afterglow of his witticism; he'd already flopped onto a velvet sofa and taken a slug of what looked like a pint of gin and tonic.

Holmes saw him and waved him over. He introduced Ryder to everyone.

'Everyone, this is Ryder.'

Then he clasped the younger man's shoulder and led him away from the entourage, so they could talk business in private. The woman from behind the bar approached.

'Either of you two drinking?'

'This is Shells, Ryder. She's the most important person in this place, apart from me. But don't tell her. I don't want her getting all big-time.'

Shells scoffed at his clowning and shook hands with Ryder. Holmes ordered two large gin and tonics, then said he was off for a piss and they should get better acquainted while he was gone. Shells shook her peroxide head.

'It's because I once said only posh people drink G&Ts.'

'Maybe he thinks if he drinks it, he might become posh?'

She seemed to find that idea amusing. 'Well, it's not working. But I think that's the last thing he'd want.'

'Maybe you should've said only wankers drink G&Ts. Then again ..'

She leant into him as she laughed.

By the time Holmes came back, she'd served up two half-pints of gin and tonic. Ryder tried to pay, but she said they were on the house – friend of Holmes and all that. Then she left them alone.

'So, have you and your partner come up with a number?' Holmes slipped onto an unoccupied bar stool. 'Cash, mind.'

He said that as if paying in cash should decrease the amount asked for.

'What we paid for it, plus fifty for our trouble.' Ryder recalled the last time he'd mentioned a number to Holmes, so he quickly qualified it. 'Thousand, that is.'

They both smiled crookedly at each other and settled into silence. Holmes raised his glass and took a sip before speaking.

'The cabinet – you stole it, didn't you?'

Ryder feigned indignation; Holmes's remark was almost true.

'Of course not!'

'Listen, Ryder, I wasn't born under a cabbage. I've made enquiries and I know you and that cunt O'Malley couldn't come up with two hundred Gs even if you were printing the stuff.'

Ryder looked around sheepishly, as if trying to find support and inspiration where there wasn't any. He caught Shells' rueful gaze from behind the bar, indicating she knew this was a contest between the pretentious pup and the full-grown dog. Ryder decided to put his cards on the table – well, some of them.

'It was a misattribution, catalogued as Georgian.'

'How did they make that mistake?'

'Backwater evaluators . . . it came in with a job lot of Georgian from a clearance.'

'So, again, how much did you pay?'

Ryder hesitated before replying, then let out a sigh to convince Holmes that he'd won.

'Eighty.'

Holmes smiled victoriously. 'That's more like it.'

He took another sip from his glass, then began writing on a serviette from the bar, stopping while pretending to think, then continuing. He pushed the serviette over to Ryder, but prevented him from looking at it, while glancing at the gin and tonic.

'I'd take a slug of that first, you're not going to like it.'

He sucked his teeth and gave Ryder a fang-like smile. Ryder picked up the serviette without touching the drink. He eyed the figure written on it, then looked back at Holmes, poker-faced. He folded the paper and pushed it back across the bar.

'You're right.'

'See, I said you wouldn't like it. That's why I told you to take a drink beforehand.'

'Needs to be a bit thicker.'

'Cash is always disappointingly thin when it's bundled up.' Holmes said this with a winsome grimace, as though it were a cause of regret to him. He reached inside his pocket and pulled out a vial of pills. He placed them on the counter. 'My doctor said I should take these if I felt I might be having another heart attack. Funny, but I feel as strong as an ox. You could pop a couple if you want. Have a drink, have a think, and tell me what you want to do when I get back.'

He slid off his stool and sauntered over to the troops. Ryder could hear him barrel straight back into the conversation. He'd come here with a rehearsed spiel and a narrow window of negotiation. This was supposed to be the big one for him. It'd seemed, back outside the shop, that Holmes had accepted the buying price and it would be a given that he and O'Malley would deserve a profit for their acumen and the risk involved in the knockout. So, £250,000 wasn't unreasonable, and he knew, with Holmes's connections, the dealer could make a nice little bundle for himself without having to lift a finger.

The offer on the serviette was £100,000, lower than Ryder would have liked, lower than what he had as a minimum. Sure, he'd make £92,000 – split with O'Malley, it'd be £46,000 profit for him, minus his half of the auction house commission. But this was his deal from the beginning – he'd spotted it and now he was getting shafted, first by O'Malley and now by Holmes. It was too low-ball!

Holmes may have been a hero to many people, but not to Ryder. Ryder didn't have heroes. Of course, Holmes was a legend, he'd heard about the deals the man had done, the famous and fortune-owning people he'd sold to and hung out with. As far as Ryder was concerned, it was mostly self-mythologising – Holmes had a talent for manipulating people, and the manipulated always aggrandised the manipulator to excuse their own gullibility. Still, it was a lesson to deal with Holmes, one of those milestones, one of those occasions that would prove irresistible to mention. The trick would be not to mention it too often – another one of those inverse laws. The potency was in the selective use. On the other hand, it sometimes nauseated him when people garnered refracted glory by just being near a magnetic force.

Holmes had been surprising in this negotiation. He hadn't approached it in a textbook way – textbook was always weak, because it was known. It wasn't wrong, but it was like 'pawn to king four' in chess – a good play, but a play with a clear and well-anticipated response. Holmes had cut all the crap. From the beginning, he hadn't played coy by pretending he didn't want it. Then he'd brought Ryder to his den, which he knew would knock some of the cocksureness out of him. He'd also done his homework and knew neither Ryder nor O'Malley had the financial clout to acquire this piece legally. And now he hadn't given him any guff about different costs – van man versus premises man. He'd made his offer in a way that appeared non-negotiable, and Ryder had to give him respect; the man had class.

Ryder sat there thinking and, while he spun his cogs, he knew Holmes wasn't doing the same thing. Though he was out of sight in the coalescing crowd, he wasn't game theorising to the nth about it. Sometimes being clever wasn't a plan – the unreasonable man, the man of instinct, had the advantage. At the same time, the rejection of a first offer was always expected.

Ryder took a deep drink from his glass as Holmes flitted back to the stool after a few minutes of regaling his audience.

'So?'

'I can't do it at that price.'

'I knew you wouldn't like it, but I'm not here to make you happy.'

'I need more.'

'You mean you *want* more. I can understand that. Did you take any of those pills?'

'My heart's fine.'

Holmes re-pocketed the pills and considered what he was going to say.

'You think you can't accept the first offer, isn't that right, Ryder? You think that would be weak.'

Ryder was about to reply. Before he could, Holmes was off his stool again and dragging him by the arm.

'Come with me.'

Ryder followed him into the commodious gents' toilets, wondering what was happening. He had a look about – a mounted moose head, heavy gilt-framed oils, a tiger pelt on the floor, other assembled deviancy.

Holmes gestured to the lines of cocaine he'd quickly chopped out on a low art-deco glass table. 'Now, that's what I call an improved offer.'

'Better than your heart medicine, I suppose.'

'There's an argument to say that, because this was probably up someone's arse, the traps might be more appropriate.'

Holmes paused, and lifted his hand in acknowledgement of an imagined audience. Then he rolled up a fifty and offered it to Ryder, with a trace of amusement on his face.

'Are you going to tell me you don't?'

'I do. I very much do.'

Ryder took the note and snorted one of the four lines up his left nostril. He lifted himself back up, then dived down again and took the fattest line up his right barrel. This time he whinnied and threw back his head like a spooked horse. With a teary eye, he handed the note back to Holmes.

'You banged the big one!'

'I did it for O'Malley.'

Holmes chuckled at that. This young guy had something about him that he liked, and that was rare. But he still needed to hear Ryder accept the offer.

It wasn't hard; it wasn't even close to hard in the end – and that was before the coke kicked in. He could have tried to negotiate further with Holmes, and he might have got a bit more, but probably not. And O'Malley was going to bitch anyway and figure he could have done better himself. Ryder, in the end, decided to accept the offer and have the night paid for by Holmes.

'Put your wallet away and come meet some interesting people.'

The rest of the evening flowed from exactly that point, as he was brought into the fold. When they went back to the table, it was as though he'd been admitted, as though the others accepted it from their king. This young guy was now part of it, at least for tonight.

Between the booze and the blow, it was increasingly difficult for Ryder to work out who was who and how everyone fitted in. Holmes started out with vague introductions, then waved it off, as though it was too much effort. Let them talk, let them work out if they like the sniff of each other. What did it matter to him?

Ryder succumbed to the defrayed circle of friends, taggers-on, joiners-in and passers-by. In the end, it didn't really matter who or what they did. The cocaine was really hitting him, cascading down the back of his throat. That was good chop – he felt its rush and was touching his face more than was necessary.

There was Rollo, whose gappy smile and hollow cheeks suggested a long-requited love affair with the night and its wares. Pavel was lairy and loud. Ryder had never met a Russian before, and the man's voice came out of him in a deep bass. He had a couple of girls with him, and they were laughing and Ryder's glass kept getting filled and they were all keyed into this thing happening right now – whatever it was. He had to stop touching his face. Was she laughing at him?

'Leave your nose alone.'

She was fit and he could feel his obsessive interest growing. She was becoming metallic in his mind – her ringleted hair and her black metal-edged dress a bit showy, a bit trampy. He couldn't tell if it was expensive or cheap. Whatever it was, it worked. He should probably have remembered which name went with which face earlier – it was too late now. His fetid imaginings were running so strong that he had the paranoid sense the others could see them jangling around in his mind like the pornographic chessmen and -women.

'I want to do more coke.'

Ryder said it out loud, then gawped with pretend shame at Metallic. She smiled with a cool seriousness and drifty eyes. 'Who doesn't?'

In the public gents, she swept her hair away to one side and leaned over the cistern. Ryder could see her dress tighten and ride up an inch or two on her thighs. She glanced at him, then went back to racking up the lines. Early coke – the paradise isles, Ryder thought, but you couldn't get back there once you were banished. You'd get somewhere else and it'd have the same palm trees and beaches and hammocks, but the sunrise wouldn't be a full-sky orange, the water wouldn't be as clear, the sand as fine. It was the now. And Ryder was caught between seeing and touching, wanting and having. He was in a weird loop of deferment – it was coming, he knew that, and he hoped he could wait.

The world had gone quiet and he didn't notice that she'd turned towards him, offering him a note, offering the choice of the lines. He let her go first and she shimmied back down and adeptly snorted a line into each perfect nostril. She quivered and then offered him the note again, with a full-watt smile. Her proximity was mesmeric and the anticipatory pleasure was almost shattering. It was a singularity. He'd only felt that strongly once before. Ryder bent down and banged the lines. She stroked his hair childishly during the strange, intimate little ceremony. He looked at her and her hand slipped down to his cheek as they moved in close together. The door opened loudly and they held, still and together. An unfazed voice called out, 'Coke or sex?'

'Coke.' Ryder answered first, followed by her, imitating a male voice: 'Sex.'

They all laughed. Sometimes beginnings were perfect.

Ryder vaguely remembered meeting Seth that night, but couldn't recall what they'd said to each other, if anything. It was lost. What he did remember was two mobile phones together on the table and a little pouch which Seth opened to reveal the sparkle inside – to Metallic. He also sensed that Seth was the only one to see him and Metallic coming back from the traps, and thought that it was amusing how people sometimes failed to spot what was going on in their midst.

## CHAPTER 9

# CRIMES AND MISDEMEANOURS

After the meeting with Holmes, Ryder felt like he'd grabbed the ladder and climbed a couple of rungs. Before they broke up at The Gasworks, Holmes had taken him to one side again and offered some advice.

'What was the lowest figure you came with tonight?'

'Two hundred thousand.'

'A hundred each for you and O'Malley?'

'Yes.'

'What if you don't square with him, then you have your hundred?' But that would be unethical. That would be against the rules. 'Whose rules?'

Ryder thought about it the next day. O'Malley knew how to find him, or so he said, and he knew some rough people, or so he said. But what if something had gone wrong – what if the piece or the cash had been stolen?

O'Malley was a sharp individual and he'd smell a scam a mile off. Ryder would have to make it real. Holmes already had a buyer for the Ming, so it wouldn't end up in his window and no one would ever know its whereabouts. How to get O'Malley to believe it and, in doing so, save himself from a broken arm – or worse.

As it happened, before he could put this half-baked plan into effect, Ryder received word that O'Malley had been in an accident and was in hospital in Grimsby, of all places. How could he cheat the man out of his money now? It'd be more than a crime, it'd be a sin. Ryder wouldn't normally have cared about committing either, but he did have some scruples. O'Malley wanted to see him, so he packaged up the man's money and headed north.

Even though he'd travelled all over the country, Grimsby was one place Ryder had never been to, and he thought about it as he was driving up the motorway. How people said things like – 'it's grim up north' and '*Grim*sby' and stuff. You got a picture in your head of dark clouded mills and satanic hills and flat caps and lurchers and coal in the fucking bath. He knew Grimsby was a fishing port on the Humber – and that was about it. He'd heard the people liked to call themselves Grimbarians, sort of like 'scowling barbarians' he supposed, and that was the picture he had in his head. He didn't know much more and wasn't interested in knowing much more. He just wanted to hand over the cash to O'Malley and get out of the place – as quick as possible.

It was five-thirty in the afternoon when he got there, and he went straight to St Hugh's Hospital, where he was told O'Malley had fallen into a coma after being involved in a hit-and-run. He didn't fancy leaving the money at the hospital.

'Does he have any family?'

'You could ask at reception.'

Which he did, and was referred to the hospital information centre, where he was given the address of O'Malley's brother and only remaining next of kin. He was in the Nunsthorpe area – or 'the Nunny', as it was affectionately known to the indigenous population. But there was no answer when Ryder knocked on the door, and a neighbour referred him to the Northern Star pub down the road.

It was getting late and Ryder didn't fancy driving all the way back to London, so he checked into the Casablanca Inn on Windward Drive for the night. He left the van in the hotel car park and took a cab to The Northern Star. It was eight-thirty by then and the place was empty, apart for a few of the local midnight cowboys playing pool in a side room. He could hear the click and clack of the pool balls and the occasional outburst of laughter or swearing behind his back as he stood at the bar and waited for service. After a couple of minutes, a barman who looked like he was chewing a wasp came out from having a tea break or a wank somewhere, and stood looking him up and down.

'What can I get yez?'

'What do you recommend?'

'I'll come back when you mek up yer mind.'

'Wait!'

The arsehole just stood there staring at Ryder, as if he'd just stepped off a day-trip coach to Cleethorpes or something. He was starting to look agitated, so Ryder thought he'd better give him the benefit of the doubt.

'I meant your beer.'

'What about it?'

'What's your best lager?'

'Northern Monk.'

'I'll have a pint of that, then.'

He looked at Ryder as if he'd never seen a man wearing a maroon Ormonde suit with a Superscreamers retro T-shirt and Scarosso tasselled loafers before.

'Two seventy-five.'

'Cheap.'

The dickhead grimaced at this last remark. He pulled a pint of stuff that looked like it was coming out the arse end of a dog with diarrhoea, and pushed it across the counter. Ryder handed him a bullseye and he studied it under the light to make sure it was real, or maybe he was reminding himself what a fifty looked like. When he brought the change back, he leaned over close and sniffed.

'A southerner?'

'How can you tell?'

'By the smell.'

Ryder decided it was best to ignore the pig.

The place was starting to fill up with people, mostly blokes coming in from work or from the dole office or from minding the kids while their wives went to their window-cleaning jobs. They all gave him a leery look before settling down with their beer. He decided it would be dangerous to advertise the fact that he was carrying £50,000, plus half the auction house fee, for O'Malley's brother. Better to stay cool and find out if the guy was here. He'd learned that the best way to get information was to buy people a drink – or several drinks, if that's what it took. At £2.75 a pint, that would be a cheap option tonight.

He noticed a group of five likely lads who might have been in or about O'Malley's age, so he thought he'd start with them. He flashed another fifty at the barman and pointed to their table. When the beer was brought over to them, the barman nodded towards Ryder, still standing at the bar. They looked him over as if he was an overdressed policeman and he lifted his glass in salute. Ryder reckoned it could go one of two ways – they'd think he was a pervert and make him drink the five pints he'd just bought before kicking the crap out of him, or the barman would tell them he was a soft southerner with loads of money to spend and they'd accept his goodwill gesture.

Ryder waited.

'Ain't seen you in here before.'

One of them came over. He put his arm round the back of Ryder and rested his hand on the bar. His breath was too close for comfort, but at least it looked like the offer of beer had been taken in the spirit it was meant.

'Never been in here before.'

'You moved onto the estate, then?'

'Nope, just up here on business.'

'What business would that be?'

'Show business.'

The guy laughed and lifted his hands, as if to say *that explains everything*.

Fifteen minutes later and he was sitting at the table and on his second pint of dog's vomit. But they were warming to him, and it seemed like his money would get him where he wanted to be. He told them he was a screenwriter, researching a plot for a film that'd be set in Grimsby and would have Sean Bean and Keeley Hawes in the starring roles. They didn't know who Hawes was, but they liked Bean.

'What's this film about?'

'It's a biopic.'

'What's a biopic?'

'Based on a true story.'

'What true story?'

'The life of Peter O'Malley.'

That's when the conversation stopped. The latest round of drinks he'd bought were placed carefully back on the table and the group turned stony-faced. Nobody spoke for what seemed like half an hour.

'What you want to make a film about that gobshite for?'

The voices were hostile now – menacing. Time to back off. Ryder wondered what O'Malley had done to piss these people off. He wondered if everybody in this bar felt the same way, that he was a cunt. And what about his brother?

'What about his brother?'

'Another gobshite!'

'I heard he drinks here.'

An incomprehensible growling sound went round the table, like feeding time for a pack of starving bull terriers.

'He don't come in here anymore.'

Ryder decided to leave it at that.

The night wore on and the group was getting a bit pissed, so there wasn't much chance of surreptitiously dragging anything else out of them. Every time Ryder mentioned the name O'Malley, they got that stony look in their eyes and he knew not to push it. They parted company out on the street when his cab came to take him back to the Casablanca Inn. Just as he climbed into the passenger seat, one of them shouted after him, 'O'Malley had a girlfriend . . .'

Ryder stuck his head out the window.

'And where might I find her?'

'She lives on an estate over near New Clee.'

'Know the house number?'

They must have thought he said 'louse from the Humber' or something like that, because bottles began to fly in the cab's direction. The taxi driver took off to the sound of glass breaking on the street behind them.

Back at the hotel, he grabbed a late-night sandwich and decided to hit the sack and drive straight back to London in the morning.

\* \* \*

Holmes had told Seth he wanted to see him – so where was he? This time the dealer wasn't so much sprawled as spatchcocked on his sofa. As ever, he'd kicked off his shoes and socks and was idly scratching one foot with the other. But he was ill at ease. Where was Seth? The letter he'd read three times lay on his lap. The first time, he'd been incredulous and then outraged; the second time he'd read it with a sense of fear; and the third with cold resolution and attempted dispassion. He'd fight – of course he'd fight. That went without saying, it was part of his instinct, his fibre. Then he weighed up the risks and thought better of it. For now, he was staggered by the stupidity of it all.

Why would you go legal?

Holmes had never thought of the law as the final say in anything, except when it could be used as a threat against certain people in last-resort circumstances. But it was ridiculous to begin proceedings against someone like him. It was fucking unheard of! Especially by someone who knew him so well, knew he couldn't be, wouldn't be, cowed.

The whole thing started nine months ago – the issue. Actually, it had probably started much earlier than that; an eternity ago. Eternal and fraternal. Holmes's brother Aloysius was older than him by twenty-two minutes. They were twins, identical in every way except temperament. Normally, identical twins got on famously with each other, wore the same clothes, loved the same music, dated the same women, telepathically knew what each other was feeling and thinking. Not the Holmes boys. Apart from physical appearance, they were chalk and cheese. Cain and Abel. And this thing had been gestating since their conception. It probably had something to do with sharing the same womb – kicking for dominance in the amniotic sac. It was always coming – and now it was here.

He'd been bunkered up ever since he got here this morning. Cassie had put her head round the door earlier and offered him a coffee.

'No!'

She knew by the tone of his voice that further intrusion would elicit a shower of expletives, so she stayed away from him after that. She'd only met his brother once, in all the time she'd known Holmes. He'd moved to New York a short while ago, and she knew better than to mention the name Aloysius since then. She gleaned from her father that the brothers had been in business together, but it didn't work out. It never would have. In the end, they couldn't even live in the same city, so Lucien took London and Aloysius took New York. Holmes was glad to see him go and hoped he'd never come back.

Seth arrived and Cassie showed him into the bunker, retreating quickly and listening at the other side of the door. Holmes held out the letter. Seth took it from him.

'From the cunt over the water.'

He slumped back heavily, hoping that his suppressed fury might fashion a metaphysical weapon that would fly to New York and pierce the heart of darkness there. Seth sat at the desk and read it. He took his time, letting the potential consequences sink in.

Holmes had been pre-warned that this was coming when Buggins came to see him. Such was the idiocy of his brother that he'd made their autistic restorer, their mild and awkward backroom genius, into an enemy – pushed him hard enough that he'd had to respond. And now this! What level of stupidity did it require to spill everything out into the open? What kind of cretin turned a mouse into a lion? When Seth finished reading, he spun round on the chair.

'Well, what are you going to do?'

'I know what I'd like to do!'

'Ruling that out?'

'I know you're going to New York soon.'

'Am I?'

'I want you to sit him down, Seth. Let him know where this will end.'

Seth knew he'd been summoned for something like this – something he didn't want to get involved in. It was one thing for the brothers to never be free of each other, but why did they have to drag him into their everlasting struggle? It wasn't even as if one was looking for dominion over the other – no, it was about denying the other outright victory, hurting them in new and various ways, being a thorn in the flesh. He had his own business to attend to in New York – he didn't need complications. But, if the shit hit the fan, some of it might land on him. Plus, he could get Holmes to pay for the trip.

Seth sighed. 'If that's what you want.'

Holmes wasn't looking at him, as though he'd already assumed the answer would be in the affirmative. He was onto the subject of the Buggins visit. He'd made Buggins an offer he thought the man wouldn't refuse, to make him whole on all the work he'd done – even to cover the work he'd done for Holmes's brother. But it wasn't enough for Buggins – he'd been wronged. Hurt. Cut to the quick. And money wasn't going to do it. He was past that, way past that. It was no longer about the money. The moment to squash the little man back into his box was gone.

That was the trouble with allowing people to take themselves too seriously – they developed all sorts of real and imagined slights, demands. People became convinced they were right and, once they convinced themselves, they believed anything they did was fine and justified. It was so ridiculous that his brother had got them here. Up on this ledge.

Seth never discovered where Holmes found Buggins. He claimed variously to have won him in a card game, bought him from a travelling fair, discovered him on his doorstep, found him under a head of cabbage – infant-sized but fully formed as a man. He embellished it all in front of Buggins, who chose to ignore it, which only served to encourage more of the same.

But all Holmes's wisecracking left out the fact that Buggins was a master 'restorer', as they called it. His 'reproductions' were uncanny, otherworldly, beyond what would be expected of any normal copyist. And, in his own very particular way, Holmes saw his genius and treated him right – not so Aloysius, who failed to see that Buggins was their golden goose, albeit small and misshapen. He'd done an imperial armoire for the brother, which Aloysius sold for two million and then shot off to America without paying Buggins for his work. Repeated requests for payment were ignored, which led Buggins to make enquiries – enquiries which confirmed that the brothers were making a huge amount of money off the back of his labour, for which he was paid what he considered to be a pittance.

Now he wanted recompense, and a grovelling apology from Aloysius. Aloysius, from the safety of New York, refused to comply. In fact, he completely ignored all communications from both Holmes and Buggins, apart from the curt and dismissive letter now in Seth's hand.

To Holmes's dismay, it had gone legal. And, in going legal, the authenticity of certain items sold by the brothers could, and most likely would, be questioned. Once the legal eagles got Buggins into the witness box, who knew what would be revealed?

Initially, it *had* been just about the money – Buggins wanted to be properly paid for the work he'd done – and everything would've been fine, would've carried on as usual, had Aloysius not tried to knock him. But then it drifted into wider complaints about his treatment in general, and the ridiculing by Holmes in front of people. He hadn't been treated with the respect he deserved. Flushed and angry, recalling the laughter at his expense, his voice became louder and whinier, convinced of his own righteousness, convinced he had been traduced, maligned – and the rest. Once people felt slighted and belittled, they were capable of anything.

Apologies were difficult to come by from the brothers – they were always an admission of something or other. Chicanery. Double-dealing. Deception. Reputation-damaging. It seemed to Seth that Holmes was at war with himself – angry, the vexation of the culpable who'd been caught unawares but determined to continue denying what was obvious to everyone else. Now Seth was being dragged into this. He didn't want to be, but he'd speak to Aloysius while he was in New York, in an effort to avoid the worse coming to the worst.

'One condition . . . I bring Ryder along.'

'Why?'

'I need a favour from him.'

'All right. Just don't tell him anything.'

Seth shook his head ruefully. 'As if I would!'

## CHAPTER 10

# NEW YORK CITY

Ryder remembered Seth Silver from the first contact they'd had at The Gasworks, even though the latter part of that night was hazy and translucent in his head. He remembered liking Seth because the man was an insider and had a direct line to Holmes, not an easy achievement. He also seemed to understand the mechanisms of the world – he saw through the lies and false rectitude. Seth had called him after The Gasworks and asked him to come look at his premises – that in itself seemed unusual, until Ryder realised it was just an excuse to go drinking. It became clear to Ryder that Seth marked himself out from the Holmes crowd, apart from them and happy to be so. He rarely went to The Gasworks because the Holmes retinue resented him. They couldn't quite fathom how he was preferred over them.

Silver was older than Ryder but younger than Holmes. Blond-haired and blue-eyed, with a round scar on his left ear that was rumoured to have been made by a bullet. He dressed variously in the period styles of the late-nineteenth and early-twentieth centuries. So much so that, apart from being inconspicuous at The Gasworks, he would've fitted in well at a Cosima Wagner shindig, or even one of Jay Gatsby's – or Al Capone's. He believed people were deluded and in denial of how things really were, and they clung to their false convictions like sheep. What he lacked in eye, he made up for in instinct. He had a dark élan about him – half Mephistopheles, half Iago. He believed everything was hackable – the shadow background. But he wasn't guilty of hypocrisy or the arch modern crime of being two-faced. He had the ability to draw people close, even if it was only to use them. Ryder realised, of course, that Seth would want something from him, and it would only be a matter of time before he asked.

Once the plane levelled out after take-off and they had their first drinks perched on their trays, Ryder poured the gin over the ice and added most of the dinky little can of tonic, swizzled it, licked the stick and sat back. Such small glasses but, hey, it was first class and they could always order more. They took it in turns to hit the hostess button. Seth thought Ryder would ask him why he'd been brought along on this trip, but he never did. As far as Ryder was concerned, he hadn't been to New York, so that was reason enough to go. How desperate to have to admit, if anyone asked, that he'd never been to New York?

They sat in silence for a while, before Seth started up a conversation about some girl he was seeing who worked in the music business.

'She checks out hotels. Flies into cities to check out hotels and tell her bosses where they should stay. It's a world of free shit.'

'For some.'

'There's a wall of money.'

'It just isn't evenly distributed.'

'Never will be.'

Ryder wanted to switch the conversation, not because he knew Seth was married and he'd met Floss and liked her, but because he was feeling a little self-conscious, suddenly aware that he was becoming too easy to see. Maybe it was the drinks; maybe the altitude.

Seth seemed to have that habit of suggestion – that there was some taint, some grubby fingerprint, to be found on everything, if you looked closely enough. As though the way to really see something was in the dark, not in the light.

He rested his head back and finished what remained of his drink. Then he told Ryder he was going to sleep. Ryder was too excited to follow suit. New York was too much of a promise. Too enticing.

Everything about the Big Apple was front-loaded, and that was how he intended to take it on. The thing he was looking forward to most of all was the first sight of it.

Seth said it was a mad, bad, crazy place and, although Ryder had never been, he knew all about it. Didn't everybody? It was a dreamscape. The image in everyone's eye. That *thing* that made people want to go there. For the first time in a long while, Ryder wasn't uneasy about being outside London and wished he'd come here many years ago. Things would be different from now on, now that he was becoming an insider like Holmes and Seth. Things would be better. Definitely better. And being here would only enhance that process, because this city was everything that was off in the world – and everything that was on. A schizophrenic city. Diseased. Genetically flawed. But beautiful. Everything that was good-bad and bad-good.

Their plane touched down at JFK around midday, and Ryder immediately felt a surge of adrenaline. They took a cab northwards along the freeway into Queens, and then west through Brooklyn and across the East River into Manhattan. But, slung in the back of a taxi with a cramped interior and low seats and a security divide, he couldn't see much as the famous skyline ducked in and out of underpasses. He caught a brief glimpse before it disappeared behind the buildings hemmed in on the expressway, then it was gone. The cab dived through a tunnel and then swung with the road and he got the full view. There it was. Perfect.

Up through Chinatown, Little Italy and the Lower East Side. Madison Avenue was in Midtown – that area of the city which was immediately and unmistakably the New York of Ryder's imagination. Skyscrapers reeled and traffic cops rolled and yellow cabs clicked and clacked and honked and swore and people swarmed like insects and vents belched steam from ancient underground heating systems – just like in the movies. Madison was sandwiched between Fifth and Park and didn't quite have the same sense of glamour as its more famous neighbours. But it was still impressive, with coffee bars and delis and big strutting buildings and street cred and superiority complexes.

Morgans Hotel was self-consciously chic. An establishment inhabited by has-beens and wannabes and handsome resting-actor staff in designer uniforms, with an air of low profile about the whole place. Holmes had splurged on the first-class air tickets, but obviously stinted on the accommodation. Ryder felt it was the kind of hotel that could be slipped in and out of without too much attention being paid to whatever it was you were doing. A mixture of multiplex and monochrome décor, just a little past its bedtime, with lizards lounging and girls calling. But their rooms were big and there was a Jacuzzi and a coffee bar and two hundred complimentary Camel cigarettes. Good enough. In the lobby Ryder spotted a poster proclaiming that The Eagles were performing a one-night-only, end-of-tour gig at the Radio City Music Hall. Were they still alive? While, outside on the street, he caught quick glimpses of himself amongst the big colourful cast.

Seth unpacked in his room, but Ryder was restless. He paced in and out of the adjoining door for a while, smoking the Camels, until he began to get on Seth's nerves, who told him to go for a drink or something and settle down. He took the lift from the fourteenth floor and strode across the lobby and out into the city's afternoon. Ryder stood on the sidewalk for a moment, wondering where to go and trying to keep out of the resolute crowd's route. He opted to head south for a while, past the Sony Building and then right, into West 55th Street. There were plenty of bars and dives of all declensions – shebeens and speakeasys and swell joints.

After a bit of indecision, he stepped inside a place called Shorty's on Fifth Avenue and ordered a pint of lager. They were used to tourists and told him to sit down, then brought him a glass of beer on tap and he didn't complain about the large head. Or the taste. It was mid-afternoon and happy-hour crowds were yet to pour in from the shops and offices. One or two other customers sat along the bar, and

an odd couple were holding a serious and psychologically demanding conversation with some arm-waving and shoulder-shrugging
and feigned oblivion of the rest of the world.

From his quiet corner table, with its back to the wall, Ryder stared
out through the grimy window at the street scene – a colourful
tableau of sight, sound and smell. He could feel the ambiance. Sense
it. Touch it. Taste it. The rich vein of electricity that ran through this
place. It might have suited him if he'd come here sooner, before he
began to grow up. This city could have been his 'hood and he might
have been its homie. Maybe he was wrong – in any case, it was too
late now. But he could feel something in the air and hear it in the
street music and smell it in the unique perfume of prosperity.

Someone sat at the next table. A middle-aged man in a business suit and a younger woman. They glanced uneasily at Ryder,
not meeting his eyes, sipped martinis and whispered secrets to each
other. Then Seth appeared.

'This is the fourth bar I've tried.'

Ryder ordered two drinks while Seth sat down, giving the odd
couple a cursory glance but not showing any interest. He looked
directly at Ryder, seemingly sizing him up and weighing in his mind
whether or not he could trust this man. Outside on the street, rush
hour was approaching fast. Ryder was eager to get the business side
of things over with, so he could relax and enjoy himself.

'Well? When do we see Aloysius?'

'Tomorrow.'

'Why not today?'

'You can't rush things with Aloysius. Lucky he's agreed to see us
at all. Well, he's agreed to see me, he doesn't know you're here.'

'So, you don't need me then?'

'Of course I do. You haven't come all the way over here just to
see the statue.'

Seth Silver watched Ryder closely. The younger man was ill at
ease. Seemed nervous. His eyes scanned the bar and then returned to

the table. He grinned awkwardly at Seth and raised his glass to his mouth. Seth continued to stare, trying to see inside the man's head. Trying to read his thoughts – understand his soul.

Ryder was wondering if Holmes had said anything about O'Malley. If Seth knew, but was saying nothing about it. You couldn't trust any of them. You had to be careful – all the time.

'Did Holmes ask you to bring me?'

'No, I asked him.'

'Why?'

'Break the monotony, I suppose. Are you complaining?'

'Of course not.'

Ryder needed to be careful what he said. Everyone was an enemy until proven otherwise.

He drained the rest of the drink in his glass and Seth called for two more. Shorty's was beginning to get crowded as happy hour approached. The place was full of what Ryder imagined to be Bronx and Brooklyn and huggys from Harlem and freebasers from Flatbush and queens from Queens and sharks from Staten Island. Martinis mixed and bourbons rocked and Budweisers and Miller Lites and Rolling Rocks and pitchers of Anchor Steam and Wicked and Samuel Adams and Molson and Dos Equis and Dubonnet straight. The two men drank and talked some more, and the friendship tentatively reinforced itself.

A dark-skinned man came and sat down on the chair next to Seth. Ryder eyed him suspiciously. He eyed back.

The man whispered to Seth, still eyeing Ryder. '*Está él contigo?*'

'*Sí.*'

'*Quién es él?*'

'*Un amigo. Él esta bien.*'

The man stuck his face up close to Ryder's and growled. '*Estas con el hombre de plata, gringo?*'

'I don't know what you're on about, mate!'

The 'mate' word again – as in, only to be used for taxi drivers and talking your way out of a fight. Sort the problem to survive. Sort the problem and survive. Sort the problem. Survive. Problem to survive. The man kept looking at Ryder with a frown – a long frown. Then he began to laugh, loudly. The frown returned momentarily to his face and Ryder thought he saw him slip something to Seth, but it happened so fast he couldn't be sure. Then the guy laughed again, even louder than before. And left the bar shaking his head.

'What was that all about?'

Seth shrugged, apparently not bothered by the weird exchange.

'It's a crazy town, full of crazy people.'

\* \* \*

Seth chose the Tavern on the Green for its view, and Ryder was glad to be out of the hotel room again. He wished he had some coke or even speed – something to get him up and out of the ditzy mood that was dogging him. He hoped everything would go right on this trip. It was important. Maybe when he got back, Holmes and Seth would help him establish himself as a fine art dealer. Things were beginning to become intolerable for him at Boulets, and he was considering packing it in there.

Seth ordered grilled chicken with a Caesar salad, while Ryder had a heavily garnished hamburger with fries and black coffee. Footpaths meandered outside the restaurant in Central Park, like snail trails through the trees. Evening was falling and the lamps gave the place a still, quiet feel, even though Ryder suspected it might be full of murderers and muggers. A few horse-drawn buggies ignored the danger and carried romantic couples for a view of the night-time skyline, to the music of Manhattan.

All the joggers and rollerbladers and street performers had gone home, in case someone stole everything from them. Everything they had in the whole world, and maybe even their very souls as well, taken at knifepoint when they were enjoying themselves and at their most vulnerable. One or two brave locals walked fierce-looking hounds out among the ponds and pavilions, while the sounds of zoo animals drifted across on the still air above the noise of peripheral traffic. The Carousel was quiet, its organ safely locked away for the night, and statues of Robert Burns and Sir Walter Scott and Hans Christian Andersen and Alice and the Angel of the Waters closed their eyes to the rapes and robberies and their ears to the screams of the innocent and naive. Away to the north, the reservoir hid the grinning skulls of those wearing concrete boots, and Latino locals fished the Meer. And around it all the clear, star-filled sky was a canopy of crystal hope that would never again become black and lifeless.

After eating, they decided to walk back to the hotel, across Fifth Avenue. Ryder was staggered but not surprised by the sheer consumer excesses of the superstores and he wanted to ask people passing by – why? Didn't they have enough junk in their lives? But he kept quiet; it was none of his business. They strolled east along 67th and then south on Madison. A late breeze blew across Manhattan from the Hudson River, and city smells and sounds filled Ryder with a familiar longing for a chance to shine on the sequined stage of life – without a handicap or heavy boots to hold him back. Without anyone. Just himself. Whole. Hearted.

Back at the hotel, Seth didn't want to go clubbing, so Ryder began to systematically empty the minibar. He was aware that something was changing, something was creeping over him. Gradually. Like a sickness. Or a syncopation. Something was either right or wrong with him and he didn't know which. He was changing from the inside. Being microwaved. Maybe his problem was the same as Holmes's? Could he have caught it from Holmes? He shouldn't be like this – not now. He should be keeping a cool head.

Seth came into the room. 'Please don't drink too much.'

'Why not?'

'Because we're here on business, Ryder, you know that.'

'The business will take care of itself. Let's go out on the town.'

'Not yet, we haven't made contact with Aloysius.'

'I thought you said tomorrow?'

'That's what I mean.'

Seth was about to say something else, but Ryder wasn't listening. He'd already finished off the bourbon and started on the scotch. He asked if Seth wanted a drink but he didn't.

'Suit yourself.'

Seth made coffee and turned on the TV. He flicked through the cable channels until he found a documentary about Mexican drug cartels, then settled back in a chair to watch and wait.

*　*　*

Morning brought a hangover for Ryder and empty miniatures all over the floor. He rose quietly from the bed and checked on Seth through the adjoining door. He was still asleep and Ryder left him there – because he didn't want to listen to any more killjoying – while he made coffee and smoked a cigarette. Midtown Manhattan was already alive outside the hotel window and singing its morning song. Hysterical traffic crawled along Madison and people poured across the gridwork of streets. Ryder felt light-headed and wasn't sure whether it was looking down from the fourteenth floor that made him dizzy, or the effects of the night before. The room reeked of booze and bewilderment. Ryder found it hard to breathe. He tried to open a window, but they were shut tight – to prevent people jumping out?

He called room service and ordered a bacon-and-egg breakfast with pancakes, which he ate in silence. He tried to read the newspapers, which were delivered to the room with compliments of the management. All the headlines were encrypted messages and he hadn't figured out the code yet. Ryder threw the papers across the floor and lay on the bed for a while, but soon got up and started pacing the room. He went through and woke Seth.

'What time?'

Seth looked up at him, sleep still in his eyes.

'What?'

'The meeting ... what time?'

'Three o'clock.'

'Let's go out and see the sights.'

'You go, I'm jet-lagged.'

The day was bright and unseasonably warm. Ryder hailed a cab on Madison and set off downtown. He wanted to see Wall Street and Chinatown and the Brooklyn Bridge and everything else there was to see in this city of dreams. The taxi drove south past Madison Square Garden. Posters shouted Knicks basketball and Rangers hockey and he insisted on getting out at Kabooz's Bar and Grill, which he'd heard about from Charlie Steel. He was still hungry, so he had an early lunch of Louisiana catfish and cornbread with Creole sauce and a pitcher of Grolsch.

Afterwards, on Broadway, he mooched round the theatres, then caught another cab's attention and travelled further south, into the Village. The quaintness there seemed genuine enough, although the bohemians were passé to the point of being trippers. The brownstoners and camp copywriters passed him by into SoHo, with its continentals and cast-iron buildings. Ryder got out again in Little Italy and walked south along the Bowery to Confucius Plaza in Chinatown, then carried on to City Hall and walked from there down to Wall Street. For Ryder, this was where it was really at. The centre of insatiability. The capital of capitalism. He could smell the money, like a narcotic, latent on the heady air. Intoxicating. This little pot-of-gold place. You could find god here, if you were so inclined. Sleep on the street. Eat off it. Become absorbed by it. Part of it. Flesh and blood and concrete and sinew and steel.

If you were so inclined.

But he had to get back to Seth and the rendezvous with Aloysius.

## CHAPTER 11

# METALLIC

Aloysius had an apartment on the Upper West Side – West 59th Street to be precise. It was surprisingly spacious inside – a small, bright reception area gave way to a more discreetly lit studio, which looked minimalist and sterile to Ryder. A highly polished wooden floor with bland colours on the walls and reproductions of Picasso and Lorenzo and La Tour.

This area of the city was salubrious and self-satisfied, and the apartment was an oasis in a crazy world. Nothing bad could get in once the door was multi-locked. Aloysius could be himself here and forget what it was that had driven him away from where he really wanted to be – whatever it was that disfigured him and made him ugly inside. In here, he felt safe behind the heavy door. Until now.

He had his back to them when they entered, sprawled on a couch in front of an imitation log fire, leaning back watching the dancing false-flames. He seemed mesmerised by the movement and didn't turn to greet them. Seth stood there, waiting for the man to invite them forward, with Ryder behind him. Aloysius eventually produced a cellophane packet and meticulously set out several lines of cocaine on a glass-topped occasional table. He rolled up a hundred-dollar note and took one of the lines up his left nostril, then passed the money-straw to Seth, who did the same and passed the note on to Ryder.

When all the lines were gone, Aloysius spoke for the first time, inviting them to sit. Ryder couldn't believe how much the man looked like Holmes – but then, they were identical twins.

Aloysius studied Ryder sceptically. 'Who's this?'

'Ryder . . . He's a friend of your brother.'

'Can he be trusted?'

'Well, he wouldn't be here otherwise.'

Aloysius poured bourbon for the three of them and made it clear that he was only granting this audience because he liked Seth. And he wasn't going to apologise to that grubby little money-grabber, Buggins.

'He thinks he can blackmail me, does he?'

'He knows things, Aloysius.'

'Things that will incriminate himself, not me.'

'Things that will destroy your brother's reputation.'

'What reputation?'

And that's how it went – Seth practically pleading, while Aloysius resisted all attempts at reason and displayed an intransigent determination to commit professional suicide rather than capitulate to someone he considered to be a lesser mortal – on a lower plane of existence.

'You didn't pay him for the armoire.'

'I did!'

'He says you didn't.'

'Then it's his word against mine, isn't it?'

During these 'negotiations', Ryder said nothing, acting as their fag and refilling the glasses from the bourbon bottle, which was now nearly empty. In the end, he became oblivious to the words flying between Seth and Aloysius. They floated round the apartment and disappeared through the walls. Some were large and some were small, some nearby and others far away, all different shades of intensity. They hummed and buzzed around his head, flew into his ears and out again. They climbed high to the ceiling and fell back down again. Some were confident and strutted out, others cowered and tried to sneak out unnoticed. Some were spat and some blown like kisses. Some intolerant and some intimidating.

Ryder shook the empty bottle at Aloysius and the man pointed to a glass cabinet, where Ryder retrieved and opened another. He was pouring when he heard something that made him take notice again.

'You've got plenty to lose too, Seth. So why don't you go talk to Buggins, instead of trying to browbeat me?'

What *did* he have to lose, Ryder wanted to know. The bourbon spoke for him and the words came tumbling out of his mouth before he could stop them.

'What *does* he have to lose?'

'I'm not saying anything about Russia, but one thing can lead to another. One exposure ..' Aloysius was looking directly at Seth as he spoke.

The silence that followed could have been cut with a knife. Aloysius didn't elaborate and neither did Seth, but Silver obviously knew what he meant – his expression changed from one of conciliation to one of hostility.

'Russia has nothing to do with this, Aloysius!'

'I'm not saying it has, Seth. I'm just saying stains spread, don't they?'

That was enough for Seth. He stood up and indicated to Ryder, poised with the bourbon bottle, that he should do the same. Ryder reluctantly put the bottle down and drained his glass. They left the apartment without another word.

*　*　*

That night, they went to Le Bain, on the roof of The Standard on West 13th Street, with its disco, bar, plunge pool and crêperie. There was a long line outside, but Seth took them right to the front and the discerning-looking doorman let them through. Ryder was impressed by the sweeping city vista and the built-in hot tub in the middle of the dance floor. Eager voices all around, indecipherable like a babel. Seth went straight to the bar, forgetting about his earlier reticence, and ordered two old-fashioneds, while sending Ryder to scout for a table. Several cocktails later, Seth disappeared and Ryder was left on his own.

'Hi there.'

He turned towards the familiar voice.

'Metallic . . . what are you doing here?'

'I could ask you the same thing.'

He didn't know how much he should, or could, divulge to her. 'Business. Small world.'

She sat and took a sip from Seth's glass, which he'd left on the table. Ryder just realised that he'd called her Metallic and she hadn't corrected him. That couldn't be her name, just what was in his head when he first met her at The Gasworks.

'Sorry, I didn't get your name . . . before.'

'It can be Metallic, if you want it to be.'

Little-girl laugh; 'come and get me' eyes, flashing across at him.

'Would you like a drink?'

'Who's is this?'

'Seth Silver's, he's gone somewhere. You know him?'

'Of course . . . Doesn't everyone?'

Ryder got her a martini and asked who she was with. She said nobody important and pulled him out onto the dance floor. The overhead lights spun like fireflies in a kaleidoscope of kismet. Ryder's arms were around Metallic's waist, hers lightly on his shoulders. She moved in closer and he could smell her hair – it reminded him of the smell of candyfloss. Her thigh eased between his legs as she steered him towards the toilets.

'More coke?'

'Not here.'

Ryder followed her into one of the stalls in the empty ladies' washroom, and she locked the door. It was cramped with both of them in there. Her body was pressed against his and she stood on the lid of the john and took off her underwear – then pushed his head down. His tongue found the right spot and she was moaning and groaning and banging the side of the trap with her fist until she came in a convulsion of high-pitched YESes. Ryder reckoned half the bloody club could hear her.

'Your turn.'

She climbed down and told him to stand on the lid and unzipped his trousers. Now he was the one yelling and banging the wall and it felt like he was floating weightless in the rarefied atmosphere of the john. Afterwards, she pulled her underwear back on and they left the washroom as if nothing out of the ordinary had happened.

Seth was at the table when they got back. He lifted one eyebrow but said nothing. He didn't ask where they'd been and Ryder didn't ask him either.

Metallic whispered in his ear. 'Let's get out of here.'

He winked at Seth. 'I'm going back to the hotel. What about you?'

'I think I'll stay for a bit longer.'

They stopped off at the hotel bar for a few more cocktails, then went up to his room just after midnight, where they did more cocaine before moving to the bed.

He stroked her hair that felt like silk and she kissed his chest. Her woman-smell drove all the demons from his head and they slipped slowly down onto the bed. Stars winked at them from outside the big window. She caressed his thighs and kissed behind his ear. Her fragrance seemed to overpower and dominate everything else in the room. In the moment. In the universe of their immediate surroundings. For now, she was that universe. A universe that was black and silky and smelled of almond and sandalwood and tasted a slightly salty life-taste and made little far-off noises that couldn't be understood and had no need to be.

Ryder heard a light knock on the hotel room door, interrupting their concupiscence. He listened. Metallic lay still under him. They waited. Nothing. Waited. No more knocking. Waited. Silence returned to the night. Ryder got up and went to the door. He listened. Nothing. Looked through the spyhole. Nothing. Opened the door a hair's breadth. Nobody. He didn't notice the eye looking through the spyhole of the door opposite. The corridor outside the room was empty, except for a package directly outside the door. Ryder looked at it – touched it with his toe. It had 'SILVER' written on it. He carried it into the room and kicked the door closed.

Metallic was still on the bed. He poured a couple of drinks from the restocked minibar. She asked him if he had any ice.

'Sure.'

She collected a glassful from the small icebox before moving back onto the bed. He tried to kiss her body, but she pulled away and pushed him down onto his back. Metallic was at the foot of the bed and she began to crawl forward, like a snake, coiling herself over Ryder until her eyes were directly above his and full of something he didn't recognise – something he hadn't seen before. Or maybe he had and didn't remember. He was about to say something, but she clamped her hand across his mouth.

Metallic straddled him with her legs and manipulated him up inside her. Then she began to fuck him. Slow strokes at first, gathering momentum. She was light – so light. Almost weightless. He could hardly feel her on top of him. Her head was thrown back and, before long, he could feel himself reaching climax. Metallic felt it too. She reached for an ice cube from the glass and placed it at the base of his balls. The cold shock of the ice had the effect of halting the climax, and Metallic continued to fuck him until all the ice was melted and she'd reached orgasm herself – how many times he didn't know.

Ryder lay on the bed in a pool of sweat and melted ice – wondering what it was that had just happened. Metallic poured them another drink and lit up a cheroot. He took the cigar from her hand and sucked in a long lungful of scented smoke.

She made no attempt to leave and it looked like she was staying the night.

Was she waiting for him to fall asleep? It seemed to take a long time. Maybe he was waiting for her to do the same. His eyelids finally fell over the intoxicated windows to his psyche and she waited just a while longer – to be sure.

*  *  *

Their return flight from JFK was scheduled for the afternoon. Ryder was tired, extremely tired, and wanted to keep sleeping. But Seth was hovering over him, shaking him awake. It took an extreme effort of will to force himself into a sitting position. Looking around with bleary, blinking eyes, he saw that he was alone in the bed and he wondered if Metallic was gone, or if she'd emerge from the bathroom at any moment.

'What time is it?'

Seth looked at an imaginary watch.

'Eight-thirty.'

'The woman?'

Seth shook his head.

'Something was left for you.'

'Something?'

'A package . . . outside the door. I brought it in.' Ryder looked around, but the package was gone – along with Metallic.

'Oh yes, I looked in on you when I got back last night and took it with me.'

Ryder reckoned he could tell when someone was blatantly lying. But if Seth was cool with it, then fuck it. And he was hungry – he needed food, and lots of it.

Seth left him alone to shower and shave, arranging to meet down in the hotel lobby in an hour. Ryder dressed quickly and looked in the minibar for something to get him moving. It was empty.

Morning people conspicuously ignored him as he went down to meet Seth, who was already eating in the large art-deco diner. Smells of the street mingled with the odours of sausage and eggs and waffles and pancakes and maple syrup and coffee. Ryder had eggs over easy with toast, for starters, followed by bacon and muffins and hash browns and more bacon and coffee – lots of coffee. The smell was overpowering, the smell of New York at that time of the morning. A just-woken-up smell of staleness from the night before, covered over with a blanket of breakfast. After eating as much as his stomach would hold, it began to get to him, the smell, as he waited for Seth to pay the bill. In the enveloping redolence.

It was the smell of shit!

\*   \*   \*

Heathrow Airport rose up out of mist as the plane approached across the Berkshire countryside. Engines went into reverse to slow the Boeing 787 down, and it taxied lazily in towards the terminal. Ryder looked through the cabin porthole and let out a low kind of moan. He wasn't totally glad to be home – but didn't want to stay in New York either. Mixed feelings. Sure, he reckoned he might like to go back to the Big Apple again, given the opportunity, but under different circumstances. Maybe as an ambassador for art as a force of nature in its own right, without the contaminating consequence of money. An emissary of the old values, when art was an expression of the artist's soul – like the pathos in a poem, or the purity in a piece of music – and not a type of currency for the wealthy to manipulate.

When he looked at a Van Gogh or a Renoir, he didn't see any price tag. What he saw was the very nature of things – the sun and the moon and the stars; the earth in all its diversity. To him, every picture reflected the divine spark of life that permeated stuff. Art allowed him to feel the correspondence between what was inside him as a human being and what was outside and around him in nature. He could feel the energy, the ether that connected all things. But would anyone listen? Maybe, if he said what he really felt and not what he was expected to say. But something told him it wouldn't happen. An entity inside said this would be the one and only time.

Seth touched his shoulder and startled him. People were disembarking.

He worried about the package that had been left for Seth, but there was no problem at passport control or customs or anywhere else, and they sauntered safely through to the arrivals lounge. Ryder sighed heavily when they were finally out at the taxi rank, waiting for the next cab to come along. The sun was shining down on London and seemed somehow to say everything was OK. All would be well. Welcome back. Ryder felt optimistic. Good as gold. Solid as silver.

Instead of the next taxi, a police car pulled up. Uniforms appeared and handcuffs were fastened behind their backs, and they were placed into the back of the vehicle and taken to separate cells at Paddington Green. Seth told him not to worry, it was a misunderstanding and they'd be released quickly. The cell door slammed behind Ryder, and he found himself alone in the steel silence. He paced up and down for a while, frustrated and trying not to panic. There was nothing he could do but resolve to ask for a solicitor. He settled down after a bit and sat on the plastic-covered bunk – head in hands.

A kind of surrealism invaded the space around him, and it was as if he was somewhere else. *They bore him barefaced on the bier: and in his grave rain'd many a tear.* All sorts of stuff was coming and going through Ryder's confused mind – not just Hamlet. It seemed to him that he'd been sitting there for a week. He thought about the expanse of the field that seemed to stretch away to infinity – and Lola saying, *like the man from Brideshead.* Maybe, like him, Ryder was looking for something that didn't exist. *But you know me, good sir.* I do, Lola, I do! *Then you know, sir, my affliction. My madness. My torment. There's rose-mary, that's for remembrance: pray you, love, remember.* I remember. *And there is pansies, that's for thoughts. There's fennel for you, and columbines: there's rue for you: and here's some for me: we may call it herb of grace o'sundays. Oh, you must wear your rue with a difference. There's a daisy: I would give you some violets, but they withered all when* your *father died.* He died? Who died? *They say he made a good end.*

Ryder woke up as the cell door opened.

Both Lola and Shakespeare ran away.

He was told he could go. His belongings were handed back to him at reception and he was shown out onto Bell Street. There was no sign of Seth. He waited for a while, then decided to leave. Walking towards the Edgware Road to grab a cab, he heard a voice calling to him. When he looked round, Seth was jogging in his direction.

'What was all that about?'

'I told you, Ryder, a misunderstanding.'

'Can we sue . . . for wrongful arrest?'

'I don't think that would be wise.'

They hailed a taxi and, as they drove east towards Regent's Park, Ryder was sure he caught a glimpse of Metallic, crossing the street behind them.

## CHAPTER 12

# END OF BEGINNINGS

Ryder was out of sorts for a while after New York. He was even irritated by Bentley – and he was never irritated by Bentley. Price often, and sometimes Steel, but never Bentley. He was hoping Seth and Holmes would be able to break him into the fine art game, but nothing was happening on that front. In fact, he hadn't seen either of them for weeks – it was as if they'd gone to ground somewhere. He made enquiries about O'Malley and found out that he'd never regained consciousness and had died from his injuries. He didn't hear anything from the elusive brother, or anyone else, and assumed that the hundred grand was now his. It was time for a change and to not be like people around him at Boulets, who he viewed with a certain horror at their acceptance of their lot. He told himself he had to harness that feeling, and make something of it.

For a long time after New York, London seemed different. It seemed lesser. It was low-rise, in an emotional sense. Unremarkable. Unspectacular. He knew it wasn't just about London; it was more about his version of London – fine, so far as it went. Then there was that thing with Seth that really jagged at him. What was in the package and where did it go? Actually, it wasn't just that – that could've been perfectly harmless, though he doubted it. It was more the dark film with which he covered his take on things. He was too good at picking shit apart, wielding the scalpel to expose the viscera behind the smooth skin and holding it up for examination.

See! We're all made of this stuff!

Out of recalcitrance and knowing that he wouldn't win, he returned to his ongoing crusade at work – which works should be considered for sale under the banner of his department. It wasn't surprising that those who'd got on at Boulets before him were the ones who chose to maintain the status quo – who wanted things to always carry on as they were. His past attempts to bring in more avant-garde pieces had been rebuffed by Charlie Steel, who always enlisted Barnabas Price when Ryder tried to pull rank on him. They would restate their objections in the same way as before.

'Just what is it you think we're trying to sell here?'

'And to whom?'

Ryder decided he'd have one more shot at it, make the case that the company was missing out, missing the shift and the opportunity that came with it – to move to something new or, at least, newer.

But, as always, Steel was dismissive. 'An antique is something that's at least a hundred years old.' Then went on to debate what they should call themselves should Ryder get his way. 'How about "vintage and retro".'

He enunciated 'retro' as though it were a neologism, like he'd coughed up a foreign object. And all because Price was present to back him up.

'We're not a record shop, Ryder. We're here to curate the past and represent the best of it to our clientele.'

That really got to Ryder – he really went off at that. He always tried to reply to pompousness with biting satire and a scathing tone. But this time he got the measures wrong and served up a bad cocktail, long on bitters. He tried to make the point that antique dealers, from the earliest days, were happy to break things up and knock things down. They were never curators. Their forebears would happily smash a house to pieces and cart off the staircase and flog it to a rich patron. Creative destruction. It wasn't a question of preserving or conserving, but of supply and demand. He hoped to make Steel look out of tune in front of Price. But the older man retaliated.

'What are we, a fucking filtration unit?'

He laughed in Steel's direction.

'One trip to New York and he's all about "new" again. New this and new that. His head's turned again.'

'And yours is stuck in a tar pit, you fucking dinosaur. People don't want to be patronised by the past!'

Ryder was winding up for his final point, which would have been to accuse Steel of being in the wrong business. If he wanted to preserve the past, then he should go to work for the National Trust.

But Price cut across him just as he was about to let fly. 'Gentlemen, I think it's a little early in the day for tearing down the gates of convention and storming the citadel of heritage.'

He separated them, which really solved nothing, but prevented Ryder from punching Steel in the throat. It wouldn't be left there, that was for sure. Ryder was more determined than ever to take another swing at it. He'd have to do the research first – drop in the evidence, make the commercial case.

He still bought the thrust of it all, more than ever – the need to find a new market, one that couldn't be seen by the old guard. His own personal serendipity. He saw himself as the creator of a need and the servicer of that market. Some arrogant divination of the taste of others, because he assumed he had the instinct for it.

He waited until the dust had settled, then went back to Price, this time armed with backup stats.

Price threw his hands out like an impatient casting director. 'The floor is yours.'

Ryder expressed himself enthusiastically – how the new millennium had ushered in great opportunity. Something was going on in London – everyone was seeing it except Boulets. Hirst, Oki, the Tate Modern, the emerging women like Mutu and Djurberg, the YBAs – there was a vibe, a sense of excitement. Even the glossies like *Vanity Fair* and *Vogue* and *Harper's Bazaar* had spotted it.

Price was giving the impression of listening but, in reality, he wasn't taking Ryder seriously. On the one hand, he wanted his young head of department to feel appreciated; but, on the other, he couldn't allow him to jump over people.

'It's all very interesting, Ryder ..'

Ryder didn't let him finish; he continued to fire out evidence of the new renaissance, even if it was cliched, until he thought he'd dug himself a promising seam.

'We've conjured a new role, sir, a new chorus. History is so yesterday, we're all sociologists now.'

Ryder stopped talking and sat down, believing he'd made his case. Price twiddled his pen. He didn't want to bear down too directly on Ryder's enthusiasm, but he couldn't ignore the lack of actual commercial content in the stream-of-consciousness soliloquy.

'It is interesting.'

Ryder saw a glimmer of hope. Time to close the deal.

'Look, sorry, I know there's nothing actionable, at least not for now. It's an insight . . . an observation.'

Price looked thoughtful. Ryder pressed on.

'At least let me play with it, work it up, come back to you with something more concrete.'

Price smiled indulgently. 'Very well – put like that, I'll allow you some leeway.'

Ryder got up promptly, as though remaining there risked a reversal. He nodded his appreciation as he made for the door.

Price wasn't finished. 'But remember, I'm naturally suspicious of these new narratives. It feels like someone is trying to sell me something through the back door.'

Ryder looked dutiful, as though he'd taken this on board.

'And do try to stop treading on Steel's toecaps, would you?'

Price shook his head when Ryder left. He tried to remember what he'd been like at that age. He wondered how anyone made it through these days – what did they know, the young? Their cynicism was only skin-deep and, in the natural world, they'd be devoured before they even made it to adulthood. If Price had to choose, it would be Steel, but he could indulge Ryder to a certain extent, knowing that he was really indulging himself.

To Ryder, there was always a sense that someone, somewhere, was having a better time. In making his suggestions to Price, he was attempting to find that elusive Erewhon for himself. It was the self-spun delusion that, somehow, he could slip off the ropes and drop them into the murk – detach himself from the gnawing, hungry vacuum of what it was to be human. The shadow that stood on street corners. The invisible worms. Emancipation of individuality. And he'd think about the gypsy woman and how her name stayed inside his head that day in Gloucestershire – so long ago it seemed. *Lola-la-la-la-la.* Calling to him. It was still calling to him. Even now. Trying to drag him back to something that wasn't real, but existed for only a brief moment on a sultry summer evening. Subliminal. Spooky.

As time went on, the arguments Ryder made for new activity in new spheres came to nothing. Price reviewed them, but only as a digression – an interesting conversation, with no basis for doing anything about it. He was left with no alternative, and Price didn't really put his heart into persuading him to stay. He just followed protocol.

It was an odd thing, young people resigning. It wasn't something they fully understood, as they hadn't done it before. Price, on the other hand, had resigned from several jobs and been fired from one – and had numerous people come to him to resign. They were often caught between the act's supposed importance to them and a desire to be talked out of it. Sometimes polite and apologetic, wanting to have at least an affirmation and some sort of blessing.

But, with Ryder, that wasn't the case. He was always going to go.

One way or another.

And perhaps it was just as well he resigned, to avoid the inevitable other. Price didn't see the point of going through the rigmarole of trying to get him to stay, and it seemed beneath both of them to even try. Now they sat facing each other, each aware, not just of the silence but that this might be the last time they ever met. It conjured up different-coloured memories – some good, some bad – and Ryder felt he ought to acknowledge Price's leadership, just as a matter of courtesy. But he couldn't find a way into what he needed to say. Price, on the other hand, felt a sense of amused exasperation and indulgence about the younger man and his past misdemeanours. It was a moment when they sat there, no longer as employer and employee, but as something altogether more personal.

'I've learned a lot from you, sir.'

'That's very kind of you . . . depending, of course, on what it is you've learned.'

There was really nothing more to be said. Price got up first – a little awkwardly. Ryder followed his lead. They shook hands and Price wished him good luck.

And that was that.

Price retook his seat when Ryder was gone. He wondered about how uneven these things were – and, while he liked Ryder, he found himself forgetting about him already. While his head of furniture had been different, in the end he was just like all those who had preceded him – and would be easily supplanted by those to come. Price wondered how many that would be and it made him feel tired, and certain that the series would continue as long as he did. A finger of melancholy touched his soul. It was as if he was watching himself grow old and, in that tableau, there would be an inevitable end.

To everything.

\* \* \*

Ryder decided to be resolutely unimpressed by the past – not to bow and scrape to it. Only to even admit it when it added value to me-here-now. It gave him the kind of cloak he so desired.

Now that he was no longer at Boulets, he saw himself riven from the normal competing desires for all manner of gratifications, attaining a piercing truth and insight into the depth of his own experience – which, itself, would illuminate those around him. A sylvan sensibility, like a meditating monk. Of course, it would have to be accompanied by a nexus of wealth and glamour and a twist of intellectual distaste for other milieus – and exclusivity. That was his Avalon. It was a heavenly cocktail.

'Fuck me, I love it. I'll take it. I want it!'

It was Friday and he decided to go out and celebrate his newfound freedom. Swan1 was in The Cross Keys, without her boss or her erstwhile twin – who Ryder had seen a few times since their tryst all that time ago, but hadn't renewed the liaison. He rhapsodised about leaving Boulets behind and Swan1 luxuriated in his enthusiasm for what would come. His pleasure became hers. And she didn't care that he was playing it up. In fact, that made it even better. Everyone wanted to be amazed. Everyone was susceptible to believing in kismet. He was having one of those centre-of-the-world moments. It was as though, by some secret operation whose mechanics he couldn't hope to understand or explain, access could be granted to anything. A portal had opened.

If a thing was worth doing or saying, it was worth doing or saying to someone else, somewhere else.

They moved on to the Arts Club in Notting Hill and she brought her unexpected boyfriend with her. Ryder was glad; it meant he wouldn't have to try to jump her. Swan1 had an adaptability. It was as though she could shift her personality in line with her changes in looks and clothes. She laughed gently when he said as much, and told him he'd said the same thing when they'd seen each other at the Royal Academy exhibition a couple of months earlier. He didn't remember and he felt foolish for repeating himself so obviously. But she didn't care. She said it wasn't ridiculous for him to have the wrong idea about her, as he'd mostly only seen her at work, apart from the odd brief encounter at The Cross Keys. And work no longer applied because she'd left Boulets a couple of weeks before Ryder resigned.

She went on to talk about how fraught the whole work thing was. She even had to coordinate what she wore with the other Swan, so they didn't clash. It was bad enough that they looked the same, without doing a dress double-act. Still, it had been fun in its way while it lasted. But better one of them moved on.

'Do you still see Anna, Ryder?'

'No, we weren't really compatible.'

'That doesn't surprise me.'

'How so?'

'I don't think you're compatible with any woman.'

He didn't know how to take that. Was it a criticism or a compliment? And did he care which?

There was a performance element to Swan1 and the company she kept. That pastime of people looking and being looked at. Of being one of the chosen.

'Are you an art dealer now, Ryder?'

'Hoping to be.'

'Let me introduce you ...'

She took him across to a young man of similar age, who was expressing himself quite vehemently to a mixed group of bohemian-looking types. Swan1 elbowed her way straight in without excusing herself, as though she was more important than them and they should just shut up and move back.

'Dieter, this is Ryder. He's an art dealer.'

'Really? How fortuitous.'

Dieter shook his hand just as vehemently as he was conversing before being interrupted by Swan1.

'I am looking for a dealer to handle my work.'

Dieter was young and ambitious, charismatic in company and able to enthral his troupe of neo-hippies. He was born in Berlin and came to London to take a walk on the wealth side and make a name for himself in the *Kunstfieber* of the new millennium. He was principled, or so he made out – something that was always dangerous in an artist. He cared about climate change and the growing divide between rich and poor and was totally against oil wars and commercial armies and invisible torture sites and believed in egalitarianism and all the camp causes that worked when it came to the art of seduction.

Ryder hadn't seen any of his work, but Swan1 said it was indefinable – a melding of modern and minimalism, abstract meets avant-garde, a marriage of pop and post-impressionism. In other words, it was whatever you made it, a style that could either drown in its own self-delusion or become the next predilection of the pseudo-aesthete. It could start a new trend. Swan1 was enthusiastic about Dieter's raw energy and anarchic talent, and Ryder wondered if he'd fucked her – was still fucking her, despite the new boyfriend.

Dieter shook Ryder's hand with a tight manly grip, holding on for longer than was necessary. Ryder squeezed back – a test of blokey strength before the cerebral contest to come?

'So, you are an art dealer?'

Ryder deferred to Swan1. 'That's what she said.'

'And who do you represent?'

'Nobody you'd know.'

'Try me.'

'Maybe later.'

Ryder ordered a round of drinks to change the subject.

Dieter had a flat in Hammersmith, with a loft above it where he made his creations. He wrote the address and phone number on a piece of paper from the bar and handed it to Ryder.

'Would you like to see my work?'

'Sure, why not.'

'Where is your gallery?'

'Let's have a look at your work first.'

Ryder put the piece of paper in his pocket and decided it was time to move on from the Arts Club. After downing his drink, he said so long and told Dieter he'd be in touch.

He knew, if he was going to be taken seriously as a dealer, he'd need a shop.

That's when he thought about Lucien Holmes and the pending court case.

# CHAPTER 13

## LOLA

Ryder was at a loose end – between Boulets and *succès d'estime*, his rightful place in the hierarchy of fine art heavyweights. Now that he had so much free time, he spent most of it thinking about the gypsy woman and, although he knew a lot of females in London, he'd lost interest in them. A shrink would tell him it was obsessive, but he couldn't help it. Ryder reckoned if he could just get with her, he wouldn't want to stay. It'd be out of his system once and for all. It was time to lay the ghost to rest. He pencilled it in with a drive around the rural Cotswold auctions to see if he could come across another misattribution like the Ming.

Late in the evening, he visited the Trout pub again, not really expecting to find any trace of her there. He took a room for the night and, at breakfast the next morning, the woman who served him spoke with a similar accent to the one he remembered Lola using.

'Excuse me . . . I'm looking for a woman.'

'As far as I knows, there's a brothel in Cheltenham.'

It was a bad start, but Ryder managed to convince her he wasn't looking for a hooker. She told him there was a caravan site in the hamlet of Bredon's Hardwick, near Tewkesbury, and if he was looking for a gypsy, he could try there.

After mooching round a few auctions without any real appetite for it, he travelled up the A38 and came across Drake Farm, which wasn't marked on any map. It was located in the River Avon valley and had its own lake, along with a caravan and camping site. It was a good place for hiking and fishing and other such plaid-shirt activities, even a local ale festival and folk-music shindig. A kind of low-budget Glastonbury. Ryder had a look around the place before going to reception, but there was no sign of a horse or a bow-top wagon. A man in wellingtons and a flat cap approached.

'Can oi 'elp you, sir?'

'Just looking around.'

'You from the po-lice?'

'No.'

'Social services?'

'Of course not.'

That's when he saw her, down near the lake edge. He left the Flat Cap calling after him as he rushed towards her before she disappeared.

'Lola!'

She turned, but didn't recognise him.

'Look, I know it's been a long time . . . I came to your caravan, bought a silver brooch.'

'The Gorgio dealer man. Ryder?'

'That's me. What are you doing here?'

'I work here.'

'Doing what?'

'Looking after the customers in summer, and taking care of the place in winter.'

Ryder noticed there was a makeshift bar and asked if she'd have a drink with him. She accepted a dark rum and he had a pint of warm lager and they sat outside on a wooden bench. She told him she no longer travelled because of the harassment and the various public order and criminal justice acts that prevented gypsies from going on the road. Most of her people had already settled down on permanent designated sites, and the itinerant life was too hard for her on her own. Ryder had his own thoughts and wondered if it was or wasn't for the best – swap their imagination for a share of suburbia?

'It might put an end to prejudice, Lola.'

'Prejudice would die out tomorrow, if only pride would do the same.'

Flat Cap intervened and shouted at her. 'Get back to work!'

Ryder stood up. 'I'll pay for her time.'

'Fifty quid.'

He handed over a crisp pink one.

She had another rum, which dispelled her reticence, and she related how her people had once been fortune-tellers and dancers. The women made lace and flowers and pegs – baskets at Easter for the primroses and elder-wood flowers at Christmas. They were crop-pickers and never came near towns – then the farmers got machines and immigrants to do the work. And 'ethnic cleansing' was a euphemism in which language disguised official violence – like 'holocaust' and 'apartheid' and 'clearances' and 'final solution'. And gypsies, over the years, had been subjected to everything that could be thrown at them. Murder and enslavement and imprisonment and extermination and sterilisation and the seizure of children and expulsion and forced conscription and laws restricting intermarriage and the banning of their languages.

The gypsy race was a mobile community trying to survive in a settled world, on the receiving end of an endless series of by-laws and acts of parliament and private bills and codes of practice and all kinds of other lopsided legislation. Hounded by town councils and district councils and county councils and borough councils and rural authorities and urban authorities and sanitary inspectors and local residents' committees and landowners and vigilantes.

'They don't want us travelling, mister, but they don't want us living next to them neither.'

'Just call me Ryder . . . no mister.'

'We're like the American Indians on their reservations. They've taken everything away from us, gradually, like a creeping death. They should make us a country, like they did for the Jews.'

Ryder wondered if he should say what he was thinking, that her problem was the lack of a common identity – a central, unifying nexus of belief and heritage to unite gypsies through time and space against the age-old enemies.

But he didn't.

She asked what he was doing here and he told her he was in the area on business and stopped in to take a look at the place. He didn't say he was looking for her. Her shift was just about over for the day, and he walked with her back to where she was living. The old bow-top wagon was gone. Instead, Lola lived in a two-berth caravan provided by the farm. He could tell it hadn't travelled anywhere for quite a while, if ever, as it was secured to its individual concrete pad, with weeds growing up round the wheels.

'You want to come in?'

'Sure ... why not.'

The interior was different too. Gone was the little stove with its blowsy embers and the scent of lilac and the shadowy silhouettes and the subliminal sound of the cimbalom. Replaced with lustre and candlewick and brightly coloured cushions, with Royal Crown Derby china cascading down the cupboards and a cut-glass mirror and a baroque little display of bowls. She found a dusty bottle of Torresilo and a bottle of old Oloroso and mixed them into two glasses – and they sat and talked.

She told him how her ancestors were a mixture of the Cerhara tent-dwellers and Chlara carpet-traders who travelled south from Romania and camped by the shores of the Van Gölü, near the border between Turkey and Iran. They crossed the Mediterranean and lived with the Gitanos for a while, before coming to Great Britain. She was the only girl in her family and her brothers treated her like a slave, so she left and went out on her own. That's when he'd come upon her the first time. Since then, she'd discovered she couldn't live alone on the road, the life was too hard, so she took the job at Drake Farm.

So, her people were dealers too – carpet dealers – and Ryder almost felt at home. And, as the evening wore on, feeling at home gave way to feeling at ease and then to feeling the chemistry that was flowing between them. She turned the light down low and covered the lamp with a red scarf, and he was back in the field with the bow-top and the laughing horse.

Somewhere in the back of Ryder's mind was the sound of the *lāu-tari* – both exciting and sinister at once. And shadows moving in the caravan where only the one dim lamp glowed, seemingly far away in the distance – many miles from the bed. His head felt light from the earlier beer and the wine mixture, floating on the scent of the witch-woman beside him and the texture of her hair and the seductive sound of her voice and the stimulating danger of the situation. Her skin was dark and felt like rough silk – warm and slightly moist in the low-light glow. Her tongue found its way around his body and her hands were electric when they touched him. He moved to the rhythm of her – the tempo rubato within her. In tune with the body of the woman, moving in syncopation to her changing positions on the bed. Her voice purring like a leopard and her words making no sense to Ryder – nor were they meant to. They were meant for herself in the crepuscule of the satyric lair.

Blood-red light leaked out through the fibres of the scarf. Ryder looked up into the beautifully demonic face of Lola – vampirish and surreal in the translucent glow. Her legs were astride him and her body undulating, up and down. She was saying gypsy words, softly, with her fingers combing through his hair and little drops of perspiration appearing on the satin skin above her cheekbones. Ryder was trying to hold on, trying to postpone the starbright light from shooting out of him and into her. He thought about Holmes and Price and O'Malley in an effort to restrain himself. But, in the end, the sybaritism of the gypsy woman overpowered everything else, and he grasped her shoulders in his moment of crisis. Blood drained down from his head and his muscles tensed under his arching back. She felt his excitement, which heightened her own and she tightened her vulvic grip.

Ryder's breath came in short spasms. Lola leaned her head back and her long hair touched his legs. Savage animals howled in the night outside, trying to get in to join the ritual – the union of Dorje and Ghanta – the synthesis of light and dark. And they came together in a rebirth of soft insubstantiality.

Hearts beating.

Lungs snatching at the blood-red air.

Lola waited. She wondered if this was the right man – to give her the child she wanted. He had to be, otherwise he wouldn't be here with her. The old people said if the Juwa admitted the Gorgio to the privilege of the Rom, the race would disappear. But Lola didn't care. This felt right to her, in accordance with the prophecy – and if it wasn't right, she'd deal with it when the time came. For now it was enough to know that the dream had come into the sunlight of waking life. Ryder looked at her, tried to speak, and his soundless words dispersed into the ether inside the dissolute caravan.

Ryder couldn't remember how long they'd been on the bed, couldn't remember if he'd slept or been awake all the time, didn't know what day or what month or what year it was. He could see faint fingers of light creeping up the windowpanes and knew it was time to go. The door suddenly blew open, which startled them both. Lola left the bed to look around outside and laughed when she realised it was only the wind. Or maybe it was the consequences of her disregard for the lines of life and the circle of Venus and the viâ lactea. Ryder wondered about the wisdom of his actions. About the consequences. The ramifications.

He left the bed and pulled on his clothes. The woman watched him, naked on top of the tousled bed coverings. Reclining in an amused position with the dregs of the wine in her glass. She frowned inwardly as she thought of her people and how they'd be so badly shocked if they could see her now, showing real affection for the first time in many years, and with someone she hardly knew – someone who could hurt her badly. She didn't believe he would, even though she had no way of knowing that for sure, or how their little liaison would work out in the end. She knew he'd come looking for her – why else would he be here? She didn't know what would happen next, or if he'd come back again, once he left the caravan. But for her to feel the way she did was sufficient.

For now.

She'd tried to depend on no one but herself, which she found she couldn't do because the Gorgio world was an unforgiving place to be alone in and she needed some love. From somewhere. Otherwise –

But now, by accident or providence, there was this dealer man.

When Ryder was ready to go, she moved from the bed and kissed his ear.

'Will you come back again, Ryder?'

'I don't know.'

'You must.'

'Why?'

'Because I want you to.'

Ryder didn't reply, but he knew he would – knew he had to. His body told him so, even if his brain had its doubts. He gave her his card before moving to the door and said he had some things to sort out. Lola followed and waved to him as he walked away.

'Be careful, Ryder. Watch out for the Beng.' Who was extremely deceitful and shadow-like and could appear in many guises.

Light was climbing in the sky away to the east; soon the sun would too. He made his way quickly down towards his parked car.

\* \* \*

It was a couple of months later when Ryder received a call from a public phone. It was Lola. She wanted to leave the farm, but they wouldn't let her. The flat-capped bullies said she owed them money for her keep and they were holding her captive until she paid, which would be never because she earned less than they said she cost them. The impecuniosity of the slave – she was worse off now than with her brothers.

It was late and dark when he reached Bredon's Hardwick and parked the car some distance from the farm. He moved on foot and very quietly – as quietly as someone could who had a very limited knowledge of the wild countryside around him and was in almost complete darkness. He recognised the outline of Lola's caravan and crept over to the side and waited, listening for any sound.

Subterfuge like this was completely outside Ryder's scope of experience, and he realised he hadn't thought it through. What if the local yokels Lola owed money to caught him? They carried shotguns in this part of the country. It was a moonlight flit without the moon, and that was dangerous. He could have paid them, of course, but it was totally extortionate and illegal what they were doing, and giving them money was against his principles as an abolitionist.

A kind of animal adrenaline flowed through him and he forgot his natural cautiousness as he listened to the whispers of the night. Knew the woman was waiting. He tapped lightly on the window.

'Lola?'

Nothing. He tapped again.

'Lola?'

She'd known he was outside even before he knocked. She could see inside the rainbow mist of latent knowledge in which truth revelled, because she had a gift, handed down from her mother, which couldn't be measured by everyday consciousness. And she knew that all people were, within themselves, gifted with infinite power and the ability to know all things. But she wouldn't tell that to Ryder.

Outside, it was as if time was standing still and had ceased to exist – replaced by a fog of sensations that could easily be mistaken for time. It was a cool night; the clouds parted and a gibbous moon shone its silver light down on the eerie surroundings of the farm, lending them an insubstantial aspect. There was so much on Ryder's mind before he came up here. So much he had to do and was in a hurry to do. Thinking way ahead – three or four events ahead. But that all stopped now. Now it didn't matter – none of it – what was to come, what was ahead. In the future. Now, only now meant anything.

Lola was ready. She emerged from the caravan with a couple of bags, which Ryder took from her and carried silently down the road to the car, with her following. She was thinking about the baby he would give her, a baby that would be beautiful and intelligent and humorous and he'd love his mother and take care of her when she grew old. He wouldn't desert her and she knew he'd be famous for something – maybe music or art or literature. It wouldn't matter which. And she would accompany him to all the best places and be introduced to all the best people and, if he was lucky, he'd possess the power – as she did.

Or unlucky – depending on how you looked at it.

On the way to London she asked about Ryder's family – his mother and father and if he had any brothers, as she did. He was reluctant to talk about personal stuff, but if he was going to live with this woman, at least for a while, then she'd need to know something about him. He told her he was an only child and his mother lived in Oxford and his father had killed himself – but that was another story, which he might tell her some time. But not now. She said both her parents were dead and she wanted to stay well clear of her brothers. And that was enough for the present. They could come to know each other later.

They didn't say much for the rest of the journey, nor did they stop anywhere. In the first place, it was too late, and they wanted to get as far away as possible before the flat caps on the farm woke up and found that she was gone.

Back at the flat, Lola watched as Ryder undressed. He was really beautiful, she thought, tanned and muscular, with reddish-brown hair and eyes a strange shade of grey. She wondered how old he was – not more than thirty, but older than her. There was something about the man, something elusive and enigmatic, and she wished it was like in the old days and she could have gone on the road with him and they could have spent the rest of their days roaming the wild world.

He glided to her on the bed, and he smelled sweet, and his teeth were white in the light of the moon, shining through the glass of the patio doors. She wanted to confide in him, tell him about her life, right from when she was very young. That she wanted all the amenities and luxuries of his world, yet to be apart from it, uncontaminated by it. But it was difficult for her to confide in a stranger, even this stranger, who wasn't a stranger at all. At the back of her mind, she couldn't help feeling that, somehow, this man might already know what she wanted. She decided not to tell him yet what she believed in and what she hoped for and what made her who she was – the woman she was.

And what hurt her.

Ryder moved with the woman. There seemed to be a unanimity between them, a eurhythmic equilibrium. And he felt something he'd never felt before – he felt like he was in love. He wondered if *fons et origo* made a man truly what he was, if his fate was sealed at birth, or if he changed with each new experience. And in the end, he became the sum of his life to that particular moment in time.

For now, he was no longer the man of the past, he was the man of the present, waiting to become the man of the future. And who would have believed, only a very short time ago, that he'd be here now, lying beside the gypsy woman and wondering when this thing he was doing would blow up in his face.

Lola kissed his neck and she was wild in her sexual enthusiasm and Ryder was lost, lost in her desire. He wondered if that desire was for him or for what he could give her – if he could give her anything, of course. Though he wondered this somewhere at the back of his mind, he wasn't aware of it at that particular moment in time, because everything was right. Even if it would be wrong at some interlude in the near future.

When it was over, Ryder lay back and smoked a cigarette and the back of his mind became the front of his mind. But he decided to ignore it anyway.

It was as it was.

And there were three ways of knowing a flame –

To be told of it –

To see it –

And to be burned by it.

## CHAPTER 14

# ROYAL COURTS OF BLIND JUSTICE

After reading every book in the flat and losing the edge of her broad accent, Lola acquired a habit of disappearing for days on end, then coming back. She was always vague about where she'd been and Ryder stopped himself from asking too many questions that might make him sound possessive and needy. She was a gypsy after all, and she was used to moving around – not being stuck in one place all the time. He figured it was her business and, to be fair, she didn't ask where he went. They hadn't been together long enough to be living in each other's pockets, and it would break some clause in the contract of early-stage relationships. Neither had any obligation to the other and, even though she was living in his flat, she insisted on paying half of everything. He didn't ask where her money came from – that was her business too.

The fact that he took it upon himself to stop chasing other women was a surprise to Ryder and something that should definitely be credited to him, even though the mechanism for gaining that credit was unclear, short of telling her 'I haven't fucked anyone else for two months, give me a prize'. And he didn't even feel like he'd given anything up, because Lola on her own was enough for him to handle. When they were alone together, it was as though the world had stopped, that their part had sheared off and slid away somewhere remote, unmoored to anything but each other. She swirled around him, she came and went like an airy spirit and, when she wasn't there, he could instantly recall her in his mind. He could reanimate her, bring back her laugh, her body, her face – above, between, beneath, below. By being absent, she became all the more compelling in the vacuum she left behind.

Now they were both silent, knowing that a single word would drop them back into time. Ryder looked out at a sky and a city that were just colours and shapes. He exhaled deeply and seemed lost, as though a thousand frost crystals had formed in his mind and would crack with any movement or thought. She slunk up behind him and wrapped her arms around his waist. Five minutes came and went and his first attempt to move was resisted as she drew him even closer.

'I have to go out.'

She didn't ask where. He disengaged himself and turned to look at her eyes, which were right up in his face – searching, locating, recording what she saw.

When he left, he leaned against the low wall outside the flat, as though the world was too suddenly upon him. He needed a couple of seconds to readjust to this side of the door, this real world where buses and taxis and people existed, before heading out into it. When he pushed off, he felt like he was a tourist, walking with no velocity or direction. On the tube, he wondered what it would be like to announce it all to the packed commuters – a disembodied voice – recounting all he'd done and felt in the last two months. He imagined the faces, as the voice, not his own, recounted his stepping outside the known world. Who here had ever experienced anything like it? It was so good that something had to be off-kilter. He had an almost performative power. He could command legions. All within a sense of temporal and experiential dislocation. He feared for the too-much of it, the without-proportion, the impossibility of imaging it, as though the shadow of doubt was what brought it about.

The Hex.

It all dissipated when Ryder arrived at the Royal Courts of Justice on the Strand and reality intruded. It was far too good an entertainment to miss out on – the prospect of it being played out in public.

They were all there, the buyers and dealers and factotums and anyone who'd heard the name Holmes – and of those there were many. They all knew their own know; little individual splinters of the whole secretaire. Now it was all going to be revealed, a shared public event. All the beans would be spilled. They were sitting together in the public gallery to witness the fall of the House of Holmes.

It promised to be one of the great public airings in the history of art dealership. And admittance was free. It was an outing – an event – with a carnival aspect to it. Colour and style combined in the outfits being walked up the imposing steps of the court. The *dernier cri* and *ne plus ultra* – the odd and the outrageous vying with the deliberately understated and the conspicuously discreet. They were all there, except for Seth.

Ryder couldn't believe they were actually going through with it, that it had gotten to this point. There were so many ways it could have been avoided.

'How many ways?'

He turned to find the Russian called Pavel behind him. Ryder gave him a half-smile as he answered. 'Thirty . . . at least.'

Pavel gave out that big Russian guffaw of his and clapped Ryder heavily on the back, almost knocking him forward.

'Have you seen Seth . . . since you went with him to New York?'

He hadn't – maybe once, at a distance, but not to speak to and find out why they'd been arrested.

'I heard you were arrested.'

'Bad news travels fast.'

'Do you know why?'

'A misunderstanding.'

Pavel laughed again and clapped Ryder on the back again. He wondered if he should get up and go sit somewhere else, but that would be disrespectful and everyone would be looking at him.

'We must meet for a drink, Ryder.'

'Sure, why not.'

'I would call you, if I had your number.'

Ryder handed the Russian his card, indicating that he was now a freelance fine art dealer.

'Where is your gallery?'

'I'm in the middle of relocating.'

The conversation was cut short by the arrival of Lucien Holmes. All eyes were on him, but he wasn't going to be hurried and he wasn't trying to pause for dramatic effect. As a matter of fact, he'd rather be lounging in the back room of his shop, with Cassie bringing him coffee at regular intervals. He was immediately surrounded by the many briefs and barristers in attendance, and seemed to be swallowed up by them. Ryder was noticing the legal array disposed against him on the other side of the chamber – and Buggins, who sat there looking down at an open pad with a pencil in his hand. He appeared to be drawing rather than writing. But who knew what went on in his mind? An introverted oddity, convinced of the wrong that had been done to him. Slighted, offended and righteous.

Three weeks earlier, Ryder got a call from Holmes, asking him to travel down to Buggins's workshop in Hampshire. He was the chosen emissary, in place of the reluctant Seth, as both Lucien and Aloysius Holmes could just about agree that he could represent their different interests. Ryder didn't care much for the honour, but he was still looking for a way into their world. He asked Lola if she wanted to go with him, but she said her brothers had many friends in the New Forest and they might be looking for her there.

Buggins had created his own little kingdom down in Hampshire. As well as being a workshop, it was a sanctuary for rescued animals. It started with one horse and grew from there, then Buggins began taking in people too. He'd gathered a group of misfits around him. Hallucinogenic visionaries and disillusioned environmentalists and political pariahs and tech-savvy savants and sexual nonconformists and religious dissidents and equalitarians and globophobes and down-and-outs and freeloaders and a few fixers like himself. The piece of land on the edge of the New Forest had become open house for philosophers and prophets and gurus and sages and seers and witch doctors and drifters of all declensions – they came and went and the renovated barns were always full of people at any time of year. They all wanted something – were looking for something. The truth. Or the pseudo-truth. Or the quasi-truth. Or the nouveau-truth. Or the neuro-truth. Or maybe just a meal ticket. And it was obviously some of them who'd set Buggins on his kamikaze course against the Holmes brothers.

Buggins took Ryder into his huge workshop, one half of which was given over to his hobby of restoring vintage cars. He was an uneasy tour guide and only became fluent when he got lost in the technicalities and processes of his trade. He was like a child writing a letter – *and then I did this, and then I did that*. Ryder reckoned he might disorder the man if he interrupted, so he didn't. It looked like a long-term hoarder had been given free rein, but there was a kind of order amidst the chaos. Lockers and shelves were numbered amongst the paints and vices and blocks of wood. Workbenches were marked and battered through industry, but arranged in a production-line manner. The forlorn frame of a large sofa was pinned with rods and grips, its ribbing making it look like the carcass of a whale or the remnants of a wrecked longship that would eventually be returned to its former glory.

Buggins announced that it was eleven and, therefore, time for tea. Ryder felt like he was being steered away from this side of the workshop and he would have liked to have had time for a rummage on his own. Who knew what he might come across? They sat and drank from Delftware mugs and ate Highland shortbread biscuits and Buggins kept on talking trivia. He'd have done that all day in order to avoid the reason Ryder was there, who should have known it wasn't going to be about money – it rarely was with people like Buggins, not that there was anyone else quite like him. When Ryder tried to broach the subject of the Holmes brothers, he became reticent and defensive and deflected the issue away from himself. As far as Ryder was concerned, everyone was just getting wrapped up in their own self-righteousness – feeling they'd been disrespected.

Buggins looked on him with suspicion. Ryder returned his gaze, trying to seem both open and serious. He figured Buggins first had to get over the trust issue, to recognise that he was impartial and not taking sides.

'Who are you, Ryder?'

'You know who I am.'

'Yes, but who *are* you? Why isn't Seth here?'

'He didn't have the time.'

Buggins made a face which indicated he didn't believe any such thing. What Ryder was really hoping for was, if or when he got through, he might get to actually encapsulate the answer to this problem, but not with a narrative of wrongs that had been done – not the puff and complaint. He needed a trophy to take back to Holmes.

He had to come up with something that had been lost in all the commotion and posturing. Something to spike the whole thing. He wondered if Buggins had a problem with prison food – that might be the tack to take. Buggins, of course, had his own ideas regarding how the matter could be resolved.

'What is it they want?'

'That's not the question. The question is, what do *you* want?'

Buggins shook his head and sighed. 'An apology from Aloysius.'

Now it was Ryder's turn to shake his head and sigh. 'You're not going to get that.'

'Then we'll go to court.'

Ryder stood up. He wanted to leave, but didn't have anything better to be doing. It was time to get serious and find out just how far this little man was prepared to go.

'You know you'll incriminate yourself.'

'I don't care.'

'Is it more money? Some new arrangement? What can you live with?'

'An apology from Aloysius . . . in person.'

'You know he's in New York?'

'I don't care.'

After another hour of trying to reason with Buggins, Ryder finally left without a resolution. Some of the weird lodgers had come into the workshop and encouraged their host not to capitulate, to stand by his guns – for his principles. Things got a bit belligerent and Ryder decided *sod it*! But not before asking Buggins if he'd consider doing some work for him, when he got set up.

He then reported back to Holmes, who threw some stuff around the back room of his shop and shouted. 'It's put-your-fucking-wigs-on time!'

This was no longer about Buggins. He'd initiated it, but he was going to be collateral damage. Ryder started to think that, like Seth, he needed to distance himself. No point in getting caught in the blast.

And so here they were, Holmes still angry that it had come to this – angry with Buggins, angry with the court and its officers, above all angry with his brother. An anger that was personal and lifelong. They would fight to the end of days, no matter what, lawsuits or not, for all the life so far and all the life to come. And Ryder could see the glint of gold in the eyes of all these £1,000-an-hour barristers. Just imagine the costs up to now – those wigs didn't do pro bono. He was glad he wasn't paying.

They looked on, in these preliminary minutes, before the proceedings proper got underway, hoping it could be dragged out indefinitely so they could bleed their respective clients dry. For all their practised hours and Latin secret-speak, how often did they come across a Holmes – or a Buggins?

As well as the Holmes fan club in the public gallery, there were some of Buggins's social outcasts he'd brought along for support and it was all getting a little rumbustious. Verbal scuffles were breaking out and there was a distinct danger that the judge would clear the court when he arrived to take charge.

Holmes hadn't said a word, as if his stoical silence made him seem strong and confident. He wanted the toxic hatred to be enough to fuel him. It didn't help that his errant brother was physically three thousand miles away. But the thing with Holmes was that, when he got into it, he was pure force. When it came down to it, once all the charm had dissipated, he was someone who would take you on, take you head-on. It was almost old-fashioned – basic, even. But effective. Holmes would gun the accelerator and keep going until he hit you, making the choice yours and yours alone. Hit me or swerve. How do you communicate that you're not going to change course? Be seen to throw the steering wheel out the window.

Your problem now!

But, as quickly as he turned himself into a great looming thunderhead, it seemed to pour itself away and level out and he felt detached. He knew, no matter how it went, it would be the end – it was going to be the end of him. Nothing would outplay the sport and squirm of a public and forensic cross-examination by a gaggle of hostile and belligerent barristers in the law courts. He imagined all those former clients, spluttering over their breakfasts: *WHAT? WHAT? You mean this is* not *an imperial armoire worth two million, but some fake cobbled together by that erstwhile leading dealer and his backyard gimp?* Would all his rich and powerful clients, on learning of being duped, come back and stick the litigious knives into him, let him bleed out from all the financial wounds and then chuck his bankrupt body on the bonfire of disrepute and dishonour?

He felt strange, transported away from this court, feeling something he hadn't felt for a long time – indifference. It wasn't shame, or the disgrace to come, none of that really mattered to him anymore. It was the pettiness of it all. This parade which had seemed to matter for so long; and, now it was finally here, it turned out not to matter much at all.

Ryder caught the strange look on Holmes's face. It was relaxed – angelic, even. He looked old but serene. Then Seth arrived. He made his way down into the well of the court and whispered something to Holmes, who waved him across to Buggins. Ryder couldn't hear what was said, except for Buggins as he pushed the learned wigs out of his way and headed for the exit. 'Give me some room, will you!'

The barristers all exchanged puzzled glances, not wanting to follow their client before the other side made some kind of move. In the end, the tension was too much and they all made a dash for the door, followed by the entire assemblage of the public gallery. Ryder looked back to see Holmes sitting alone now, removing his shoes and socks and putting his bare feet up onto the cap rail in front of him.

Ryder emerged to see Aloysius, flanked by Seth, down on one knee in the open area inside the railings, between the Strand and the law court steps. Buggins stood in front of him, as if he was bestowing a knighthood. When Aloysius stood up, they both shook hands and walked away together, much to the dismay of the public-gallery onlookers – the tricoteuses, up for the spectacle to watch what they wouldn't have to participate in. Well, there would be no bloodied edge of guillotine today. And that was that.

Ryder lit a cigarette and smiled to himself; somehow he knew that Holmes had managed to engineer this reconciliation between his brother and Buggins. He didn't know how, but that didn't matter now.

It was Holmes through and through, to be able to overturn the inevitable. Only he could get away with something like that. His charm and latent graciousness, which was almost menacing, allowed it. And how was Seth able to fire-walk between the Holmeses? When and how did he become so indispensable? No doubt his singular talent for self-preservation played a part – even if it couldn't prevent him making it back from Moscow in a worse state than those on the ignominious retreat with Napoleon in the winter of 1812, as painted by so many artists that the scene was almost ubiquitous. And would it now be open season on Seth? Now that Holmes was being toppled, would his confidants follow? That's why Ryder had to be careful and distance himself from the fallout – it would do him no good to be seen as sullied.

He wondered why, if Holmes had indeed the means to set up the apology to Buggins from Aloysius, which was obviously what had happened – why did he leave it till the eleventh hour? Was it grandstanding – displaying his power in front of the watching art world? Or was it, in the parlance of psychoanalysis, a deep-seated need to expose himself and be caught? What was the point of doing something great if no one knew you'd done it?

Wasn't there a delight, not just in the duping, but in making sure they knew they'd been duped? Didn't we all want credit for our crimes? Wasn't any deathbed confession nothing more than a boast?

Ryder felt a tap on his shoulder. He turned to see Pavel standing behind him.

'We should have that drink now.'

## CHAPTER 15

# THE TELLING OF THE MOSCOW INCIDENT

The George was just across the Strand from the law courts. It was a gastropub, with a clientele of pinstripes and the carriers of pink-ribboned briefs, in which Ryder would never normally be seen. But Pavel was insistent, so he conceded. The place was packed, but they managed to secure a small corner table after ordering a pint of Neckinger and a large Johnnie Walker single malt.

Ryder was the first to speak. 'Holmes certainly did a Houdini there, don't you think?'

'A Houdini?'

'An escape.'

'Not really, the damage has already been done.'

Ryder took a long slug from his pint and wondered – if that was the case, what was the point of it all?

Pavel elaborated. 'Well, I suppose he has escaped prison. But you should know, Ryder, the world of art dealing is a small one and, as you said yourself, bad news travels fast.'

'So, what will happen to Holmes?'

'No one will trust him again. I heard he has already moved all his stock from that shop or gallery or whatever it is.'

'Where to?'

'Who knows? You should ask Seth.'

Ryder wondered just how much of Holmes's dealing had been in fakes – and how much this Russian knew about it. Maybe he should ask him about Seth. He'd heard about some trouble in Moscow – was it connected to what happened when they returned from New York? Pavel was sure to know about it, but the Russian was still discussing Holmes.

'I think "fake" is the wrong word, Ryder. I think he just got carried away in the restoration.'

Like Theseus's boat. The paradox that, after each part of it had been replaced, could it still be said to be the same boat?

'What happened to Seth in Moscow?' Ryder just blurted out the question.

Pavel gave him a curious look before replying. 'You do know he is a smuggler? Of course you do, otherwise you would not have gone to New York with him.'

'Of course,' Ryder lied.

The Russian went to the bar and brought back more drinks, before telling his story in that demonstrative way which only Russians know how to enact.

Pavel's words morphed into mental images as Ryder listened.

\* \* \*

Seth made his way towards the arrivals gate at Sheremetyevo International Airport. The place was practically deserted and Christmas carols played musakally over the loudspeakers in all the lounges. It was snowing outside and there were no taxis at the rank. A cold white world. Clean and clear. He waited a few minutes and lit up a cigarette, contrary to the signs on all the walls. From away in the half-light, a silver Citroën made its way slowly in his direction. It seemed like a mirage at first, coming out of the whiteness. A snow mirage, becoming clearer as it drove closer and stopped at the taxi rank.

A tall, well-built blond man in his forties emerged and shook hands with him.

'Seth.'

'Pavel. *Privet*. It's been a while. You have somewhere for me?'

'Yes, my cousin runs a little place on Zhukov Proyezd. It is small, but very comfortable. He has kept you a double room.'

'Thanks, Pavel, one I owe you.'

'I will think of something so we can be, how you say, square. Yes?'

'Sure.'

Seth climbed into the front of the Citroën and Pavel drove off south along the A104 highway. They didn't speak during the twenty-minute journey, and Seth looked out the window at the snow scenery while Pavel stared straight ahead – directly through the windscreen, to a distant point of concentration. He seemed preoccupied, lost in the penumbra of midwinter. Concentrating on something specific but nothing in particular.

Moscow was a sprawling city, one of the world's biggest, and coldest, and home to the highest number of billionaires in Europe. Red Square was a landscape vista as well-known as Manhattan, and Gorky Park, St Basil's Cathedral and the Kremlin were all names that conjured up a history from ancient tsars to *Doctor Zhivago*.

Seth reached over and touched Pavel on the shoulder. 'What do you know about Garage Valley?'

'We call it Shanghai. Dangerous. Is that why you are here? Be careful.'

'Listen, Pavel . . . I need a gun.'

'I am sorry, Seth, my friend. I don't want any trouble with the *militsiya*.'

'For old times' sake?'

'My friend, I would not know where to find a gun these days. After the muscle game, I put my savings into art. That is what I am now, an importer and exporter of art.'

Seth wondered if he was telling the truth. There was no way of knowing for sure. But routine comforts calmed anxiety, like the feel of a semi-automatic against the skin.

'OK. Don't worry about it.'

'I can get you a hotel room, Seth, help transfer funds, or give you advice on a Picasso. Nothing else. I cannot take chances. Chances are for foolish men to take.'

'You're right, of course, Pavel.'

'I hope so, Seth . . . but I wish you well in your venture.'

The Citroën pulled away north-westward along Zhukov Proyezd, leaving Seth standing on the snow-covered pavement. He waited and watched the silver car disappear into the silver afternoon and, even then, waited some more, as if he expected Pavel to turn round and come back and toss a silver handgun out the window. Then he shivered and walked across the pavement to the golden entrance of the Black Crocus Hotel.

Pavel's cousin was a gregarious type of fellow, and every courtesy was extended to the Englishman. The hotel was full of tourists and the ambiance excessively Christmassy. Too much so for Seth. He hated all the fucking fuss at this time of the year. Too much tinsel and togetherness, sycophancy and shite, kissing and cuddling and hugging and handshaking. It reminded him of small days gone by when all these things – these child-type things – were not for the Silverman family. Fuck the *ben zonas*!

Warm smells of game and pancakes floated out from the dining area, and Pavel's cousin handed him a large sports bag as he made his way to the double room that had been laid on for him. It was spacious, with a king-sized bed and antique furniture. Sheepskin rugs spread themselves over the wooden floor and this made Seth feel more at home. He threw his overnight case and the sports bag into a corner and flopped onto the bed. The walls held a strange alignment of prints by Serov and Shishkin and Vrubel and Filonov, as if someone had bought a job lot and just thrown them up there, in no particular order. Home-grown artists. They stared at Seth – knew him, knew what he was here for. And they frowned.

Silver flecks of snow blew against the silver window, and down in his silver art cellar, Pavel drank a bottle of silver Sauvignon and laughed and laughed and laughed.

The rendezvous, in a small cul-de-sac off Pleshcheeva Street, just to the north of the Garage Valley area of the city, was set for 9:00 p.m. and it was now only 2:00. Seven hours to go. Seth rose from the bed on which he'd been resting and took a look at the sports bag that the cousin had given him. He unzipped it and was about to check the contents, but decided not to bother. He zipped it back up and placed it carefully under the bed, leaving the overnight case he'd brought with him in full view. Then he went down to a late lunch.

Deeper into the evening, the hotel ordered a taxi and Seth travelled away from the beaten track and the holiday revellers and the lights of the centre. He was nervous about this arrangement – would have preferred Pavel to drive him, someone he could trust. But his friend wouldn't do it anymore – couldn't, because he was now an honest man with a reputation.

Or so he said.

The further they went, the more surreal the landscape became. It was a quiet, white area of town, disguising the danger, and he told his taxi driver to wait as he walked down along Pleshcheeva Street and turned right into the cul-de-sac, checking the piece of paper in his hand for the correct address. Seth came to a dark door with the barely readable number '22'. He hesitated, looked up and down, then knocked four times in slow succession, as instructed. There was no response.

He waited. The taxi also waited down on Pleshcheeva Street, and Seth saw the driver glance at his watch. The door opened suddenly and a middle-aged man with a black beard looked out – Siberian?

'*Ty muzhchina?*'

'What?'

'*Ty muzhchina s den'gami?*'

'Speak English!'

The man waved Seth inside and made him raise his arms – frisked him and took the sports bag. Then he led the way up steep narrow stairs to a room at the top, bare except for a wooden table and one wooden chair. Another man sat on the chair – also Siberian-looking, with shoulder-length hair tied back in a ponytail and a large tattoo on his neck that came up from under the collar of his shirt and looked like some kind of black snake. A velvet sack and a counting machine sat in the middle of the table. The seated man opened the sack and took out an icon of St Nicholas of Zaraisk and motioned to Seth to inspect the merchandise, which he did with a small flashlight and a magnifying loupe.

The first man placed the sports bag on the table and the seated man smiled at Seth, exposing several gold teeth.

'*Chetvert' milliona?*'

'English, for fuck's sake!'

The seated man unzipped the bag and began stacking the notes inside it into the counting machine. When he'd finished, his smile turned to an angry frown.

'*Eto korotko!*'

'What the fuck are you going on about now?'

'*Vsego dvesti tysyach!*'

The man rose from his chair and smashed his fist against the table. The second man pulled out a Heckler and Koch semi-automatic pistol and pointed it at Seth.

'*Gde ostal'nyye?*'

'I can't understand what you're fucking talking about.'

Snakeneck struck Seth across the face with the back of his hand. Seth recoiled, then grabbed him by the throat and swung him round into the gunman's line of fire. He sunk his teeth into the man's neck and a fine spray of blood erupted from the snake tattoo and spread over the room. The gunman pointed the Heckler and Koch and his finger tightened on the trigger. He tried to get a clear shot, but the blood was on his face and in his eyes. That slight hesitation was enough. Seth twisted Snakeneck's arm up behind his back, dislocating it at the shoulder. The man screamed and tried to hold in the spraying blood with his good hand. The gunman panicked and fired, hitting Snakeneck in the face. The bullet came out through the back of his head and Seth felt it pass through his ear. Snakeneck stopped screaming and struggling. The gunman was trying to get off another shot. Seth flung the dead body across the room, knocking him off balance and sending the semi-automatic flying from his hand. They both reached the weapon at the same time and each man held on to the other's grip on the gun, in a desperate struggle for life – or death. The man was stronger, and a left cross sent Seth flying backwards towards the door. He pointed the gun as Seth scrambled through the exit and down the stairs and out of the cul-de-sac onto Pleshcheeva Street, leaving the money and the icon behind. The taxi was gone – everywhere was white and silent in the stillness of the Christmas night. He scooped up some snow and tried to stop his ear from bleeding, then ran out of Garage Valley.

There was no sign of life anywhere, except for some shivering souls doing eight-hour shifts on their cold street corners. Everyone else was in the bars and clubs or at home for the holiday. No vehicles of any sort ploughed through the virgin snow in this part of town, and only distant sounds of music and laughter were audible in the cold air. It was as if the whole world was inside hibernating – safe in the warmth of its den and afraid to move out amongst the gunslingers and jugular-biters.

Seth didn't know which direction took him back to the Black Crocus Hotel. If he got picked up by the *militsiya* he'd be in big trouble. He knew the cab came here in a north-westerly direction, so he kept going south-east. Buildings loomed and the sky lowered itself to street level, and snow stuck to his shoes like quicksand and tried to pull him down. Each step was an effort and his breath came hard and rasping up from burning lungs. Shadows hid round every corner, trying to grab him and hold him, like the snow, until the ghouls came to rip all the bones from his body and leave the rest of him in a bloody heap on the ground. Silver-red, like a shed snake-skin, staining the whiteness.

Then he saw the bright sign outside the Black Crocus, shining like a silver star to guide him. It was only a hundred metres away now and he quickened his step through the snow. Reception was closed and laughter drifted out from the bar and dining area. Seth was careful not to be seen as he hurried to his room and into the shower, washing the gore from his body and changing his clothes.

\* \* \*

That was the tale Pavel enacted for Ryder in The George on the Strand.

Ryder didn't know whether to believe the Russian or not. Then again, he'd seen the scar on Seth's left ear. Pavel needed more drink and Ryder obliged – he wanted to hear the rest of the story.

'What happened after that?'

'My cousin, he called me. I drove to the hotel.'

Pavel said he was shocked when he saw Seth; his ear was bandaged with torn strips of a shirt and he looked like a Van Gogh self-portrait. He'd asked him what happened and Seth told him they didn't speak English but it was his guess that the money was short. And now he'd lost it all. Pavel and his cousin managed to get hold of a dodgy doctor, who disinfected the wound and patched it up properly. Then they got Seth back to the airport and out of Moscow while Christmas was still being celebrated.

Luckily there were no problems at Sheremetyevo, because it was Christmas night and everybody'd had a vodka or two and Seth was late and the plane was waiting and he was rushed through passport control and boarded with hand-luggage only. Heathrow was relaxed and seasonal too when he arrived back after the four-hour flight, most of which he slept through after taking two little pills given to him by the dodgy doctor, which rendered him back home as if he'd been teleported.

Ryder didn't know anything about icon smuggling and he wanted to know how it worked. Pavel told him that some Russian pieces were regarded as priceless and many were to be found, not in the Hermitage Museum, but locked in government buildings in the Yakutia region of Siberia. Maybe an icon of St Alphege, or

St Porphyrios of Kavsokalyvia, or the miracles of Christ, or a Fabergé imperial egg belonging to the Romanovs that disappeared when the Bolsheviks took over. It was a place about five times the size of France but with only about a million inhabitants. People there were generally poor and were prepared to steal icons and sell them at a fraction of what they were worth on the international black markets.

Ryder tried to get his head round it. 'But who buys them?'

The Russian leaned in closer to him. 'Let me give you a hypothetical situation.'

Pavel took a mouthful of whisky, swirled it round his teeth and swallowed. He told Ryder to imagine some guy from the Colombian Banco de Comercio who wanted to invest money in art. Nothing wrong with that, and art dealing was chic, because everybody figured the market was less prone to the cyclical price fluctuations typical of many commodities and it substantially outperformed oil and gold – and the strength of the art market was reckoned to continue into the foreseeable future, with the outlook for prices staying positive, particularly for the rarer, more obscure pieces like Russian icons.

'The Colombian guy represents some Medellín syndicate that wants to lose a couple of hundred million dollars.'

Both of them knew Pavel was talking about drug money, and the Russian could see Ryder's disapproving expression.

'It is all business, Ryder. Nobody cares.'

If Seth didn't do it, somebody else would. So, he and the Banco de Comercio guy do business in a roundabout way, breaking the ice so neither of them got the jitters. They talk about new orders of investment in the global economy and how the *démodé* capital guys who were traditionally the largest providers of money had all but disappeared, and Seth might say there was always someone prepared to part with their money – as long as they could be shown the advantages. When both of them were sure that the other wasn't Customs and Excise or DEA or FBI or some other interfering agency, the Colombian guy tells Seth there's a Zurich account in the name of Empire Developments, and the icons could be deposited there as collateral for a loan made by Empire Developments to an unspecified company. This company would disperse the loan money amongst various secret accounts and then go bankrupt. The icons would be appropriated by Empire Developments and transferred to a front company.

'It is done all the time, Ryder.'

Pavel went on for a while longer about how the clean money would get back to the original 'investors' and how nothing illegal could be proved about what they were doing – immoral maybe, but not illegal.

'Pavel, are you telling me that the money Seth lost in Moscow was cartel money?'

'I'm not saying that at all.'

'No?'

'I am just outlining a hypothetical situation.'

'How much was involved?'

'Two hundred and fifty thousand American dollars.'

'Jesus!'

'A mere trifle, my friend.'

They drank up and left The George.

And Ryder knew he'd look at Seth Silver in a different light from then on.

## CHAPTER 16

# DEATH AND DIETER

Ryder expected more – for the foremost dealer to be found out, he'd expected howls of protest and claims in the courts! But the Holmes effect turned out to be a ripple rather than a tsunami. Hardly a sex tape? In the end, it just slipped away, along with Holmes himself.

Pavel was right, Holmes had moved all his stock abroad – some said to New York, where he set up again with Aloysius. It was supposed to be a condition of Aloysius coming to the law courts and bending the knee before Buggins, but Ryder wasn't sure about that. That might have been just rumour and gossip from those who were trying to make up for the lack of aftermath.

To the trade, it was as if a large boat had slipped under – scuttled and sunk. And, as its carcass folded and dived for the depths, it left only a suck of eddies and vortexes, gradually subsiding, to be replaced by the rippled inflow of the surrounding body of water. Unremarkable, only a few minutes after the event. All the venom and noise that was expected from outraged clients never materialised and it became a non-story. News barely for a day. The lawyers got paid and the world moved on. Where was the outrage? Where were the clients demanding satisfaction? Ryder had expected a slew of them to emerge from the shadows, hitherto holders of immaculate imperial pieces, now sullied with accusations of fakery.

But it didn't happen.

Seth explained the dilemma to him – that, in seeking recompense, they'd announce they'd been stupid enough to allow themselves to be conned. Also, there would be no recompense, rather a financial disadvantage. They'd no longer be able to claim that they had a Picasso or a Ming or an Ormolu. Did it matter that it was a fake? If it was such a good reproduction, then why not carry on with the pretence? If they weren't planning on selling, then why write the insurance value down? Even if they did sell, half the so-called experts out there couldn't tell a Myatt from a Matisse. No, the best thing to do was let it wash out – run its course. Least said, soonest mended.

Ryder wondered if Holmes had perhaps always wanted it that way – to be proved right? To be proved right was to be revealed to be right – to reveal yourself. The final part of the final act. Look at what I've made you believe. Look at what I've conjured. Seth tended to get annoyed at the speculations of lesser mortals about Holmes's psychological make-up. By raising the subject of psych profiling, Ryder was trying to poke him into saying something about Moscow, without coming out and telling him what Pavel had revealed all those weeks ago. But Seth wouldn't bite, just gave an off-hand dismissal that suggested he didn't know what Ryder was talking about.

Holmes's shop had been locked up for several months and Seth had helped Ryder acquire it – along with the services of Cassie. Now he had a place of his own – a shop, a window, a display. Now he was a real dealer, even if he had nothing yet to display in that window. The £100,000 he'd made on the Ming and taken from O'Malley was dwindling fast – in fact, it was almost gone. What made it worse was not that just about everyone he knew was getting rich, but that they kept insisting he must be finding it easy to make money with all this wealth landing in London. There was this presumption that people had when they were speaking – that what was happening to them was happening to everyone else too. It was a lack of imagination so far as Ryder was concerned, but it didn't seem to be holding them back.

Seth arrived, phone to ear. He held up a hand, as much to tell Ryder to be quiet as in acknowledgement. Ryder watched as he paced up and down and eventually finished his call. Seth looked more and more the part of what he was – a dealer-cum-smuggler. In the age of the dress-down, no-tie professional, he'd gone to the ground they'd vacated. Less of the period styles of old and more of the flauntingly expensive whistle – of the kind that could be found on display in the windows of Darcy's or Aidan Sweeney or Handsome Dans. Then again, he was always going to lean towards looking money rather than looking art. He was late, and Ryder was irritated from being left with offcut time that he couldn't usefully fill.

'Why do you always look like you could go to a funeral at the drop of a hat?'

'Drop of a corpse, surely?'

'In under thirty seconds.'

'Always be prepared.'

'Let's get going.'

The funeral service was set for 11:30 a.m. Seth offered to drive, to make up for his lateness, which was fine by Ryder, as it meant he could drink as much as he liked. He regretted accepting the offer as soon as they were in traffic – Seth was sucking the bumpers in front of him. He had a system of tearing up to them, then holding off a way back, which seemed to Ryder a modified threat, sitting behind a nominal politeness. Look. No flashing. Some space. For now. Look in your mirror! See that grille! Move in! He surged past those who did at speed, making clear the wisdom of their choice. He crept up on those who didn't, as though the leading edge of his bow wave might cause them to be tossed into the inside lane.

'Why are you going, Seth? You didn't know Barnabas Price.'

'Funerals are always good occasions to meet people.'

People of sufficient importance.

Ryder hadn't seen Price in a couple of years, and he'd found it rather sad when they did meet. Price seemed diminished, scrabbling for something noteworthy to talk about, as though he were still in the flow. The conversation always limped in an embarrassing way, and Ryder felt bad for the man who used to be his boss and mentor. He'd expressed enthusiasm over Ryder's progress in the world of pictures and was still keen to impart advice. But it was all a bit faded and seemed to Ryder that, now he'd grown old, nothing much interested Price anymore. And now he was gone, it was as if he'd taken the principles of it all with him. All that secret code, which wasn't really secret – or useful. But he liked Price and what the man stood for. Each had seen through the other – seen the pretence. And anyway, it all seemed a small vanity now.

Midway through the service, he looked around, over the sea of faces. Each had made a decision to be here – had put themselves out and made the journey. Taken the time. His vision blurred as a tear formed. He didn't want to touch it – to touch it would be to acknowledge it. He changed the subject in his mind. Funerals were better than weddings; they were as close as you could get to transcendence – as though a channel opened up – a glimpse into the hinterland of the dead. It transmitted through him like a point source wave through a body of water. A revelation that Price, in his life, had been many things, most of which were unknown to those who knew him – or thought they did.

But maybe it was all just another conceit?

And, afterwards at the reception, the world closed in again. Someone said something witty and, glass in hand, Ryder felt the need to reply. His shard of quintessence melted away and everyone was back to what they were – ambulant talkers and drinkers and eaters. He introduced Seth to a couple of people and Seth introduced him to a few others. It was an alternative court. People just seemed to come into frame around Seth, as though drawn by an unseen force. He, in turn, pronounced with a speedy intelligence and spry detachment to acquaintances and strangers alike. Ryder almost expected people to get out pencils and paper to take notes.

Seth turned to him in the middle of a group discourse.

'D'you think there should be concern about the amount of money in the art world?'

Ryder wasn't expecting it and it put him on the spot. After all, he was part of that world and he wanted some of that money – a lot of it!

He decided to reply with his abbreviated fable of the bees.

'There are two beehives, one full of vanity and the other full of dour righteousness. The former buzzes with energy, while the latter is dull and lethargic.'

'I had no idea that's what bees did.'

'They don't. It has nothing to do with bees.'

Seth turned to the assembled gawpers, as if looking for an explanation. Ryder continued, irritated by Seth's feigned incomprehension.

'Public virtue comes from private vices . . . the desire for wealth and fame can be yoked and turned towards the common good.'

Seth grinned widely and lifted his hand, as if having a eureka moment. 'Well, give me the boisterous beehive any day. Buzz, buzz, buzz.'

They all laughed, not at Ryder's analogy but at Seth's response.

Ryder stared back with his nothing face, trying not to be held responsible, denying what he just said was anything other than a bagatelle.

'Where's that wonderful wife of yours?'

Ryder couldn't tell who asked the question – someone in the surrounding melee. He wasn't going to answer, but that would just lead to more enquiry.

'She's attending a bare-knuckle boxing match.'

Silence at first, then a crackle of laughter, like breaking glass. But it shut them up. Ryder, in fact, didn't know where Lola was. Her excursions away from the flat had grown more frequent and for longer periods of time. And he remembered her answer when he'd first asked her what she thought of the place.

'It's fine, but it has these terrible walls.'

Swan1 intervened. She touched his arm and indicated that he should follow her outside for a smoke.

'I wanted to see you before I left.'

'I didn't know if you'd be here, Katie. I haven't seen Anna?'

'She's in Paris, with her new beau. Are you disappointed?'

'Of course not, I'm married now.'

'So am I, Ryder.'

She said it with just a hint of regret in her voice. It had been several years since he'd seen her. The last time was at the Arts Club with her unexpected boyfriend. She must have married the guy.

Ryder picked up on her chagrin. 'How did that happen?'

'I wish I knew.'

They laughed and fell into an easy-mannered chat. The conversation staccato and witty, as though each was trying to get as much in as possible before the cut-off.

She didn't remember him the way he was now. Back then – well, they'd only started to know each other when they both left Boulets. She only became real to him by turns. Once he liked her she was fully formed, whereas before she and her sidekick were just eye candy that had been fashioned into an element by Swanson.

'And we never were lovers.'

Her remark surprised him – threw him. They were never close to being lovers, so why would she say such a thing?

She was caught now between wanting to stay and the need to go. It was funny – in its way, dissatisfying – to be skirting around the bigger issue that she'd initiated with her earlier remark. Then they were interrupted by Swanson sashaying up to them. He could be such a fucking nuisance sometimes. He enquired after them both in a predictable fashion, making a point of asking Ryder the same questions he asked her, as though his scrupulous even-handedness should be noted – even if his gaze remained mostly on her. Swan1 repeated her need to leave. Ryder caught her arm as she turned away.

'What did you need to see me about?'

'Sorry?'

'Before you left . . . you said . . .'

'Oh yes . . . Dieter. Did you two ever connect?'

'Not on a commercial level.'

'You should.'

And then she was gone, leaving him with Swanson.

They carried on for a few more minutes, each of them wishing for someone to come and provide an interruption.

'I saw you with Seth Silver.'

Ryder expected him to follow up and ask how he knew Seth or what they had discussed. But it was just a set-up for Swanson to launch into his own opinion.

'He's quite an enigma.'

'Quite.'

Ryder took a decent swig of his drink and resigned himself to settle in for a while. Maybe going for a refill was going to be the only way out. Still, he was interested to discover what Swanson knew about Seth – if anything at all.

'We've been to New York together.'

'Really?'

'And we got arrested when we came back.'

Of course, Swanson would already know that, even though he feigned surprise: 'Why, pray tell?'

'A misunderstanding.'

'I see.'

He didn't – see. Neither did Ryder. It was something to do with smuggling and money laundering and Colombian cartels, but he didn't much care to impart that information to Swanson. Careless talk could cost careers and, as some pugilist once said, *everyone has a plan, until they get punched in the face.* Ryder wasn't sure if it was even true, or just a story made up by a Russian to impress him. And he didn't want to unnecessarily diminish Seth's aura of éclat by branding him as a common miscreant. Holmes was bad enough.

Ryder couldn't afford to make enemies. He was still rehearsing his lines in the move to dealing pictures. He'd made a decent fist of it but he wanted more. To get it, he needed something to break for him. It seemed there was a wall of money landing in London and not enough of it was landing on him.

Maybe Dieter would be the answer.

It was getting late. Seth had drifted off somewhere else and there were very few people left. Ryder felt a little half-seas-over, after drinking a wide selection of beer, spirits and wine, with very little to eat in between. He reckoned it was time to go home – see if Lola had returned from her latest excursion to who knew where.

He was on his way out the door when he got the phone call.

'Ryder, are you still at that funeral?'

'Just leaving.'

It was Dieter, wondering if he'd like to meet for a drink.

'Why not?'

Swan1 had called him and told him Ryder was the man to solve his problem, but he didn't say what that problem was. It could wait till they were face to face.

He'd bumped into Dieter a few times since that first introduction and he liked the guy, which was saying something, because Ryder liked very few people in the art world. The German had a wickedly dry sense about him and that's why Ryder never pushed on the work side; it might have threatened the easiness between them when they met. Ryder thought about putting something on at his gallery, but had never really pursued it.

They met at the Larrik Inn on New Kings Road. Dieter looked harassed and got straight to the point, unlike his normal chilled persona, saying he needed some professional advice.

'Why do people have to be such kunts?'

'What are you, the new Holmes?'

'What do you mean?'

'Nothing . . . sorry.'

Dieter let it all out – blew himself out and eventually rounded off with a string of expletives in German.

Ryder was trying to work out the way to go on this. He ruled out levity after the Holmes comparison, as it would just go over Dieter's head – and, anyway, the young artist was too furious for smart-alec facetiousness. He looked sullen and bruised, as though he and his entire world view had taken a kicking.

'What can I say, Dieter? They're out there, cunts and cockroaches and all kinds of cads.'

Ryder smiled inwardly at his extempore alliteration.

Dieter didn't know what a cad was.

'It's a . . .'

'How can he just change the deal?' the artist interrupted, hearing Ryder's words only as noise.

'Look, whatever you think about it, it's happened. What's important is how you go about it from this point.'

'But he says if I don't sell all of them, he doesn't want the one we agreed on. Do you know how much they cost to make, even before my hours and effort?'

'OK, I'll buy it on the terms you agreed with him . . . if it comes to that. But first let me talk to him, see if I can get him to be reasonable.'

'Would you do that?'

'Yes, so you can stop looking like an abused child.'

'The terms I agreed was twenty thousand.'

And that was the trouble with a grand gesture. But there was no point in getting all lawyer-tight now. Besides, this was an opening for Ryder.

'One condition . . .'

'What condition?'

'I exclusively handle all your work from now on.'

'Of course! Please do!'

Now Dieter had some insurance, some reassurance, he was ready to agree to anything. He could stand back and let his agent deal with the buyers – remaining unsullied and wilfully disengaged from the grubby commercialism of it all. Ryder would keep him clean by getting down into the vulgarity himself.

For Ryder, it was a capture operation, locking up a relatively unknown artist's catalogue, brokering it. It was a form of gambling that might pay off.

Or might not.

It was very late when he got back to the flat, and he could see that Lola was home and sleeping. So he tried to make as little noise as possible, even though he was fairly pissed.

Rain outside the window was playing with the night.

And, if it wasn't wrong – it had to be right.

## CHAPTER 17

# HALLUCINOGENIC

Taking on Dieter was proving to be a good move for Ryder. He wanted to properly thank Swan1 for setting it up – and to take her comment that they never were lovers to a higher level of consciousness. He called and offered dinner – she chose the Star and Gator Steak House in Bayswater for its anonymity – she and her husband were known in all the chichi places where the urbane people went.

On the way there, in the back of a taxi, she took out a little silver box and opened it up. Inside were some pills and she popped one into her mouth.

'What is it?'

'Not sure . . . DMT, or maybe LSD, or PCP . . . or a combination of all three.'

'You're not going to freak out, are you?'

'Of course not. You want one?'

Ryder wasn't sure. He was OK with cocaine and a toke of weed from time to time – and amphetamine to keep going – but he didn't like taking something he hadn't sampled before. On the other hand, he didn't want to seem a drip in front of Swan1.

'OK.'

He'd never been to the Star and Gator before and it had a definite rough edginess to it. He thought it a bit pretentious for what it actually was. The manager spoke American with a Lithuanian accent, and the waiter had the kind of septic smile which Ryder had only seen once before, in an old black-and-white Boris Karloff film.

'Your table will be ready shortly. Would you care to have a drink at the bar while you wait?'

Of course we would.

Swan1 ordered a dirty martini and Ryder asked for a pint of Carlsberg. The barman told him they didn't have any lager on draught, only bottles, for which they charged corkage.

That in itself was enough to infuriate Ryder.

'Shouldn't that be cappage?'

'I'm sorry, sir?'

'Bottles have caps, not corks. And anyway, corkage should only be charged for drink not purchased on the premises.'

'House rules, sir.'

'What kind of pub is this?'

'It's a restaurant, sir.'

Swan1 intervened, before things became ugly.

'He'll have a whisky.'

'What kind of whisky, madam?'

Ryder answered for her.

'Famous fucking Grouse.'

The barman sneered – bow tie around his unconscionable neck and half the fucking till in his pocket. He hesitated before getting the drinks, making them wait. Payback for Ryder's unreasonable arrogance. Then he placed the drinks on the counter with a well-practised flourish.

'Dirty martini for madam. Whisky for . . . sir. Thirty-five pounds please.'

'How much?'

'That doesn't include the service.'

Ryder, in retaliation, deliberately made him wait while he counted out as much small change as he had in his pockets. Four pounds seventy – eighty – ninety. Five pounds.

Swan1, in a low voice, said she'd pay. Ryder stayed her hand as it went for her purse.

He smiled at the barman. 'Do you take dustbin lids?'

'We normally take debit or credit cards, sir.'

'I'll bet you do.'

The man obviously had no sense of humour. Ryder told him to put it on the dinner bill, and he swept the change back off the counter.

'That didn't include the service, sir.'

The barman continued to stand and stare. Ryder stared back. Swan1 tapped him on the shin with the toe of her shoe.

'What was that for?'

She tapped him again.

A whisper. 'He's waiting for a tip.'

'I'll tip him on the fucking ear.'

The barman overheard and quickly withdrew to a safe distance from the glowering Ryder, who was so irritated that he wanted to crack open his skull and dance on his small mind.

'Don't make trouble, Ryder.'

'I'm sorry, but I can only tolerate extortion if it's accompanied by a threat of violence.'

The waiter returned in the nick of time, a cloth over his arm and a walk that once might have been used to follow funerals.

'Your table is ready now, sir.'

The dining area had log-cabin-style wooden tables, with the light soft as a sedative. A stuffed alligator occupied one wall and an assortment of old flintlock guns and Confederate swords and Bowie knives adorned the others. Trying hard for the American frontier look, with a big bison head behind the bar and other animals of obscure origin on pedestals in crouched corners. Stars and stripes forever, and three cheers for the gunslingers and god-fearers.

'It's not so bad in here, Ryder.'

'Bit primitive for the prices.'

'Stop being so grouchy.'

'Where's that waiter got to? He's ignoring us.'

The pill Ryder had so recklessly consumed on the way there was now affecting his measured cynicism. Instead of being pithy and droll, he was becoming loud and belligerent.

'Hey, you!'

'Yes, sir?'

'Can we have something to read while we're waiting?'

'Certainly, sir. Here's a menu.'

And one for madam. And see if you can keep that obnoxious escort of yours under control, my dear, because we have some sensitive people in tonight, who tip us well for our trouble.

Swan1 hugged his arm in an attempt at mollification and gave him a light kiss on the cheek. Ryder felt the wildness in his blood cooling down – until he drank the whisky.

'Would sir like to order now?'

'If you've got nothing else to do.'

'Very good, sir.'

Swan1 decided on the filet de bœuf en croûte with spinach and chestnut mushrooms. Ryder discarded the menu with a disinterested flourish.

'Steak and chips for me.'

'And for hors d'oeuvres?'

'I'll have burrata ... Ryder?'

'Chicken noodle soup.'

'Where's your imagination?'

'With the waiter's titubation.'

The waiter took their order, with a twitch and a snigger at the chicken noodle soup. Very interesting, sir.

'And would sir like some wine?'

'Madam will have a bottle of your very best Beaujolais, if you're fucking quick about it.'

Ryder watched the green velvet curtains on the small-paned windows as they spoke to the sound of rain on the bottle-bottom glass.

She jokingly reprimanded that she couldn't take him anywhere. He replied that she could – and did – all along the primrose path that ran through the dream of life and led to inevitable obscurity. And where that path began, he couldn't remember. Somewhere back there was a marker, on the turnpike between Boulets and this dive. And he knew there was no going back, because there was nothing to go back to.

She was trying to understand when he told her that conscience and fidelity faded fast in the swirling mainstream of this gobbling, grunting hog of a world. He knew too that, eventually, he'd step over the line she'd drawn on the ground with her remark at Price's funeral.

'Hey, you!'

It seemed to Ryder that the waiter was avoiding his eyes – ear closed to his calls. The clamjamphrie discriminating against itself. Awful fucking ignorance.

'Where's the food?'

'Don't shout, Ryder.'

He knew he had to shout to be heard in this lousy life. Had to push and shove and barrack and bite. Those who didn't would have it done to them.

'I could do with another drink.'

'He'll be back with the wine in a minute.'

'We'll be lucky if he comes back at all. I'm off to the bar.'

'Wait ..'

Ryder bounced back up to the barman – who was, in his hallucinating imagination, telling everyone that he didn't tip and ignoring his finger in the air – demanding service. Swan1 came and got him and led him back to the table.

'Ryder, are you all right?'

'Never better.'

'Maybe we should go.'

'Not until we eat.'

He scanned around for the waiter, who was serving someone else and looking positively on the perverted side. Ryder imagined him standing in a raincoat with cut-off trouser legs tied with twine around his knees, and his tie and shirt terminating under his armpits – waiting to jump out from behind a bush and throw open the coat and frighten the very eye-whites out of some unsuspecting woman.

'No wonder the world's in such a state.'

'What?'

Ryder pointed towards the table that was being served.

'What with this kind of overt favouritism and politicians practising what they preach against, and all the upper echelons of the civilised world thinking with their pricks. And the fucking clergy too!'

'I think we should go.'

'Burrata for madam.'

And a snigger for sir.

Ryder stuck a foot out, and over the waiter went. Slip-sliding away, with the chicken noodles held high over his head. A stagger and then a sprawl across the next table. Arse in the air and face in the food. Swan1 glared and Ryder tried to look all innocent and oh dear how the fuck did that happen?

'Waiter, what have you done with my soup?'

There was a huge commotion at the next table. Frozen peas on the floor and look out, you clumsy clown. The waiter apologised and wiped and scraped and what the fuck's that all down my wife's best dress?

'Chicken noodle soup, sir.'

The manager came, mortified, to the scene.

'If sir and madam will just wait a minute or send me the cleaning bill ..'

'Don't worry, our fucking solicitor will!'

The manager's face was now purple, screaming at the waiter to clean the mess up. A warm feeling came over Ryder, as the last of the whisky slid slowly down his throat. Ready now for a taste of the wicked little wine.

'Wasn't that exciting.'

'Ryder . . .'

'Yes?'

'Why are they staring at us?'

'Who?'

'The bouncers.'

'Casts in the eye, I think.'

After mopping up the floor, the waiter could be seen telling the manager that an object, which felt very much like a foot, was thrown deliberately into his path, with the definite intention of causing chaos.

Ryder lit up a cigarette while waiting for the main course. Swan1 frowned again.

'You can't smoke, Ryder.'

'Sure I can.'

'You know what I mean . . . it's banned.'

She was beginning to annoy him now. Life was nothing if not about compromise, and he was quite happy to give and take.

'I saw you trip the waiter.'

'You definitely did not!'

The manager interrupted over his shoulder. 'Is something the matter, madam? And could you please put that cigarette out, sir!'

He flicked the butt from Ryder's mouth, who immediately grabbed him by the bent-down bow tie, but it was only a clip-on and it came away in his hand. The manager made a startled retreat, with his bow tie being flung after him across the floor.

The manager returned a few seconds later. This time he had his doormen with him. To Ryder, at that particular moment and in his hallucinogenic state, attack seemed to be the best form of defence – something, under other circumstances, he would never have attempted. Before he knew it, his fist flew up into the manager's face. A scream stifled in the guy's throat as his teeth bit into Ryder's knuckles. The doormen closed in and customers scampered for safety. Ryder grabbed an antique sabre from the wall and swung it round his head.

'Get back, you fuckers!'

A crunch of glass breaking off the bone. He felt something warm running down the back of his neck – Beaujolais or blood?

Days could sometimes disappoint, no matter how hard you tried. And people could turn like snarling dogs on the innocent bystander. Though the police, when they came, were uncommonly decent about it all – and he wondered if Swan1 had anything to do with that. She knew a lot of people.

He had his head patched up at the hospital and then they were allowed to go. By the time they got back to the flat, the effects of the hallucinogenic were wearing off and Swan1 suggested he take a barb to calm himself down. She insisted on coming in with him, just to make sure he was all right. Luckily – or unluckily as it happened – Lola wasn't there.

'Would you like a drink?'

'I think tea would be the best thing for you, Ryder.'

He banged about in the kitchen, but wasn't able to make tea. When he came back, Swan1 was stretched out on the Nepalese rug he'd recently acquired. She patted the place beside her as she slipped off her shoes. The buttons of her Isabel Marant blouse opened all by themselves and the Balenciaga skirt zipper slid down noiselessly and unaided. She moved to him – her pink lips on his eyes and ears and his head full of rainbows. Her breasts caressed his bare chest and she whispered something indecipherable in his ear, then turned her body to take hold of his hard-on with her candyfloss hands and guided it through the luscious lips and white teeth onto the licking tongue. Another delicate twist and her legs went around his neck, urging his face up into the secrets of her woman's body.

And here he was, at the centre of the earth and the street corner of the universe.

\* \* \*

As daylight struck the outside of the patio, a key turned in the front door lock. Ryder looked up from the blanket he was wrapped in on the floor, to see Lola's ankles next to his nose.

'Why are you lying there?'

He tried to remember why, but couldn't.

'What time is it?'

'Nine o'clock ... Where were you last night?'

He thought that to be an unkind question; he hadn't asked where she was. His brain cells fought for survival – where was he last night? Then the fog began to lift and expose an even more serious question – where was Swan1?

Lola went to the kitchen. 'I'll make the coffee – you look as if you could do with some. And put some clothes on, Ryder, I could have been anybody.'

Maybe she'd nipped off home during the night – or crept away, blowing back a kiss, before the dawn broke. He just hoped she wasn't in the kitchen.

Ryder stood up, the blanket wrapped around him. Oh no! Women's clothes fell to the ground – tights and other tiny things. She was still here. The toilet flushed and Swan1 appeared, standing in the bathroom doorway, her naked silhouette framed against the frosted glass and a husky voice saying –

'Ryder, we overslept.'

He could hear the sound of coffee cups smashing in the kitchen, and saw Lola storming past, knocking him sideways onto to his unfaithful arse.

He jumped back up and tried to grab her arm.

'Lola ... wait!'

'Get away from me.'

'I had a few drinks and it's certainly not what it looks like.'

But she was gone through the front door onto the morning street, with Ryder running after her, still wrapped in the blanket.

'Lola ..'

'I said, keep away from me, Ryder!'

She turned quickly on her toes and brought a hard knee up full force into his bigamist balls – obviously a tactic she'd learned from her bare-knuckle brothers.

He felt his whole life flash before his eyes. The blanket fell to the ground and she kicked it away with contempt, down the street in front of her fury. Ryder couldn't straighten up to follow her – or the blanket. A crowd was beginning to converge, laughing and pointing at his exposed privates. He hobbled up the street towards the flat as the phone cameras clicked, just in time to see Swan1 sliding out through the front door.

'Got to go, Ryder.'

'Wait ..'

'Don't need all this publicity.'

She pushed her way into the crowd just as a siren sounded. Wide grins spread across the faces of the young officers, who looked as if they'd just graduated from coppers' kindergarten.

'I can explain everything, Officer.'

'I certainly hope so, sir. Where do you live?'

'Just here.'

'Shall we go inside and get some clothes on?'

The police weren't really interested in the whole truth of the matter. Their main concern, in Ryder's biased opinion, was to make an arrest and an example of some poor unfortunate person. He tried to reason with them, but they wouldn't listen to his lies.

And finger wet, finger dry, cut my throat before I die!

## CHAPTER 18

# DIETER'S WORKSHOP

Ryder searched everywhere for Lola. He went back up to Gloucester-shire, to The Trout and Drake Farm, then down to the New Forest and to a few gypsy camps. He looked around London and enquired from gypsy liaison groups and the Gypsy Council. But it was as if she'd disappeared from the face of the earth. In the end, he reported her to the police as a missing person, but there was no joy there either.

During all this time, he was neglecting his job and his clients and, most important, Dieter. He was belligerent and antagonistic towards anyone who he deemed to be distracting him from the business of finding his wife. Even Seth felt the brunt of his self-vexation.

'Was that you I saw on YouTube?'

'No!'

'Some guy naked in the street, trying to cover his face and phallus.'

'It wasn't me!'

'OK, no need to get so shirty. Can you drop me off somewhere?'

'Am I wearing a fucking cap?'

'No, but I can get you one if it'd make you feel better.'

It wouldn't. The only thing that would make him feel better would be Lola coming back.

Ryder missed her. Their relationship wasn't conventional – in fact, it was probably the least orthodox arrangement that any married couple could have. But that's what he liked about it – the sheer uncomplicatedness, the easiness, the convenience. No, it was more than that; he missed her presence, her essence in the flat, even when she wasn't there. The realisation that he might never see her again bruised his very soul.

Ryder wondered why she got so angry about the lost night with Swan1. He didn't know what she did when she went off – maybe she was fucking someone else too?

'I need a favour from you, Ryder.'

'Not now, Seth.'

'It's for Pavel.'

'Why can't he ask me himself?'

'He's shy like that.'

'Is it because you owe him for helping you in Moscow?'

'What d'you know about Moscow?'

Only what Pavel had told him, and Ryder didn't know if that was the truth or not. But then there was New York as well – and if you put two and two together . . .

If Pavel wanted a favour, why ask Ryder personally and end up owing him, when he could get Seth to do it, who was already in his debt? Quid pro quo.

'He wants to get his son into Charterhouse; he thought you might be able to help.'

'Why would he think that?'

'It's your alma mater, isn't it?'

'There is a test and an interview, you know.'

'Yes, yes . . . but with a recommendation . . .'

Ryder didn't want to do anyone any favours, especially if it was to pay off someone else's debt. He also had a meeting with a collector who wanted to buy one of Dieter's paintings, which he didn't want to attend either.

'I'll see what I can do.'

He dropped Seth off and drove to the Connaught Hotel in Mayfair. He was being squeezed by Dieter on the one side, and on the other side by some serious hard-nosed buyers. It made his hair hurt. Ryder arrived early and ordered coffee in the lobby bar. By the time the buyer arrived, he'd settled down and draped his jacket over the side of his chair.

'I'm Pieters. You must be Ryder.'

They shook hands and Pieters sat down, trying to remember where he'd seen this dealer before. He sat forward in his chair, as though this wasn't going to take long – so why get comfortable? He'd found out what he could about Ryder, which wasn't much, and now he surveyed him.

'My wife bought a number of pictures directly from Dieter, you know.'

'That must have been some time ago?'

'Yes, but I'm wondering why he's decided to sell through you.'

'I'm his dealer.'

'Really?'

Ryder was becoming irritated by this person. Did he want to buy or not? It was becoming obvious that this wasn't going to go as smoothly as he'd thought.

'I offered twenty thousand.'

'That was the value of his work when your wife bought.'

'And now?'

'Fifty thousand.'

'Since you became his dealer?'

'Since his work became popular.'

Pieters turned this over in his head. 'Popular' also meant prolific, which lessened the uniqueness of the purchase.

'People like my wife made him popular; he should show some gratitude.'

'It doesn't work like that. It's fifty thousand or nothing.'

'Well, then it's nothing.'

Ryder had expected him to push a little on the price, but Pieters just shrugged and got up. He extended his hand again and Ryder hesitated before shaking it. Then he was gone, signalling that it wasn't worth his while to haggle, that he had better things to do with his time.

It almost impressed Ryder. It was another example of the exercise of power that money granted to itself, but not entirely. No, it was more than that, he mused; it was an example of the need for money to exert its control over a purchasing process in which it felt it might be the weaker party – that need to accept it in the terms first offered.

Ryder sat back down, in no hurry to report this failed sale to Dieter.

His rule of thumb was, the richer the client, the more demanding they were. And if they were famous as well as rich, that was even worse. If they came into his shop themselves, they expected the pool of light they cast on the world to warrant red-carpet treatment. After their visit, they sent their reservoir dogs to batter down the price, on the basis that they were doing the artist a favour and their glow was transferrable to the work. Nothing was ever simple with them – late payments, arrogance, ignorance – and this Pieters guy had read the book, or at least an article about Saatchi.

Although it looked like he had a good deal of money, Pieters was twenty years too late on that score. He probably didn't have a clue about Dieter's work, its essence, but was buying just to humour his wife. Maybe the guy had a mistress somewhere and the picture was an attempt to placate a nail-spitting spouse? Of course, he could just go find another artist, but if his wife really wanted a Dieter, he'd be back.

Fewer and fewer things surprised Ryder about it all. He didn't think he'd really set out to move into the primary art market. His world of furniture was one thing; this was quite another. A world of endless promotion, of expense, of luck and uncertainty – a game that played out for the few powerful gallerists and owners. Buying art, or at least non-established art, seemed like a reckless investment. But he'd got himself into it now, and he wouldn't have swapped it for anything else – except, maybe, Lola.

He doubted if even Seth felt like he did, if he ever fell over himself to have something, ever fell prey to *la grande romance*. And maybe that's why Ryder had taken on Dieter – not because of the odds, but in spite of them.

Maybe that's why he married Lola.

\* \* \*

A flat, sarcastic female voice came over the intercom when Ryder pressed the button outside Dieter's place in Hammersmith at one o'clock in the morning.

'Come on up, unless you're a vampire.'

The voice was distorted – a kidnapper's voice. No further instructions followed.

Ryder heard the buzz and leaned into the heavy metal door. He'd had enough to drink when he left The Cross Keys at closing time, after he got a text from Dieter saying he was in his studio and would be all night. It was as good a time as any to tell him about Pieters.

It was the first time he'd been to Dieter's workshop, so he was curious. Once inside the metal door, he walked a few paces away from the street lighting and found himself in the darkness of a kind of courtyard. He stopped, listening to the faint sound of music being drowned out by bursts of a whining noise like a small sawmill. He climbed a set of metal stairs, at the top of which a stern young woman gave him an initial cursory glance. She pointed in the direction of the blasts of noise.

'It's that naked guy who was on YouTube!'

'That wasn't me!'

Ryder entered the workshop. It wasn't what he expected – certainly like no other artist's studio he'd seen. Dieter stepped out from behind some plastic strips, looking like a cross between a forensic scientist and a proto-raver. He had a pair of ear defenders up on the sides of his head, and a face mask which he swiped away.

The girl flicked Ryder a minimal smile, as if there was some use for his presence after all.

'Don't mind Anya, she is angry. Not a permanent state, just temporary because of the noise of my creations.'

'Creations?'

'*Ja*, Ryder. First I make them, then I destroy them.' Dieter wiped his hands on the front of his white boiler suit and took a swig of water from a bottle on the worktop. 'Come and have a look.'

Ryder followed him through the plastic strips.

'I didn't know you sculpted, Dieter?'

'If that is what you want to call it. And I should have said half destroy – build them, then half destroy them with a sand blaster. You could call it establishing a patina.'

What was a space of work for Dieter was a world half remembered for Ryder. He hadn't been in what he could call a proper studio since he left school. It was the smells – oil paint and solvents and other agents of uncertain origin. Dieter was rattling on, but he was only half listening.

'It is the illicit act of creative destruction ... looking for an effect that makes it both older and more alluring. *More interesting*, you would probably say, Ryder.'

Dieter had cordoned off the area he was working in with paint-stained sheets, hung off the wrought iron supporting the glass roof.

'You have not asked why, Ryder.'

'Why?'

'Because they look better half-destroyed. But it is not just that ... I have not worked it out yet. Maybe I will know when I find the best process.'

Ryder walked up to the constructed visage that was being held in a vice, its upturned face serene, like a martyr before the pain of the flames.

'Masks?'

'*Ja*, lots of masks. Like those that Picasso was interested in. Like Basquiat. Some more ancient phase ... comedy, tragedy. Masks from the ancient gallery.'

Ryder looked closely at it, trying to work out what it was made of. It was amber in colour, like resin, but darker and more dense. There was a metal plate deep within it – a frame on which it was cast?

Dieter interrupted his mental observations.

'It is just a huge lollipop, really. Without the stick, I cannot make them . . . they just fall apart like *kandierter apfel*.'

'I like it. What's the material? It's like a Messerschmidt . . . Franz Xaver, of course, not the aeroplane.'

'*Ja, ja* . . . though not so *gefickt oben*, I think, as his works.'

He strained his face into an impersonation of the hyper-realist sculptor, rolling his eyes and jutting out his chin and pushing his tongue into his bottom lip.

'Ahh, but you haven't half destroyed it yet.'

Dieter looked at Ryder manically, as he pulled down his goggles and ear protectors and shouted wildly. 'Anya, you are going to hate me!'

Her reply was shouted back. 'Permanently!'

'Nothing is permanent.'

'I'm going!'

Dieter flicked on the power to the sandblaster. Its motor fired up and, after a splutter and a whine, hit a steady note. He swung the nozzle round and placed it close to the glossy cheek of the face. He pulled the trigger and the engine noise was obliterated by the sound of air and sand hitting the surface, as he set about destroying what he had created.

Ryder felt the irony.

After a brief moment, Dieter stopped. As an afterthought, he went and got another pair of ear protectors and handed them to Ryder, then resumed his work. Even with the headphones, the pitch of the noise was ear-splitting. Ryder winced and screwed up his eyes, but stayed close enough to see the face rip and blister and peel away as the structure began to burn. Dieter kept going for a minute or so, then stopped again to survey the depth of the damage and its effect. He put his hand on it and felt it, then fired the blaster again, directing it round the area of the wound, blending it, grading it with its surroundings. Eventually, he decided he'd done enough. He put the blaster down and lifted the ear defenders onto his head.

'I have to remember to stop. I destroyed the first two so much there was nothing left, just stumps. Totally ruined. Into the skip.'

Ryder wondered what that would do to a real human face. He could taste the smell: a dryness – a burned meat smell – roast pork. Like a suicide on the underground once. Dieter talked about the effect he was looking for and all the processes he'd tried, to make it look both created and destroyed. He talked about wanting to see into the head, to give it translucency.

'The metal plates look polished, not messed up like the faces.'

Dieter cocked his head at this. He hadn't thought of it. Ryder was right. He fixed a base plate into a vice and found a lump hammer and chisel.

'You hold it, I will hit it.'

'No, *you* hold it and *I'll* hit it!'

Dieter handed him the hammer, then placed the chisel on the metal and held it firm. Ryder rehearsed the swing a couple of times to line it up, looking more concerned than Dieter, then let loose. After managing several strikes without breaking the artist's hand, they played around with a variety of different tools. Dieter had a focus and intent that didn't seem to admit anything else. Maybe that's why he was the artist – a need, a monomania, a compulsion. But some worm inside Ryder's head stopped him believing it was worthwhile.

He didn't know how long they were in the workshop – it was as though they'd been conveyed outside the normal framework of hours and days. Ryder had stopped contributing and was sitting back watching Dieter. There was a quality about him; he had what Ryder saw as an educated European formalism. The intellect and emotions were connected, not shorted or circumvented by the British disease of crass humour. He could have asked anything of Dieter and the young man would have seen it as failure not to be able to respond. And he would never resort to taking offence.

After three cigarettes, he interrupted the work. 'Do you ever feel like you've made the greatest mistake of your life?'

'Many times.'

Ryder paused, unsure whether or not it would be prudent to continue. 'Do you know, I haven't told anyone my marriage is over.'

'You have told me.'

'When?'

'Just now.'

Dieter put down his tools, grabbed one of Ryder's cigarettes and sat back against the wall. Neither man spoke for a while and it was as if something intimate and personal was being shared in the silence after the ferocious noise. Ryder didn't want to go back to a normal register, but Dieter asked the inevitable question.

'What about Pieters?'

'He'll be back.'

'Are you sure?'

Ryder wasn't sure, but he was more than tired, he was fatigued, and didn't want to have to explain. He stood up.

'Do you intend to sell these masks, Dieter?'

'A collector saw an early one. He wanted to buy it, but I would not sell. He said I should make him twenty and name my price. Crazy, yes?'

Ryder was shocked back into reality by this. He was annoyed that someone was trying to tie up this work without his involvement.

'How many have you done?'

'Maybe a dozen or so that I am happy with. Do you want to see them?'

'Of course! You must tell me about these things, Dieter!'

Dieter looked scolded, like a child. He unlocked the door to a large walk-in cupboard. On the shelves were these looming faces that had been there in the dark. The light cast them like some Italian family ossuary, and, in that moment, Ryder imagined he saw them blink. Dieter removed them and surveyed them on the floor, like they were a miniature Renaissance Easter Island.

'They shouldn't all be sold to one person; they're far too good.'

Dieter remained silent, as if he was testing Ryder's sincerity, trying to elicit more from him before deciding if he was being bona fide or not.

'Who was the collector?'

'Somebody called Pork, I think.'

'Do you mean Perk?'

'*Ja*, maybe.'

# CHAPTER 19

# FROM SELLING MASKS TO ST-HILAIRE

It was as if Perk hadn't bothered to wait for age to weather him; he'd gone and done it to himself. He'd sacked his own temple with partying and drugs and lordly excesses of drinking and dining. He wasn't old, he just looked that way – and it seemed he'd always looked that way. It was hard to believe he'd ever been slim, but he was, at least in the good-time pictures littered around his house. That was then and now he had some proper heft to him, some girth, and his face had that jowly roundness, like he was a lump of unkneaded dough. His fleshy plumpness rubbed out any chin line and pushed his eyes in like currants. When he smiled it was slow, and his eyes retracted even further. In fact, he looked like he didn't give a shit about anything, then or now. And that was in his favour.

Ryder knew Perk even before his name was mentioned by Dieter. Seth had intro'd them at some soiree or other. He'd bought a fuck-off pile up in Lincolnshire on a whim and now he needed to fill it with stuff. Seth had thrown the work Ryder's way as compensation for being arrested after New York. What Ryder liked about Perk was that he just threw it all out there, put it all on show, let it sort itself out. He conspicuously wanted to have a good time and for others to have a good time with him. They got on well from the start. Perk still talked about the time he objected to Ryder's van being parked next to his AMG Merc, and Ryder went out and moved the Merc rather than his van.

Perk had solved the problem most rich people had of not knowing how to trust non-rich people. He got their loyalty by showering them with attention and extravagance. Still, for all that, he was smart and he'd seen the potential value in Dieter's mounted masks. They were new and different and Dieter was a – if not unknown – not well-known artist, who might just hit the big time in the future. At worst, the pieces wouldn't lose any value and, even if they did, they'd be interesting talking points in his house. Ryder, of course, played them up, saying that, in the end, who knew anything? Playing down the risks was the way to go.

'No one can say, Perk. He may be nothing in ten years, but they're big and good. And, fuck it, they'd be great in the house, or even in the grounds.'

'Where did you meet him?'

'At a Hirst party.'

Perk smiled a little at that, knowing Ryder had been waiting to get it in.

'Yeah, yeah. If that's the case, then I'm a sheep in a shark skin.'

Ryder tried a different tack. He told Perk some hedgie sort was also interested and Dieter would prefer if he could sell to several buyers. That way, his work would get more exposure.

'How many has he got?'

'About a dozen at the moment, but there will be more.'

'I did want twenty.'

'And you'll have twenty, Perk, in time.'

Perk ruminated on this for a moment or two – it was all part of the game they were playing. Ryder was good at it, Perk not so good.

'So, how much is he asking?'

'Mates rates to you, Perk, and he'll let you have six . . . to begin with, of course.'

'How much, Ryder?'

'Fifty.'

'Each?'

Ryder smiled, indicating that he wasn't talking about a bullseye apiece. Perk was a rich man, but £300,000 of anyone's money was something that needed at least the pretence of ponderance.

Ryder pushed on.

'I've seen them and they're really, really outstanding. I'd buy them myself if I had the money. Well, I could . . . just, but it would tie up all my working capital. I told him I'd buy one and try to sell the others.'

'You're buying one?'

Ryder lied. 'I am.'

'Bit of a departure for you, isn't it?'

'Maybe, but it's there in front of me. Besides, if people only stuck to what they knew, you'd still be organising parties.'

Perk nodded his head in agreement – he'd always been on to the next thing, the bigger thing. He had a penchant for the loud and garish, as many big people did. Vintage T-shirts, rare editions, luminous shorts, multicoloured socks. He complained that there was too much mud in the country for him to wear his Balenciaga trainers. His clothes were an acknowledgement of his past identity, now that he'd moved on from organising parties to the more conventional role of property developer and country squire. He'd invested in a private members' club and a couple of nightspots, but he knew it was to his advantage to play up his colourful past. Otherwise he was just another rich fat guy – and there were plenty of them.

Perk was more interested in the next ten million than the first. But it didn't matter how he made the rest, his story would always be the maiden money. He'd started out throwing parties back in the eighties. He organised them for posh schoolkids, him being a bit older and with greater access than his target clients. He was good at it and made more money than anyone else his age, even those in front of the blinking green screens in the City. The parties gained a notoriety, which was great – until they attracted the attention of the tabloids.

The offspring of the rich and famous, drugs and underage drinking, who was seen with who – it was manna for the rags. Perk had no problem with the notoriety; it made him even more money. But, after a few years, it lost its cool, as all these things do, and it was over.

So Perk moved on to the rave scene and took his growing-up customers with him – done with wearing parachute pants and listening to crap music. The scene went massive; it became bigger and bigger. But for all the supposed glam of the illegal, you were still pissing about in motorway service stations. Fun maybe once or twice, but something for the summer at best. Where do you go for the rest for the year? Perk decided to do it bigger and better – decent sounds and decent loos, proper bars and not some skivvy upturned-crate affair. The way he told it, he always knew when it was time to move on, and that was the secret of his success.

'You should remember that, Ryder.'

'I will.'

Time for business.

'All right, I'll take the six for now.'

He said it with a flippancy that belied its finality. And business was done. Now they could get back to all the other stuff in the world and not have to talk about art.

Perk walked Ryder through the house and showed him his plans for restoring it to its former infamy. They clicked through the marble hall and opened tall doors onto one large empty room after another. Ryder was listening to Perk telling his tale. He'd told it a hundred times in a hundred different ways. The trick was not to interrupt, just look interested. But, although Ryder's ears were listening, his eyes were sizing up just how much stuff this guy needed to buy.

'By the way, someone said they saw you on the internet. Indecent exposure or something?'

'It wasn't me.'

'You sure?'

'Of course I'm sure.'

'Nothing to be ashamed of.'

Perk ordered a Thai takeaway and they drank Drambuie and Cointreau cocktails. Ryder stayed the night, as he was too tired, rather than too drunk, to drive back to London.

\* \* \*

Meetings, meetings, meetings. His life was becoming one interminable series of them – catch-ups, progress, rescheduled. Even the breaks between them were merely opportunities for updates on upcoming ones. Neville St-Hilaire was hard pressed to remember a time before them. And if it wasn't meetings, it was receptions or presentations or introductions or informal drinks or formal dinners. He wouldn't mind, he really wouldn't, if it could ever be about the thing that had excited him in the first place. It led to him thinking of himself in the third person – as a means of separation, of committing to the role.

For a moment, his mind freed itself from the confines of the ceaseless issues that were done to death by people he no longer knew, and he could feel as free as the peregrine falcon he saw briefly through the window, soaring in the infinite sky. Instead of being tethered to the wrists of these dry and ceaseless committees, he longed to gimble and spire in his own element. There those who might have said that St-Hilaire had something of the hauteur and imperiousness of a falcon. After all, was he not at the apex? Had he not assembled and promoted and pushed this capital city to the forefront of the art world? A man of pre-eminence, who'd brought London into the cultural vanguard of the cosmos.

Over five million people had walked through the doors of the London Gallery in its very first year. Now, of course, it was a major tourist fixture, rivalling the Tate Modern, and having housed works by the most famous as well as the most obscure. With its expansion almost completed and due to open to the public the following June, he was looking for someone to assist him, to take on some of the load. St-Hilaire didn't want one of the old guard, the art establishment. He wanted someone new and fresh – someone with a bit of flair, edginess, dash. A maverick who'd cause controversy and attract attention. This was London, after all.

Would it be too much for his metrics of success to be afforded a little latitude? Indeed, some belief that it might be a good thing to back him in his quest? Were it not for his enterprise and the force of his vision, London would still be a dilettantish backwater. Yet the board still continued to question his proposal, to rerun the same old worn-out arguments and objections. He wondered if everyone of vision was so beset on all sides by morons?

Still, at least he'd be in Venice in under two weeks – away from the growing pains of the project, away from the mess of public money, away from committees and planning and strategies, and from the constant demand to tap people up for funds. It was only in Venice that he could get back to what he once was. And he was determined for Ryder to come with him. Of course, Ryder didn't know that yet.

Or that he was being considered for the job.

St-Hilaire spun his pencil listlessly on the desk in front of him. The speaker hesitated before continuing, but without the confidence he had up until then.

St-Hilaire interrupted. 'Right, thank you for your thoughts and presentation.'

He dragged all the attention onto himself and no one noticed the chagrin of the speaker, who sat down.

'I think we have enough to be getting on with. I myself will not be here next week, but we can pick it up again when I get back.'

Molly Bradford, his éminence grise, whispered to him. 'And don't forget, you have the thing with the would-be benefactors.'

'Oh god, really? I thought that had been moved?' He sloped his shoulders in half-joking disappointment. 'Shoot me now, but only once you've shot them. And find out if they've left any bequests in their wills.'

Molly smiled, playing along with his whimsy. 'So far as I know, they have not.'

'That is a considerable shame.'

He liked the confederacy in their repartee, as though what was said between them somehow fortified him to go back out there and do what needed to be done.

'Better not shoot them yet, then.'

'I'd mind less if these would-bes were gonna-bes, but some are so mean.'

She wondered if, one day, he'd tell her which ones he meant. But he was disappointingly scrupulous on such matters. It might have been his background, or maybe he'd acquired it in order to perform his role. He often told her that he preferred to cajole private money from the rich, rather than perform genuflection in front of the pygmies of public money. Indeed, such abasements could only be justified in the service of the greater good.

What would have been awkward for him personally was made far easier by the prominence of his position. There was a time when asking for money seemed somehow dirty and beneath him, such that his embarrassment tainted the transaction and neither he nor the giver felt good about it. He'd always centred on what he was familiar with – established wealth, great families, traditions of philanthropy, patrons of public good. And he became very good at it. The trick that made it work was the presumption he brought with him. It sounded simple – to ask often and loudly for money, and to let the personal motivations of the benefactors operate on them. He stopped trying to involve himself too directly in their decisions. Rather, he saw his role as removing obstacles from their way, instead of whipping them into giving. It was the sort of thing a big man did. And he was a big man.

But was he the high priest in the temple, or was he overturning the tables?

They all had their own reasons – to get onto the rungs of the altruistic ladder; to see their name on benefit-dinner guest lists; to rub shoulders with the righteous; to reinvent themselves as Ryder had; to have access to wealth and power; to showcase themselves; to repay some of what they'd stolen – reasons too various and subtle for him to divine. Of course, there were a few who did it for the love of art.

The only way to describe St-Hilaire in Venice was with the word 'doge', because that's what he was there – enthroned, feted, elevated. Outside of Paris Fashion Week, Venice was the absolute pyramid of eminence, where everyone knew their place in the chain of being. There, he was the sun and the rest were the planets circulating his splendour. He pretended to be phlegmatic about it all, be professional and detached, as though the art came before everything else – even him. He couldn't ignore that it was awash with wealth and its display, but there were limits to money – it could buy itself in but it still had to kiss the ring of the less temporal powers, to genuflect in front of the high priest. It was the rich guy not being able to walk into a gallery and buy a painting off the wall. Money wasn't enough. Normal rules didn't apply in the art world.

Molly Bradford was envious; she'd been to Venice with St-Hilaire and now he was proposing to take someone else, this Ryder person, who sounded both unsuitable and unsavoury.

\* \* \*

Ryder was in the Chelsea Arts Club on Old Church Street when he heard the news. It came from Seth, who was holding forth at the bar, before any formal invitation from St-Hilaire.

'I'm telling you, things can just spontaneously generate, under certain conditions.'

Ryder thought he knew what was coming next, even if no one else did, not even Seth. It was such an ingrained pattern and, for the most part, you didn't see your own patterns. He didn't blame Seth – well, not much. Everyone was on a loop, weren't they? Some people's were just longer than others. And some you'd heard too often.

Seth was in full swing.

'Take wealth, for instance. It's a scientific fact that money in certain concentrations, particularly on boats in the south of France, can lead to the spontaneous generation of long-limbed Russian hookers.'

It wasn't that Ryder was bored by Seth; it was just that he'd heard it all before. He knew how it ended. Seth had that vulpine smile, at once amused and scornful, that made people afraid to seem square and conventional in his presence. That was his appeal; he was the man who could mess up your night but, if you hung around, you could take a trip with him, hear some stories, stay up late, see in the dawn.

'Or take Ryder here – one minute a down-at-heel art dealer and the next he's off to Venice with St-Hilaire ..'

Ryder gave him a warning look; it wasn't funny.

'Who told you that?'

'. . . as a prelude to being offered the job of the great man's second-in-command.'

There was a certain malice in Seth's tone, as though he believed the position should be offered to him, not Ryder.

Seth had heard the news through channels that were only open to him, and Ryder believed it was one of his psychodrama charades until he got back to the flat in the early hours and found the envelope inside the door. It was franked with the London Gallery mark, and Ryder tore it open quickly. Inside was an invitation from the personal assistant of Neville St-Hilaire, to join him in Venice for the International Art Fair, with an order to RSVP immediately. Ryder sat down – was this some kind of joke? A candid-camera-style TV hoax where some minor celebrity jackass would jump out from behind a door and all his friends would be there laughing and pointing at the plonker? Seth was obviously behind it, so Ryder threw the invitation to one side and went to bed.

The next morning, he nursed a hangover as he drank a cup of strong coffee and tried to eat a piece of French toast, but couldn't.

The phone rang.

'Mr Ryder?'

'That's me.'

'My name is Molly Bradford. Did you get the invitation?'

'What invitation?'

He could vaguely remember the envelope with the red franking.

'From Mr St-Hilaire, the Venice invitation.'

'Oh, yes . . . I have it here.'

'Well?'

'Well what?'

'Do you wish to accept?'

## CHAPTER 20

# VENICE

'Open your mind and let the world pour in.'

That's what Lola said to him when she first moved into the flat and was reading everything she could lay her hands on. Those words echoed in Ryder's head on the flight to Italy from London. It wasn't as if he'd kept the world at bay or anything, although he did have a tendency not to engage with people unless he really had to. If he took the job with St-Hilaire, he'd have to engage with them a lot more, and he wasn't sure he was up to that. But it would open doors for him – doors that would otherwise remain closed. He'd never been one to go off-limit, compulsively committed to staying under the public radar. Even now, he was inclined to recoil from the strange proposal he'd received from St-Hilaire.

His flight departed on time and the journey was uneventful. He tried to concentrate on what was before him and the decision he'd have to make, but fell asleep and dreamed he was at the Uffizi Gallery in Florence. Lola appeared, naked and standing in a shell, with her long black hair covering her womanhood. She'd become Sandro Botticelli's Venus, emerging fully formed from the sea at birth.

Lola, since she disappeared, was no longer flesh and blood to Ryder. She was a phantom – a chimera, beautiful and exotic, conjuring up the emotional storm that came with that kind of obsession.

He woke as the plane was on its descent into Marco Polo Airport. The terminal was packed with tourists and students and Ryder was grateful to get out, away from the disorganisation. Henry James once wrote that Venice was best approached by sea, so, after collecting his luggage, Ryder took the Alilaguna *motoscafi* via Murano, Fondamente Nove, the Lido and Zattere, to Giudecca Island to the Molino Stucky stop, which was only a few minutes' walk from the hotel.

Venice seemed somehow apart from the Italy he'd visited before, as a child, on holiday with his mother, but without his father. The mountains, the vineyards, the cypress trees, dogs lazing in the road, the slow pace of life, warmth – long days in the sun, long nights in moon-filled rooms. The deep feeling of longing inside the psyche. Calling. *Come back!*

Come back!

Venice was different. He threw the memories out of the boat.

At Hotel Cipriani, St-Hilaire had an exclusive suite with a vast balcony, which connected to Ryder's junior suite next door – really just a double room, but very rococo. He thought about indignant tabloid headlines – 'British Public Funded Arts Institution's Lavish Expenditure' – completely ignoring the wasted zillions on bombs and other bullshit.

The art fair was a forum for a direct exchange of ideas between leading and emerging international artists, photographers and designers, arts professionals and collectors, with some live performances thrown in. Its purpose was to provide artists and exhibitors with an opportunity to present their work to curators and gallerists who were interested in encouraging talent. For St-Hilaire, it was an excuse to get away from London and recharge his batteries; for Ryder, it was uncharted water. To be seen in the company of St-Hilaire would enhance his professional reputation immensely, especially after the naked-in-the-street debacle. On the other hand, he'd always had an aversion to the public and the political, and didn't see himself fitting into that bureaucratic milieu.

The fair was organised by communications companies in collaboration with events agencies and the Palazzo Ca' Zanardi, and held at a variety of venues over a period of a month. Of course, neither St-Hilaire nor Ryder could spare that much time, but a week would be long enough for them to conclude what needed to be pacted between them. Ryder had never been to Venice before, and he was eager to experience the city of Othello and Shylock, where Constance Chatterley went to get pregnant and Sebastian Flyte took his namesake. Where Childe Harold pilgrimaged and Candide was disillusioned with humanity. Where Von Aschenbach became obsessed with Tadzio, and where Ryder could maybe find a part of himself in the ghost of the loveless Jeff Atman, only aroused from his torpor by the possibility of free booze and invite envy.

Hotel Cipriani had been dreamed up in the same era that gave the world romantic films like *Roman Holiday*. Its appeal, allure and charisma shouted Hollywood glamour and it was a magnet for movie stars, and its gardens were where Casanova once wooed his lovers. Ryder dumped his bags in the room and went down to the alfresco ambience of Cip's Club – with its view across to St Mark's Square – to meet St-Hilaire.

The great man was already there, sipping a vodka and cranberry cocktail. St-Hilaire stood up and shook hands, then offered Ryder a drink.

'It's called a Buona Notte, created by George Clooney.'

'Sounds superfluous.'

'You're probably right.'

Ryder had one just the same, to humour him. No sense in getting off on the wrong foot. It was 7:00 p.m. and, although a little early for dinner, St-Hilaire decided to make an exception, as Ryder was hungry after his trip.

They adjourned to the Oro Restaurant, where St-Hilaire had a reservation. Ryder decided to forego the recalcitrance he'd shown at the Star and Gator and ordered the blue lobster with baby artichokes and pistachio, while St-Hilaire had the sea bass with ash-baked turnips and fermented citrus sauce.

An uneasy silence fell as they finished with a couple of negroni cocktails. The arts-establishment doyen and the maverick upstart measured each other across the table. Ryder knew that St-Hilaire was renowned in the art world for his rhetorical gifts and perspicacious instincts. He could silence a strategy meeting just by clearing his throat. An intimidating potentate who could play the hardball needed to control committees and who sometimes seemed like he'd just stepped into a poker game with five aces up his sleeve. He was the focal point of what was happening in London, and to be invited here by him was to have arrived in insider-land.

St-Hilaire broke the ice by asking how Ryder's business was doing, and was told it was doing fine. The conversation remained cordial for a while and Ryder waited for him to get to the point.

'What happened with Hugo Swanson's girl?'

'She's not Hugo's girl anymore, and nothing happened.'

Ryder wasn't surprised by the question – it was waiting to be asked. All the same, for a man of infinite diplomatic skills, this was rather direct. Then again, he was only doing what came naturally. Ryder wondered just what he'd heard and who he'd heard it from. But most of London had seen what the nosey fuckers had put up online. A lot of it had been taken down by now, but the speculation remained, like a revenant, haunting him.

'Not that I care, personally, mind you.'

'Then why mention it?'

'Because, Ryder, you're a married man and I'm offering you a job in the public eye.'

'Separated.'

'Really? I didn't know.'

'It was a lapse of judgement.'

'What ... getting married, or the Swanson girl?'

Ryder didn't answer. He didn't intend to get into a conversation about his marriage, and the Swan1 incident was old news. He wanted to forget about it.

St-Hilaire leaned in. 'It's just that . . . there's opposition to your candidacy.'

'Then why am I here?'

It was a rhetorical question. They both knew the answer.

'Look, Ryder, I want you for the job. I want a fresh outlook, a fresh mind. London is in a unique position in the world of art at the moment, and the city needs people who are willing to take chances.' He paused. 'And, of course, the fact that you went to Charterhouse will be a huge asset.'

'Exactly what *is* the job?'

'It has a wide remit – Molly will fill you in on the details. But, basically, I need a right hand . . . a man Friday, a Tonto, a Watson. The salary is generous and I'll be too busy to interfere.'

'What about my dealership?'

'You'll be free to carry on with that, as long as your public role comes first. Of course, you'll have to declare any conflicts of interest.'

St-Hilaire went on to explain that, because of the amount of work on his plate, Ryder would be expected to cover for him at functions, meetings, presentations and the like, but he'd also have a say in what would be displayed in the new extension. He'd be consulted on budgetary matters and have his own deputy, who'd liaise with Molly Bradford and brief Ryder on the day-to-day stuff.

They spoke long into the evening, until St-Hilaire got a bit tipsy on the liqueurs and had to go to bed. Ryder was relieved to see the end of the quasi-compromising and retired shortly afterwards. But he found it difficult to sleep because of the turmoil in his mind.

And he still hadn't said he'd take the job.

The next day, he went with St-Hilaire to attend a number of events. It was like being in the train of a monarch, as his would-be boss held court in the spotlight and Ryder stood off stage in the wings. In the evening, St-Hilaire suggested somewhere off the beaten track for dinner.

'Did you ever see the film *Don't Look Now?*'

'With Donald Sutherland and Julie Christie?'

'Yes.'

'Very atmospheric.'

So they went to the Ristorante Roma in Cannaregio, near the Ponte Scalzi, over the Grand Canal, where some of the movie was shot. The owner was a heavy bald man with a thick black moustache who welcomed them at the door, then began an animated conversation with St-Hilaire in Italian, gesticulating so vehemently that Ryder thought they were arguing. His daughter was short with straight black hair and bushy eyebrows, and a thin line of hair under her nose that reminded Ryder of Frida Kahlo.

After his frenetic but friendly exchange with Moustache, St-Hilaire sat down in the low-ceilinged room, which had images of the movie that made it famous on the walls. They ate in the company of about a dozen people who'd obviously been tipped off that St-Hilaire would be in attendance. The respect that Italians paid to their meals was almost ritual, a sacred ceremony – the importance attributed to conversation, the relish with which they drank. It was as if they'd invented and owned time itself. Ryder was used to the lifestyle in London, eating a rushed sandwich in front of a computer screen or during a meeting. So, although he appreciated the opportunity to leisurely taste the flavours of the pasta and the wine, he had to force himself not to keep checking his phone for messages.

Several hours later, after feasting on prosciutto e melone, pasta bianco and litres of red wine, St-Hilaire was settling into a singing competition with Moustache and the tenors and baritones of the restaurant's clientele. As midnight drew close, Ryder had enough of the renditions of 'Faccio Quello Che Voglio' and 'Non Ti Dico No' and 'Nessun Dorma'. He looked for an escape, and found it in the form of Daughter Moustache.

'The red ghost in the film . . .'

She looked at him quizzically.

'*Il fantasma rosso . . . nel film . . .*'

She seemed to understand, nodded her head and beckoned for him to follow her.

Soon they were deep into dark, crumbling, off-the-beaten Venice. He followed her over narrow humpbacked bridges and along wet, canal-edge cobbles. Spectres played hide-and-seek across the shimmering water – ghostly hands touched him with cold fingers. Fleeting shadows disappeared when he turned his head. He wished they'd leave him alone – the buried memories of his childhood. He'd come to terms with what happened to his father, and wanted to leave all that where it belonged – in the past.

They followed the Calle di Mezzo to the gates of the Palazzo Grimani a Santa Maria Formosa, where John Baxter confronted the red-coated figure in the film. Daughter Moustache led him through the gates and across to a small chapel. The heavy wooden door creaked when she pushed it open, and they stepped stealthily inside.

'*Qui viene trovato l'assassino del cappotto rosso.*'

Ryder's Italian was hit-and-miss, but he thought she'd said something about a red-coated killer.

'What is this place . . . *che posto è questo?*'

'Chiesa di Santa Maria dei Miracoli.'

It was then that Ryder noticed candles flickering close to the altar. They cast an eerie light over a coffin and bier, standing motionless in the gloom. The sight gave him a start and his first instinct was to leave – quickly. Instead, he moved forward, taking each step as if he'd have to turn and run at any moment. He came level with the coffin. It was closed, with wreaths and cards resting on the lid.

Ryder tried to read the cards, but they were all in Italian and he could only get the rough gist of what they said. The word *padre* appeared a lot, so he assumed someone's father had died and was lying in state until the funeral, which would probably be the next day. A sudden wind blew in and Ryder heard the loud slamming of a heavy door. He turned, but Daughter Moustache was nowhere to be seen. He made his way back to the entrance, but the door was jammed and he couldn't pull it open.

'Hello! Anybody there? *Ciao! Qualcuno là?*'

Nobody answered. Ryder looked around and noticed another door, near the chancel, but that was locked. He took a candle from the altar and went back to the main entrance and tried again. It wouldn't budge, no matter how hard he tried.

Ryder sat down and lit a cigarette. Daughter Moustache had probably gone for help and she'd be back soon. No need to panic.

He waited. Waited. She didn't return. He looked at the coffin – there was nothing to be afraid of, was there? Nowadays people hid death; they put it away where it couldn't be seen and didn't speak about it. Yet it was as much a part of life as breathing. It was the only inevitable and universal thing that linked all life on the planet.

He began to light more candles, placing them in a ring so that he was soon encircled by the flickering flames.

The wine he'd drunk was making him drowsy, but he believed he'd be safe within the circle. Outside was darkness, but he was protected within the ring of light – protected from what, he didn't know.

Time meant nothing in this place, so it stood still. Every time a candle began to burn down, Ryder replaced it with a fresh one. And then he was seven years old again, standing outside the door to his father's sanctum. He heard the hysterical screaming of his mother and he opened the door. His mother was inside, sobbing, so he put his arm around her to console her. She lay against him, trembling and crying. The wall behind his father's desk was splattered with blood and bits of brain, and his father lay crumpled on the ground.

Young Ryder didn't really understand what had happened. He looked at his mother for some kind of explanation, but none was forthcoming. She retreated quickly, leaving him alone in the study with his father, and he could hear her on the phone, crying softly into the mouthpiece. He could hear his own heart beating loudly and he knew he should leave the room too, but he didn't. He just stood there, looking at the ground.

Now, the wreaths and cards on top of the coffin began to move, as if there was a tremor in the ground underneath. They fell to the floor and the lid of the coffin began to slide. Ryder waited. Waited. Waited for his father to emerge. The circle of light flickered violently and he rocked to and fro in his pew. He hummed a tune from his childhood, one his mother used to hum. All the darkness outside the circle was filled with ghosts. They moved around the ring of light and asked to be let in. Ryder told them to go away, but they wouldn't. He shouted at them and they disappeared for a time, but came back again and again.

Eventually, there were no more candles left. He heard the banshees howling. The ghosts were getting in! More candles were burning out and more ghosts were getting in. It felt as if he was in some time machine which began to whirl – slowly at first, but with increasing speed. He stepped outside the circle and went to the coffin, climbed inside and lay down beside his father. Then he slept.

Ryder felt a hand on his shoulder, shaking him. He looked up and saw Daughter Moustache standing over him. '*Dobbiamo tornare indietro*.'

'Where did you go? *Dove eravate?*'

'*Ero qui*.'

Ryder looked at the coffin. The lid was closed and the wreaths and cards were intact on the top. There was no circle of candles. He stood up and followed Daughter Moustache to the open entrance. Outside, he turned his collar up against the chillness of the air. He though he heard a sound behind him as he walked away from the old chapel and he looked around quickly. But it was nothing – just his imagination.

When they got back to the restaurant, St-Hilaire was ready to go. The other customers had already left and Moustache was closing up.

'Where have you been, Ryder?'

'Sightseeing.'

'Well, it's been a fabulous evening, but we must go.'

Moustache called for a water taxi and they climbed in, St-Hilaire rather unsteadily. Its engine throbbed as it pulled away from the Ristorante Roma. Daughter Moustache stood alone on the side of the canal and waved to him. The undulating light from the water distorted her face.

He waved back.

## CHAPTER 21

# RISE & FALL

Ryder was glad to get back to the reality of London. He told St-Hilaire that he'd sign up for a probationary period of six months. If it didn't work out, then they could part company without the legal implications of a public divorce. St-Hilaire was amenable to that, and the paperwork was signed. Ryder was given an office in Bankside and a deputy called Lucy, who was both bright and efficient.

His first foray into the mire of public life was with St-Hilaire at a board meeting of financial types at Millbank – letting them all see him, that he'd arrived. The unfortunate speaker didn't realise what he was doing when he mentioned the Bilbao Guggenheim. In the following moments, everyone else sneaked as much of a look at St-Hilaire as they dared. He leaned forward and rested his forearms on the boardroom table, intermittently tapping his pencil, but refraining from speaking – for now. The financial guy was going on about indicators and metrics with endless data and graphs, all designed to outline, by siege rather than elegance of argument, the hard realities of how art was being utilised to brand cities around the world.

St-Hilaire interrupted his spiel about the financial models that allowed for the extension and enshrining of their brand. 'Where did you say the Guggenheim is?'

'Bilbao.'

'I think you'll find that *the* Guggenheim is in New York.'

Corrected, the speaker checked himself momentarily, then continued rigidly with his prepared script.

St-Hilaire sat back and allowed him to speak for another minute or two before interrupting again. 'Do you know how many visitors we've had in the past year?'

The guy shook his head, half afraid to comment.

'I'll tell you ... five and a half million. I think we might need to remind ourselves that London is not Bilbao.'

The speaker stood there dumbly, unsure if St-Hilaire had finished or if he should continue.

Ryder decided he had to learn this kind of subtle impatience. That the managerialism of ruthless efficiency had to be grafted onto him. St-Hilaire was in the habit of regaining, from those competing for his attention, the time he gave to artists. For Ryder it was more *why do I have to listen to these people?*

'I think we've heard enough.' St-Hilaire let the finality of that remark stand for a moment before relenting. 'For now. Perhaps some lunch?'

He'd given the consultant a chance and the guy hadn't taken it, so it was on him. Maybe he thought this was just a break in proceedings and he'd get to resume.

The point was to keep things moving at a fair clip, like a boat, its velocity establishing its direction. Or like a shark – after all, weren't they supposed to die if they stopped propelling themselves forward? Ryder wondered if he could work that into some droll Hirst reference in future conversation. He could see that, to some of these people, the extension was a big overwhelming project, but to St-Hilaire it was just a sideshow – even if it was a big one. Did they really need to hear about Frank Gehry and Koon's floral Scottie dog anymore? They knew about all that; they knew about templates for re-imaging a city and about raising profiles and about branding. London wasn't Bilbao and the London Gallery certainly wasn't the Guggenheim.

Ryder accompanied St-Hilaire to lunch. They passed by his office, as he wanted to leave some papers. Molly saw them coming and smiled.

St-Hilaire threw up his hands. 'Don't ask.'

'Ah, that bad?'

'Terrible.'

'A circle of hell?'

'Yes, exactly that. And I fear the planning for a further circle is already on the drawing boards.'

Ryder could see that St-Hilaire trusted Molly with all his little indiscretions and remarks about the goings-on and the people he came into contact with. It was that privilege of inside knowledge, and a relief for St-Hilaire to be able to share in confidence all the stuff that clogged up his days. Being within earshot, Ryder was now also privy to such revelations, which made him valuable to a lot of people. He'd been grossly underestimated up to now, but that would all change. They'd be queuing up for an audience with him.

Ryder thought his hiring might have proved to be a flashpoint for Molly, but the lieutenant had accepted him cordially and gracefully. It was clear St-Hilaire needed a vice-captain as his world had become more global. Not just travelling to places that required his presence, but his days were extending like a plane flying west at full speed, chasing the sun. It wasn't feasible for one person to be looking after him and his itinerary.

'Right, we're out to lunch . . . literally, not metaphorically, of course.' She laughed.

'Enjoy the food, at least.'

He muttered back to her on the way out. 'The eighth circle. The eighth circle.'

St-Hilaire's driver dropped them outside the Ham Yard Hotel in Mayfair, which had a small piazza with tables and chairs scattered round one of the abstract sculptures called 'Rational Beings' by Tony Cragg. Ryder wasn't aware this place existed and it was refreshing not to have to make decisions, to allow himself to be led into the unknown.

St-Hilaire was escorted to a table for three and Ryder followed him and the maître d' into a room dominated by four large Balinese stone mirrors, with ambient light-classical music providing a satisfying background for his growing feeling of well-being.

St-Hilaire picked up the menu and ordered three macchiatos. The background music became a waltz by Shostakovich – the one from the Jazz Suite that appeared in the Kubrick film *Eyes Wide Shut* in the scene where the lounge lizard tries to seduce Alice.

A tall, bald-headed man of about sixty joined them. Ryder instantly recognised him as Vladimir Gazmonov, the Russian businessman and philanthropist. St-Hilaire introduced them and they shook hands.

'Ryder, eh? I think you may know Pavel Muransky?'

'Yes, but not well. Is he a friend of yours?'

'A close acquaintance.'

St-Hilaire ordered Dorset crab and cherry tomato linguini, with crème brûlée for afters. Gazmonov said he'd have the same and Ryder fell into line with them, not because he didn't have a mind of his own but for convenience.

'Wine?'

Gazmonov suggested the 2011 Albariño and St-Hilaire ordered a couple of bottles.

Gazmonov was a billionaire who'd contributed a substantial amount of the £200 million cost of the new extension. After the initial success of the London Gallery, it had undergone major extensions over a dozen years, the first part being five thousand square metres of new display space in the south-east of the complex. After that came the tower extension to the western section, built over some old storage tanks, which were converted into a performance art space.

The initial budget was £175 million; £50 million came from the government and £7 million from the LDA, with private donations from the Sultan of Oman and a number of other luminaries. Even then, it fell short, and Gazmonov gave St-Hilaire the rest. The tower extension would provide over twenty thousand square metres of additional interior areas for display and exhibition, performance, education, catering and retail, as well as parking and external public spaces.

And now it was going to be Ryder's – or so he thought.

For Gazmonov to be present at this lunch, St-Hilaire must have something else in the pipeline. Ryder wondered what it might be. Or maybe it was some private project? St-Hilaire had been with the London Gallery for over twenty years and he was retirement age. Maybe time for a change – time to accumulate some of the money in his own pockets? If that was the case, who would his successor be? Ryder was getting ahead of himself.

Gazmonov was the first to speak after eating. 'Is the time right, with everything that's going on?'

'There's simply no way I'd countenance a delay. The time is now. I have everything in my favour.'

Ryder didn't know what they were talking about, but he was listening intently. Inside knowledge.

'Well, not everything.'

'Maybe not everything; there are uncertainties.'

'There are always uncertainties.'

A silence followed while St-Hilaire considered what to say. Ryder remembered a passage from a bio of Kissinger, talking of persuasion as being set in different time scores and needing different registers. He reckoned St-Hilaire had read it too and adopted it instinctively.

The doyen flicked his hand out towards the east. 'I've never been tied to what they do in the City. It's about something more than money. We're not part of that.' He sat back and threw his hands up to suggest that he'd finished. Then he leaned over to Ryder. 'You wouldn't want to be associated with something that was second-rate, would you, Ryder?'

'Certainly not.'

'I mean, what would they say about you in a hundred years?'

'Fifty, even.'

'What will they say about us when the new extension opens? You'll be able to tell me, of course?'

'You'll be there too . . . won't you?'

St-Hilaire smiled at him. It took a while, but it induced a reciprocating smile from Ryder.

The great man took out a pen and drew a rough sketch of the Sydney Opera House on a napkin. He pushed it across to Gazmonov. 'Remember how much that cost?'

'No.'

'Neither does anyone else.'

Gazmonov eyed St-Hilaire closely. He was taking the point, whatever it might be, and Ryder could see he was being charmed into submission. But hesitant, as though this would then stand as his position for all time. Agreeing now was implicitly agreeing at all future points.

Ryder was wondering if he should ask what they were talking about or leave it alone, knowing he'd probably find out soon enough. Maybe he wasn't meant to know, or maybe St-Hilaire was testing him, seeing if he had the balls to ask. It was a dilemma. He decided to keep schtum for now. St-Hilaire got the waiter's attention and asked for three more macchiatos and the bill, which came to two hundred and sixty pounds. He paid a straight three hundred, including the tip.

'Do you know three artists who have changed the landscape?'

St-Hilaire began to answer Gazmonov's question. 'Dali, Warhol . . .'

Ryder provided his choice for the third. 'Pussy Riot.'

Gazmonov gave him a hard look.

St-Hilaire stood up. It was time to go.

'We should exhibit her.'

The other two laughed loudly.

When they got back to Millbank, after saying their goodbyes to Gazmonov and Ryder promising to give his regards to Pavel Muransky, he thought he saw a woman watching him from a doorway on Atterbury Street, where St-Hilaire's driver dropped them off. She didn't look familiar and Ryder thought it might be his imagination, so he put it out of his mind.

Inside, Molly gave them her usual cordial smile. 'How was lunch?'

'Much better.'

'Than?'

'The morning.'

'And the afternoon?'

'It won't match lunch, but better than the morning.'

'You hope.'

'I most certainly do!'

St-Hilaire took Ryder out onto the vast rooftop for a smoke. It was indeed an honour, as only he was allowed access – not even Molly ventured out there.

'I call this my balcony.'

He liked the privileged view, the prospect it gave. It was where he did his best thinking. How could you look out over London and not draw from it? All its jumbled history, all those centuries told in tides and in buildings and in its myriad forces. For all the interminable meetings and glad-handing, for all of what weighed him down, out there he could see what it was and what it could become.

Still, the view wasn't without its blemishes. St-Hilaire frowned as he fixed his eyes on the encroaching mass of banker buildings. He'd never cared much for the financial centre that was the Square Mile. The elements of the guildhalls and the ancient regimes were being overwritten by the clasp of modern finance. Even in his time here, he'd seen the march of the financial institutions like obscene chessmen – looming bishops and squared-off rooks and gherkin pawns and shard knights, all clustering around the squat and immobile queen, the old lady of Threadneedle Street. Were they her protectors or attackers?

He knew for sure which side he was on, even if it meant he had to go amongst the money men. It was a price he'd accepted, one that he'd borne. His role was to persuade them that they should support his causes. And those causes were a series of globally eminent institutions that would command respect and admiration. From donors to artists – from sponsors to trustees – a network of arts organisations and other institutions, major auction houses and super-dealers, regulatory bodies and charity boards.

And he would be the Doge of London – as well as Venice.

His thinking on finance, like most people's, was a couple of generations behind the times, but it was the lack of recognition outside the art world that really galled him – the underplaying of the role of art in reinventing a city. He needed to believe he was apart from the valorisation of wealth – and, yet, it wasn't that simple. His uneasy truce with money was only made possible by the philanthropic tithe he demanded, again and again. And he took the work very seriously. It wasn't a question of enjoying it, or even liking it – it was just to be done. He shouldered it, long ago realising that the stand-or-fall decisions weren't about one bad acquisition, but rather category events like the failure of a major project. Everyone was always so delighted to be associated with the big, sexy parts – the glitzy, spotlight parts. But it was the guts and the innards that made it all work.

It surprised St-Hilaire how easily he'd become au fait with the terminology of economics – fluent in what, until a few years ago, would have been the preserve of others. Much as he decried to Molly the endless round of tapping up people for money, he'd resigned himself to knowing it was the job. He joked, half seriously, that he was no more than a shakedown artist – the artistry coming from knowing when to do it. But he didn't want to be the kind of man people jumped around corners to avoid. He saw himself more as the one who did the jumping.

Now Ryder would do it for him. And he could always throw him to the Stuckists.

\* \* \*

During the six months of his probationary tenure, Ryder rose to the heights, rubbing shoulders with the super-rich, partying with the powerful, pictured in all the arts magazines. Major players were vying for his time – people who would have slammed the door in his face only a short time earlier. Unfortunately, he was neglecting the minor artists he represented as an agent, especially Dieter, who'd helped him make the transition from furniture to fine art. He never did find out what St-Hilaire and Gazmonov had been talking about in the Ham Yard Hotel, and it didn't seem like St-Hilaire was going to resign any time soon. But it didn't matter; Ryder was indeed on the way to the top.

So, when he fell, he fell fast and the drop was deep.

The new extension had its official opening in June – and it was hailed as the most important new cultural building to open in the UK for twenty years. It featured over two hundred artists from twenty countries, and revealed how art had evolved from the studios and salons where modernism was born, to the live, interactive and socially engaged projects of the day. Works by Picasso, Beuys, Rothko, Choucair, Gaba, Meireles, Gowda, Abakanowicz and Weerasethakul were just a few of the artists on parade. Speeches were made, then applause, music, more speeches, more applause. It was a glorious gala and everyone who was anyone in the art world was in attendance.

St-Hilaire introduced Ryder as a new face for a new phase in art, and he stepped up to the microphone to make a short but scintillating speech. He just about managed to thank St-Hilaire for his trust before the shouting started.

'Thief!'

Ryder tried to see who the screecher was. It looked like a woman. He'd seen her before, but couldn't remember where – maybe watching him from a doorway on Atterbury Street? Maybe she'd go away.

'I'd also like to thank—'

'Robber! That man stole fifty thousand pounds from my fiancé.'

'And he was naked on YouTube!'

Some of the dignitaries attending thought it was all part of a performance piece, and they stood there with bewildered looks on their faces.

'Remember Peter O'Malley?'

'Ryder had him killed!'

'For fifty thousand pounds.'

St-Hilaire pulled Ryder away from the mic and pushed Molly Bradford forward. She tried to calm the restless crowd.

St-Hilaire took Ryder to one side. 'What's this all about, Ryder?'

'Anarchists, probably.'

By now the barracking and catcalls were increasing in volume and capacity.

'Criminal!'

'Murderer!'

'Pervert!'

St-Hilaire took him away from the stage altogether, out of view.

'You must leave, Ryder. You'll ruin everything.'

He was hustled away by security. They took him to a remote exit and put him in a car, which drove him from the venue. It was a day before his probationary position was due to be confirmed as permanent. Apparently, gossip – false, of course – had circulated that he was somehow involved in the accident that killed the prominent antiques dealer Peter O'Malley, and that Ryder had profited from his death. It was all innuendo, of course, spread by some malicious and anonymous rumour-monger. St-Hilaire called him later, saying how much he liked him and how he didn't believe the allegations for one second. But this was public office and dirt like that tended to stick, Charterhouse or no Charterhouse.

Ryder's job was not confirmed.

Three months later, St-Hilaire announced his retirement.

He was succeeded by Molly Bradford.

## CHAPTER 22

# SETH

It took Ryder a long time to recover from the fall. People he knew drifted away and didn't want to be associated with him – except for Dieter, who stayed loyal. But it was difficult to find buyers for his work. He thought about packing it all in and following Holmes to wherever Holmes was. Seth didn't desert him either, even though he kept his distance for an appropriate time after the debacle. But now he was on the phone, looking for a favour.

'Another one? I already got Pavel's boy into Charterhouse.'

Seth was hosting a party that night and his wife was coming down to London.

'There's nobody else I can ask ... or trust.'

'Why can't you do it yourself?'

'I have a meeting and she'll be there in an hour.'

Ryder was always going to do it, he just wanted to press home the point that this was going in the book. Sometimes it was better to do stuff without asking for anything immediate in return – the gratitude was greater for not being quid pro quo. Although maybe not with Seth. Gratitude had always been an issue for him; it wasn't his natural state. But it was as if he and Ryder were now somehow partners in crime, blood brothers, fellow felons. And that generated some trust.

Twenty minutes later, after a taxi ride across town, Ryder was letting himself into Seth's apartment and keying in a ten-digit code to disable the alarm. Who used a ten-digit code? He guessed Seth would reset it, now that he knew it. He flicked on the lights and headed up the stairs, into a long corridor. Walking down it, the floorboards seemed to scream *intruder* at him, and he felt one part burglar and one part voyeur. He'd been here many times, but not like this.

Seth told him where to find the pictures, stashed on the top shelf of the wardrobe, behind the spare duvet. There was a slither of admiration for Seth, along with a slight disgust. It wasn't just substituting one woman's photos for another's; it was replacing one relationship with another – one set of vows and promises and lies in place of another. Until it was time to change them back again.

Why not be honest about it and say, *Look, I'm fucking this other woman – do you mind?* Then again, *he* hadn't been honest with Lola, had he? But that was a drug-induced one-off. At least his betrayal was hot-blooded – the sybaritic sexual appetite that was in all males, that restless internal energy that had no connection with merit as a civilised human being, the primal, animal carnality. The second greatest instinct, after fight or flight.

At least, that was his excuse.

This was different – this was devious and calculated and continuous. A clinical manipulation. Ryder, who'd always been impressed by self-serving but not self-denying behaviour, felt a tinge of sourness in his throat as he hid the framed photos of Seth's music-business mistress and replaced them with the ones of his wife and young children. Seth was quite open about the intrigue. He made a virtue of its orchestration, that he had what most men wanted but were too craven to acquire – a normal weekend life in the shires, and a fast-and-loose midweek London life. And some travel thrown in, which could be with one or the other. Or neither.

Ryder felt that his own marriage might have lasted longer if he hadn't known people like Seth – not that he was blaming Lola's departure on anyone else. But it was the lifestyle. He'd kept listening to the whispers of what was possible, available, desirable. The idea that only a common man would be constrained by flimsy convention; only a manqué, a beta. He should have changed it, but he didn't, and that's why she went off on her own at times – because he wasn't there. He should have met her halfway. Wasn't that what any relationship was about? On the other hand, it was the art world – there were a thousand and one temptations. How dull and pedantic you'd be, if you didn't act on your desires.

He regretted it now, of course.

After substituting the photos, Ryder sat on the bed and looked at them. There was one of who he assumed to be Seth's parents – even though he'd never spoken of them in all the years Ryder had known him.

\* \* \*

What Ryder didn't know was that Seth's name wasn't Silver; it was Silverman. He'd changed it to sound less Jewish; not that he had anything against being Jewish, he just did it because it suited him. His family didn't know about it because they were quite orthodox and it was like he was Seth Silver in London and Seth Silverman in Canvey Island. He was the youngest of three kids – his parents had him late in life and he might have been a mistake or a moment of Chanukah craziness.

His childhood in North London, before his parents moved to Essex, was pretty uneventful and typically Jewish. He didn't remember his circumcision, but Passover and Purim and Rosh Hashanah and Yom Kippur and Sukkot and Simchat Torah were all part of it, and he went to the cinema twice a week with his father and they all picnicked on Hampstead Heath in summer. Then there was his bar mitzvah and he was a man and going to Hasmonean High School. Seth's father was a rabbi – he was retired now and in his sixties. His grandfather came over from Poland after the war – he was in Auschwitz-Birkenau as a child but never spoke about it, as far as Seth could remember. And he didn't remember him that much. His mother's people went way back – they came over with William the Conqueror from Rouen. Or so she said.

Seth's father would have liked him to become a rabbi like himself, because he couldn't afford to send him to university – he still owed money from sending his two older children to Chichester. In high school, Seth joined the Hillel Jewish club, to further his knowledge of his religion and deepen his spirituality. He was a straight-A student and on the Academic Challenge Team and joined the Youth Partnership Scheme and the In-School Program and the Summer Institute. There was one teacher he was very close to – Mr Sattler, who told him a place at university could be arranged for good Jewish kids with potential. Mr Sattler encouraged him to join Habonim Dror, and he learned about the Code of Maimonides and Halacha and Gush Emunim and read the words of Rabbi Kook and became a junior member of the flying squad – invading anti-Semitic meetings and burning anti-Jewish literature. He was a dedicated bnei akiva without seeing the irony of it – a small-action star – and, in return, his parents were told he had a scholarship to go to Oxford.

There was no Mr Sattler at Oxford, but after Seth got checked in and found his room, some guy called Murray came to welcome him. He said he was a representative of the Oxford Protection of Israel Society and he hoped Seth would have a successful stay. He gave him a bundle of forms to fill out and a list of the society's activities, then he left him to unpack, saying they could talk later. His roommate was another Jewish student called Greg Waxman – Seth didn't know if it was deliberate that he got a Jewish roommate, or just a coincidence. But it didn't matter to him either way.

He studied politics in his undergrad year and the curriculum included Political Theory and Middle Eastern Politics and Political Science and Comparative Politics and International Relations. He was much more interested in studying something artisan, but it was a condition of the private scholarship. Still, he managed to sit in on some lapidary and other craft classes and he visited a lot of galleries and exhibitions. Murray came back to see him again and he joined the society and was soon involved in all kinds of stuff – like encouraging discussion about the issues facing the State of Israel and its relationship with the rest of the world, as well as promoting political activism within the university community and beyond. He was on awareness creation committees, debating teams and part of a group of dedicated students concerned with the welfare of Israel and the Zionist movement. Seth never saw Greg Waxman at any of the guest talks or events or rallies or briefings or forums he went to, and they rarely came into contact – except at night, when they slept in the same room.

Seth liked university. He made lots of friends there, and not just Jewish friends. He made the rowing team and did some work for the student magazine. He drank beer and dated girls and his best friend was a Catholic. Well, his parents were Catholic, but he said all that religious shit was bollocks and he didn't go to Mass or anything. His name was John Francesco Kennedy – his father was Irish and his mother Italian, so they were very devout. But Kennedy didn't care and said there couldn't be a god because, for heaven to exist, everyone would have to be equal there, otherwise you'd always have someone trying to be the top dog and there'd be no peace – just like on earth. And, if there was no peace, then it couldn't be paradise.

As well as that, he reckoned the Pope was living in the dark ages and expected Catholics to do the same, and the priests were all paedophiles and masturbated in the confessional and all the Vatican-roulette-birth-control junk and no abortions were designed to keep people poor and ignorant. And even though his parents were so devout, they still used contraceptives and his sister had an abortion because she fell pregnant when she was sixteen. So they were all hypocrites at the back of it. And everyone talked about everyone else behind their backs and that wasn't very Christian, was it? And Seth wondered how that could happen – how anyone could go against their parents and traditions and values and everything they'd been taught. And he said it'd never happen to him.

But he still liked Kennedy because there was something about him, something natural and disparate and transparent and crazy and dangerous, like you could see all of him and there was nothing hidden or underhand – like he listened to no one or nothing, except what was inside himself. It was a rare thing and not everyone could be that way. And Kennedy liked Seth as well, even though he knew he was Habonim Dror and active in Zionist groups. Well, he didn't exactly like what Seth was, he just liked *him*. It wasn't in any latent homosexual way – not on Seth's part anyway. And Kennedy was popular with the girls and boasted he'd fucked ten different women before he was seventeen. Sometimes Seth thought he tried too hard to prove he was straight, but then why would a natural, disparate, transparent guy like him be afraid to come out with it if he was gay? It didn't make sense.

Seth liked the way there were always good-looking girls around when he was with Kennedy. He played rugby and did some boxing and he was a real all-rounder. Murray didn't like him hanging around with John Francesco, and a rumour started that Kennedy was involved with an underaged kid from the town and, even though the rumour was proved to be false, the shit stuck and Seth never saw him again.

Seth was a good student, and his graduate curriculum included Comparative Political Analysis and Public Law and Political Systems and Analysis. Murray didn't know it, but Seth was also taking the craft courses and interfacing with Art UK and the Arts Society and the Fine Art Guild and other such organisations. He was particularly interested in precious stones – there was always an air of anticipation when he was close to them, like with some girl he'd met for the first time. He looked at the colours and ignes fatui and phosphorescence and noctilucae and facets and clarity and all the intermediary phases between dark and light. They whispered to him about ecstasy and agony and honesty and deception and pain and pleasure and true, true beauty – like he'd never seen before.

One day, Seth was in town and he saw Greg Waxman sitting at a bar. He went over to say hello, even though he wasn't his roommate anymore and he hadn't seen him for some time. Waxman couldn't remember who he was.

'Seth Silverman.'

'Oh yes, that right-winger guy.'

'Right-winger?'

'Into all that Gauleiter shit.'

'What Gauleiter shit?'

Waxman was getting on his nerves – he was no Gauleiter. What gave him that idea?

The guy bought him a drink. Seth didn't want to take it because he'd just been insulted, but he wanted to know where he got his ideas from.

'All that Gush Emunim stuff and fundamental expansionist shit, land-centred nationalism and messianic fulfilment bollocks.'

'What are you, Waxman, some kind of self-hating Jew?'

'I believe in human rights, man. That's all.'

To Seth, it seemed like Waxman was in on some joke and he wasn't.

The people he was with asked him who he was talking to and he said nobody, just some guy he used to room with. But he just couldn't get Waxman out of his mind. How could he be a Jew and a Jew-hater at the same time? He reminded Seth of Kennedy the Catholic. The more he thought about it, the more confused he got – the less black looked like white.

Seth was like that – once he got something into his head it wouldn't leave him alone until he did something about it. He found out where Waxman was rooming; he wasn't on campus anymore because he got blacklisted or something like that. He had a room in town and Seth went to visit him with a bottle of whisky. They sat and talked, and the more they talked the less confused Seth was, and the more black looked like black and white looked like white.

By the time Seth was in his final year, Murray had gone and been replaced by someone else, who came round to ask him why he didn't turn up for meetings anymore and why he wasn't dedicated like he used to be.

'Are you no longer a child of god?'

Seth told him it was academic pressure and he had to put his studies first. The guy said he understood and there was a job waiting for Seth in the Foreign Office when he graduated. But Seth didn't want to go into politics; he wanted a career in gemmology. His handler told him he should take a year off and get that nonsense out of his system. But when he got back, they'd be waiting for him – because he owed them.

Seth continued to meet up with Waxman, who introduced him to other people – people involved with Yesh Gvul and Sadaka-Reut and Peacewatch and Amnesty International and Neve Shalom and Givat Haviva, but he was getting fed up with all the politics and wanted to get away from both sides – not to be involved. He got the feeling he was being followed; just a feeling. But, when he looked around, there was no one there. Then, one night, he went to meet Waxman but the guy wasn't at home, even though Seth had phoned the day before. The landlord said he'd moved out, just left without saying anything. Seth tried the pubs in town for a couple of weeks, but he never saw Greg Waxman in Oxford again.

He wasn't really sorry that Waxman was gone because he was getting too close to him and his liberal friends. It gave him an opportunity to stand away from all the political activist stuff that he never really cared for in the first place. So he began making approaches to people for an opportunity in the antique jewellery business, and that's when he met Lucien Holmes.

His family came to his graduation and his father was disappointed he wasn't going into the synagogue after him, but he convinced them there was money to be made in antiques – if you had the right connections, and he was already halfway in. He found himself a flat in London and, when his mother showed him the graduation photographs, he noticed that Murray's successor was in most of them. He had one arm around Seth's father and the other arm around Seth's mother and he was looking straight at the camera – without smiling.

One night, when Seth got back to his apartment after a drinking session with Holmes and some others at The Gasworks, there was someone waiting for him when he switched on the light.

'Good evening, Seth.'

'Who the fuck are you?'

'My name is of no consequence.'

'How did you get in?'

The man laughed and rose from the chair where he was sitting. Two others emerged from the bedroom. One of them was carrying a Glock G17 handgun.

'Are you Shabak? You have no jurisdiction here.'

'We're not secret police, Seth. You know who we are.'

'Mossad? MI6? CIA?'

'Maybe. Maybe all of them, maybe none of them.'

Seth tried to get to the door, but the two tough guys from the bedroom beat him to it. One of them punched him hard in the stomach. He fell to his knees and threw up on the floor. The one from the chair stood over him.

'You let us down, Seth. We invited you into our club. We invested time and money in you and you threw it back in our face.'

'What are you talking about? What do you want from me?'

He was hit again – harder this time.

'You just don't get it, do you, Seth? It's a messianic thing.'

Seth tried to answer, but his stomach was churning and words wouldn't come to his mouth, just pieces of vomit. They pointed the gun at him.

'You have to look at it in an eschatological context, Seth. We expected things from you; you had the potential to become one of us. Instead, you became a mealy-mouthed, lily-livered liberal neturei karta.'

Seth managed to struggle back to his knees. He looked up at the one who was doing all the talking, but he still couldn't speak.

'We're not Jews, Seth. We're soldiers. Religion is just a weapon; one of many. Unlike you, most people don't get the chance to examine the founding principles of their ideologies. If they did, they'd be shocked at the secularity of it all.'

Seth managed to find his voice. 'Who *are* you fucking people?'

'I told you – we're soldiers, defenders. We're the hijackers of religion, much more than the evangelicals or the end timers. Much more. You can't beat us, Seth. Nobody can. We'll win every time.'

'What do you want from me?'

'We don't want anything from you. We have to make an example of you. Debts must be paid, one way or another.'

The one with the gun forced the muzzle right into Seth's mouth. His whole life didn't flash before his eyes – just the last fifteen minutes of it. The one from the chair crouched down close to him.

'Here's the way it is: we have to make an example in case some other little twat thinks he can just do as he likes.'

The gunman tightened his finger on the trigger. He pushed the muzzle into Seth's cheek and it hurt. The talking guy stood back up.

'Before you shit yourself, we're not going to kill you. You can still be useful to us.'

'How?'

'By helping our friends in America to clean up some of their assets.'

The sound of metal striking skull bone. Seth slipped away into darkness.

When he came to, a photo of his family lay beside him on the floor.

## CHAPTER 23

# DIAMONDS AND FLOSS

Until then, Ryder was just doing what Seth had asked of him. But now – well, he was on his own in Seth's flat and this was probably the only time he'd ever have this opportunity to snoop. He tried to imagine where a devious, naturally suspicious, slightly paranoid game-player might hide his secrets. There was no question of accessing his laptop or anything that required technical skill. He didn't have a plan, so he started with the art-deco chest of drawers – socks, underwear, collar stiffeners, cufflinks, nothing that could be considered contraband.

He looked under the bed and pulled out a lacquered box – a pair of velvet-covered handcuffs, some knotted sash rope, crimson ribbon, lube, two eye masks and a couple of vibrators, one small and one a great thrusting phallus, designed away from the naturalistic. It looked as though Philippe Starck might try to squeeze a lemon with it. It was more than a starter kit, and it seemed that each item had been added as required. Ryder wondered if this should be hidden away too, or was it for both wife and wench? Seth hadn't given any instructions about it, so Ryder pushed it back and smoothed his hand over the bed, where he'd left an imprint.

He opened up the cupboards behind the full-length mirror, seeing his own reflection first. He expected to find that confederacy of half-empty bottles and ointments and nail-cutting implements that somehow made us all the same. But not Seth; his was designed to be looked at as an artwork, designed to be opened – ordered and spotless. Which, of course, meant that somewhere else was a cache of all the normal stuff which remained unseen. Ryder was now at a loss. The frisson had gone and, with it, the momentum. He closed the mirror doors, to see himself reflected again. If that was all he was going to find, it did him little credit. In fact, it made him feel a bit shabby, throwing his moral superiority away for little advantage. He'd learned more about Seth by switching the photos.

Ryder did a quick once-over to check he'd not left any obvious signs of his furtling around, then headed downstairs. In the kitchen, he poured himself a glass of wine from an already-opened bottle and moved through to the living room. He looked limply at Seth's collection of vinyl while humming an aimless tune, then sashayed over to the books. A cursory look at them, then a flop onto the sofa. It wouldn't be long before Seth's wife arrived, so it was time to make himself scarce. He drained the glass and was about to return it to the kitchen when his attention was drawn to a discreet office with a desk. If there was a secret, it was bound to be hidden in there.

There were drawers on either side, inlaid with delicate figurines of Japanese design. Very nice. The top drawer on the left was locked, but the one underneath it opened – it was disappointingly empty. The bottom drawer contained some hanging files, arranged in alphabetical order, which he flipped through – Accounts, Family, Floss, Holmes, Home, Pavel, Ryder, Shabak, Will & Testament, Winona. He didn't have time to look through them all, but opened the file with his name on it. It was thin: some press cuttings of his time as St-Hilaire's right-hand man; a note from Pavel thanking Seth for getting his son into Charterhouse, which irked Ryder, seeing as he was the one who'd done the favour. There were some documents he couldn't read, as they were in Russian, and one in what he thought was either Hebrew or Yiddish. He photographed them with his phone.

On the right side of the desk, the top drawer contained some indifferent paperwork, along with the usual pens and stationary paraphernalia, a passport and some cash, mainly foreign. He found a little box in the middle drawer, which he opened to find two wraps of cocaine. He was tempted, but put them back. Also blister packs of various prescription drugs – Xanax, co-codamol, paracetamol, ibuprofen, some Viagra, along with an old Lesley Garrett gift collection CD, obviously of sentimental value.

The bottom drawer was full of bubble wrap and seemed to contain nothing else, until Ryder noticed something in the corner, pushed well back. It was a key. He retrieved it and tried it in the top left-hand lock. It worked. Inside the drawer was a small purple velvet bag. He took it out and emptied the contents onto the desk – blue diamonds. The lights were dim in the room and Ryder felt an air of anticipation, like he felt when he discovered a misappropriation. He looked at the stones, picked some of them up – examined the colour, the sparkle. They felt surprisingly heavy in his hand and it was as if they were alive, had some soul of their own. Dark and disturbing.

He heard a car pulling up outside, so he carefully put the diamonds back into the bag, trying not to drop any on the floor. He relocked the drawer and replaced the key where he found it, arranging the bubble wrap over it. But it was too late to get out of the flat; Floss was already through the front door.

'Ryder, what are you doing here?'

'I heard there's a party.'

'You're early. And how did you get in?'

'Seth gave me a key. He asked me to come and sort out the food and drink.'

'He asked me to do the same.'

'Let's do it together, then.'

\* \* \*

Ryder was hanging out in the kitchen, wondering whether he should mention the diamonds to Seth. If he did, he'd expose his snooping. If he didn't, he wouldn't be able to get them out of his mind.

Eventually, he took himself back into the sitting room, where Seth was holding forth and flicked him a quick glance from midstream. He'd been surprised when he arrived and found Ryder and Floss together. His naturally suspicious temperament wondered what was going on and Ryder had to do a bit of quick ad-libbing. Others had turned up shortly afterwards and the two of them hadn't had time to talk.

Ryder poured himself a glass from one of the bottles on the go. He didn't care to interrupt Seth, who was getting animated, off on what Ryder thought of as his favourite hobby-horse – the whole soft conspiracy theorising about the world and how it was understood. But, after listening for a minute or so, he couldn't help butting in.

'A bit early for conspiracy hour, isn't it?'

'Maybe we should just carry on sleeping, based on your observations of time, Ryder, as though the nature of truth changes according to the hour?'

'I don't know, maybe the midnight hour?'

Floss stifled a snigger, then tried to look serious.

Seth was obviously irritated, more so than usual, and Ryder put it down to finding him in the flat with his wife when he should have been gone.

'Do you ever think that mocking and sneering might be something that limits you?'

'I didn't realise it was appraisal time. How did the others do?'

'You know, if you could just suspend your cynicism' – Seth hesitated, distracted by something across the room – 'you might find it's the thing that stops you from succeeding.'

'I'm sorry for interrupting. I'm not here to light a fuse.'

Ryder immediately lit a cigarette, smiling dumbly as he did so. Seth sniffed the air, not looking at all happy.

'Not all of us choose to believe the world as it's commonly defined.'

After a pause to make sure Ryder wasn't going to continue to be obtuse, Seth circled back around to where he was before the interruption and, with the herd back under his control, he could restart the drive.

'As I was saying, some people just accept what they're fed. And why do you think that is? They can't be bothered to think for themselves; it's much easier to let the populist media do it for them.'

Ryder had heard it many times, seen it rehearsed and prepared, added to and illuminated. Of course, he agreed in principle with Seth – that we were all force-fed a diet of tripe and trash – but repeating it ad infinitum just defeated the purpose of stating it in the first place. In any case, people were increasingly mercenary; as long as they were all right, they couldn't care less about anything else. So why bother? It was just a pointless ceremony, repeated and attested to in an evangelical tone.

If Seth really wanted to do something about the state of the world, he should go work for Médecins Sans Frontières or donate his diamonds to Children in Need. There was nothing worse than the bourgeoisie pontificating about situations they themselves were responsible for.

Seth carried on regardless.

'So, the issue shouldn't be, are you paranoid, but do you question enough? What are you not being told and why? Why do you believe what's being served up by the government? The lying government, which you know to be lying!'

He finished and sat back to let it hang for a while, but he'd aroused his own simmering anger and frustration.

His silence seemed temporary, the only question being: was someone going to respond, or were they cowed enough by the vehemence he was still trying to hide?

Ryder couldn't let it go. 'Why don't you tell us about Russia?'

'I'll tell you what they hate about us: the double standards.'

'And there was me thinking they just liked our football clubs.'

'What you think isn't important, Ryder. What I won't be a part of is the uncritical acceptance of lies. If people look, they *will* see.'

Ryder hadn't known this in Seth before. This was a development. He got up to get another drink, not wanting to provide the counterpoint. Any argument he gave would be deconstructed and interrogated and inevitably be seen as a traitorous act.

Some half-drunk people were leaning on him and he didn't like it. They looked grotesque – images from a fairground hall of mirrors, all distorted and out of shape. Their voices sounded shrill and intense, getting on his nerves. The flat was full of all sorts: chics and shits and snow-noses and pseudo-intellectuals and dope-heads and drunks and poets and pimps and a general collection of cunts and creepy customers. At least, that's how it seemed to Ryder – half the fuckers looked to him like they'd been awake for weeks.

He turned to see Floss dangling an empty glass from a hand which was crossed over her chest. Ryder straightened the glass and filled it for her. She smiled at him, in that disarming way of hers.

'What he's really saying is, look at my logic, look at my display of logic.'

'I know that, Floss.'

'So, Ryder, you don't think it's all an inside job?'

'Was it that obvious?'

'Let's just say there were indications.'

'Unless, of course, it's the lizard men with their Mossad handlers, because everyone knows the lizard men love their oil.'

She grabbed his arm and led him through to the office with the desk he'd rifled through earlier. It was quieter in there, and she skinned up and handed the spliff to him. He took a long drag, just to be sociable. She sat close to him and they passed the joint back and forth, then she retrieved a little packet of whizz which she took up each nostril like snuff and offered to him without speaking. He decided *why not* – it would keep him on his feet for another couple of hours, if nothing else. Her arm was resting on his knee and her face was very close to his – eyes looking directly at him.

Floss tilted her head and looked away. Were they both just scoffing in a secret collaboration that made them feel somehow intimate? Pretending it was just the politics that stayed safe and locked up? Too dangerous to drag out into the light. Too disruptive. Inconvenient. She seemed in a playful mood.

'But what if he persuades them, Ryder? Maybe you need to silence him, assassinate him before he gets the truth out?'

'That would make you a loose end.'

'Only if you were a lizard.'

He stuck his tongue out.

'See, no fork.'

'In-fucking-controvertible.'

'We can shapeshift like fuck, but we can't hide our true nature.'

'Achilles had his heel.'

'And I got this tongue.' He said it behind his hand.

She raised her glass to drink to it. He clinked his against hers.

'I should start running.'

'But you won't.'

And she didn't. Not for a while – until she'd finished her drink.

They hadn't been speaking for long, but it seemed like they'd said a lot. She remarked that she knew who he was. And he asked if she knew who *she* was. She answered that she was just like him, and all those other people weren't; they were full of fear. And words were the worst of all weapons. He went along with that, remembering what O'Malley's fiancé shouted at him when he was about to become king. Now he was getting drunk and a little high, but he thought Floss might have said she was inside him, part of him – something like that – or maybe she just said they were indivisible from each other in some way that only she knew. It was all very existential and Ryder couldn't help thinking there weren't many women as interesting as her – apart from Lola, of course. Or maybe she was just drunk like him. She told him everyone was changing, constantly, minute by minute – it was implicit in nature, in all tribes and religions and moral principles. He knew he shouldn't be listening.

After she left, he wondered if he'd jumped to a conclusion here. If it was nothing, why did it feel like something? Should he chalk it up as one of those little amusing things, not even a flirt? Wasn't that what people liked to do, have those charged little conversations? Maybe it had something to do with Seth, then maybe it was nothing to do with him at all.

Ryder was really looking for a way to make himself out to be better than Seth. It wasn't hard to do, based on the events of the day. But trying it on with Floss would've been a clear way to hand back that advantage. Wouldn't it? Maybe. Had he got her number? Even if he had, would he call? The one thing he shouldn't do was the one thing he wanted to do.

Maybe it was time to go.

He decided he'd taken enough intoxicating substances into his body for one day – that heaving fat barge of all-day drinking, along with the weed and the speed. He moved out of the office space, looking for the toilet. Two a.m.

Ryder came to slowly, lying face down on the bathroom floor. He could hear someone banging on the door to get in. He gradually pulled himself into a kneeling position over the lavatory bowl, spat down into the urine and then stood up. He ignored the banging while he washed his face and hands, combed his hair and brushed down his clothes. Then he opened the door. Floss came in and asked if he was all right.

'You look like you need to have a lie down, Ryder.'

He looked at the time. Three a.m.

She took him upstairs, not to the bedroom where he'd switched the photographs earlier that day, but to a smaller room with a single bed. He held on to her as she tried to keep him steady, then he kissed her on the lips. It was an awkward thing; Floss pushed him away gently and he complied. The impulse took them both by surprise – almost like an ambush. It had given no warning and it was wrong. Ryder knew he should go, leave the room, get downstairs and out the front door, but his feet were rooted to the floor. Floss should have told him to go, but she didn't. Instead, she moved back in and kissed him. Her arms were around his neck as they moved closer to the bed.

Clothes were in the process of being removed when the door creaked open and Seth was standing there, a bottle in his hand.

'What the fuck?'

Ryder jumped unsteadily to his feet.

'I can explain, Seth.'

'Doesn't look like there's much to explain.'

'It's my fault. I deserve ..'

'You deserve a punch in the face, Ryder.'

Seth came at him from across the room, swinging the bottle. Ryder picked up a pillow to block the blows. They circled each other in a surreal, drunken dance, while Floss escaped through the door and ran down the stairs. Round and round, Seth swinging the bottle and Ryder ducking each wild swipe that came his way, until fatigue finally ended the Pythonesque pas de deux.

'Get the fuck out of here!'

'Nothing happened ... It was my fault ... Don't blame Floss.'

'Get out!'

The tempo in the living room had slowed down considerably when Ryder got to the bottom of the stairs. A tenor saxophone blew late-night blues from Seth's turntable and the few people who remained standing clung to each other for support, as they dragged their feet around the floor. Others were slumped in chairs or on the stairs while the smell of dope could have choked a carthorse and rolled-up notes of all denominations littered the powder-strewn glass-topped occasional tables.

Outside, the early morning air blew some of the shit from Ryder's brain. He looked up and down the street, unsure of the best direction to walk in to find a taxi. He chose left, because he could hear the sound of traffic noise coming from that direction. It was semi-dark as Ryder stumbled along, falling over a dustbin that had been placed in his path by some inconsiderate resident and frightening the cats. He wondered if Capote was one of them. A couple of sanctimonious lights went on and net curtains were peered through by disapproving eyes, at the derelict who was disturbing the peace of their precious little promenade. Ryder ignored them and drifted on, until he found the orange light of a cab and sat back to see the waking city flash past his window.

Ryder was tired when he got back to the shop. He was now living in the bunker at the back of the premises, having lost his flat in the financial turmoil that was the aftermath of the London Gallery fiasco. It had been a traumatic upheaval and it took all his mental resolve to hold himself together. He'd felt as if he were shattering, like glass. Dissolving into the despair. There was a certain dread in that ending of an episode in his life. It had felt like an excommunication – like when his father died. An exorcism. It had brought reluctant tears that he wiped away irritably with the sleeve of his jacket, and also a piercing note into his ears, clear and high in pitch, which resounded around his head.

After leaning his forehead against the window, before fumbling attempts to get the door open, he felt it would be enough to shatter the glass and the shards would slice open his throat.

This is your life. No, this is your bed, mate.

Ryder was back in his plastic world – in some vestigial drug playout. Some ghosting, imaging, unzipping – he felt like he was unzipping. Was it a panic attack? Panic – now a word – now a thing. Could the word induce the thing? And where would it lead? What would it bring?

Oblivion? His father had done it, when things got too strange.

That night, he fell into a fretful sleep and dreamed about Lola. He wanted so much to see her again, even after the long time they'd been apart. They were an odd couple – a cynical, self-obsessed art dealer and a fey, mercurial gypsy. She hadn't asked for much from him, just to be protected from the rest of the exploiting world. And she'd accepted him at face value and didn't look for the man underneath. The man she saw in front of her was good enough – until Swan1 came along.

No sentimentality and no shit. Lola was happy, as long as Ryder was there when the world tried to take a bite out of her.

But he wasn't.

## CHAPTER 24

# ASHOOK

Ryder was surprised when Seth came round the next morning – well, afternoon to be more precise. At first, he thought the bell was that rare beast, a walk-in. He struggled off the sofa to find that Seth had come round to square off matters from last night. Always good about bringing things up, he had a way of dragging stuff into the light. But, if there was light, then there was always shadow with him. *Darkness visible.* So things were never simple.

At a different time, Ryder would have made a joke of it, maybe even told him where that phrase came from to prove a point. Calling him Satan in words other than those of Milton, throwing in Belial and Mephistopheles and a few others for good measure. But there was none of that today. Today was serious.

Seth, rather too politely, asked him what he was busy on. He gave some limp answer, which was accepted for the preamble it was, and Seth enquired no further. In any case, it was for him to make the running; it was him who'd come around. And why would Ryder tell him what he was up to, even if he *was* up to anything?

'Thanks for doing that favour yesterday.'

'No worries. You'd have done it for me.'

Maybe, but he'd have wanted something in return.

'So, Ryder, are we squared away then?'

'Squared away?'

'That thing with Floss . . .'

'My fault, a drunken mistake. She was pushing me away, resisting . . . when you came in.'

'I thought it might have been a problem for you, switching the pictures, and you were trying to make up for it.'

Ryder got up and offered him a whisky. He accepted. Cassie was gone, no longer able to be afforded, so he had to do everything himself.

Seth elaborated. 'I mean, if it's a problem for you, Ryder, then it's a problem for me.'

'Please, don't worry about it.'

'But, say I do worry about it?'

Ryder had a sense of something being extracted from him.

'All I can do is apologise . . . most sincerely.'

'So it's not an issue, not a problem?'

'It's not a problem for me, Seth, if it's not a problem for you.'

'Good.'

Seth sipped the whisky, hanging about awkwardly, as if there was something else on his mind. Ryder was hungover and not in the mood for a debate, either about the diamonds or about Floss. But he knew he wouldn't be able to rest until he'd speared what happened yesterday, on both counts. Unless he could pin it like a butterfly, he knew it would flit inside his head and keep distracting him from trying to get back on his feet.

There was something about Ryder that never took things at face value. He spent so much time thinking about angles and intrigue that his shabby, serviceable mind was always at work – always looking for some connection. It was as though all things should be in the service of his desires, or working some play. Wasn't it true that everyone else had been put on the earth for his convenience and didn't have a purpose of their own?

It was then, for that reason, he had a sudden flashback. He remembered the first time he'd encountered Seth, at The Gasworks all those years ago, when he was trying to sell the Ming to Holmes.

He remembered two mobile phones on the table and a little pouch which Seth opened to reveal the sparkle. He was drunk and crunked back then and it was all very hazy. But it was a way in.

'Did I remember seeing some diamonds?'

Seth stiffened, like a deer that heard a noise in the forest.

'Where?'

'Oh, way back, in The Gasworks, when Holmes intro'd us. You had a little pouch and were showing them to Metallic.'

'Metallic?'

Ryder forgot he didn't know her real name. He left it hanging.

'Do you deal in diamonds, Seth?'

The question was so direct, Seth sensed there was more to it than a distant memory. He thought about it before answering but – OK, if Ryder wanted to get naked.

'Have you been snooping, Ryder?'

'Snooping?'

'I know you're guilty when you answer a question with another. Has Pavel told you about the Russian icons?'

Seth didn't wait for Ryder to go Socratic again.

'Of course he has. Well, the source of supply dried up, so I made the move into diamonds . . . just as a sideline, mind. Much more compact.'

'I don't understand.'

'Of course you do, Ryder, you just want me to spell it out for vindication, don't you?'

Seth went on to give more or less the same explanation as Pavel had in The George on the Strand, after the aborted court case. A Swiss account is set up and the diamonds deposited as collateral for a loan. The money is then dispersed, the diamonds appropriated and trans-ferred to a front company, et cetera, et cetera. Seth was more sketchy with the details than Pavel.

'Of course, it's more complicated than that, but I don't want to bore you.'

'But where do the diamonds come from in the first place?'

Seth didn't answer that directly, just threw out some spiel about the DTC, which meant De Beers, controlling prices by controlling supply – and how the diamond market was strong, particularly for the high-quality alluvials and blues.

'Is it money laundering?'

'That's an ugly phrase, Ryder.'

'Why do you do it, Seth?'

'Why do you do what *you* do, Ryder?'

'Out of necessity.'

'And there you have it.'

Seth finished his drink and stood up. He made his way slowly to the door, then turned, as if he'd just had an afterthought.

'I almost forgot with all this speculative talk, the reason I'm here is to return the favour.'

'How so?'

'There's a client called Ashook; he wants to do some business and I thought I'd throw it your way.'

'What kind of business?'

'The art kind. Are you interested?'

Ryder was interested. He needed something to get him out of the crosshairs of the receiver.

'Of course.'

'Good. He'll buy you dinner. Tonight. Eight o'clock, at the Reform Club.'

Seth was halfway through the door when he turned back again.

'Oh, and . . . in future, Ryder, leave my wife alone.'

\* \* \*

The Reform Club was a private member's establishment on the south side of Pall Mall. It used to have an all-male membership, but let women in back in 1981. It was once the traditional home of progressives, like radicals and whigs, but was no longer associated with any particular political ideal and many of its members were conservative.

It also attracted a significant number of foreign members, such as diplomats accredited to the Court of St James's, and Commonwealth business types. It was a place of outstanding architectural importance, with its kitchens designed by Charles Barry in 1838.

The elegance of the club immediately impressed Ryder, as he was shown to the columned Coffee Room – a high-ceilinged place of chandeliered splendour where Ashook was already seated. He was looking forward to the svelte service and the promise of good wine, coupled with the possibility of making a lot of money.

The client was a tall Anglo-Indian in his early fifties. Ryder suspected that any sense of discomfort astride that divide had been eliminated by Ashook's success in business, and further diluted by London having become a Babel. They shook hands and he seemed convivial enough to Ryder – someone he might just be able to get along with.

He hadn't been given much information by Seth, but he'd done his research and risked joking that Ashook was becoming a sought-after commodity himself. How he'd developed his own patina – something that distinguished him from the everyday.

'Are you likening me to a piece of art?'

'Maybe.'

'I don't know how I should feel about that.'

'I suppose it depends on the piece.'

They laughed together – always a good sign.

Ashook kept up the art theme. 'Strange, how things can acquire characteristics after their creation.'

'Is it strange?'

'Well, with art, in that an incident like a theft or a scandal can elevate it, make it famous, more celebrated.'

Ryder was eager to get down to business, but Ashook seemed more inclined towards a tête-à-tête. Maybe he was sizing Ryder up – getting a feel for him, so to speak. Seeing what he knew.

'The Cézanne . . . *Bouilloire et Fruits* – lost for twenty-one years, then it reappears. I was there, you know, Sotheby's in 1999. It was electric, that sale. And yes, because it had been stolen and then leapt back into view, its allure was all the more.'

'The same with people.'

'I suppose so. It only matters who you used to be to lend you allure.'

'We're all narrative whores, Ashook. Do you know what Cézanne said about that painting?'

Ashook signalled to the waiter. 'Shall we order first?'

He had the wild mushroom goat's curd for starters, then the rare-breed ham hock terrine, with fried quail eggs and straw fries, and lime sugar madeleines for afters. Ryder ordered the roasted celeriac and chestnut soup, followed by Scottish smoked salmon with horseradish cream and toasted soda bread, with caramelised walnut crumble for pudding.

'Would a bottle of the 2005 Sine Qua Non be appropriate?'

'With anything and at any time, Ashook.'

At £700 a bottle, Ryder would enjoy this.

'You were saying . . . about Cézanne?'

'*With an apple, I will astonish Paris.*'

'Wasn't it Paris who presented the Apple of Discord to the most beautiful goddess?'

'Yes – it's a joke, a pun.'

Ashook was enjoying himself. Ryder was proving to be exhilarating company – so much so that the business they were there to discuss could wait.

'Who were the three . . . Aphrodite, Hera and . . . ?'

'Athena.'

'Thank you. And let's not forget the winner was the one who offered the best bribe.'

'And let's not forget they all tried to bribe him.'

'And let's not forget, he took Aphrodite's bribe . . . Helen.'

This display of classical knowledge put Ashook in an expansive mood. Glowing, in fact. So much so that he decided to order another bottle of the Sine Qua Non. He joked that he'd at last found a use for the classical history he'd learned at Eton.

'You should judge a beauty competition, Ryder.'

'I would if I was offered a bribe by a goddess.'

'That would rather spoil it. And look where it got Paris – no end of trouble.'

'At least we got literature. And who should I choose, the one with the best face or the one with the best figure?'

'Neither. You can't choose the one *you* think is the most beautifuk.'

'You said beauti*fuk*.'

'I did not!'

'A typo, then. A Freudian quip?'

This was turning out better than Ryder had expected, and the expensive wine was quite potent, making them giggle like giraffes at their own equivocations. Ashook had forgotten the point he was trying to make – the puzzle he was setting for Ryder – but he stumbled on.

'You have to work out who everybody else wants to win, not you.'

'What if everybody else doesn't want the same one?'

'The majority, then.'

'I don't know . . . you're talking game theory now, Ashook, and maths is always about iterations.'

'It's all about averaging, Ryder. You're trying to average other people's choices.'

'One man's blonde . . .'

'Is another man's bombshell.'

'That observation alone stops us from being total philistines.' Ryder looked at this client intently, pleased to see him enjoying himself, being a human instead of a predictable shicer.

Ashook's interest in art derived more from his English education than any hereditary or cultural vocation. In fact, he'd kept his collection away from his extended family. His parents were Indian before they were English and, although they approved of ways in which their son could be more Anglified, they probably didn't have spending millions on fine art in mind. And now it was no longer novel – no longer nouveau and exciting. He had to pretend it was still a pleasure to look at.

Ryder believed there was something a bit 'Uncle Tom' about expressing too much love for a foreign culture. Trying to outdo them at their own game was to accept the rules of that game. His twin nationality made Ashook a bit of a curio – adoption by one made him suspect by the other.

They were on the Irish coffees before either of them realised they'd been talking around the contrarieties of art instead of talking about art itself – which is what they were there to do. Ashook said he wanted to sell a number of paintings – he didn't explain why.

'Sell them and I'll tell you, Ryder.'

But they had to be sold privately.

'I don't want everyone knowing my business, if you understand.'

Ryder understood. And there would be a very generous commission in it for him, much more than the industry standard. Ryder didn't mention that he'd lost most of his erstwhile contacts, but there was always Seth's money launderers.

He didn't mention that either.

'What have you got?'

'A Picasso ... *Nature Morte*. A Richter, a couple of Warhols, a few of Van Gogh's early drawings of his mistress, Sien Hoornik. A Gauguin, some miniatures. I think one or two Hoppers, maybe a Malevich ... definitely a Degas.'

Ryder stopped him there. He was already talking about many millions.

'I'll have to come and see them.'

'Of course.'

'When would be convenient?'

'They're in Switzerland.'

'Well – maybe not today, then.'

Back at the shop, he wondered why Seth had sent Ashook his way. It was probably because Ashook would expect market value for his paintings and wouldn't sell them off for a song, unlike the Russian icons or the dodgy diamonds. But they'd still be useful things to buy with dirty money, if you were prepared to hold on to them for a while and then put them out on the market. Maybe the Medellín cartels didn't look at long-term investment opportunities; maybe they were just into high liquidity and cash management and cut-and-run control. If Ryder couldn't dispose of the collection by legitimate means, he'd have to consult with Seth on those issues.

But who knew the workings of Seth's mind? There was something just so unrelenting and adamantine about the guy. Ryder had never seen him blunted by anything, until last night. His all-encompassing view on the world applied, and applied again. An application of the will. An application of the urge. A true believer in zero-sum and, for sure, he wanted to be on the plus side of the final fuck-all equation. He may not have Ryder's eye, but he had all his own teeth. At least, that's how Ryder saw him – but Ryder didn't know everything, even if he thought he did.

He sometimes saw Seth as another person he might have to fall out with – leave behind. But that brought him no comfort. He knew it was open-ended. Things were only concluded when they were concluded.

And, even then, it wasn't the final word.

## CHAPTER 25

# SWAN2 REVISITED

The selling of Ashook's collection was the big opportunity Ryder was waiting for. The way back. The path to redemption. He had to make it work, no matter how. But, in doing so, he had to endure the temerity of the euphuistic and the artificial, the smug and the specious. Like the intense investor on the other side of the table, whose inflated opinion of himself was taking the dialogue away from the purpose of buying some pictures.

'I've got a theory.'

Ryder reckoned it was a theory about whether he only existed if someone was listening to him. He clenched his teeth behind his tight, fixed smile. And was it really a theory, or was he just calling it that to accord it greater status than it deserved? Maybe it was just a thought, or an observation? Maybe the same could be said of him!

'Which is, we're living in a new paradigm. There's been a paradigm shift.'

Still, that wasn't the annoying thing. The annoying thing was that Ryder had to listen to him, faking interest.

He'd had enough of the self-promotion, the dashed-off pose of the guy's position that was just a restatement of the tech-savvy, business-literate dimension of the suits. The financialisation of everything. The remodelling and reduction of the world. Ryder was beginning to treat the meeting as a sociological experiment, as if he was an anthropologist. It worked for a while; he could see how people who attributed their success to their own foundational excellence believed their insight was transferrable from their supremely specialist advantage. Maybe he was becoming a kind of anthropologist of wealth but, as far as he knew, anthropologists weren't supposed to harbour homicidal thoughts for the objects of their study.

'What I'm talking about is a shift in distribution – a stage of global development where more and more will amass and concentrate in certain places and to certain people.'

The guy spoke as if this was a new phenomenon, forgetting that, once, wealth and power were the property of the aristocracy. A certain amount of levelling had occurred during the twentieth century, but now the dynamic was returning to a kind of feudalism.

'It's a brave new world, Ryder – an alpha one.'

'Do you know where that comes from?'

'*Brave new world*? Shakespeare's *Tempest*, of course.'

'No.'

'No? Where then?'

'Aldous Huxley.'

'Who's Aldous Huxley?'

'Jim Morrison named his band after him.'

'The Doors?'

'Of Perception.'

The man fixed his eyes on Ryder, trying to weigh him up. Did this guy want to shift some paintings or not? He was supposed to fawn and flatter, not come out with all this cryptic shit.

'The difference between me and you, Ryder, is that I see the world as something still to come, not something to be looked back on.'

'Is that why you want to buy pictures that were painted in the past?'

'I'm not buying for myself.'

'Oh, you're a dealer then?'

'A financial advisor.'

Ryder grimaced. Nothing said 'progress attained' like a spreadsheet.

Swan2 came back from the ladies' room.

'How are you two getting along?'

Neither of them spoke. She suggested a cigarette break on the balcony. The financial advisor didn't smoke, so they left him alone to google Aldous Huxley.

'How's Swanson?'

'Older.'

'Thanks for this intro.'

'He hasn't bought anything yet, has he?'

Ryder lit her cigarette and she took in a long drag.

They were at Bar Termini in Soho and, after reconnecting recently, Ryder was using her as a sounding board. She had the access he'd lost: a tier of connection to people and wealth through Swanson, who she still worked for, even though the other Swan had left Boulets years ago. She operated in a different dimension to him now – a different realm, where things seemed to flow to her.

'I heard you were in Paris.'

'For a while. And I heard about your downfall, and saw you naked on YouTube.'

'That wasn't . . . It was Katie's fault.'

'It was your own fault, Ryder.' She blew smoke at him.

'It wouldn't have happened, Anna, if we'd stayed together.'

'I think it would.' She decided to change the subject. They'd had that week together that seemed so long ago now. After which he'd dumped her. She looked older, but it suited her and Ryder reckoned he'd stayed more or less the same – according to himself. 'You know they're doing funds now. You can invest in top-end art. I remember when pictures were things you put on the wall to look at.'

'Tell that to the Popes.'

She wasn't put off.

'Now you can have fractional ownership of a piece, like a race-horse, with an investment profile, or whatever. You can buy a Picasso and they'll lend you money against it as security.'

Ryder thought of Seth.

'You only need thirty per cent. Painting mortgages.'

'It's a mixed-up, muddled-up, shook-up world.'

'*Except for Lola, la-la-la-la Lola*'

She stopped singing abruptly, realising where she'd gone.

'Sorry.'

'Don't be.'

They finished their cigarettes in silence, then made their way back in. She tried to lighten the mood. 'You know, Hirst once put a cigarette in his penis.'

'He might have painted with it too.'

'That I would pay to see.'

'Why would you pay to see that?'

'So I could tell people about it, of course.'

'If you're in the right place, you can see it for free.'

She linked her arm through his as they approached the table. The financial guy was still there, even though Ryder hoped he'd fucked off. Ashook's paintings could wait another day.

They sat down and Ryder ordered three marsala martinis. He and Swan2 continued their conversation while the financial guy shook his head and put up two fingers to the waitress, indicating that he wasn't drinking – at least not alcohol.

Swan2 kept talking. 'Tell me this, Ryder, do you think a good liberal arts education is a total waste of time?'

'Why so?'

'Well, given the limited opportunities to indulge it, without being considered pretentious.'

'Is that your experience, Anna?'

'My experience is that art has been refashioned as an accessory.'

'Different Popes for a different age.'

The financial guy looked at his watch. He stood up and kissed Swan2 on the cheek and said they should get together more informally in the near future. 'It looks like you two have lots to talk about.'

He shook Ryder's hand. 'It was good meeting you. Let me report to my people and revert. I have your card.'

Then he was gone. Ryder sighed. 'I think I blew it.'

She didn't confirm or deny. It was a fucked-up, mixed-up, financialised world.

Ryder wasn't sure he'd seen the level of the game. In trying to sell Ashook's paintings, he'd been increasingly dealing with the representatives of rich people. He didn't mind them per se, but they took him further away and put him at a remove from the principal. Of course, some were all but unbearable – the butler being haughtier than the master.

Words were cheap and endless. Even experience couldn't save him from inferiority in front of money. Wouldn't it have been better not to have tried to play at the top table? His distaste for the financial screen-jabbers seemed to be eroding his belief in it all. He'd got himself invited to some dinner a while back, where the host stuck a massive kitsch Jeff Koons monkey in the hallway. It was so large it was difficult to get past. It seemed ridiculous to Ryder, until he realised he was missing the point. *Look! Look at my Jeff Koons!*

'Would you come work for me?'

'*For* you, Ryder?'

'With me, then.'

'Can you afford me?'

'Not at the moment, but maybe.'

She laughed, not because she thought the proposition was preposterous, but because she saw the irony in it. He didn't know why he asked her; it wasn't something he'd thought about and the words just seemed to speak themselves, without his approval or consent. But it could get lonely in the shop on his own; more than just the hours he spent there, it was the isolation and lack of corroboration. Sure, he could talk to people, but it was just trade stuff and he needed more than that.

Ryder didn't feel much like going home – well, as much as the back of his shop could be called home. So when Seth texted to say Pavel was in town and wanted to buy Ashook's Picasso, he accepted the offer of drinks at the Connaught Hotel. Ryder had always assumed Seth's history with Pavel was closed, but it seemed it wasn't so done after all.

He asked Swan2 if she'd like to tag along and she said why not.

They were in the cocktail bar when Ryder and Swan2 arrived. Pavel called the waiter while Seth kissed her on both cheeks.

'Anna . . . you two back together again?'

'Not romantically.'

'She's helping me with some contacts.'

Ryder shook hands with Seth, then the big, clasping hug from Pavel, who went on to enquire who the beautiful lady was.

'An old flame of Ryder's.'

'And you let her go? How careless of you!'

Ryder put his head to one side and gave a rueful smile. He'd always wondered about these two – was Pavel involved in Seth's close shave with the bullet? He could imagine the Russian back then – his shrug, the plaintive hands, the curled-out lower lip, the *what could I do?* Maybe Seth had been played? How would anyone ever know? But there had to be something more – some other angle.

'And, Ryder, thank you so much for Charterhouse.'

'How's your son doing, Pavel?'

'Very well. For him, like Pip, we have great expectations. Who knows, he might even acquire some Englishness.'

'God help him.'

Pavel laughed. 'You, Ryder, would make a good Russian.'

'And you, Pavel, would make a lousy Brit.'

Pavel took that as a compliment.

Ryder wondered what else sat behind the decision to send his boy out of their native Russia. Pavel was a man who liked the idea of the cold and the hardship being the mould that made him – the elements that had made him what he was.

'I owe you a big favour, my friend. That is why I want to buy your picture.'

'The Picasso?'

'If you say so.'

'It's not mine. I'm just the broker.'

'But you will make money?'

Ryder couldn't help feeling that everything Pavel said contained a subliminal coded threat – or maybe it was just the way he said it. The Russian called for more cocktails.

'Don't you want to know the price?'

'Of course not. I trust you, Ryder. I am only here for two days and tomorrow I have to attend a charity event . . . which you must all come to, I insist, as my guests! You don't have to buy anything, just eat and drink for free.'

'So how will we . . . the Picasso . . . ?'

'I will be in touch. Just don't sell it to anyone else.'

They sipped their drinks and Swan2 decided to vary the conversation. Seth and Pavel were sitting either side of her and she was intrigued by their unlikely alignment.

'How did you two meet, if you don't mind me asking?'

Ryder wasn't sure if she should have asked that question – or if there would be a satisfactory answer. Both of them went quiet for a moment, then Pavel threw out that big laugh of his.

'Will you tell her, Seth, or should I?'

Seth gave him a lowered-eyebrow look. 'You do it.'

It came as a surprise to Ryder that Seth had worked, as a graduate intern, for the British diplomatic mission in Moscow, after his brief flirtation with the gem trade. According to Pavel, Seth had walked out of the Beta Hotel Izmailovo and stuck his hand out for a taxi. Back then, any number of private enterprise cars would rush to a halt and offer their services – all of them just wanted the dollar. He never had to say where he was going; that got sorted out on the move. Pavel pulled over just as he was getting into another car. He caught Seth's attention by speaking good English and he told the other driver to fuck off. Ryder thought it smacked of a set-up, but he said nothing.

From then on, they had sort of adopted each other. Pavel found in Seth an excellent new toy, as he put it, and Seth found in Pavel a conduit into things beyond the confines of the Ministry. He got cache and status from having access to Pavel's set; he could go places other people couldn't.

Back then, it was hard to say what Pavel even did. As a front, he traded in anything he could get his hands on, but he had connections in dark corners – with the seraphic shadow-men who turned black into white. The ones who never came into the light; who sowed the grapes of wrath from the recesses of secret places; who spread their disease across oceans and continents and turned lies into truth. Of course, Pavel didn't say that to Swan2. Nor did he disclose his affiliation with Yisrael Beiteinu, the aliyah of Russian immigrants who, in turn, had links to the Shabak, who used the shadow-men to threaten and intimidate.

In those early days, Seth's handlers were tiring of the strictures and policy documents which pushed him too far away from the decision-making. So, with Pavel's help, they put into effect the money-laundering part of their plan for Seth, who was spending more and more time 'beyond the wire'. Until it all went wrong.

Ryder had a question for Pavel. 'How many times did you stop to pick people up?'

'That was the only time.'

'How come?'

'Well, I suppose you could say, it was the only time it mattered.'

'Whatever happened to those foxes you always talk about?' Seth changed the subject – happy, if not eager, to divert the course of the conversation.

'Oh, the foxes – you remember them, of all the things in the world? They were always more trouble than they were worth. But what do you expect, they were fucking foxes.'

'I need a cigarette.' Ryder didn't want to hear the story.

Seth insisted. 'Anna hasn't heard it.'

Pavel turned to Swan2.

'Let me tell you about them.'

The Russian insisted on having a full glass if he was going to undertake to do the story justice. And, although he might have seemed like a caricature sometimes, Ryder hadn't forgotten how clever he was; and not just at telling stories – how educated he was. How all his academic knowledge percolated amidst the strange landscape of his history. Ryder always thought the greatest propaganda of the Cold War was that Russian men were invariably thick peasants wearing potato-sack trousers and carrying unread copies of *Dialectical and Historical Materialism*. Yet here was Pavel, whose rough-hewn sophistication was an anomaly.

But now it was time for that smoke.

Ryder and Seth left a captive Swan2 listening to the unexpurgated narrative of Pavel's grandmother and her quest to housetrain wild foxes. Seth seemed pensive and Ryder wondered if he still had the hump over his little flirtation at the party with Floss.

'Are you still sore about it?'

'About what?'

'Me and Floss.'

'I don't know what you mean.'

It was clear that Seth was irritated by Ryder's insinuation that he should have got over his fit of pique by now.

'If you need me to say it again, I will.'

'Say what?'

'Sorry . . . for what happened.'

Seth wanted to get off the subject. Hearing Ryder made him feel petty and childish. Like he was being chucked some birdseed. But he also realised some good could come of it. The favour bank – the long-term play.

'I don't need an apology.'

'What, then?'

When they returned to the bar, Pavel was asking Swan2 if she knew a good lawyer in London, and she was recommending one or two. He didn't explain why he wanted legal advice – at least, not to Seth or Ryder.

They drank some more and it got late and there was nothing further to be gained from the meeting. Swan2 said she had to go and Ryder said he'd share a cab with her. They left Pavel and Seth with a couple of for-the-road brandies and Swan2 asked him in the back of the taxi if he still lived at the same flat.

'Not exactly.'

'Where, then?'

He gave the cab driver his address and she recognised it.

'That's the address of Holmes's shop.'

'It's my shop now.'

'Are you living there, Ryder?'

'Temporarily.'

She told the driver there was a change of destination and gave him the address of her flat in Chelsea. Ryder was about to object, but thought better of it. She smiled.

'We'll be more comfortable there.'

## CHAPTER 26

# A LITTLE CHARITY
# GOES A LONG WAY

The charity fundraiser was held at the function suite of The Dickens Inn on St Katharine's Way. Pavel had taken one of the extortionate tables at the event – it was the price that needed to be paid to play at this level. Pay up or fuck off! The point was access – and who wanted access unless it was denied to others. Ryder didn't relish it, but he came along all the same, mainly to solidify the sale of Ashook's Picasso to the Russian. Swan2 came with him and Seth arrived suitably late and alone.

Pavel had brought a party of six, mostly model-type women who caused a stir when they arrived. The wake of people tried not to look, or tried not to be seen to look. Some pretended to ignore the entourage, like they'd ignore a flash car in the street, so as to deny any satisfaction to the driver. If this was Moscow, it would've been unremarkable, but here it threw various groups into mild consternation. It disturbed them. Pavel liked to expose the weird social hypocrisy and crippling anxiety of the West, and he played his role with relish.

'I love the way the English are embarrassed by everything.'

Perk came and sat next to one of Pavel's women, whose name was Petra. Perk, Petra and Pavel – it sounded like a firm of alliterative solicitors, and Ryder smirked inwardly at this silent observation.

The charity auction part of the evening commenced, which Ryder saw as a flatulent and slightly gross display of wealth. But tonight he was happy to let the others at the table do the bidding.

The auctioneer was a neat little man with a nifty line in humour and some real front. He knew who was out there, who had to be needled and cajoled when they went a bit quiet. He wasn't above reminding them why they were there – to raise large amounts of money for good causes.

He told some calculated asides and trowelled it on about the generosity of those who bid heavily, which had the desired effect of making their peers want to match their philanthropy. He was like a dancing weasel, out to transfix and mesmerise those who wanted to play in the moment.

'We have a bid from the lovely lady on table six.'

Petra had raised her paddle for a Roman bronze figure of Asclepius, god of medicine and healing. It was amusing as far as Ryder was concerned – proximity to the action without having to cut a cheque. Normally, he'd be attempting conversation about the tasteless ostentation of it all – but hey, why not sit back and enjoy the show before having to face reality again.

He watched as people craned their necks, following the bidding; saw it return to Petra, for whom the auctioneer had developed an obvious *coup de foudre*. The little guy smiled when the bid returned to her and scowled when it went elsewhere. Her paddle allowed her to be the momentary centre of attraction, not just an implacable beauty with impossible geometry. When she bowed out, Perk jumped in and won it, standing up and waving like it was an unexpected victory for the underdog. When he sat back down, he said he didn't really want it and only got it for her. It was a £40,000 piece of fun and he was rewarded with a kiss. It was a sick joke as far as Ryder was concerned, one that turned him this way and that and then confirmed what he held to be true all along. He hoped some people were appalled by it – the conspicuous element of it – but of course they weren't.

Pavel caught him giving Perk a slow handclap. Ryder leaned over and whispered, in response to the Russian's quizzical look. 'We have an expression, *pissing on someone's chips*.'

'In this case, I think lobster and chips.'

Pavel raised his glass in a gesture that seemed to suggest it had nothing to do with him. After all, he wasn't the one bidding.

Ryder sipped his whisky, observing the tables, the auctioneer and his saccharine cajoling, the slightly fuck-off quality of it, like watching tycoon tennis, heads swinging wildly, seeking out play.

Later, Perk collared him in the toilet.

'When will Dieter have the rest of those masks?'

'I'm not sure. I haven't seen him for some time.'

'Are you still his agent? I mean, I heard they all deserted you like the proverbial rats.'

'I'm still his agent.'

'Could you make an enquiry, please?'

They went on from the charity bash to a drag evening at the Phoenix Arts Club off Charing Cross Road. Seth was ebullient; he'd obviously taken something.

'I went to a party in a flat that had a *Never Mind the Bollocks* poster fastened to the wall with a Versace brooch and a Cartier tie pin.'

Was this Seth trying to act his erstwhile age – trying to prove to Ryder that he had the biggest testimonial? The experiences of the young got commodified in the not-so-young. The 'I was there' syndrome. Reckless behaviour was a test of purity in a *Tropic of Cancer* sense – in a Baudelaire-Verlaine context.

'Sex Pistols' *Never Mind the Bollocks*?'

'What else?'

'Bollock Brothers' *Never Mind the Bollocks*.'

'If I lived there, Ryder, I'd have no choice but to batter my girlfriend and then overdose.'

'The only way to keep your dignity.'

'I've had enough of people parlaying their rebellious youth. I mean, when does a spotty naff teenager convert into outsider cool?'

'Never. You have to be cool from conception.'

It seemed, after the previous edginess, that they'd fallen back into their easy company, even though Ryder was keen to avoid just about everything connected to Seth at the moment. At least, until he knew for sure what was going on.

Everything about him lately seemed to be imbued with a dark tincture. Of course, it might just have been that Ryder was down and Seth was up – or seemed to be – and that made him galling on most subjects. Ryder didn't want to get dragged back into it, the easy familiar territory, as if they were each other's confessors or confidants; it smacked too much of intrigue – and not just chichi bafflegab, but something insidious. Ryder still wanted to maintain an open line of communication, as long as there was clear demarcation, a limit, keeping himself clear of Seth's dodgier dealings. Hang out with him too much and he might be dragged into something he'd regret.

To Ryder, Seth seemed to do most of his business in the margins – always something underway, some scheme; more ear than eye, in the argot of the dealers. Ryder, by his own reckoning, was more eye than anything – and eye was considered the highest ranking of the senses.

Now Seth was being funny, talking about the Sex Pistols, and it would've been easy to fall back into their old routine. People tended to grab hold of a past that never really existed – before long he'd be talking about cultural necrophilia at the fountainhead of youth.

Looking over from the bar at the party of people drinking, Seth was being coy and Ryder didn't believe his stated reluctance to join the others.

'I suppose we're going to have to go amongst them.'

They walked across the room from the bar and languidly joined the throng. Was there anything more outré than people showcasing what they were while watching drag queens being risqué and rudely impudent? No doubt there was, but it was all rhetorical.

Ryder wondered how he'd got to such a dissonant state. He shook his head as he observed the airbrushed allure of his company – a crowd that was enraptured by itself, a congratulatory beneficence extended to those who extended it back. A mutual buffing and glamourising.

Pavel was getting a little drunk and more than a little loud. He decided to take on one of the more vocal queens on the small stage and it was developing into somewhat of a slanging match, with the queen winning the exchange. She bowed to the Russian in the manner of addressing an aristocrat. 'Ladies and gentlemen, the masturbator of Moscow. The faithful lover of the Widow Wrist.'

The crowd laughed. Pavel wasn't amused; he usually won arguments and this was belittling his manhood in the presence of the ladies in his entourage.

He shouted back. 'And you are the easy lay of London, and a cheap one at that.'

'You know a lot about whores, then?'

Pavel was surprised by the answer, unused to people standing up to him.

The queen wasn't finished with him. 'Ah yes, I remember you from the Chelsea Cloisters – the ladyboys there said you had a tiny penis. They had to look for it with a magnifier.'

With that, Pavel jumped up onto the stage and tried to pour his drink into the drag queen's mouth. Now, she wasn't as strong as the Russian, but she'd been performing in rough clubs long enough to know how to handle herself. She brought her knee up hard into Pavel's testicles, and he fell to the floor holding his groin and groaning. The drink he tried to pour down the queen's neck spilled on top of him and he now looked like he was grovelling at her feet. The whole club was laughing now but, before Pavel could get back onto his feet, security arrived on the scene and the company was ejected onto the street amidst howls of protest from Pavel and catcalls from the queens.

It was getting late and Ryder had had enough entertainment for one day. Pavel was threatening to have the club burned to the ground and the management was threatening to call the police. It was time to go. He hailed a cab out on the Charing Cross Road, and Swan2 came back with him to the shop. She was shocked to see the conditions in which he was living and expressed concern about his erratic behaviour.

'What erratic behaviour?'

'Being naked in the street.'

He opened a bottle of Semillon and put on some music and they danced together. They danced slowly and he could feel her breath on his neck. Ryder was happy to be away from the crowd – away from people in general. They moved round the back room, her humming to the music. His lips brushed against hers and she pulled away slightly. Almost apologetically.

Ryder was a bit disorientated from the amount and variety of alcohol he'd drunk during the long day, and really all he wanted to do was sleep. But he went through the motions. Her humming retreated further and further away from him, until it was off somewhere in the distance. Then he couldn't see her anymore because everything went black.

When he came to, she was on the floor beside him, holding a glass of water to his lips. It took him a moment or two to realise who she was.

'Anna . . . what happened?'

'You collapsed. I should call an ambulance.'

He sat up. 'No! I'm all right!'

'You're not all right, Ryder. Are you eating properly?'

'I'm eating, sleeping and drinking properly. No ambulance!'

That's *all* he needed. It'd get around – something wrong with Ryder. The ignominy.

He got to his feet and she helped him to the sofa. He drank the water and felt better after it. It was nothing, just too much alcohol.

'Too much alcohol, that's all.'

'Are you sure?'

'Positive.'

She stayed that night, just to make sure there wasn't a repetition of his blackout, then left in the morning, after making him tea and some toast, which she insisted he ate. Swan2 was concerned for

Ryder – about his mental state as well as his physical health – so she got in touch with Swan1, who trawled around, but nobody wanted to get too deeply involved except Dieter. He immediately offered the use of his flat.

Ryder didn't want to go; he considered it deeply infra dig, and he didn't want to be seen as some kind of degenerate Dieter groupie. But they agreed it would be temporary, until he sold some of Ashook's pictures. And Pavel had already agreed to buy the Picasso, so maybe a couple of weeks – certainly not more than a month. Ryder made a strange vow of sanctity that he'd always stand by Dieter. An uncharacteristic splurge of sentiment that would soon evaporate.

Dieter let him in and helped him with his bags into the lift first and then into the flat. Anya wasn't there on this occasion and Ryder was glad of that. Dieter showed him his room, then asked if he was hungry. He wasn't, but he could do with a drink. There was an open bottle of Pinot Noir in the sitting room and the television was paused during an episode of some reality show.

Dieter tried to be upbeat. 'You have caught me being normal. In flagrante. Do not tell anyone . . . bad for my reputation. Are you sure you don't want to eat?'

'A drink is fine.'

'You look pale, Ryder. And you could do with a shave.'

'I'm fine.'

'Very well, but just one drink . . . or two. And I need to take any sharp objects . . . and your belt, please. Don't want you swinging from the chandelier, if I had a chandelier.'

'There was a time I could have sold you some.'

'Just as well I don't need one, then.'

Ryder sat heavily on the sofa. Dieter poured him a large glass of wine. An uncomfortable silence ensued – they were two individuals who were used to their own space and now it was being invaded, on both sides.

'Thank you for this, Dieter.'

'You do not have to thank me.'

'Perk is asking for more masks.'

'Fuck him. He can wait.'

Ryder looked at the television.

'What's this?'

'Nothing, just a repeat of *The Osbournes*. Did you ever see it?'

'No, put it back on.'

They watched for a while. Ryder caught Dieter flicking his eyes across to see how he was reacting. He tried to laugh, tried to animate his expression, so Dieter wouldn't have his entertainment curtailed by worrying if he was enjoying it. Wasn't that just like a marriage? But no, in a marriage he'd have just left, or sat in sullenness. That was when you still cared about the small things.

Dieter pointed at the screen. 'I like that there is no claim being made about it, other than it is shit. It has no purpose. It has no design, by design.'

Ryder's distraction turned to actual interest. He couldn't shake the sense that it must be staged. How did they get to that level of dysfunction? How did they agree to it?

When Dieter turned it off after two episodes, Ryder swung round to look at him, as if to say he could do another one.

Dieter shook his head and got up. 'Help yourself to whatever you want. Goodnight.'

Then he went, as though he'd changed his mind about having a lodger and was sorry he'd agreed in the first place. Ryder continued to sit there for a while longer, then went to bed himself. Of course, he didn't sleep much and, when he did, it was fitful and restless.

Next morning, the atmosphere had changed. Dieter seemed antagonistic about everything connected to London – the place, the art, the money, the people. He seemed angry that he hadn't become part of the inner sanctum. Ryder put it down to the volatile temperament of all artists, who felt it was within their compass to shift the world and reverse its very motion. It was ridiculous, of course, but it didn't stop the wild accusations of deceit, corruption and connivance. Even when it blew through and Dieter calmed down, it was still there in the aftermath, as if it left a residue of rankle on every surface.

Ryder had seen enough people behave badly down the years, and had contributed to the file, no doubt. His normal reaction would have been to do a body swerve, but he was in this thin-ice situation, living in Dieter's flat. He considered moving back to the shop, until Dieter made it easier for him to stay.

'I am going back to Berlin.'

That settled the tension down somewhat, at least temporarily.

'Of course, Ryder, you must keep living here . . . in case I decide to return.'

Ryder didn't try to convince him to stay.

They actually got on better during the month before he left for Berlin. They tiptoed around their friendship, arguing only about Perk's masks, which Dieter refused to do, saying he was finished with that kind of sculpture and wanted to move on to something new.

'It's money in the bank, Dieter.'

'Is that all you care about, Ryder?'

'Of course not!'

'Well, it's what it seems like.'

'If that was true, would I be here?'

'Probably.'

But it was amiable, like being students again, sharing an unruly dorm. They swapped books and argued points of view and criticised each other's taste in music and drank a lot of wine. The unsheathed ego of the artist versus the acerbity of the natural-born cynic.

Ryder's irritation at having to be what he considered the reasonable one.

'It comes to something when I'm the pragmatist!'

Dieter's threats to find another dealer.

'Fine, try it and see how cold it is out there!'

Ryder's frustration at seeing his protégé falling away, after all the work he'd done to promote him.

'What have you done?'

'You don't know the half of it!'

'That's right, I don't!'

They would avoid each other for a while, as far as that was possible – Dieter going to his studio and Ryder going to his shop, each allowing the other to go through their wild and far-flung ideas, or their bouts of indignation and smouldering irascibility. Ryder wanting acknowledgement for his part in the strange half-success Dieter had achieved. Dieter seeing it as something unfinished, the early part of the arc. What did he suppose – that everyone made it? How would that work?

Ryder not agreeing that he would have done better if he hadn't been blinded by the lights of his association with St-Hilaire.

'Look where you were before me!'

And then it was over.

Dieter left for Berlin and Ryder was alone again.

## CHAPTER 27

# COMING HOME

So far, Ryder had been unable to sell any of Ashook's paintings. Dieter was back in Berlin and his business was firmly in the crosshairs of the receiver. The odd thing was, he felt strangely calm – in fact, he was trying to isolate and identify what he felt. The closest he could come to it was a strange, resigned equanimity. It was as though the sentence had been handed down, but was yet to be executed.

That was before one of his young artists came into the shop all riled up – fired up and angry. Jaffa was Ryder's wild card amongst his roster of the undiscovered and unsuccessful. Despite his insistence that his work couldn't be categorised, it fell under what would be termed 'street art'. He had a certain following and a volatile reputation.

'This is bullshit, man. You and I had a deal and you're … Why're you fucking me like this?'

'I'm not fucking you.'

'You are! You're fucking me!'

'I'd only be fucking you if I was making money, and you weren't.'

Jaffa shut up, looking sullen rather than angry for the first time. Annoyed by the logic contained in that statement.

Still, he didn't like Ryder's tone, or that thing he did with his hand. It looked dismissive, as though he was being patronised.

'Why can't you be straight with me, man? You said this was going ahead.'

Jaffa had got in front of himself on the telling people he was going to have the exhibition that Ryder promised him. He'd told all his friends about it and now it wasn't happening. He was going to look like a right clown.

Ryder was conciliatory. 'Look, I'm not saying it won't happen. What I'm saying is just that now's not the right time.'

'You're saying no one has any money?'

'Would you buy a car now?'

'If I needed one.'

'Would you buy a *new* car?'

'I'd never buy a new car. I'm not an idiot!'

'How about a new artist?' Ryder said it with an open-handed gesture, which annoyed Jaffa. All his gestures annoyed Jaffa. Still, the artist couldn't get around the fact that, if one of them wasn't getting paid, the other wasn't either. But, if he couldn't stay angry, he wanted to hang on to his annoyance.

This wasn't how it was meant to be. This wasn't part of the plan. He wouldn't be the first artist Ryder had dropped – or the last. Maybe it was time to get out?

Ryder laughed, lightly, so as not to antagonise Jaffa and flare him up again.

'For a moment there, I thought you were going to clump me.'

'What would you have done if I did?'

'Hit you back.'

'Fair enough.'

Ryder wondered what really would have happened if they'd got into it. He liked Jaffa in his way, even if he'd almost had a fight with the guy. Being clever didn't mean you were right. Just wrong in an acceptable way.

And that was the story of his life. There was something charmingly naive about looking back. It made him wince to think about the veil of ignorance behind which he'd laboured for so long. Still, he'd thrown his lot into that space and it was like a sea captain complaining about the weather. He knew how it could get before he set sail. It wasn't that he didn't care about his artists but, as he told himself, when it came to the push, he was the one out there hustling – not them. Maybe that's what he needed – some angle. Some catalyst. He had his own ideas about how the market had changed, how tastes had changed; that wasn't hard, even if you didn't have eyes of your own. He'd heard the complaints from the loose confederacy of dealers, especially when they drank. Endless complaints about how it was getting worse – and it was all true. But somehow he sensed that he'd come out of it. It was just a matter of tying himself to something that floated. He needed a tool – something to kick-start his comeback. But what was that going to be?

Speaking of tools –

'Listen, Jaffa, are you able to use a sandblaster?'

'I think so.'

'Lump hammer and chisel?'

'Sure, man.'

Ryder made himself a coffee when Jaffa left before calling Perk. He needed to think – how much should he ask for? Would Perk still want them or had he gone off the boil? He was fickle like that – today's trophy was down tomorrow's toilet. With Perk, you had to strike while the blood was up, while the champagne was spraying.

'Perk, my dear chap, how are you?'

'Ryder, what do you want?'

'It's more a matter of what *you* want, Perk.'

There were fourteen of Dieter's mask sculptures outstanding. Perk only had six of the twenty he originally wanted, which left unoccupied spaces in his house and grounds. Ryder told him he'd be taking delivery of the other fourteen and he was giving Perk first choice – if he still wanted them.

'I thought your man was back in Berlin, Ryder?'

'He is, but I've persuaded him to honour his commitment to you.'

'How noble.'

Ryder told him the sculptures would be arriving in Dieter's London workshop in two months and there would be no more after that. It was a limited-edition offer.

'I'm not sure I want them anymore, Ryder.'

'But he's already shelled out for the materials.'

There was a pause on the other end of the line, while Perk thought about it. It could go either way.

Ryder had to press – close the deal.

'You'll have twenty original Dieters, Perk. No more after that. Think about it, they're only going to go up in value.'

'All right, Ryder, I'll take ten.'

'Just ten?'

'That's all I want. How much?'

There was no point in trying to push any further. If he did, Perk was just as likely to tell him to fuck off and keep the lot.

'Seventy . . . each.'

'I only paid fifty each for the six.'

'Like I said, there won't be any more. These will be exclusive, especially if Dieter dies.'

'Is he likely to die?'

'There's a rumour . . .'

'What rumour?'

'That he went back to Berlin because he has cancer.'

Ryder didn't like denigrating Dieter's health and tempting fate. That was low, even for him. But Perk needed a last push and that was it. He'd do penance for his perjury at a later date.

'Sixty.'

'Done!'

Ryder called Jaffa and told him to come to the workshop immediately.

\* \* \*

Two months later, Jaffa had made the masks in the style of Dieter and Ryder delivered them to Perk's stately pile in Lincolnshire. Perk gave him £600,000 for the consignment and Ryder paid Jaffa £100,000 for his good work, leaving himself with a cool half-million.

He was back!

To celebrate, instead of going out and getting wasted, Ryder decided to be sensible for a change and take a little break to go visit his mother in Oxford. It was Christmas after all, and his mother would be alone. After he told her and she said she was looking forward to seeing him, he started having second thoughts – but it was too late to back out. Unlike his father, Angela had a past that he was part of. His father had no past – he must have had a past, of course, but it wasn't part of Ryder's. Their pasts didn't intersect; not in a significant way. She'd told him his father was a magician – so good he made himself disappear. That's all he knew. He could have been anybody, anywhere. Except that he was dead.

Ryder's mother, on the other hand, was still there, in the past that was now the present and perhaps into some of the future. She was an aristocrat, or so she said, and when Ryder was young they'd lived on an estate that she'd inherited from her family – the Courtenays, who went back to Edward Courtenay, the lover of Mary Tudor, the first Queen of England, who was banished to Venice where he drowned himself. Ryder's father wasn't an aristocrat, of course, just a common conjurer, and the family didn't want Angela to marry him. But she did, because of his mesmeric powers.

When he was very young, before Charterhouse, Ryder had gone to a local boarding school for boys. His mother was an attractive woman and she was very good friends with the headmaster. He seemed infatuated with Angela in a kind of devotional way, and he saw in her son some of her ethereality and even introversion. They confided in each other and the head was concerned about young Ryder's unsociability and lack of friends. Angela was also worried; not about his unsociability and lack of friends – that kind of thing was natural for aristocrats – but about his obsessive preoccupation with the byzantine and the baroque. She spoke to young Ryder's father about it, and his only response was that his son had a gift, like himself, and it wasn't to be interfered with – otherwise some disastrous consequence would occur. Angela believed that was just a lot of superstitious nonsense and the boy should be encouraged to consider financial subjects, as was the tradition in her family.

The headmaster grew even fonder of young Ryder's mother as time went on, and they became close. His life had been an academic one for the most part – never much time for personal relationships. Consequently, he'd done very well and he was one of the youngest prep school heads in the country. He was proud of his achievements but, now and then, felt he'd missed out on something along the way. This dearth, this absent stratum of experience, this lack of complete character development, prevented him from relating fully to Angela. Sometimes he wanted to say more to her, to do more for her, but he didn't know how.

He was afraid of things he didn't understand. Perhaps if Angela had been alone? Young Ryder was somewhat disconcerting to him – the offspring of another man. A father. Blood into blood. The man's aura could sometimes be felt – vague, esoteric. The headmaster couldn't compete in such an arena, so the relationship remained at a respectable distance. And even though little rays of hope and loneliness shone out, they couldn't quite connect.

One evening, young Ryder was brought into the headmaster's office for absconding from the school to visit a neo-expressionist exhibition in Oxford. The head shouted at him and, after several attempts to communicate, young Ryder told him he wasn't his father and he could fuck off! The head lost his temper and told the boy that his mother had enough to contend with and he, like his father, was breaking her heart. If things carried on, he'd be taken away from her and put into a children's home.

Young Ryder's father found out about this threat and there was a huge argument at the school. The headmaster got punched in the face and the police were called. Young Ryder's father was arrested and a charge of GBH brought, which could result in a prison sentence. Judges took a dim view of illusionists beating up the heads of distinguished prep schools in Oxford and the penalty would undoubtedly be severe. The headmaster resented being stashed on the nook in front of his impressionable charges, and young Ryder was expelled. Angela did nothing but cry for a long time after that, and his father's photograph was in all the papers and the estate was surrounded by reporters all the time – others kept calling on the phone and trying to get an interview.

The headmaster stayed contritely away – until one night, when he received a wild phone call. He could get no sense from Angela, except that he must come to the house immediately. She was sobbing when she opened the door, so he put his arms around her to console her. She lay against him, trembling and touching his shoulder. She asked him to come to her husband's sanctum, as he called it. Young Ryder was already standing there, the magician's accoutrements splattered with blood and bits of brain, and his father, with a large hole in his head, lay on the floor, clutching a gun he used in his act.

The headmaster was horrified. He held his hand over his mouth to prevent himself from vomiting. Angela was hysterical – in a silent, motionless way. The headmaster retreated quickly, leaving Angela and young Ryder alone in the room with the body. He could hear her crying softly, as he stood outside the sanctum door, above the wild beating of his own heart. Then he was suddenly seized by an uncontrollable terror and he rushed out of the house – never to return again.

After the suicide, Ryder was sent to Charterhouse and, from there, to Oxford University. After he graduated, his first job was in the settlements section of a private investment bank in the City of London. But it was so bloody boring and he couldn't stand it – the same thing every day. He wondered why he'd studied all those years and achieved a double first, only to end up in a boring job like that. He wanted to run away – fly away to somewhere exotic. Somewhere colourful, away from the boring monochrome of banking. There was more to life than money. More to work than money. Wasn't there? Work to live, or live to work – which?

So he joined the furniture department of Boulets Fine Art Auctioneers & Valuers.

But now he was back, for the first time in a long while. These days, his mother lived in a modest detached bungalow, surrounded by gardens. She was rather quiet when he arrived, not having much to say and not enquiring why he was there or how he'd been. Just in a world of her own. Ryder suspected that she'd always blamed him for the suicide, though she never said as much. She was still very elegant, wearing a two-piece by Gharani Strok and shoes by Carvela and some understated jewellery by Boodle and Dunthorne. She had money, which she made on the sale of the estate after her husband's death. Ryder never felt comfortable here, but he came just the same, though not very often. It was just that he imagined it would be nice for his mother – to spend Christmas with her.

Why did anyone do anything? It was just a whim – something he did – and he wasn't going to be sorry for doing it.

'Have you seen my old headmaster, Mother?'

'No, not since . . . He's not at the school anymore. He moved away after . . .'

She didn't want to talk about it.

'I want to drive up to the estate and have a look around. Would you like to come?'

'It'll be closed up for the holidays.'

But Ryder was determined to go, even if it was just to stand at the gate and remember. It wasn't far away, just a mile or so down the A420. The house was built on a hill, so it could be seen from the bungalow.

When he got there, the place was open after all, because they had some Christmas festival going on at the estate theme park. He drove up along the approach road and parked the car. Inside it was all changed, of course, and nothing was the same as it was back then. The sanctum was now a games room, and all the blood and bits of brain had been cleaned away, which was a good thing. He didn't stay long and, afterwards, he drove past his old school. The boys had gone home for the holidays and the place looked forlorn and lonely without them. Stark and grim – at least to Ryder. Had it been the same back then? He couldn't remember.

Snow was beginning to fall over the fields of Oxfordshire, and the county looked so old-world and splendid and unmoving. Suspended in time. Quiescent. Growing dark in the midwinter gloaming. He saw some figures on the road up ahead so he slowed down and dipped the headlights. As he passed, he saw it was a woman leading a horse.

And he thought about Lola.

Back at the bungalow, his mother had prepared a small traditional Christmas dinner – pheasant with brussels sprouts and roast potatoes and a rich gravy. The aroma was evocative and they ate to the sound of carol music on the radio. Ryder was trying to be a son to her, trying to be nice and make something up to her. Trying to make her happy, at least for a little while. It wasn't her fault – what happened. She was always quite a delicate, fragile woman – frail now, so many years later. He wondered if he loved her and it was difficult to know. Did he even know what love was and, if not, how could he know if he loved his mother? Maybe he loved his father and it died when he died – disappeared when he disappeared?

After dinner, they had a couple of sherries together, then Angela said she was tired and went to bed.

Ryder left early the next morning.

# CHAPTER 28

# GENEVA

Money goes to money. It was an old adage, but a true one. No sooner had Ryder got back on his feet financially than Ashook's paintings began to attract buyers.

He stood outside the Geneva Freeport looking at the unremarkable building. It wasn't so very different to any of its neighbours, or any of the ones he'd passed on the ten-minute cab ride from Genève Aéroport. Ryder checked his watch – he was early, so he began to walk away, slowly and reluctantly, that pointlessness of covering distance he knew he'd soon re-tread on his way back.

He was glad to be back in the groove – in the swing. Nothing invigorated him more than proving people wrong, especially those who thought they were something but were never all that much to begin with. There was a certain smugness in witnessing their crumbling conceptions of him. It left them marooned, gossip-wise, and flopping around like fish that had missed the tide. They were nothing special; they just made the wrong predictions and now the game had turned. He'd regained that sense of being special, while a lot of those people were just mediocre. It was as if some magnetic field had reversed. He didn't gloat or give them a hard time; he just took what was due to him.

After walking around the building, he was now back at the front entrance. He looked at his watch again but he was still early – he knew that even before he checked. There was a sudden slap down on his shoulder and the sound of Ashook's voice.

'Doesn't look like much, eh?'

Ryder turned. They shook hands and headed towards the entrance.

'Let's see if we can even get you in here.'

It was Ryder's first admittance to the Geneva Freeport – a warehouse complex for the storage of art and other valuables. It was the oldest and largest freeport facility and the one with the most artworks, estimated at over a hundred billion dollars. It was where Ashook stashed his collection, and now he got to behave as though he was introducing Ryder to his club and in some way vouching for him.

He tour-guided his guest through the various levels of security that had to be negotiated before getting admittance. 'They say you need your passport for security reasons. It's not true. You need your passport because you're leaving the country. I always think they should check it again on the way out.'

Ashook left Ryder to it because it was taking too long to get him processed. As it was his first time, he had to submit to a whole series of checks. He'd done a lot of it online, but he still needed to have his fingers, face, palms and iris scanned. He had to declare all passports and nationalities before being issued with an ID card and allowed to go through.

He found Ashook jabbering into his phone, with a leg thrown over a low sofa. He rounded off his call and got up. 'When people say "offshore", I still think of oil platforms. That's how out of date I am, Ryder.'

Ashook made his money in some real outposts, and he could be gone for months on end. He thought Ryder spent too much time in London. Life was out there, at the frontier, not in some gallery or restaurant or English idea of the country.

A guide appeared. 'I will take you to Monsieur Ashook's facility. Please follow me.'

She walked in front of them and they followed her clicking heels through the polished marble atrium, to what looked like an access point for goods in and out of the building. Two overalled workers were clearing up a pile of debris. The guide frowned and seemed on the point of apologising, as though this should not be exposed to sight. Ryder couldn't help noticing broken frames – good ones at that – prised off and discarded in such a way that indicated there was no interest in keeping or reusing them.

Ashook drew his attention away. 'If you knew what space cost here, you'd do it too.'

They faced each other in the lift when the doors closed and it moved so quietly that Ryder didn't know if they were going up or down.

Ashook was trying to make conversation with the guide.

'Do you ever wonder what's being stored here?'

'Not really.'

She maintained her non-committal exterior.

'I suppose it's all normal to you?'

'I wouldn't know about that.'

He gave up. 'Fair enough.'

The lift door opened and they resumed their walk, deeper into the building. The corridor was close and tight, but why wouldn't it be? Space was what they were selling here – it was the commodity itself. Ryder looked at the guide and wondered how many people and how much net worth had done the same. Maybe she was more surveyed than any of the items stored here. She was the one thing that connected them back to the living world outside this inert, ionised, regulated place. Humidified – sterile – dead.

They passed some Gulf state Arab in his treasure box. He'd left the door open, and their walking by made him look up with an angry glower. He seemed compromised amongst his haul.

Ryder knew there were other facilities like this around the world, and Ashook caught a flicker of expectation on his face as his strong-room was opened up. It was smaller than the one Ryder had half seen with the Arab. The guide said they should call her when they were done, then she removed herself to somewhere unknown.

'So, tell me, Ashook, why do you have one of these?'

'Why do I have one, or why does anybody have one?'

'Well, both.'

'I'm never in one place long enough, and if the stuff is here, I know it's not decaying or being stolen. Besides, some of it was already here when I bought it.'

'And anybody?'

'Anybody being those who like to have an enormous safe deposit box that no one else can look inside. I can't think of a reason. Why would anyone want that?'

Ryder felt a bit naive for asking a question to which he already knew the answer.

The kitsch crowd was always relentless about the need for art to be shown, for it to be displayed and seen. The underpinning of public good was never far away. They had some mismatched ideas as to how access and exclusivity worked together. To them, the high point would be to endow it all to a museum of standing, even if that meant other exhibited works being withdrawn, boxed and carted down to the storage vaults.

For them, this place was an anti-museum. He'd read a piece by an overheated journo about the advent of freeports being an artistic apocalypse – an overturning of some fundamental right. About how, if all was revealed, this place would match the best museum in the world. Of course, the register of stolen or missing works would itself populate many museums. It was just impossible to say where they all were.

Of course, Ryder believed art should be seen, and by as many people as possible. He loved art for its own sake and not for its monetary value. So, in that respect, he wanted it to be free – available on the streets, like Banksy or Stik or Phlegm. Hung from the railings along the Bayswater Road or the Place de Abbesses in Montmartre. But then, if that happened, he'd be out of a job. It was a catch-22 of constancy. A principle quandary. A shtook, as Seth would say.

Over the years, Ryder had observed how certain paintings which had mouldered away – overlooked and untended for years – made their way back into circulation. As if they'd resumed their travels. Originally, maybe bought and resold, then stolen by the Nazis, then looted by the Red Army or the Americans. Then, after a significant gap, stolen or liberated and sold again, clambering their way back to respectability by stages – give or take some competing claims and legal antagonisms.

'Did you start out in pictures, Ryder?'

'No ... furniture.'

'How very English.'

'Like yourself, Ashook.'

Ryder reckoned he'd come a long way. He felt that was at least part of the reason he and Ashook got on so well. They'd both seen an aspect of the world that fell outside most people's settled metropolitan view. It was as though they could stand the patronising of the luminaries of the art world, because they knew things the worthies didn't. So Ryder thought now would be a good time to ask.

'I'm going to meet a Russian client soon, the one who wants to buy your Picasso. D'you want to come?'

'Hmmm ... I don't know if I like Russians very much.'

'Even if they're buying your paintings?'

'Particularly if they're buying my paintings.'

Ashook thought of Russians as being like a virus that gains access by imitating some other cell, ignoring the correlation with his own milieu. Ryder believed Pavel would take such a simile as a compliment.

'All right, let's look at the Degas.'

'And the rest.'

\* \* \*

The guide wished them well as she held the door open and they stepped out of the facility almost an hour later – after Ashook had signed all the paperwork giving Ryder joint access to his collection and permission to come and go as he pleased, and to remove items for sale as and when required.

They decompressed back into the world of direct sunlight, traffic and breeze. Ryder was glad to be out; it was like emerging from a five-star submarine. It would have given him a headache had he stayed much longer in the scrubbed air that had something of an aircraft or hospital about it. A kid could easily become a bubble-boy in there, dehumidified in the allergen-inducing sterility. Would it be allowed to take a space satellite dog in, he wondered, or a canary from a coalmine? Or Van Gogh, who was called the Christ of the coalmines?

Ashook was still thinking about their guide.

'I'm pretty sure she was a cyborg.'

'A sexy cyborg.'

'What do you say we go have some dinner, Ryder?'

'And some drinks.'

'Of course.'

They were booked into the Hôtel de la Cigogne on Place Longemalle, and they went back there to eat. Ryder had Älplermagronen and Ashook had Zürcher Geschnetzeltes, both with vegetables of the day, and Bündner Nusstorte with meringue buttercream for afters. All washed down with a couple of bottles of Cabernet Franc.

It was still early and Ryder was restless, so he suggested they go out somewhere for a few hours. Ashook chose Le Baroque on Place de la Fusterie.

The ambience in the club was dark and degenerate, like 1920s Berlin, and Ryder half expected a grotesque and face-painted Joel Grey to usher them to the small table with black suede seats.

A couple of young blondes sat close by. Ashook gave them a good looking-over.

'I bet they're high-maintenance.'

'We've just walked in and you're already testing the talent, Ashook.'

'I have a radar for beautiful women, Ryder. I inherited it from my unscrupulous father, so don't blame me.'

Ryder guessed it was more *I'm rich and I get what I want*. He too could spot a beautiful woman from a distance, but with him it was just human nature.

A waitress came, dressed like Liza Minnelli in *Cabaret*. They ordered Asbach manhattans, to be in keeping with the German *mise-en-scène*. After a while, Ryder noticed the two blondes looking over at them and smiling provocatively.

He tapped Ashook on the shoulder.

'They're looking at us.'

'Really? How exciting!'

Ashook called the waitress and sent a couple of cocktails over to the blondes, then lifted his glass in acknowledgement. One of the women came across to their table.

'My sister wants to know if you would like to join us.'

Her accent was unfamiliar to Ryder – perhaps Hungarian, or Romanian?

Ashook was grinning widely at the girl. 'And what about you?'

'I too, of course, would like it.'

He turned to Ryder. 'Shall we?'

He didn't wait for an answer. He was already on his feet and crossing to the blondes' table. Ryder followed, a little worried about where this was going to end up.

The blondes introduced themselves as Mustique and Mystique and they said they were sisters. Ryder doubted if either was true, but he went along with it. They drank some more and, when Ryder went to the gents, Mustique followed him in. They went into one of the traps and snorted cocaine off the cistern, but this was gear unlike anything he'd experienced before. It must have been very pure, because he could feel it hitting his throat – chalky, like a bad medicine taste. Within seconds, he had a massive rush, his eyes bulged and his heart felt like it was exploding in his chest. It was as if he was outside himself, outside the loo, outside the club. Nothing or nobody could touch him. He was invincible.

Indestructible. He was famous. He was a movie star – and everybody loved him.

When they came back, Mystique and Ashook took the same trip and the girls asked if they wanted to go somewhere more exciting. Both of them were up for anything after the coke and they found themselves at a downbeat pole-dancing club in the red-light district of Pâquis. The place looked like a cattle market to Ryder. The clientele was rough, like the bar itself – drunks and old men in dirty raincoats and an unruly stag party, munching on Fleishtortes and slurping down pints of Kronenbourg while watching the dancers perform. The girls on the poles were wearing flimsy maids' outfits, which consisted of a black minidress with a white frilly apron across the middle and a feather-duster thing to titillate the male clients. How very conventional, Ryder thought – and not at all original or remarkable.

It was a free-for-all. There was no stage and the drunks could get right up close to the performers. This made for trouble, and the bouncers were constantly pushing them away or throwing them out. Ashook seemed to be enjoying the unaccustomed stridency of the place, but Ryder had enough after one pint.

'Let's get out of here!'

'Where's your sense of adventure, Ryder?'

'With my sense of self-preservation.'

They eventually moved on and the next club was more upmarket, if that term could be applied to it appropriately, with glitzy silver décor and kitsch chandeliers and a revolving disco ball. The music was techno and there was a stage for the dancers to perform on. They wore basques and fishnet stockings, with bleached white hair and scarlet lipstick, and the clients were more subdued than in the first place. Ashook was definitely in the groove.

'Let's have a private dance.'

'I don't think that's a good idea. I mean with the ladies here.'

'We do not mind.'

Mustique and Mystique joined them in a private room, while two of the pole dancers performed. Ryder could never see the point of pole or private dances. All you did was sit there while some woman shook herself in front of you. You couldn't touch her and it was really just a prelude to masturbation.

He was glad when it was over and they were out of there. By now the rush of the cocaine was wearing off and they had to be at the airport early the next morning, so he suggested going back to the hotel. Ashook wanted to keep the night going and asked the blondes if they'd like to come too.

'Can we? Thank you.'

Ryder felt a little disorientated as they travelled up in the spacious lift. Their suite was large and dazzlingly white, in a mini-malist style, with a partition between the two beds. Ashook poured champagne, while Mustique set out more lines of cocaine on the low glass table. They snorted the coke and then the blondes stripped to their underwear and circled the men like birds of prey. They seemed to be gliding around the room on a cushion of air, laughing and strangely animated. The room grew more surreal as time went on, then Ashook collapsed into the bath when he went for a piss and nobody could get him back out.

Mystique looked worried.

'What about our money?'

'What money?'

'Do you think we do this for free?'

To be honest, Ryder didn't know much about anything by that stage. He took Ashook's wallet out of his pocket.

'How much?'

'Five hundred dollars . . . each.'

He thought that was a bit steep but, hey, it wasn't his money. And, as Ashook was the one who wanted to keep things going, it was only right that he should pay. Both women lay with Ryder on the bed, undressing him, then getting astride him – one at each end.

He could hear laughter coming from somewhere and he thought it was from the bathroom. It ebbed and flowed on the tide of the strange and surreal scene. Fingers caressed Ryder's scalp, moving to the spot where the third eye was located – caressing, manipulating, mesmerising. Suddenly, Mustique bent her head and sank her teeth into Ryder's shoulder, eyes rolling in her head, as Mystique slid vermiform from the bed, her hair in a fury around her crazy face.

It seemed like some macabre ritual, and Ryder tried to get off the bed but couldn't. He rolled over and over, hoping he'd come to the edge and fall onto the floor and the impact would bring him back to reality. But the bed went on and on – it had no dimensions, no beginning and no end, and he was lost in its vastness. His eyes began to close, even though he tried to keep them open. He didn't want to succumb to sleep, or whatever trance he was falling into. But the pull was too strong and he was unable to resist.

It was morning when Ryder woke. Light illuminated the room and amplified its whiteness. Everything was white, except for a red stain of blood on the bed. He rose and searched the suite and found Ashook still in the bath, but the two blondes were gone. He looked in the mirror. There was a cut on his shoulder – more than a cut, a wound where the skin was broken and blood congealed. He splashed water on his face, then hauled Ashook out of the bath.

'What happened, Ryder?'

'The sisters . . . don't you remember?'

'Not much. Where are they?'

'Gone.'

And so was all their cash.

## CHAPTER 29

# EVERYBODY WANTS A PIECE, INCLUDING SETH

Apart from the thousand dollars Ryder paid the blondes, Ashook had another two hundred in his wallet and Ryder about four hundred more. The sisters had taken it all and cleaned out the minibar, which cost them another two hundred. They'd left the cards and passports and other personal documents, like the authorisation from the freeport. So, when Ryder thought about it, they were lucky and got off lightly. It could have been a lot worse.

By the time they boarded their flight back to London, Ashook had already forgotten about it and was deep into conversation on the subject of everything being connected. A huge, global public relations conspiracy, as he called it, managed by advertising executives. He said there were greater forces at work behind the scenes in the world, behind the ideal, behind the cynosure, behind the political and the correct, behind the face, behind the word, behind the gesture, behind the essence and the quintessence. He said that Ryder should know about it more than most.

'It's all connected, Ryder.'

'Maybe you're right.'

At that particular moment, Ryder didn't care. The sound of Ashook's voice was beginning to offend him.

They said goodbye at Heathrow, as Ashook was catching a connecting flight to Canada. Ryder promised to keep him up to date on the sale of his stuff and caught a cab to Dieter's flat, where he went back to bed and slept for what seemed like a week but was, in fact, only twenty-four hours.

When he finally woke, he remembered there was a Hirst sale at Christie's and he'd promised to meet Seth there. It was an evening event, which gave him time to find his bearings and recover from the strange night out in Geneva. He didn't really want to go, but all his rehearsed defences for not doing so had been countered by Seth, who said his attendance was important. In the end, he agreed because he didn't want to seem like a cultural Luddite – a dumb disconnect. But he wasn't going to buy anything; just turn up as another gawper.

Seth came dressed for the occasion, and clearly not keen to have any transfer of foreign material onto his immaculate satin jacket. He stood back and looked at Ryder, still fairly dishevelled even after a shave and a shower.

'I can only assume, Ryder, that you hope to get in as one of the porters?'

He didn't wait for a reply, just carried on as though he was Prospero in a bad production of the dream play.

'By that I mean to the after-party, not the auction. There are only five hundred invitations.'

He waved his, making it dance in front of Ryder's eyes like Violet Beauregarde with her golden ticket. Of course, for someone to be so delighted, someone else had to be disappointed. Seth touched Ryder's arm and said he'd extend every effort to get hold of a spare invitation for him. 'But it's who you keep out as much as who you let in.'

'It's who wants to stay out as much as who wants to get in.'

'Touché.'

'What's so important about me being here, Seth?'

'Later. Are you going to buy?'

'No!'

'I think I might.'

He said it in a matter-of-fact way and shrugged his shoulders as he did so. Ryder couldn't work out whether it was an acknowledgement of it just being another purchase, or some urge to own a Hirst – to *have* one. To Seth it was just another acquisition – well, that was how he wanted it to appear. He liked it when he could be so casual about something others might think of as serious, making it seem reckless and carefree. But, as Ryder pointed out, if he was so careless about it, why was he seeking direction and validation in his selection?

'I'm not.'

'Then why am I here?'

'I didn't want you to feel left out.'

Seth wasn't sure that Ryder got the real proprietary joy of ownership. How could he? Everything just passed through his hands and nothing was retained – even his wife. He might be a highly educated aficionado with a depth of interest and appreciation, but he couldn't have the ownership, the territorial assertion – the conquered land. Contrarily, Ryder could see that, after the decision to *have* something, everything else fell away. He could see it in Seth and replicated across a whole class of would-be purchasers. They had some irrational need to play, to have some kind of stake in a game that most of them didn't understand.

It was a bit of a zoo, the last couple of hours of public viewing before the evening's sale. Full of last-minute hordes. Ryder didn't want to be part of it – even more so now he was here. There were too many of them. The force of people and money and entitlement. Anything but art. This was art as phenomenon. This was pharaonic. The art-money-fuck nexus. The be-all and the fuck-all.

And there was the man himself, older now and balder – next stop sixty. Not the curled-lip, fresh-faced, goat-god of former times. Tucked away on high and smiling, imbued by it all, the full-spectrum deification. Money and art and drama – god of skull and gold. It was a splurge, a latter-day hand job, more an orgasmic squib than a monumental ejaculation.

'Not as big a frenzy as "Beautiful Inside My Head Forever" in 2008.'

'You remember that?'

'When we were young, Seth.'

'Younger.'

'I can't work out if it's the end of something old or the beginning of something new.'

'Probably both.'

'What about this one?'

'Listen, Ryder, if I'm going to have a dead animal in my house, I should at least have shot it myself.'

Seth padded on down the line of works, his arms crossed and one of his hands extended up to his face. He occasionally tweaked his chin or rubbed his cheek against the static open hand, or ran it through his thinning hair. The more he liked something, the more he was inclined to slow down but never quite stop. Ryder kept up with the pace, hoping to get through it quickly and go back outside for a cigarette. It wasn't like he didn't know where it was going to end, and he assumed Seth did too. It was always going to be spots; always going to end with a spot painting. It was standard. Was this what he'd come here for -- to help Seth choose what he'd already chosen, an antiseptic package of urbanity for his white wall? A signature, an instantly recognisable style, an acme of minimal, an announcement of wealth. Buy it because it's expensive!

The auction itself turned into an event, a spectacle, with tiered levels of play, which the room was structured to represent. Everyone wanted a piece. The red carpet. The appearance. The heat. The elixir. Yet everyone was equally afraid of being duped, of being the fool in the room. It meant that most people were trying to work out the rules of the game. What very few of them realised was how much was going on in private. It was no longer about art, but about money and the edge. Seth knew that, about it being toppy, inflated. So why was he here?

'Do you ever ask yourself why people buy art, Ryder?'

'Used to. But even the question supposes an answer.'

'Maybe more than one.'

'Well, you know my theory on it.'

And Seth did. Ryder had told him more than once.

Ryder reckoned it was all a cosmic piss-take. What he couldn't work out was whether the artists themselves were taken in by it, or just the collectors. Of course, it could be both. What he did know was that people just wanted some of the exuberant, over-the-top feeling. The comedown, the hangover – well, that was for tomorrow, or tomorrow's tomorrow.

Seth shook his head. 'I don't know whether to buy one or slit my throat, listening to you.'

'You could do one and then the other.'

But now he wanted something else – something from Ryder. 'You got time for a coffee?'

What Ryder still didn't know was that Seth's handlers had intervened when he lost the cartel's quarter-million in the ill-fated Moscow deal all those years ago. They had prevented the cartel from exacting the kind of retribution that they'd normally have meted out in such circumstances. The money wasn't short when it was handed over to Seth and he must have appropriated it himself. Of course, Seth denied doing any such thing and insisted it must have been tampered with in transit. 'In transit' meant Pavel.

The money had been transferred by Seth to an account in Russia, and Pavel withdrew the quarter-million and bagged it and had it waiting for Seth at the Black Crocus Hotel, to avoid it having to be carried through customs. There was only one point at which it could have been tampered with. Seth hadn't bothered to check it before setting off to make the deal, as Pavel had spent a lot of time beforehand gaining his trust. Because of the shadow-men's intervention, Seth was then deeper in debt to them than ever before, and it looked like he'd never be free of their control. This, he reckoned, he owed to Pavel.

In the bistro at Christie's, he ordered two Americanos and sat opposite Ryder, not speaking until he'd taken a sip and grimaced, as if the coffee was too bitter for his taste.

'This Picasso you're selling to Pavel ..'

'Yes?'

'When's that happening?'

'Don't know. Waiting for Pavel to organise. But it needs to be soon; Ashook's stuff is going fast and there could be another buyer.'

'Where's the painting?'

'In the Geneva Freeport.'

'So, Pavel will need to travel to Switzerland?'

Ryder shook his head, wondering why Seth was so interested in this.

'Not necessarily. I have access and can bring it to him.'

People were coming and going from the gallery and Seth seemed nervous, looking around every now and then as if to make sure no one was listening.

'Surely he'll want to view it before buying?'

'I expect so.'

Seth reached over and touched Ryder's hand – an uncharacteristic gesture which made Ryder feel uncomfortable, so he withdrew it and lifted his cup to his lips.

'I need a favour, Ryder.'

'Another one?'

'I did give you Ashook ... and Perk.'

'I suppose so.'

Seth asked Ryder if he could organise Pavel's viewing of Ashook's Picasso at the ski resort of Verbier in Switzerland.

'It's only a hundred and fifty kilometres from Geneva ... two hours.'

'Up a fucking mountain, Seth.'

'While you're there, you could kill two birds, so to speak.'

'How so?'

'Remember the diamonds you came across when you were snooping round my flat?'

Ryder didn't acknowledge or confirm that he'd done any snooping, and Seth didn't really need him to. The diamonds had been deposited in a Zurich bank, as collateral for a loan. That money had been dispersed via a number of scattered accounts and the diamonds had been appropriated by the original account holder. They needed to be collected and brought back to London.

'Is this stuff legal, Seth?'

'Of course!'

He said it in an indignant fashion, which insinuated that he would never dream of doing anything that smacked of contraband.

'I don't know about this . . .'

'Look, Ryder, I'll make it worth your while.'

'How much worth my while?'

'Half.'

'Of what?'

'The diamonds. They're superfluous now, and worth a lot of money.'

Superfluous diamonds – Ryder reckoned he'd heard it all now. The whole thing smelled badly – stank, in fact. He didn't trust Seth and he wanted nothing to do with it. He was an art dealer, not a diamond smuggler.

'It's not smuggling.'

'What is it, then?'

'Completely legitimate.'

Seth assured him he wouldn't have to go to Zurich. A courier would collect the diamonds and deliver them to him in Verbier. All he'd have to do was put them in his suitcase and carry them back. Seth would meet him at Heathrow and they'd split the cache and that would be that. Simple.

'Who exactly owns these diamonds, Seth?'

'We do . . . now.'

'Who originally owned them?'

'You don't need to know that, Ryder.'

'I think I do.'

Seth rose from his chair and looked down at Ryder, rather like a disappointed schoolteacher would at a delinquent pupil. Ryder knew Seth had helped bring him back from the financial brink, but it was his own ingenuity in using Jaffa for Perk's sculptures that had really turned the tide. All right, Seth also set up the Picasso deal with Pavel, but Ryder had been selling the rest of Ashook's stuff through his own skill and experience as a dealer. Nevertheless, he felt he still owed something to Seth and, if this was all above board, then what was there to lose? He knew very little about diamonds but, from what he'd seen in the velvet bag in Seth's flat that day, they could be worth a considerable amount.

Ryder had made money from Perk and was making money from Ashook, but he was still living in Dieter's flat. He needed a place of his own, and not somewhere shared with a flatmate, like with Jonnie. No, somewhere exclusive to him, that no one could take away, no matter what happened. He wanted it in case Lola came back – something to give her, a home of her own with some land around it so she wouldn't feel hemmed in. Maybe a horse and a bow-top wagon for her to feel safe in if she wanted space. The diamonds could do that.

He put up a final show of reluctance.

'Why don't you go collect them yourself?'

'You'll be going there anyway, so there's no need for both of us to make the trip.'

'I don't know ..'

Ryder was weakening and Seth could sense it. He just had to close the deal – hammer it home.

He sat back down. 'If you don't want to do it, I'll ask Perk.'

'Perk?'

'Sure, he's always up for a quick killing.'

'Too unpredictable. Who knows what he'd get up to?'

'Well, if you don't want it ..?'

Ryder rubbed his chin, considering it.

Seth knew he was closing in for the kill. 'I give you my word, Ryder ... it'll be fine.'

It was too crowded to go back in so, in the end, Seth chose the piece he wanted to bid on by simply going through the catalogue. As a reward for Ryder, for agreeing to do the favour, he appropriated a spare ticket to the after-party for him. The event was buzzing and Hirst was there, greeting people and posing in that easy way which celebrity lends.

Seth could walk the walk too, and many people wanted to be near him, including Vladimir Gazmonov, who Ryder had previously met at the Ham Yard Hotel with Neville St-Hilaire. The Russian kissed him on both cheeks and asked how he was, particularly after the unfortunate scenes at the opening of the London Gallery extension. Ryder assured him he was fine now and had completely recovered from the setback.

'Have you seen Pavel lately, Vladimir?'

'No, I have not. But then, Pavel is a very hard man to – as you would say, pin down. Do you not have his number?'

'I do, but he's not answering.'

'If I see him, I will tell him to call you.'

Seth had left him to it and was mingling – handling those who approached him with equal ease. Never patronising and never getting a signal wrong. Looking like one of the stars. Conversing easily on any theme. Smiling the smile, laughing the laugh, shaking the hands, riffing the raff. Ryder watched him standing with Hirst for a while, letting them all see that they knew each other. Being there!

Later in the evening, Ryder caught a glimpse of Swan1 out of the corner of his eye. He turned his head slightly to see her looking across the room at him. He was going to ignore her, but thought better of it. After all, it wasn't her fault Lola left. Well, it was indirectly, but not intentionally.

He walked towards her, feeling as if he was moving in slow motion, and his words sounded long and vowel-heavy when he spoke them.

'Would you like to dance?'

The musicians were playing Peter Tchaikovsky's 'Chanson Triste', which was one of her favourites. She was pleased he remembered.

She smiled and took his hand and he led her away from her husband.

'How is your wife?'

'Never saw her again, after that morning.'

'I'm so sorry.'

The dance ended and they stood together in silence, not really knowing what to do next. He walked her back to her group.

'It's such a tragedy, isn't it, Ryder.'

'What is?'

'That we'll never be young again.'

'Almost unthinkable.'

He thought he saw a tear in her eye, and he put it down to the emotion of the occasion.

## CHAPTER 30

# FROM BERLIN TO VERBIER

Ryder felt the plane begin to drop in altitude. He hit the service button overhead, hoping to squeeze in another drink before the trolly dolly announced the end of play. He was stopping off in Berlin to meet Dieter on his way to Switzerland – he needed to find out what the artist wanted to do with the flat and workshop after Ryder left. The steward-ess brought his drink and he polished it off quickly and jammed the plastic cup into the seat pocket, causing it to crack. He'd never made it to Berlin before. It felt like an omission, but he hoped it wasn't the beginning of an undisclosed bucket list. Equally off-putting was every-one telling him he should go, expounding on their own experiences – less Third Position, Brandenburg, Reichstag, sex and fetish, party-party-party, curated decadence, organic this and green that. Fuck it.

He booked into a hotel for the one-night stay, rather than rely on Dieter's hospitality. He hadn't offered it and Ryder preferred not to rekindle the unruly month they'd shared as flatmates in London. Dieter had been generous back then, at a time when it was much needed. Despite their differences, that was when their relationship became friendship rather than just the commercial.

They met at Bar Tausend in Behrenstrasse, close to the Rocco Forte where he was staying, and Ryder regretted making a joke about his beard. Dieter just smiled and bashed him on the shoulder and ordered a couple of Tschunk cocktails, then shrugged as if to say, *here we are.* They were caught unawares for a moment, unprepared, not really knowing what to say.

Ryder broke the impasse.

'A few years ago, I nearly jacked it all in.'

'What would you have done?'

'See . . . if that was me, I'd have asked *why*, not what.'

'Sorry.'

'Don't be. It was you who saved me, Dieter.'

'Did I? How?'

'I mean by taking me in when I was deteriorating, desiccating, dehydrating.'

Their conversation, once started, continued without pause as they reminisced and discussed and compared and elucidated and drank too much. They went for a walk to clear their heads and it was as if they'd fallen in with each other again. The stories and ideas and jokes came tumbling out – a state which neither wanted to interrupt with any outside concern or agenda.

'It's funny how we . . .' Ryder began, then seemed to lose track and tried to gather his thoughts. 'Well, you know . . . when we were young, we were told that life would take something from us, exert a cost. But that was what people who'd already lost something said. It didn't seem like a certainty.'

'When I was young – I mean really young – I was convinced I could not be poisoned.'

'And did you ever test that theory out?'

'No, but that did not stop me from believing it was true.'

'It's like the expression, *life chips bits off you*. What are we, lumps of rock?'

Ryder could feel himself getting diverted. But what if he wasn't stone, but a metal edge that was ripped and left ugly and jagged? He wished sometimes that he could shut down the traffic in his mind.

'I think the point is that it takes off the edges. It smooths things out. But in your case, Ryder, it just revealed another set of edges.'

They were back to the twin-strand rope that connected them – that Ryder had played for advantage at times.

'Do you ever, Dieter, think about that thing, that important thing, that would reconcile you with everything . . . if it happened?'

'You mean, like success, validation?'

'I mean more like love. My world now consists of selling expensive objects to rich people who have no knowledge or interest in anything, other than how it will make other people view them. I've become a remora.'

'I thought remora just stick to one bigger fish?'

'So I'm promiscuous, even in metaphor.'

'And what is the thing that would reconcile you?'

Ryder was occasionally on the point of voluntary confession, then recoiled from it. He'd looked down at Lola in her delicate and vulnerable little sleep. He'd felt the heat of her happiness and touched the almost-smiling corners of her mouth. He thought he knew her dreams so well, knew who she was and what made her little tock tick – the unreality that was real and the fantasy that was fact. He believed he knew where her small feet walked, but was there a ghost following close behind – or were her dreams the same as her nightmares? 'Love' was a word he'd never really understood, but once, he'd been warmed by something other than the sun and felt as if he could cry. Alarmed by his own apprehension, he'd taken the sentiment by the throat and carried it back to its cage and locked the door.

It was time to change the subject.

'I always believed in you, Dieter, that you'd be feted . . . famous, even.'

'And that would have been it for you – my success?'

'Does that sound so odd? I'm not one of those repressed artist dealers. I like the people part, and I know you hate it.'

They went to Dieter's place in the Neukölln neighbourhood, to see his new art. It was absurdist neo-dadaism, creating for creation's sake – and Ryder considered that to be the truest art form of all.

'Someone's been busy. Do you have a dealer?'

'You are my dealer, Ryder.'

'Still? You never told me.'

'Just because I am in a different country, does not mean I need a different dealer. Art is universal.'

'So it is, my friend. So it is.'

Anya arrived and made them coffee. She didn't like Ryder in London and that hadn't changed.

'She's still with you?'

'Does that surprise you?'

'I'm not sure. Then again, if I wanted certainty I would've done something else. And here I am, saying this to an artist. The world is so far away from where we started out, Dieter.'

Ryder told him he did the right thing getting out of London – told him about the triumph of branding and about exclusion and money. Asked him what he wanted to do about the flat and workshop.

'Are you moving out?'

'I was thinking about it.'

'Well, when you are ready, just stop paying the rent and notify the leasing agent.'

'What about your stuff in the workshop?'

'I will send Anya over. She can hire a van and drive it back here.'

They drank some beers and talked till late and Dieter accompanied him back to his hotel. Ryder found himself looking at the weave of the artist's hand as much as what he was saying. He jumped readily from thought to observation, interlaced with disclosures about his life and experiences. He hardly mentioned London, which made Ryder believe there was no open sore, but maybe some scar tissue. He thanked Dieter for his loyalty and promised to be the one to break him into the new level. He'd inject heat!

'Just send me your catalogue, when it's ready.'

They shook hands outside the Rocco Forte and said goodbye.

\* \* \*

Ryder hadn't expected to be here this long. He'd been waiting two days for Pavel, and Seth's courier hadn't shown up either. Should he call it all off and just leave? He decided to give it one more day. He felt stuck – stuck in a ski resort with no intention of skiing. All that vitality. All that activity, all that pursuit. And for what – to get back to where you started? It reminded him of T. S. Eliot's 'Little Gidding' and seemed a ridiculous parade – although, put like that, almost a familiar one. But why should he bother to understand it? It could remain one of the few activities beyond his appreciation, like gambling.

He'd had enough of looking at the yellowing wood of his hotel room ceiling and its matching pine walls. He had to get out, even if it meant enduring the cold again. Waiting had become his *métier* – waiting on rich people to make up their minds and finish playing their games. He left his key behind the desk, around which an old woman popped her head and smiled. He smiled back imbecilically, in that way he suspected people did when abroad. He didn't know where he was going, which meant he would inevitably end up in the bar, like he had yesterday. He'd put on all the clothes he had for the trip down the hill, which wasn't enough to keep out the chillness.

Walking in the tracks made by tyres through the snow helped. His feet got cold, but not wet. Cold was tolerable – cold and wet wasn't. Ryder could see the crowd outside the bar; they did like their drinking, the off-piste sorts. People were milling about, still in their ski suits, boisterous and smoking furiously. He slipped into the breath-warm bar and threaded his way through the pressed bodies, which gave way. Space opened then closed around him. It was like being a student again, in a crowd that was in the process of getting drunk – merry, but not yet messy. Maybe they were all agoraphobics who'd suffered terribly that day and this was their group therapy? If people were the problem, they were also the solution.

He got served quickly and didn't want to give up his place at the bar and have to muscle his way back to it. Then he made the understandable mistake of letting a pretty girl through. He was like a detached barnacle, kicked off its rock, and he looked about to see if there was another he could latch on to.

'Ryder . . . what on earth are you doing here?'

He turned to see the flushed face of Jonnie, his erstwhile flat-mate, who gave him a hug then stood back to look at him, as if he was an apparition. A blast from the past.

'I didn't know you skied.'

'I don't.'

'Jesus, then why are you here?'

'I was misinformed.'

Jonnie was with the girl who'd pushed through, and he'd come to help her with the round of drinks for the table. They brought Ryder back with them and introduced him to the others, whose names he instantly forgot – except for Rosie, the girl he'd made room for at the bar. He wondered where Jonnie's fiancé was.

'How's Sophie?'

'She's fine, as far as I know.'

'Did you marry her?'

'We came close.'

'Was it because I said she could be our cleaner?'

'It had nothing to do with you, Ryder.'

Ryder had to shuffle up tight into an alcove – where he'd been directed by Jonnie, who took the only vacant stool. He squeezed in next to Rosie, who didn't seem to mind, and nor did he. She gave him a full-set-of-teeth smile.

'So, if you don't ski, then what are you doing here?'

'Waiting.'

'For what?'

'Someone to arrive.'

He could sense the swell of her breast on the back of his arm, which made him feel old, but good. She wouldn't let the subject of his presence go.

'It must be lust or money.'

He leaned back and felt the press of her, returning the smile she'd given him.

'And why not love?'

'Isn't that covered by lust?'

The rest of the group had become interested now and were leaning forward in their seats, so he had to give them something.

'I'm here to sell a painting . . . so I suppose it's a combination of love for art and lust for money.'

Rosie said she was going to dance. She slipped out past Ryder, using his shoulder as a balance. He watched her go and wondered if he was supposed to follow. He'd have known for sure when he was younger – been able to interpret the subtle nuances of flirtation. But he didn't want to dance, especially with someone as young as Rosie, so he bought a round of drinks instead, which ingratiated him with the company and prompted Jonnie to invite him to dinner with them.

Two or three drinks in and it was easy to fall into line. The music and dancing, the waitresses sashaying through the suggestible crowd with trays of beer going out and trays of empties filing back in. Maybe skiing wasn't the most ridiculous thing in the world after all. He tried to remember why he'd hated these people just a couple of days ago, with their preening display of fake adventurism. He was never going to be one of them, but he liked this particular bar, the light-headed altitude feeling and the acceptable claustrophobia of the ambience.

Jonnie was getting a little animated. 'Better take it a bit slow. What are we, Ryder, pushing forty and pissed up before seven.'

There was no 'we' as far as Ryder was concerned. And he hoped this wasn't going to go down the misremembered-times-of-their-youth shtick. The wheeling-out of anecdotes, especially in front of Rosie. It would be both lame and fake. There's to be no bullshit about the past here!

'So, who are you meeting?'

'My Russian.'

'Ah, Russians,' Rosie intoned in a hanging, needling way, as though she had the scoop on them. 'Is he a millionaire?'

'Who said he's a he?'

'Is she your lover?'

'He's a billionaire.'

'Or bullionaire?'

She said it with a heavy Russian accent, the 'aire' rippling on her lips. In truth, Ryder didn't know if Pavel was or wasn't a billionaire, but it sounded good.

The group went to Restaurant La Grange for dinner, where they had fondue and traditional raclette and Zürcher Geschnetzeltes and drank Glögg and cherry juleps. Ryder was enjoying himself for the first time since he'd arrived and was thinking about his chances with Rosie. That's when the text came from Pavel, asking him to come to his chalet and bring the Picasso. Ryder asked if it could wait until morning, but Pavel didn't reply, so he thought he'd better go – he didn't want to do anything to jeopardise the sale.

He said goodnight and hoped that he and Rosie would meet again. She said what about tomorrow? He said he'd call her. Then he took a cab to his hotel to pick up the painting and went from there to the chalet.

After knocking and getting no answer, Ryder entered through the unlocked door. Pavel was nowhere in sight, so he deposited the painting in the living room and stepped out the back, into the Alpine night. He could see footsteps in the snow, leading off into the cold, deserted darkness. Where the fuck was the Russian? He saw the flare of a match and moved a few paces forward, to be free of the interior light. Pavel was sitting on a kind of log seat, lighting up a cigar. Ryder knew it was him by the shape of his skull and the outline of his body. He looked like a man who was waiting for something – something he knew was inevitable. Waiting for Godot, or maybe Golgo?

Pavel saw him and beckoned him over. The Russian filled two glasses from the bottle he was drinking out of. Ryder brushed snow from the log seat and sat beside the bigger man, taking an exploratory sip from the glass, hoping it was whisky. He nodded approvingly when he discovered it was – and good whisky at that. Single malt. The Russian sat up from his slumped position, trying to rouse himself. Ryder noticed the bottle was almost empty.

'I have kept you waiting . . . Sorry, business.'

'I've been amusing myself watching people having what they consider to be fun, going up in mechanical lifts and then returning to where they started.'

Ryder didn't mention that he'd just started to enjoy himself, and the company of Rosie – something that Pavel had unfortunately interrupted.

'Did you bring the painting?''

'It's inside.'

They continued to talk and drink out in the cold, and Ryder wished they could go in, but didn't say as much. His clothes weren't designed for being outside in the freezing night and, if it weren't for the whisky, he was sure he'd have died from hypothermia by now. But the deal wasn't done yet, so he was prepared to put up with a lot.

Eventually, Pavel suggested they go inside, where they opened another bottle and Pavel gave him some more suitable clothes with which to endure the mountain climate. The Russian was in no hurry to get to the point of the meeting and seemed to be deliberately delaying, telling Ryder the story about his grandmother and foxes that he'd previously related to Swan2 at the Connaught Hotel. It was as if he was looking back on his life and reminiscing – more for himself than his reluctant audience. It was a strange scenario and almost surreal, not what Ryder expected. He'd hoped he could clinch the deal quickly and get back to Rosie at the Restaurant La Grange. That wasn't going to happen now.

Eventually, halfway through the second bottle, Ryder decided to ask Pavel to take a look at the Picasso the next time he went for a piss.

'I've left it out for you to see.'

Ryder left him alone to contemplate and, when he joined Pavel, the painting had been hung on the wall and the Russian was sitting on the sofa, facing it but not really seeing.

Ryder didn't want to rush him.

'Take your time.'

'Leave it overnight. Come tomorrow.'

## CHAPTER 31

# DID HE JUMP
# OR WAS HE PUSHED?

Morning broke and Ryder reckoned it had all gone very well the previous night. It wasn't until he got to within thirty yards of Muransky's chalet that he realised something was off. He'd already seen the police car, but it wasn't until he turned the corner that he encountered the group of officers standing outside on the driveway. Their attention was immediately drawn to him.

'*Qui êtes-vous, monsieur?*'

Ryder considered answering in French, but better to be straight from the beginning, to avoid any misunderstanding later.

'My name is Ryder.'

The policeman resumed in English. 'And what are you doing here?'

'I have business with Monsieur Muransky.'

'What business?'

'Art . . . he's buying a piece of art. Can you tell me what's going on?'

'Wait here, monsieur.'

A detective emerged from the chalet and asked if he'd be prepared to accompany them to the *poste de police* at Sembrancher to answer a few more questions.

'Am I under arrest?'

'No, no . . . of course not.'

Ryder considered refusing, but he didn't know what was going on and, until he did, it was better to cooperate.

A couple of hours later, he was shown into an interview room and given coffee and an ashtray. The detective from the chalet, who introduced himself as Sergeant Bernier, sat opposite him.

'We are hoping you may be able to help us, Monsieur Ryder.'

'If I can.'

'We want to establish what happened at Monsieur Muransky's chalet last night. Any assistance you can provide would be appreciated.'

Bernier's method of interview struck Ryder as direct, polite and reasonable. He wondered how many British policemen would be able to have an equivalent conversation in French or German, or even strike that tone in their native tongue.

'I'll help in any way I can, but it may not be much.'

Ryder was eager to know what happened – and not just that. There was also the not-inconsequential matter of a three-million-dollar painting hanging on the chalet wall. He thought about saying, if he wasn't under arrest, then he'd like to leave. But that wouldn't look good, and it wouldn't help him retrieve the Picasso.

Bernier's questions seemed to be in a sequence to tie down a timeline, and he knew that Ryder had been with Pavel for a good deal of last night. Ryder gave him the answers he wanted – straight, factual, checkable as needed. He showed the detective the text he'd received from Pavel and the receipt he'd obtained from the cab company that picked him up from the chalet. He demonstrated his willingness to cooperate. He'd gone to the chalet after receiving the text – he'd drunk and talked with Pavel for a length of time. His departure was confirmed by the taxi receipt. All very straightforward.

'I wonder what you two had to talk about for three hours? Was it normal? How well did you know him?'

'I knew him as a business associate. We met in London a couple of times. He's a very talkative man, especially when he's drinking.'

'And was he drinking?'

'Yes, quite heavily.'

'And you?'

'I had a couple of whiskys.'

'Just a couple?'

'Yes, just a couple.'

Ryder thought this was a good time to bring up the subject of the Picasso. He was worried about it being damaged or stolen.

Bernier was non-committal. 'So, you went there to sell him this painting?'

'At his request.'

'And you brought the painting with you?'

'Yes.'

'A very valuable painting?'

'Very valuable.'

'Did you not think that was rather rash, Monsieur Ryder, to be publicly transporting such a valuable piece of merchandise?'

'Not really, it's done all the time. I mean, it was in Switzerland to begin with, I just had to transport it from Geneva to Verbier.'

Bernier asked Ryder if he was the owner of the painting and was told he was the dealer – the representative of the owner, with full authority. The detective asked to see the paperwork and Ryder showed him the documents from the freeport and from Ashook.

'I need some assurance that the painting is safe. Can you do that for me?'

'Where exactly is it?'

'In the living room. I put it there for Monsieur Muransky to look at.'

Bernier left the room. He returned fifteen minutes later with more coffee and nodded his head. 'The painting is safe. Did Monsieur Muransky actually purchase it last night? I have to establish legal ownership, you understand.'

'We were to finalise the deal this morning.'

'In that case, there may be a delay in returning it.'

'But I have to leave Verbier very soon.'

'We will give you a receipt.'

Ryder was becoming more than a little agitated. A receipt wouldn't be enough to leave a Picasso in the hands of a bunch of provincial policemen. He'd worked hard to recover from the London Gallery disaster. Ashook would go crazy and this would knock him back again.

'I'm afraid I can't leave the painting; it must either be paid for by Monsieur Muransky or come with me when I leave.'

Bernier didn't respond, but carried on with his prepared line of questioning.

'So, you talked for three hours?'

'Yes – I've told you, people become talkative when they're drinking.'

Ryder tried to second-guess the detective. He was anxious to finish this and get out of there; to phone Pavel to find out where he was and what was happening.

'If you're asking me what his state of mind was – well, I'd say he was a little melancholic. Is that an answer?'

'A very good answer. Thank you.'

'In truth, I try not to get involved in my clients' lives. I keep a professional distance.'

'Very wise.'

'Are you able to tell me what's going on?'

'Monsieur Muransky took his own life last night.'

Ryder's mouth fell open. The revelation knocked the wind out of him for a moment or two and Bernier could see he was physically shocked.

'How?'

'He hanged himself from one of the beams in his chalet.'

Bernier seemed satisfied. He sat back and closed his file. It gave finality to the interview – the correct chronology had been established and Ryder had convinced him that he wasn't involved.

Back at the hotel, Ryder called Ashook and told him what had happened and he wasn't sure when the Picasso would be returned.

He couldn't hang about in Verbier and didn't know what he should do about it.

Ashook took the news calmly – more calmly than Ryder had anticipated.

'Did your guy pay?'

'Unfortunately, no.'

'All right, look, it's insured. Actually, for more than it's worth.'

'But, I'm sure we'll get it back . . . in time.'

'You don't really believe that, do you, Ryder?'

Ryder didn't know whether he believed it or not. What he *did* believe was that Pavel hadn't killed himself. Why would a man like him do that? And what about his son in England? The whole thing stank, and Ryder couldn't wait to get the fuck out of Verbier as soon as possible.

Ashook said he'd send some insurance documents to the flat in London and Ryder should say the Picasso was confiscated. He'd need something from the police to confirm they'd kept it, and also an incident number.

Ryder didn't want to go back to the police station in Sembrancher, but he equally didn't want to owe Ashook three million dollars for losing his painting. He went down to the hotel bar to have a badly needed drink and a think about what had happened and what he should do. He was on his third large scotch when a woman approached him. She looked familiar, but his disorganised mind couldn't quite place from where.

'Ryder . . . good, you're still here.'

It was Metallic. What was she doing in Verbier?

'Sorry to be so late, but there was a delay in appropriating the diamonds from the bank in Zurich.'

Ryder was even more confused now – what had Metallic to do with the diamonds? Was she the courier? He needed to ring Seth, but she told him not to.

'No need to ring anyone, Ryder, everything's cool now.'

She took a package wrapped in colourful paper from her bag and made a bit of a show of handing it over to him.

'Happy birthday, darling!'

She kissed him on the lips and quickly ordered him a drink.

'Now, I must go. See you later.'

Ryder watched her from the hotel window. She crossed the street and got into the back of a black Mercedes with tinted windows. The car drove away, slowly and deliberately. He watched until it was out of sight.

He tried to put the pieces together. Seth had insisted he meet Pavel in Switzerland – now Pavel was dead. Everywhere Seth was, Metallic seemed to appear also. Now she'd turned up with what he assumed to be the diamonds. When he came back from New York with Seth, he was arrested and taken to a police station – what would happen when he came back from Switzerland? In his room, Ryder opened the box and, sure enough, inside was a purple velvet bag. He emptied out the contents – three dozen blue diamonds. He didn't know how much they were worth, but he reckoned it must be a lot. The thing was, if Metallic had come over to retrieve them from Zurich, why couldn't she take them back to Seth? It didn't make sense for her to bring them to Verbier for him to transport.

Ryder didn't like any of this. He decided to get out of there the next day, before anything else happened. But first he had to see Bernier about the Picasso. Travelling to Sembrancher now was out of the question, so he decided to go back to the chalet. Maybe Bernier was still there and, if not, some other policeman might be able to give him what he needed for Ashook.

Next morning, when he got there, he was surprised to see that there were no police cars present. He knocked on the front door and waited. Nobody answered and he was walking away when he heard a male voice calling from behind. 'Can I help you?'

He turned to see Vladimir Gazmonov standing in the doorway.

'Ryder? What are you doing here?'

'I was hoping to find a policeman.'

'Ahh, you know about poor Pavel?'

'They interviewed me.'

'Really? Why would they do that?'

'I was here the night he died.'

Ryder deliberately didn't say 'the night he killed himself'.

Gazmonov invited him into the reception area and asked why he was there that night and did he know why Pavel had done it. Ryder explained about the sale and said he had no clue as to why Pavel would have done such a thing.

'What are *you* doing here, Vladimir?'

'I was in Vienna. Pavel's son called me and asked me to come. There is no other family. I am here to have the body released.'

'Will it go back to Russia?'

'Certainly not. Pavel has not been anywhere near Russia for many years, Ryder.'

'How come?'

Gazmonov lowered his voice, as if someone might be listening, then explained to Ryder that Pavel was somewhat of a fugitive. He always kept his whereabouts secret and only confirmed appointments at the last minute, for which he invariably turned up late.

'I don't understand . . .'

'To be honest, Ryder, I don't really know. He was a very secretive man. But, if I was to guess, I would say there was some kind of . . . how you say, contract, or fatwa, or price on his head.'

'Don't you think his so-called suicide is suspicious?'

'That is not for me to say. I do not want to be involved, and neither should you. I am only here to arrange for the body to be flown to the UK.'

'The UK?'

'That is where his son lives now. There will be a cremation.'

Gazmonov stood up, indicating that it was time for Ryder to leave. Passing the living room, he noticed the Picasso still hanging on the wall and the painting that Pavel had taken down and put to one side was gone.

'That painting . . . that's the one I brought for Pavel to buy.'

'And did he buy it?'

'No.'

'So it is yours?'

'Yes.'

'You must take it.'

'Listen, Vladimir, I won't ever see Pavel again. Do you think it might be possible for me to pay my last respects before I leave?'

Ryder intended to catch a late flight to London, but the situation had changed. He thought about bringing the Picasso with him, as a dealer, he had a licence to transport art. But he wasn't sure what would be waiting for him when he got back.

He dropped the painting off at his hotel room, then made a quick purchase of a box cutter and a sack needle and some synthetic thread at a hardware store, before linking up with Gazmonov again.

They arrived at the morgue, and Vladimir Gazmonov showed his authorisation papers to the attendant and slipped him fifty dollars to allow Ryder to be alone with his friend to pay his last respects. The body had been prepared the night before and was in a small room off the main area of the morgue, waiting to be flown to the UK for cremation. Pavel lay in a wooden box that was a cross between a coffin and a tea chest, and he looked indifferent – taking death as he had taken life.

Ryder put on a pair of rubber gloves and unbuttoned the dead man's shirt. The autopsy cut, down the chest and stomach, was still fresh, and he took the box cutter from his pocket and opened a small hole in it. The stench of formaldehyde almost made him vomit, but he knew he had to be quick. He took the velvet bag of diamonds out of his pocket and stuffed them in between Pavel's intestines. Then he sewed the autopsy cut back up with the sack needle and synthetic thread.

Gazmonov was still talking to the attendant when he emerged. Ryder thanked them both for their assistance, then the Russian dropped him back at his hotel.

Ryder had three options: take the late flight to London as he'd intended; go to Geneva and deposit the Picasso back at the freeport; or the third – which he took.

He boarded the train to Berlin at 10:30 p.m., made his way to the sleeping cabin and settled in for the twelve-hour trip. Although he felt exhausted, it took him a long time to drift off; even then, the night was filled with ghosts, and several times he got up and paced the corridor. The train pulled into Berlin Central at 10:00 a.m. the following morning and he took a taxi to Dieter's apartment-studio in Neukölln, where the artist was surprised to see him so soon after his previous visit.

'You look terrible, Ryder, what has happened?'

'Nothing. I just want to leave this here.'

Dieter looked at the painting.

'Is that *Nature Morte*, the Picasso?'

'A copy. Look, Dieter, I don't want to have to lug it about. Do you think Anya could bring it over when she comes with the van?'

'Of course. How about some tea – you look as if you have not slept for a week.'

'I can't stay, Dieter. I have to get to the airport.'

Because the crematorium flames wouldn't wait.

## CHAPTER 32

# INFERNAL AFFAIRS

Back in the UK, Ryder disembarked from the plane and collected his suitcase from the baggage hall. He expected to see Seth at arrivals, but he wasn't there. He left the terminal and reached his car – Seth wasn't there either. Just as he was unloading his case from the trolley, the sound of screeching tyres tore up the car park and blue flashing lights appeared out of nowhere. Uniforms advanced cautiously and Ryder's hands were handcuffed behind his back. He was placed in the back of a police car. His suitcase was placed inside another. They were taken to Paddington Green police station.

Déjà vu!

Ryder was shown into a cell at Paddington Green – it looked like the same one he'd been held in the last time he was arrested, after being in New York with Seth. But then, they were probably all alike. The uniformity of custody – there was no penthouse here. Was it a coincidence that every time he was associated with Seth, he got arrested? He didn't think so. Just as well he'd anticipated something like this happening. He'd had a premonition it might – a Lola-esque forewarning. Maybe she'd sent him a subliminal tip-off from wherever she was?

Nobody came to the cell for some time, and he assumed they were searching his luggage and his car. He tried to stay calm, just sitting and waiting. He remembered the last time he was arrested – he remembered reciting *Hamlet* to pass the time. They couldn't keep him here forever. They'd have to come and open the cell door at some point. And they did.

Ryder was brought to an interview room, where he waited again. After about fifteen minutes, two detectives came into the room and turned on a tape recorder. He told himself there was nothing to worry about – after all, Seth had said there was nothing illegal – his friend would be coming to the station with a lawyer. They told him they had information that he was smuggling contraband into the country and that's why he was arrested.

'What kind of contraband?'

'We're not at liberty to say.'

'And where did that information come from?'

'We're not at liberty to say.'

'And have you found any contraband?'

'Not yet.'

After that, Ryder was strip-searched but nothing was found. He was returned to the cell and he waited some more, before banging on the door and asking for a lawyer. He was ignored.

Some hours later, the cell door was opened by a uniformed policeman and he was taken back to the interview room, where the same two detectives questioned him again.

'What were you doing in Switzerland?'

'I was there on business.'

'What kind of business?'

'Selling a painting. I'm an art dealer.'

'And before that, in Berlin?'

'Visiting a friend.'

He refused to answer any more questions until a lawyer was made available to him. They said that wouldn't be necessary as they had no more questions – for now. The detectives left the interview room and, a few minutes later, he was released. He was given back his suitcase and picked up his car from the station car park. The vehicle had obviously been gone over, good and proper – and, as he left by the rear exit, he thought he saw Seth talking to one of the detectives who'd interviewed him. Then again, maybe not – maybe just someone who looked like Seth. All scumbags looked alike.

Ryder went home to Dieter's flat and poured himself a large whisky. Next morning, he telephoned Vladimir Gazmonov and asked if Pavel's body had been safely returned to the UK.

Midnight fell on the city and the sky was dull and starless. Aliens crossed the street in front of his headlights. They didn't know he knew, or maybe they did but didn't care. Maybe they knew the theory of everything, as he did. That temperature was radiation and radiation was energy and energy was matter and matter was man. And that each question asked spawned another, and that empty space wasn't empty at all. And that Merlin was baptised by Blaise and beguiled by Nimue and entangled in a thorn bush by the Lady of the Lake, where he still was to that very day. And his voice could sometimes be heard, on still, starless nights.

Ryder drove west through the sleeping city to the Wellbeloved Funeral Home in Willesden. The night was dark and dense and no one was aware of his mission. He hoped. He had to be quick, before the diamonds were incinerated with Pavel in the crematorium. He turned the car into Leighton Gardens, near the sports centre, and waited. After making sure nobody was about, he got out and walked in silence a short distance to the back of the funeral home on Chamberlayne Road, and climbed over a low brick wall. Then he made his way to the rear entrance, where he forced the flimsy lock. He looked around by torchlight until he found Pavel's coffin, which looked like a tea chest. Undoubtedly, they would install him in something more appropriate for the funeral.

Ryder unscrewed the coffin lid and looked down at Pavel – still looking indifferent about it all. He half expected the Russian to sit up and slap him on the back and laugh. He covered his mouth and nose and cut the stitches to the dead man's stomach. Then he reached inside. He couldn't find the velvet bag at first and he had to feel around through the intestines before locating it. As he was about to withdraw it, the smell of the place seemed to grow more powerful. It began to get the better of him, overpowering him, crawling on him like a living thing. He tried to brush it off – the smell of death – as Pavel's features detached themselves from the rest of his body and became entities in themselves. Nose and ears and eyes and mouth. Ryder told himself to concentrate. Slow down. Stay cool!

Everything about him was dull and colourless. A sad colour. The colour of melancholy. Monochrome. He began to shake, convulsing and dropping his torch. He bent over and everything went black. Like the night. Like death. Ryder tried blindly to find the exit, but the entire funeral home had become one thing. An entity in itself. A live-dead thing. It swallowed him like Jonah and he couldn't find his way out. Everything was shimmering and alive-dead – carpets and furniture and floors and ceilings. Almost transparent. Non-existent. Ghostlike. Hypothetical. He felt his way around the soft flesh-like walls, until the crematorium furnace opened up in front of him and he fell into it.

Ryder felt the jets of pure flame hit him from all sides. They became a swarm of red-hot needles, biting into his skin, blinding him, ripping him to pieces.

Wait!

Slow down!

He lay still on the floor, until he could see the hazy outline of the room. He vomited as he waited in the oppressive heat and oppressive smell. He felt claustrophobic and panicky, but he waited – for the effects of the formaldehyde, or whatever it was that had caused him to collapse, faded. It was in that moment that he realised the real meaning of life was death – and the real meaning of death was life. But it was transitory – momentary – and he'd forget; he knew he'd forget.

His watering eyes cleared and he could see the outline of Pavel's coffin above him. Ryder got to his feet and tried to brush the vomit from his clothes. He didn't know how long he'd been lying there; he found the torch and shone it on his watch – 2:30 a.m. He got to his feet and looked into the coffin, reached inside the corpse and pulled out the slimy velvet bag. He tidied up the dead man as best he could and replaced the lid.

And said *sorry Pavel – and thank you*.

Outside, the early-morning streets were unnaturally quiet. No people moved up or down and cars stood silent and stationary in the road. The wind lay quiet behind Willesden Junction, as if it was in hiding. Ryder walked quickly back to his car – he could almost taste his own apprehension. He shoved the velvet bag into the glove compartment and started the engine. It sounded louder than usual, almost startling him, and he hoped it wouldn't wake the entire neighbourhood, like his van when he worked for Boulets.

Light and laughter were the flowers and dreamscapes at the moment of expiration. And god – god, who was the supreme fascist. Australopithecus. Zinjanthropus. Olduvai Gorge. Lake Turkana. Laetoli. Hadar. And it wasn't enough to say the earth went round the sun; he had to know why. And the more he knew, the more he didn't know.

'Ryder.'

'Ophelia . . . ?'

'Ryder!'

Ryder woke to a hand shaking his shoulder. A deep feeling of guilt came over him, as if he was responsible for every fucking thing in the fucking world. He tried to focus on where he was, but it was lost in the shambles of the situation. And because the situation was serious, Ryder sent it away and concentrated on the surreal. He began to panic – until he heard the familiar voice again.

'Wake up!'

His eyes gradually focused on Anya's face.

'What day is it?'

'Friday.'

Christ, he'd been asleep for three days – or maybe not asleep, but certainly in some on-and-off state of oblivion.

He roused himself and swung his feet onto the floor. She was holding something – it looked like a painting.

'Dieter sent this. D'you want some tea?'

'Yes, thank you. How did you get in?'

'I still have keys.'

She leaned the painting against the wall and went to boil the kettle. Ryder checked his phone – thirty-six missed calls and twenty-one text messages, most of them from Seth. He drank the tea and took a shower, while Anya loaded the list of items Dieter had given her into the Mercedes-Benz Sprinter. After she left, handing over the spare keys to him, he called Seth.

'Ryder, where the fuck have you been?'

'In bed.'

They arranged to meet at The Crabtree, by the river in Fulham. Ryder explained how he'd been arrested by the police again and kept locked up for twenty-four hours before being released without charge.

'What's going on, Seth?'

'You tell me, Ryder. Where's the merchandise?'

'Where do you think? It was in my case but, when I got it back from the coppers, it was gone. This is very similar to what happened after New York, and you told me it was all above board, Seth. If I'd known this was going to happen, I'd never have agreed ..'

'All right! All right!'

Ryder managed to sound as irate and indignant as possible, while Seth grew more and more agitated.

'I have a man on the inside. I'll make enquiries.'

'Inside where?'

Seth didn't answer and Ryder wondered if this set-up, and it certainly seemed like a set-up, was in some way meant to punish him for trying to fuck Floss. Hypothetical situation, as Pavel would put it:

Seth tips off the police so Ryder is arrested and charged and found guilty and either fined or sent to prison or both. He knows he's been grassed and he knows why. It would be a very heavy price for Seth to pay for that slice of revenge, but his admission of a 'man on the inside' meant that he'd be able to retrieve the diamonds either by producing some documentation or by paying a price that he considered worth it.

That was the hypothesis, but what happened when Seth's man on the inside told him that Ryder didn't have any diamonds? He obviously knew that by now, which explained his agitation.

Seth walked away from their table and Ryder could see him talking on his phone and waving his free arm around. He came back over after about ten minutes.

'Where are the diamonds, Ryder?'

'At the police station, I assume.'

'Christ, Ryder, I don't believe you! Why did they let you go?'

'Ask your man on the inside.'

Seth threw his glass across the room. The bar staff asked them both to leave. Outside, Seth grabbed him by the collar. Ryder pushed him away.

'If you ask me, Seth, your man on the inside is bent. Either that or the merchandise got stolen from my case en route from Verbier to London.'

'Or when you stopped off in Berlin.'

Ryder was about to reply, but Seth was already storming away up the street, half turning and pointing his finger back in an accusatory fashion.

'You saw what happened to Pavel!'

And then he was gone, round the corner.

\* \* \*

Ryder was busy over the weekend. He decided to keep Dieter's flat and workshop and to give up Holmes's shop. He moved his stuff there and rehired Cassie to take charge. The workshop would be his gallery and he'd have it renovated for display purposes. He also phoned Ashook to say he was unable to get the documentation from the Swiss police because he had to come back before arranging it with the detective in charge. He promised to get back onto it as soon as possible. Ashook told him not to bother. Pavel Muransky's suicide was common knowledge by now and his insurance people would handle everything. He apologised to Ryder for any inconvenience that might have been caused on his behalf.

On Monday morning, Ryder took a cab down to Hatton Garden, the Diamond Row of London. The smell of money was everywhere – secret money, furtive and fraternal. Esoteric. A polished brass plaque read simply the company name, and the modest entrance belied the spaciousness of the interior. Ryder was dressed in a three-piece suit by Aquascutum with a pale blue Prada shirt and a brightly coloured Miu Miu silk tie, with matching handkerchief cascading from his top pocket. He had coffee from a silver tray with china cups and cream and brown sugar, and he showed them the diamonds. There were a lot of rapid words in Yiddish and some arm waving.

This was where deals were done, in this nondescript grouping of little streets between the West End and the City. A security camera scanned the room, while a uniformed guard escorted Ryder and the dealers to an elevator with iron-mesh sliding doors. All access points inside the building were fitted with digital-pulse induction detectors. The guard adjusted the pulse signal, which allowed them to get into the elevator. There was barely enough room and they were crushed uncomfortably together for the descent into the underground passageways. Ryder seemed to be reacting rather nervously to the security guard's Old Spice aftershave. He was sweating slightly and licking his dry lips.

The elevator reached the bottom of the shaft and, when the door was swung back, he was first out – gasping for air. The guard led them down a long corridor, with neon lights set into an arched ceiling. He halted outside a white-tiled room with prison-cell bars separating it from the corridor. Another guard stood just inside the barred door. They talked to each other briefly – perhaps giving some kind of password or something – and the barred door was unlocked. The men from the shop above went inside first, followed by Ryder, while the first security guard stayed outside.

The ceiling vibrated as traffic passed overhead and Ryder looked up nervously. Several white-coated jewellers worked inside the room. Precious stones of all colours and shapes and sizes were scattered around a variety of benches. Scientific-looking apparatus and gem-cutting equipment were set up around the white-tiled walls, and they all stopped what they were doing when Ryder's diamonds were displayed.

An old man with grey hair and half-spectacles balanced on the end of his nose examined the stones under an illuminated loupe, then spoke to his associates in a low voice – using words like 'prisms' and 'faceting' and 'cleaves' and 'fractures' and 'atomic structure' and 'octagonal cabochon' and 'pendeloque'.

One of the dealers from the shop above turned to Ryder. 'He says his analysis will take a little time. You have seen the security arrangements; will you trust us enough to leave the stones here?'

Ryder shook his head.

'If the diamonds stay, then I stay with them.'

'The analysis could take several hours.'

'I said I'll wait.'

'Very well. Shall we at least adjourn to the office? You'll be more comfortable there.'

The men who brought him down led the way back upstairs, accompanied again by the security guard. In an office looking out over that part of London, Ryder was offered a choice of cognac or liqueurs, which he declined and settled for some tea. The talk was about money routes and the speed at which electronic cash travelled these days, and its defiance of the global financial systems in the face of all attempts at regulation.

And although money travelled fast, time travelled slowly for Ryder. An offshore account was discussed and details were determined and some documents produced for signing. Ryder was reluctant to put his name to anything, but the jewellers assured him that they were bona fide dealers and there would be no double-crosses or deceptions of any kind.

'You didn't think, Mr Ryder, that you were going to walk out of here with a suitcase full of cash?'

That was exactly what Ryder thought. But then, he was a dealer himself, albeit in a different marketplace, so he understood the rules to a certain extent.

After a couple of hours, the dealers took a call from down below and one of them listened without speaking, then put down the phone. His face was inscrutable and he took a sip of liqueur before saying anything.

'The stones are very unique indeed – flawless, in fact. Because of the quality, each stone is estimated to have a value of eighty thousand pounds sterling. After commission, the total amount due to you, Mr Ryder, should you agree to do business with us, would be approximately two million pounds.'

Ryder knew that, if they were telling him the diamonds were worth a couple of million, then they were probably worth a lot more, but he wasn't in a position to bargain.

'OK.'

They shook hands and the deal was complete.

## CHAPTER 33

# THE SONG OF WANDERING RYDER

Ryder looked at himself in the gilt mirror he'd found at the back of Holmes's shop when he was clearing it out. The label was still attached and it was the only thing of any value that Holmes had left behind. Maybe he didn't like the sight of himself after the aborted court case – maybe his reflection in it accused him of some unforgiveable misdemeanour? A conceptual Dorian Gray – the Caravaggio of The Gasworks. It belonged to Ryder now. He wouldn't sell it; it would remind him of its ostentatious owner. And it would detract from his role as a primary art dealer if he did.

He reckoned he looked the same now as when he'd taken over the lease all those years ago. Without harsh down-lighting or a large photograph for comparison, he'd be hard pressed to say how he looked any different. Did he feel sorry for those contemporaries who'd lost their hair or got fat? A smile broke across his face – of course not! It was his fortieth birthday in a couple of days, but that was the least of his concerns. He'd let go of certain cherished ideals over time – like staying forever young.

Ryder couldn't face going back to the numbing VAT return, so he picked up the *FT* supplement, 'How to Spend It', and lounged on the sofa, Holmes-style. He'd taken to buying it on a Saturday, when it pretended to be a normal paper and he pretended to be interested in it. He had to force himself to read the rest of it before he could have some pay-off with the supplement. He even stopped pretending to be offended by the tone of the rag. He read it in the same way he was told to read *Cosmopolitan* – to learn how the enemy thinks. But what once had a sociological codicil was now more an exercise in luxe porn. To him, they were selling an impossible lifestyle, much as the images of women in regular pornography were photoshopped and one-dimensional.

Of course, if they had categories, then he was good on bars, late-night clubs, restaurants and exotic women – not porn-mag exotic, more existential and unintegrated. He was less good on skiing, polo and four-figure leather luggage. Property as a fashion item wasn't a game for him – was it for anyone? Was this their ideal reader – one so rich and credulous that they could be bounced into purchasing something that made them look fatuous? Yet that was rather hypocritical of him, because it was exactly the type of client he was dealing with. And that was the thing about Ryder – he despised dissimulation in others, but tended to deny it in himself.

After selling the Picasso and transferring that money to the offshore account set up by the gem dealers, Ryder was now a rich man. Not obscenely rich, in the parlance of the modern billionaire class, but rich enough to relax. As a birthday gift to himself, he decided to take some time out and lie low for a while, in case Seth sent someone to sort him out. Cassie was looking after the business quite competently and he didn't need to be there in person; he could deal with difficult queries over the phone. In any case, he found that paucity gave him an air of mystique – the more unavailable he was, the more people wanted to deal with him.

And his presence at Pavel's chalet at the time of the Russian's death had given Ryder an added kudos – an air of intrigue. Everyone wanted to get close to him, to see if the renown rubbed off. He had acquired what he always wanted. Notoriety.

He considered somewhere abroad: maybe New York to visit Holmes, or Venice to relive his visit there with St-Hilaire, or back to

Berlin to shoot the breeze with Dieter and Anya. But Dieter's place had been broken into while the artist was out one night, and Ryder reckoned it might not be a safe haven. In fact, he'd be better off staying in the UK. But where? Where could he be insular and anonymous?

Trawling the internet, Ryder came across a website called Wanderlusts, where you could hire a wagon and travel along new horse-drawn routes that were being established in rural areas. This appealed to him as a sanitised version of what life must have been like for Lola when he first met her, all those years ago.

After some instruction on how to drive a bow-top and handle the friendly horse, Ryder set off from the first camp. There were inns and facilities every few miles to cater for him and his animal. The weather was good and he even started to enjoy the solitude and self-exile of the backroads and lanes. The lifestyle was a lure – not just for jaded business types, but all kinds of others – and he came across performers and magicians and jewellery makers and druids and drop-outs as he chugged along at a leisurely pace.

His route took him through the Forest of Dean in Gloucestershire, where he came across a glade with mushrooms growing. He wondered if they were the hallucinogenic kind and he decided to try some, hoping they wouldn't poison him. They didn't, but he got lost and seemed to be going round in circles. His next scheduled stop was a place called The Stables, which was marked on his map; but, instead, he came to a clearing with a ramshackle cabin. It had a thatched roof and timber walls and a gabled stone chimney. Ryder approached the door, to see if it was occupied – maybe they could direct him to The Stables. Nobody answered his knocking and the door was slightly ajar, so he went inside. There was a beamed ceiling with lots of glass jars hanging from it – no furniture, except for a single wooden table. It had an earthen floor and a brick fireplace full of ashes and the whole structure made strange noises, as if it had a life of its own.

It was getting dark, so Ryder unhitched the horse, gave it water and allowed it to graze, while he settled down for the night inside the bow-top. The next thing he knew, he was over in the trees, look-ing at the wagon and horse from a distance. He could see the cabin, but had some sense of not wanting to approach strange buildings because of the danger from dogs and guns and loud voices.

Lola watched for a while from her cover at the edge of the wood-land. She saw herself tending to the horse and an old man with long white hair coming out of the cabin and both of them drinking some kind of green liquid from one of the glass jars. It looked like a scene from *A Midsummer Night's Dream* or maybe even 'Tattercoats'. Maca-bre. Moonlit. Mind-altering.

Next morning, Ryder was woken by a couple of men in a Land Rover, one of them carrying a shotgun. They faced him as he emerged from the wagon and nothing seemed to move for a short time. No sound could be heard, except for the silence, which was both unnat-ural and appropriate for that mise en scène in the wild clearing – in the strange satyr of isolated forest.

'Who are you?'

They said they were from the FDNPA.

'And what's that?'

'Forest of Dean National Park Authority.'

They'd had a report of gypsies camping in the area.

'I'm not a gypsy.'

He said it loudly, like it was some kind of vindication, exoneration, exculpation. Assuagement of a conscience that had been bothering him for some time.

'You'll have to move on. No camping here.'

'I got lost. I'm trying to find The Stables.'

They offered no help or direction and seemed quite hostile. Ryder didn't want any trouble – it was outside the parameters of what this carefree holiday was supposed to be – so he hitched up the horse and swung himself onto the driver's seat. He turned the animal's head towards the trail that led into the trees and began to move out. He wasn't the master of his own destiny, even if he believed he was – even here, at the very edge of time and space.

Ryder was nervous, so far away from what was familiar and so close to eternity. As he moved through the trees, something moved with him – it seemed to be either side of him in the forest. He couldn't see it, except for brief glimpses, but he knew it was there. He felt that he ought to stop, see what or who it was and what it wanted – but he didn't. He kept going.

Ryder eventually found his way out of the woods and, a little way up a country lane, he came upon The Stables Inn. The proprietors there were glad to see him. They'd been expecting him and were worried when he didn't show up. They'd sent people out looking, but no one could find him.

After lunch and a few large whiskies, he went out into the garden for a cigarette. There was a woman smoking a joint; she was about the same age as Ryder and, after the weirdness of the previous night, he thought a bit of company might get him back to reality. She offered him the doobie and said her name was Holly and she was into alternative medicine.

It was all about forms of energy that were alien to the laws of physics – forces that were outside the realm of the material universe. Ryder listened and pretended to be interested. To him it was like a melting pot of paganism and folklore and parapsychology and guess-work. It was a sprawling landscape of alternativism, where wishful thinking was an industry and faith was the ticket and death a transi-tion. But what was wrong with that? At least they weren't dropping bombs out of drones. She told him about pranic healing and flower therapy and holistic systems and biosonic repatterning and blood crystallisation and chiki energy-flows and acupuncture and esoteric toning and shaman stuff that could restore us all to sanity. Ryder reckoned it might have been a good thing for him, if he'd known about it earlier.

Then she asked if he'd like her to tell his fortune.

He thought, what the hell – it was summer and they were in a nice garden smoking weed. She looked at his palms, then placed her hands on his head. It felt weird, like a very mild current of electricity passing through her into him.

'I have to tell you about your past before I can tell you about your future.'

'I know all about my past.'

'Do you?'

She said his circle of life was fragmented by negative energy. He had to get back to what he was before, but it would be difficult – there were too many distractions, too much artificial light blocking out the stars. She said materialism made him vulnerable to the negative energy and he'd moved away from the thing he called humanity. The thing that made him human. The negative energy was spreading in him like a virus, blinding him.

'You have to go back to the beginning, Ryder.'

'But what about the future?'

'The future is in the hazel wood.'

Then she got up and went inside.

Ryder didn't see Holly again. He left the following morning, for the next staging post. On the way, he got a text from Cassie, asking when he was coming back. He replied that he didn't know. There was something he had to find first.

'What's that?'

'I don't know.'

To Ryder right then, it seemed like there were a million circles of life, all trying to connect at the same time, all the small circles trying to combine to form a circle of total life – the big picture. The total circle would get more powerful as it expanded, and negativity would get weaker. Otherwise, it was a further descent down into greed and fear and self-obsession – until there was nothing left.

Ryder didn't know what he wanted to do – get back to civilisation or stay out on the road. His time with the horse and bow-top was coming to an end, and he'd soon have to be making his way back to the camp from where he'd started out. And Cassie couldn't hold the fort forever. The important issues needed Ryder's personal attention.

In the end, he went back and sorted out what needed to be sorted out. He hired a young guy to help Cassie, then rented a small cottage in the Vale of Evesham, where he lived alone through the following winter, hardly ever coming into contact with another human being. He read a lot of books and did a lot of thinking and, all the time Holly's prediction kept coming back to him.

*The future is in the hazel wood.*

He believed it was a reference to a poem called 'The Song of Wandering Aengus', by W. B. Yeats.

There was a lot of snow in January, and below-zero temperatures. Ryder had enough food and fuel, so he didn't need to go anywhere and could sit it out. Late one night, he heard a knock on the door – faint at first and he thought it was just the wind. Then it came again, a bit louder. He wondered who'd be out there at that time of night. When he opened the door, he couldn't see anyone out there in the darkness. It was snowing a blizzard, so he shut the door to keep in the heat. After a few minutes, he heard the knocking again. He thought maybe it was someone pulling a prank – maybe some kids from the nearest village testing the hermit, so he ignored it. Then it came again, very loud. When he opened the door a second time, a woman he vaguely recognised was standing there in a long coat and boots.

'Metallic?'

'Ryder.'

She looked older than he remembered.

'What are you doing here?'

'Are you going to ask me in?'

He took her coat and offered her a chair by the open fire. She'd come by taxi as far as she could, then trudged the rest of the way on foot. After knocking a couple of times, she went round the back; that's why he couldn't see her when he opened the door. She'd come back around after he closed it. She saw the light and knew someone was home, but she thought he might be asleep, so she knocked louder.

'You took a chance.'

'I've taken many chances, Ryder.'

He made coffee and she warmed her hands on the cup. He had a bottle of the local moonshine and he poured some into the coffee.

'Can I stay here tonight?'

'Sure.'

The moonshine seemed to have a narcotic effect on Metallic. She sank back into the chair and let the exertion of getting there flow away. He could see her drifting on the mixture of malted barley and treacle and the smell of witch hazel. They drank some more and burned wood and he wondered when she was going to tell him what she'd come for.

'How's Seth?'

'He's in Haifa, working for the Knesset.'

'A permanent thing?'

'Hmmm ... maybe.'

'And you're here because ...?'

'I have a proposition for you.'

'A proposition? From who?'

She took another sip of the moonshine and smiled at him in that minacious way of hers.

'What happened to the diamonds, Ryder?'

'I don't know. Either stolen or pirated by the police. I told Seth ..'

She laughed, in a way that indicated she didn't believe him.

'No matter.'

'What's the proposition?'

'You come work for us ... take Seth's job.'

'Us?'

Metallic yawned and asked if she could go to bed, she was very tired. He told her to take his room and he'd sleep on a cot he had in the loft. Later, when he was sure she was asleep, he looked in her bag and found a 9mm Glock handgun.

Next morning, Ryder woke early and fried up bread and mushrooms and tomatoes and made fresh coffee. Metallic found him in the small kitchen.

'Breakfast?'

She looked at the food and her nose twitched. 'No meat?'

They ate in silence and there seemed to be some kind of understanding between them. Words would have been somehow superfluous – would have got in the way of their nexus. It was still snowing heavily and there was no way for a taxi to get through, so she'd have to stay until the weather cleared.

'When will that be?'

'Who knows?'

At lunchtime, she found some potatoes and root vegetables and other stuff and cooked up a kind of vegetarian stew, which they ate with thick slices of soda bread. He acknowledged her effort. 'You didn't have to do that.'

'I like to earn my keep.'

He told her he didn't eat much these days, and she said no wonder he was so skinny. When they finished, he tuned the radio to the weather station and the forecast was for the snow to let up the following day.

That night, they sat by the fire together and drank more moonshine, this time mixed with hot water, brown sugar and cloves. They listened to some classical music on the radio – Beethoven's 6th and Massenet and Debussy's 'Clair de Lune'. Metallic slipped down from her chair onto the mat in front of the fire and Ryder joined her there. She was quiet, meditative, listening to the soft piano, letting the drink take hold of her, smiling with her eyes. He put his arm around her, as the clock hands turned and time slipped by surreptitiously – in harmony with the moonshine and the fire and the music.

'Have you thought about my proposition?'

'Yes.'

'And?'

'No thanks.'

Ryder got up early the next morning and started breakfast. He waited for Metallic to come into the kitchen, but she didn't. The snow had stopped falling, just like the forecast predicted, and the low clouds had dispersed, leaving the sky an early colour of corn-flowers. He waited; the breakfast was getting cold. When he looked into the bedroom, Metallic was gone. There was a note. It read: 'DON'T COME BACK!'

Outside, footprints led down in the direction of the village.

\* \* \*

A month later, Ryder left the cottage and bought himself a horse and bow-top wagon. He read the Yeats poem again. It was about a Celtic god called Aengus who, in the hazel wood, caught a little silver trout. But when he went to build a fire, it turned into a beautiful girl who called him by his name, then disappeared into the air. After that, he spent all his time trying to find her again – through hollow lands and hilly lands – to find out where she'd gone, and kiss her lips and take her hands . . .

*And walk among long dappled grass,*
*And pluck till time and times are done,*
*The silver apples of the moon,*
*The golden apples of the sun.*